In two steps he was before her, towering over her like one of the masts of the ship.

❋

With one finger he tilted her chin up so that he could look squarely down into her face.

"Now listen to me, Lady," he stormed. "As long as you are on this ship, you will do as I tell you."

Eugenia shivered beneath his piercing gaze. She had no doubt that he would be capable of forcing her compliance, no doubt that those strong hands could compel her into obedience. The thought was frightening... and just a bit exciting, though she was loath to admit it. The power and sheer magnetism that emanated from him were exhilarating, and the temptation to defy him, to experience that energy unleashed, to stir the smoldering embers of what she was sure would be a blazing temper, was almost irresistible...

*   *   *   *

A Lady No More

WARNER BOOKS EDITION

Warner Books, Inc.
666 Fifth Avenue
New York, N.Y. 10103

A Warner Communications Company

Printed in the United States of America

First Printing: August, 1987

10 9 8 7 6 5 4 3 2 1

❋ Chapter 1 ❋

Of the seven people gathered in the book room of Latham House, Grosvenor Square, only one could be said to be at his ease. But as Mr. Brinkley was a gentleman far advanced in years, his tendency to doze off in the comfortable wing chair surprised no one. Nor did it disturb anyone, for his presence, as an executor of the will of the late earl of Latham, was purely a formality at this meeting.

The two primary combatants faced each other across the cherry-wood library table. The one, a middle-aged gentleman of portly build and sallow countenance, glared in undisguised dislike at the flushed face of the young woman seated opposite him. He was in no mood to appreciate the fine blue eyes that sparkled in defiance of his latest demand, nor would he agree that her ivory and peach complexion or the glossy dark curls that brushed her shoulder were the least bit attractive. If he considered the matter at all, Mr. George Wolverton would have declared that he admired only fair women; he certainly found nothing to admire in his cousin, Lady Eugenia Wolverton.

The animosity was mutual. Though Lady Eugenia had been raised in the tenet that a lady did not betray an excess of emotion, at the moment she found herself sorely tried to

adhere to it. There was a very great deal at stake here and, although she kept it well hidden, she was afraid.

"You are rushing things a trifle, are you not, my dear cousin?" she inquired in tones of honeyed sweetness.

"Rushing things! Really, Eugenia, it has been six months since Latham killed himself!" her dear cousin exploded. "I should be Latham now!"

A tremulous sob escaped from the only other female in the room, a frail lady, fair complexioned, whose pallor just now appeared unnaturally enhanced. She lowered her face into delicate hands, and her shoulders quivered.

Genie rose, knocking back her chair in her angered haste. "I will thank you to watch your tongue in my sister-in-law's presence, George!"

She strode across the room to the countess of Latham, the silken skirts of her gray half-mourning gown rustling about her as she knelt beside the Queen Anne chair. "There is no need for you to remain, dear Charlotte," Eugenia said gently. "You are not yet fully recovered. Go and rest, or see how little Louisa goes on."

The countess of Latham clasped Genie's hand, tears filling her eyes. "If only she had been a boy!" Her soft cry wrenched Genie's heart.

"Nonsense! Don't ever regret Louisa. Robert would not, you know," she told her sister-in-law kindly, if untruthfully. "And we shall find Edward." This last was said with more confidence than she felt.

"Perhaps I shall lie down for a while. If . . . if you do not mind being left alone?" she added in a whisper.

"For heaven's sake, do not worry about me. I have Mr. Mackelson to support me, and I assure you he will do so very well. Now go and rest."

With a last uncertain look at Eugenia, Charlotte stood unsteadily. "If you will excuse me, gentlemen?"

The men, except for the somnolent Mr. Brinkley, rose to their feet and remained standing until the countess left the room.

"Lady Eugenia!" Mr. Martin Rotherby recalled her attention.

She turned to face a little man she had no trouble

disliking. Just the sort of person she would expect her cousin to employ for this deplorable business, she reflected. She straightened herself to her full height, regarding the man with a haughty air that her ex-governess had almost despaired of ever drilling into her and that made her appear much taller than her five feet four inches.

"Yes, Mr. Rotherby?"

He cleared his throat, running suddenly nervous fingers through thin, slicked-back black hair. "I believe you, of all people, my lady, are aware of the many repairs—indeed, the many expenditures—necessary for the improvement of the estates."

"You perhaps forget that they have been in my management since my brother's death. Our good bailiff here can tell you that nothing has been allowed to suffer." She gestured towards a gentleman of advancing years, who looked acutely uncomfortable.

"He can also tell *you,* Cousin, that nothing is able to flourish either!" George Wolverton pointed out, a thin smile of satisfaction curving his lips as her color rose. "You are not permitted to make any of the alterations that are needed so badly."

"I never knew you to be so concerned with the Priory!" Genie's pretended surprise caused an angry flush to spread across her cousin's rotund countenance. "But surely," she went on, rubbing salt into a very sore wound, "is it not for the rightful heir to decide what improvements to make?"

"Who is to say that I am *not* the rightful heir?" he demanded.

"Edward!"

"Then let him step forward and say it!" George declared, looking triumphant.

Genie bit her lip, vexed with herself. That was an unforgivable slip on her part, to give George such an opening. Her inexperience, her youth, and her fiery temper, so deplored by both her brother and governess, had betrayed her once again.

"There is no proof that the Honorable Mr. Edward Wolverton is dead," Mr. Mackelson, her brother's solicitor, now her own, pointed out. He settled back in his chair,

folding his hands over his protruding waistcoat, scowling at the assembled company from beneath bushy gray eyebrows.

"There is no proof that he is alive!" Mr. Rotherby shot back. "Six years, without a single word to his family? That's doing it much too brown, you know. If he were alive when the war broke out with America, why did he not come home then?"

"I do not believe he would have found it an easy thing to do," Mr. Mackelson pointed out. "And it is quite possible he was well away from any conflict, or even any talk of it. America is a very big place."

"It is indeed. Even if we were to admit there was a chance he was still alive—which we do not, of course—you might never find him."

"Inquiries are being made," Mr. Mackelson informed his rival with cold hauteur. "This was quite unexpected, as you know. Latham was just turned thirty-two and in excellent health. No one could have predicted his death in the hunting field."

"You should have started your search then!" George exclaimed.

"We did, sir, but we could only act discreetly. It would have been most improper of us to do anything more. At that time, as you must very well know, we had no idea whether or not Lady Latham's child would be a boy, and the new earl. This whole situation might never have arisen."

"Well, it has, and it cannot be allowed to go on indefinitely," George threw in.

"I wrote to Mr. Reginald Jessop in America at the time of the earl's death," Mr. Mackelson told him, as if that settled the problem.

"Jessop?" George frowned, directing a glare at Eugenia. "That would be your mother's brother, would it not?"

"Yes, he moved to Rhode Island shortly after Mamma was married, about thirty-five years ago. Soon after their revolution ended, I think Mamma said. He has become quite influential, you know," she added, pleased to be able to put George back in his place. "If anyone can locate Edward, I am sure he can." The two cousins eyed each

other across the wide expanse of table, with perfect understanding.

"If he is alive," George said as he continued his solicitor's argument, "why has he not written in all this time to let you know where he is?"

Genie took a deep breath. "George, how well do you remember my brother?"

Mr. Wolverton considered. "Don't believe I saw him many times. He was at Eton, then Oxford, was he not?"

She nodded. "Perhaps you don't remember, then. My brothers were almost exact opposites, and there was no love lost between them. As soon as Robert married, Edward began talking of America. Then when little Jonathon was born, and Charlotte was expecting another child, he felt certain he would never come into the title. So he left." She kept to herself her conviction that Jonathon's death from typhoid, just before his third birthday, had broken the gentle Charlotte's heart and caused the miscarriage that robbed her and her husband of their second son as well.

"That still doesn't explain...," George began again, querulous.

"But it does," Eugenia cut him off. "Edward was—still is, for all I know—as careless and casual as Robert was reliable. He would never want to write to Robert, and it would never occur to him that either Sophia or I might like to hear from him. The last we heard was when he arrived in Providence and stayed with my Uncle Reginald."

"He actually wrote?" George asked with a malicious smile.

"Write? Edward? I doubt he knows how," Genie answered with airy unconcern. "Uncle Reginald wrote. He, at least, has kept in touch with us, even after Mamma died." George did not look pleased, and Genie mentally awarded that round to herself.

"This is getting us nowhere!" George leaned back in his chair, turning his malevolent gaze upon his solicitor as if demanding this individual to produce a solution.

"There is little we can do until we hear from Mr. Jessop," Mr. Mackelson explained, and Mr. Rotherby, despite his client's obvious displeasure, was forced to agree.

"It has, after all, been scarcely three weeks since Lady Latham was delivered of a daughter, and the question of the heir became critical."

Mr. Wolverton drummed his fingers on the table. "It is all well and good to say it has only been three weeks, but the Priory has been without a master for six months. And as *your good bailiff* will tell you, it cannot remain that way forever!"

Genie lowered her eyes to study her hands. That was quite true, and none knew better than she how desperately the entailed estates needed attention which she was not permitted to bestow upon them.

"The mail service to America is not very fast, I fear," Mr. Mackelson said with dry humor. "Nor is it very regular. It may be another month or more before we hear any news. I believe America to be a very large country, without the excellent roads to which we are accustomed. It may take Mr. Jessop some time to obtain word of his nephew's whereabouts."

George glowered but said nothing, merely sinking lower into his chair.

"We will await word from Mr. Jessop," Mr. Rotherby decided, ignoring his client's glare. "But if he has been unable to find any trace of Mr. Edward Wolverton, then, for the sake of the estates, we must act."

Mr. Mackelson's lips firmed. "We will wait upon Mr. Jessop, to be sure." He stood, and the others followed suit. Gently he shook the sleeping Mr. Brinkley's shoulder, rousing that elderly gentleman from his repose. "We shall take our leave of you, Lady Eugenia. Pray convey our compliments to Lady Latham."

Genie crossed to the bell pull, ringing for Langley, the butler, to show the men out. They seemed to take forever to depart, but finally she stood alone in the book room. Gratefully she sank down onto the sofa, leaning back against the pillowed softness of its long back. Her eyes closed in exhaustion.

The battle had barely begun, and it would be long and bitterly fought if she knew her Cousin George. He would not easily let an earldom, the estates, and the considerable

income from the numerous entailed properties slip through his fingers. And considering he was the father of a large and hopeful family, she supposed she could hardly blame him. To have two sons up at Eton at the same time, with a third shortly to join them, must be a terrible drain on his purse.

Genie could not like him, though, try as she might. He was possessed of a disagreeable manner and a propensity for gaming that kept him under the hatches and in constant jealousy of his more comfortably circumstanced cousins. That Latham's considerable fortune owed a great deal to the earl's temperate ways and careful investment served only to irritate Mr. George Wolverton even more.

The door opened and a pretty, piquant face framed by glossy dark curls peeped around the corner.

"Here you are, Genie. I heard them leave. What has happened?" Lady Sophia Wolverton, ethereally delicate in a flowing lavender muslin gown, tripped lightly into the room and settled on the edge of the sofa beside her elder sister. "Did you put that beastly George in his place?"

"Sophia, you must not speak of him like that. He is our cousin."

The younger girl wrinkled her nose. "Oh, do stop being so stuffy. You sound just like Minty, or . . . or Robert! And you didn't answer my question."

Genie sighed. "But it is most improper. You know that propriety of manner is expected of someone of our station. Minty has told us often enough. But oh, Sophie, I came so close to—to forgetting myself! George brings out the absolute *worst* in me. Never have I been so—so cattish!"

"Genie . . . ," her sister began threateningly.

"It is as we thought." Eugenia yielded. "Nothing can be decided until we hear from my Uncle Reginald."

Sophia lounged back in a most unladylike manner that for once failed to provoke a rebuke from her sister. "Well, I must say, it will be much more pleasant around here once we get the whole thing settled. But from what I remember of Edward, I almost think we are better off without him."

Genie tried to feel the shock she knew to be proper for such a statement, but failed. "I must agree, he does lack the . . . the *dignity* one would wish to see in the earl of

Latham,'' she managed to say, though the idea of her jovial, wayward brother in this august position appealed to her reprehensible sense of the ridiculous. She tried to quell it, as she knew she ought, but still felt its stirrings within her.

"Oh, *do* stop talking like Minty! Why wrap it up in clean linen? Edward was a . . . a loose screw!''

"Sophie!" Genie cried, honestly shocked. "Wherever did you hear such an expression?''

Her sister shrugged her delicate shoulders. "Well, ramshackle, then.''

"Well, would you have *George* become Latham?''

Sophia considered, then giggled. "Lord, what a . . . a *leveler* for the title, if it were to go to such a man. *George*, to succeed Robert, and Papa. I would much rather have Edward. At least he was not a gamester. *And* he was a man of honor.''

Genie turned a fascinated eye on her sister. "I was only thirteen when he left, and you were only ten. How do you remember so much about him?''

"Minty. She is forever holding him up as a Bad Example to me. But, Genie, do you not remember what fun he could be? Always laughing, always willing to play a game with us? Not at all like Robert, with his so-precious dignity and pompous ways.''

Eugenia thought it best to ignore this withering summation of their dead brother's character. "I wonder what Edward will be like now?" she said instead.

"Do you really think he is still alive?" Sophia sat up again, regarding her sister with uncharacteristic seriousness.

Eugenia nodded. "I am sure of it, though I don't know why. I can see him getting into a great deal of trouble, but I am quite sure he could bluff his way out of anything. And it would not be at all like him to get involved in anything really dangerous.''

"An accident?''

"It is possible,'' she conceded. "Perhaps I just don't *want* to believe him dead. And it is not just because I couldn't bear to see George as Latham. Edward is our brother! We must find him.''

"Well, let us hope it does not take too long. I cannot bear

the way Cousin George walks about the house, touching things in *such* a way, as if he were calculating their value.''

"How is poor Charlotte?" Eugenia abruptly changed the subject. It was most improper of her to be in such complete agreement with her shockingly outspoken sister. What Minty would say if she heard her!

"She is asleep. I looked in on my way down. Her mamma is sitting with her."

"I wish she had been able to remain at the Priory to have the baby," Genie said with a sigh. "She would be much more comfortable there."

"It is a very long way from the Priory to her physician on Harley Street," Sophia put in unnecessarily.

"I cannot blame her mamma," Genie agreed. "After two miscarriages and one stillbirth . . ." She let the sentence drop. "I am glad she had the best doctor possible."

"Genie," Sophia said after several minutes of silence. She glanced up at her sister through lowered lashes. "We are only in *half* mourning now, are we not? And this means we shall be able to go about a little this Season, doesn't it?"

"*If* Aunt Lydia is willing to act as our chaperone," Genie conceded. "Charlotte is certainly in no state to go about. And you, my little sister, are only sixteen. You are not to be brought out until next year."

"*Next* year! Why, I will be almost on the shelf before I have had a chance! Can I not attend just a few very quiet little gatherings?"

Eugenia considered the eager face gazing anxiously up into hers. "It *might* be a good idea, I suppose. That is all it will be proper for us to attend, at any rate. And this way you may become accustomed to Society before you are properly brought out." She warmed to the idea. "I do hope it may make it easier for you. I remember my first *ton* party with horror! I knew not a single soul, and I was so afraid of saying and doing everything wrong."

"You, a Wolverton of Wolverton Priory, behave with the least impropriety?"

Genie allowed herself a slight smile at this perfect imitation of their governess's outraged tone. "Yes, is it not shocking? I was terrified I might do something to put Robert

to the blush. You know how he *demanded* that I be such a . . . a pattern card of perfection!''

"How dull." Sophia dismissed her sister's trials as ancient history. "Whatever could have induced a man like Brockton to dangle after you if you always behaved in such a . . . a soppy and dutiful manner?''

"Sophie!'' Soft color tinged Eugenia's cheeks. "If you cannot speak with at least a modicum of propriety, you shall surely remain in the schoolroom this Season!''

Sophia ignored this. "May we pay morning visits to let people know we are back in town?'' She eyed her sister with a sideways glance. "I wonder if Lord Brockton has returned to London yet?''

"I am sure I have no idea,'' Genie informed her coolly. "And we shall not pay morning visits, at least not yet. We shall go shopping and walk in the park.''

Sophia clasped her long, slender fingers in delight. "Oh, when may we go? My gowns are only fit for the nursery! If I am to go into Society, I shall need new ones!''

"We both shall,'' Genie decided, glad to have something so worthy of thought to divert her troubled mind from Edward—and the long-absent Lord Brockton. "But remember, in another six months we will be putting aside our mourning completely. It will be necessary to do more shopping then.''

A footman was dispatched to the lending library, and upon his return the two young ladies were soon in possession of a number of back issues of *La Belle Assemblée*. They spent the evening engrossed in the serious occupation of leafing through these pages, examining the various fashion plates and exclaiming over every gown that took their fancy. By the time Eugenia retired to bed, her mind was too full of satins and muslins, flounces and trims, to dwell long on her brother's whereabouts.

* Chapter 2 *

The following morning Genie and Sophia ordered Lady Latham's comfortable barouche to be brought around promptly after breakfast and, accompanied by the stern-faced Miss Minton, who still kept Sophia in charge, they set forth to tour the shops. Their first stop was naturally in Bond Street, at the showroom of Madame Clarisse, a *modiste* who had become an overnight sensation with the *ton* two years before when she first opened her highly expensive doors.

Genie felt a comforting sense of familiarity as she stepped into the opulent front room, for Madame Clarisse had made the many ravishing gowns she had worn during the previous Season. She swept Sophia along with her, allowing the girl little time to take in the gilt-framed mirrors, the thick Aubusson carpets, and the plush furnishings.

In a moment Madame Clarisse herself hurried out from the back room, welcoming with obvious pleasure such a valued client. Their needs were quickly discussed and, although she had little made up in colors suitable to their state of half mourning, several gowns were to be found in white and lilac, which could quite easily be trimmed in black.

It was while Sophia was being fastened into a particularly

ravishing white cambric walking dress that two more cus-
tomers entered the shop. Recognizing the voices of Lady
Clayton and her daughter Amabel, Genie excused herself
and ventured back into the front room to speak to them.

Miss Amabel Clayton turned from her examination of a
gauze and lace gown displayed in the window. "Why, Lady
Eugenia! I had no idea you were in town." She came
forward smiling, extending her hand.

Genie took it with warmth, relieved to be slipping back
into safe and well-known routines, meeting with old friends.
"We only arrived the day before yesterday. I had not
expected to see anyone I knew so early in the year. The
Season has not yet begun." She turned to greet Lady
Clayton, who bestowed a warm greeting on her.

Miss Clayton threw a roguish look at her mother out of
the corner of her eye. "Mamma could not bear to be buried
in the country for another week, so we have come early
also. And we are not the only ones! Why, I have already
seen Miss Saunders and Lady Bevington. You will meet
many acquaintances, I assure you."

"Genie?" Sophia called from the next room. "Do come
and see! It is ever so lovely."

"You must excuse me. Do you remember my sister,
Sophia? She is bearing me company." With a promise to
bring her sister along to pay a morning call one day soon,
Genie left them.

"Yes, quite exquisite, my dear," Genie heard Lady
Clayton murmur to her daughter when they believed her to
be out of earshot. "But I very much fear it will prove to be
too expensive."

A wave of pity swept over Eugenia. How terrible to be so
purse-pinched as not to be able to buy whatever took your
fancy! She herself had always enjoyed a generous clothing
allowance, enough to cover her needs and more. Robert,
tight-fisted though he might have been on most matters,
recognized the necessity for a Wolverton to be elegantly
gowned on all occasions. His sister must always appear the
epitome of good taste and breeding, no matter the expense.

She froze, her suddenly nerveless fingers sliding off the
door she had just opened. She remained rooted to the spot,

her eyes widening as the color drained from her cheeks—exactly where would their money be coming from now that Robert was gone?

"Lady Eugenia!" Her ex-governess, never failing to use her title in public, rose from her chair and hurried across to her, taking her hands. "You are ill. Where is that vinaigrette?"

"No, I . . . ," Genie began. "I mean, yes, I am ill. No, pray, Minty, do not bother." She waved aside the small silver perforated box that the governess extracted from Sophia's reticule.

"Yes, you will, Lady Eugenia," Miss Minton informed her, pushing her down into a chair and waving the sharp-smelling box under her nose. "For all it is Lady Sophia who is the sickly one, see who needs the smelling salts now!" she declared with obvious, if perverse, satisfaction.

Genie recoiled from the pungent odor. "Sophie?" She looked up to find her sister hovering solicitously just behind Miss Minton. "I am so sorry, my dear. Would you mind if we come back another day? I . . . I am afraid I do not feel quite the thing."

"Oh, Genie!" Sophie exclaimed. She took one long, last, lingering look at herself in the glass, then sighed. With the help of the *modiste,* she began to unfasten a beruffled half-robe of lilac silk.

A few minutes later, Genie settled back into the plush cushioned seat of the barouche. Miss Minton again offered her the vinaigrette, while Sophie attempted to chafe her sister's wrist. Vexed by all the unwanted attention, Genie shook them away.

"No, please, do leave off! I don't want that!" She freed one hand from Sophie's hold and batted away the silver box. "I am perfectly all right, I assure you!"

"But . . ." Sophie sat back, surprised. "But you went quite *pale* in there. I saw you!"

"And so would you have, if you suddenly had the realization that I just did." She glanced at Miss Minton and knew there was no hope of keeping anything from her erstwhile governess. And what she was about to disclose would most likely come as no surprise to the woman, who had enjoyed the earl's full trust and confidence with regard

to his sisters. "Oh, no, Minty!" she exclaimed suddenly, noting that the coachman had begun to retrace his route to Grosvenor Square. "We are not going home. I very much fear we must go to Layton and Shear's, Bedford House."

Miss Minton gasped. "To think of a Wolverton of Wolverton Priory having to be reduced to this! I dare not think what his lordship would say, may he rest in peace, though how he should, when his affairs are left in such a state and his sisters must employ such strategems, I know not."

"A linen draper!" Sophie cried, only to be hushed by her sister. "But whatever for?" she demanded in more modulated accents.

"Sophie, how much money do you possess?" Eugenia turned to her sister, fixing her with a steady eye.

"Why, I have no idea! Why should I? Do you?"

Eugenia nodded. "Let me tell you, Sophia, that your entire income for a year would not have purchased that last gown you tried on."

"But . . ." Her sister stared at her, aghast. "But Genie! You *always* buy your gowns from Madame Clarisse! And not just one or two either. Why, you bought as many as five at one time, at the beginning of last Season. I remember!"

"The bill went to Robert, dearest. You know he would never have permitted me to appear shabbily gowned. A Wolverton must be at the height of fashion, you know. It is expected." She repeated that oft-quoted dictum with a hollow voice. "He paid for all of my gowns—out of the income from the entailed estates."

"An income which now belongs to . . ." Their eyes met in understanding. Not a penny of those sums could be spent until their rightful owner could be determined.

Sophia sank back against the squabs, letting out a long breath. "Oh, Genie, what a . . . a *bind* we are in."

"We owe it to ourselves and our name to maintain appearances," Eugenia said with a sigh.

Miss Minton nodded approval of her onetime pupil, who had learned so well the lessons repeatedly drilled into her. "Of course you must. And as there are so few people of any consequence in town, I believe it will be quite unexceptionable to visit Layton and Shear's—this once."

She turned in her seat and gave the order to the coachman. "You will select a number of dress lengths," Miss Minton went on, "and then we shall engage the services of a seamstress. I believe one may have dresses made up at very little cost."

"Should we . . . do you think we ought to go to Grafton House?" Genie asked. In spite of her training that such places were ineffably beneath her, she felt a twinge of curiosity to see this bargain emporium that so excited other young ladies of her acquaintance who apparently had lesser standards to maintain.

"Certainly not!" Miss Minton exclaimed. "It is frequented by quite vulgar persons. A Wolverton has nothing to do with a place like that."

"I believe a lady can buy almost anything she might need there, and at ridiculously low prices," Genie murmured.

"It certainly sounds like we *should* go there," Sophie commented cautiously. "Would it be so very bad?"

"It would indeed," Miss Minton informed her in a voice that brooked no argument. "If it comes to that, I shall go and make the purchases for you. The appearance of a Wolverton at Grafton House would give rise to the very sort of gossip that is most repugnant. Your dignity must be maintained at all times, girls. Remember Who You Are."

Genie sank back in her seat, that familiar refrain repeating over and over in her mind. She knew who she was, she knew her family's consequence, she knew what was expected of her. Miss Minton and Robert had seen to that. But just once, how she would love to escape from it all! It was probably too deeply ingrained within her, too deeply drilled in, she reflected sadly. She was Lady Eugenia Wolverton, and she could never turn loose that disreputably free spirit she knew lurked, well hidden, in her innermost soul.

It was with mixed feelings of mild distaste and secret excitement that Eugenia entered the vast rooms of Layton and Shear's. The foremost of these emotions quickly evaporated at the sight of so many bolts of cloth, all so surprisingly inexpensive. Sophia, less restrained than her sister by the tenets of her upbringing, hurried from bolt to bolt, exclaiming over the multitude of colors and fabrics.

In the end, the visit proved more than satisfactory. A lilac cambric and a white muslin proved so affordable that Sophia was encouraged to purchase an olive green silk twill to be made up into a redingote, as well as several ells of sprig muslin and a delectable peach crepe that she simply could not resist—for later, when they were out of mourning.

"That was wonderful fun!" Sophia exclaimed as they settled once more into the barouche. A number of parcels now occupied the forward seat, leaving little room for Miss Minton. "I do wish we might visit Grafton House as well, if it is anything like this!"

Genie peered carefully at her sister's flushed countenance and glittering eyes. "Are you tired?" She reached over, pulling up her sister's shawl. "The breeze is turning chill. Are you quite all right?"

Sophie nodded. "Of course I am. I have not had such fun in ages!"

Eugenia sat back but kept a watchful eye on the girl. In spite of a frail and sickly constitution, Sophia appeared to be holding up quite well under the demands of their shopping expedition. It was not unknown for her, though, to suddenly become cross and headachy under the least strain. It was as well that they should return home before this inevitable stage was reached.

They were greeted upon their arrival in Grosvenor Square with the news that Charlotte was once again resting. They therefore retired to the Gold Saloon with the copies of *La Belle Assemblée* and resumed their study of the fashion plates with renewed interest.

The consultation with the seamstress, whose services were procured by the surprisingly knowledgeable Miss Minton, took the remainder of the day. It was with considerable regret that Eugenia was forced to postpone their walk in Hyde Park for, although Sophia had entered into the plans for her new dresses with an energy that surprised her concerned sister, the day's activities had now taken their toll. While Eugenia was of the firm conviction that a gentle airing could only do Sophia good, this opinion was shared by neither the sufferer nor her governess.

It was not until the following afternoon that Eugenia was

able to order the barouche to take them to the park. It was the hour of the fashionable promenade, and those members of the *haut ton* who had already arrived in London were to be found here. Already a number of curricles, phaetons, and barouches proceeded along the drive while horsemen rode along the tanbark beside it. Eugenia requested the coachman to set them down and, under Miss Minton's careful chaperonage, she and Sophia joined the growing number of pedestrians along the path.

If Lady Eugenia's sole objective had been to encounter acquaintances and exchange news of the winter months, she must have been pleased. There was only one face, though, for which she scanned the passersby, one tall, broad-shouldered figure she particularly wished to see.

"Genie!" Sophie's voice came out as a whispered hiss. "Is that not Lord Brockton driving unicorn in that curricle? There." She gestured. "Talking to Lady Renly."

Genie's eager eyes flew to the vehicle, noting the three restless horses, one hitched before a pair, held tight by a firm hand. "Oh, if that is not just like him! I wonder if he hopes to set a fad!" she exclaimed, relieved to have found him at last.

"Shall we go and speak to him?" Sophia asked.

"Of course not. That would be quite forward of us." Genie's eyes dropped. *A lady does not display emotion,* she could almost hear Miss Minton declare. *Nor does she display unbecoming eagerness.* But Genie had not seen Brockton since Robert's death, and she admitted to herself how very welcome his capable presence would have been during the intervening six months.

Lord Brockton, ending his conversation with a fashionable matron, glanced up at that moment. "By all that is holy!" his deep, laughing voice declared. "The lovely Lady Eugenia. Are you back to grace Society with your presence once more?"

His bantering tone was not quite what she expected, nor did it please her, for it was not what she was accustomed to hearing from him. She managed to smile up into the cynical face of the biggest—and most notorious—prize on the Marriage Mart for the past several seasons.

"Why, Lord Brockton!" Her finely arched brows rose slightly. "I hardly expected to find you in London in March. Could you find no more amusing sport?"

"But I have. There was a most entertaining prize fight near here less than a fortnight ago. And that, of course, inspired me to pay a visit to Gentleman Jackson and the Daffy Club—well, you see how it is."

"Odious man," she responded promptly. "You should rather say that you missed the enjoyable company you find in London."

She studied his expression with care. There was a gleam in his dark eyes as they rested on her, a fact which pleased her, as she had dressed with care. But something was missing, something that should have lain much deeper than that surface appreciation; she could detect no trace of the earnestness that customarily underlay his manner when he was with her.

Six months ago, before her brother's death, she—and most of the polite world as well—would have sworn that this noted Corinthian and leader of the *ton* was on the verge of making her an offer of marriage.

Something must have altered in her expression, for his eyes narrowed and he gathered in his reins. "You must excuse me." He favored her with a glittering smile that for once failed to warm her heart. "I believe I see Waverly up ahead. Quite delightful to see you again." He nodded to both girls, gave his horses the office, and proceeded on his way.

"Genie!" Sophia exclaimed after staring after him for a minute in stunned silence. "He . . . he acted as if you were no more to him than the merest flirt!"

"Perhaps I am, now," she replied with an attempt at a casualness she was far from feeling.

"But he had become so very particular in his attentions to you!" Sophia declared hotly. "He was forever turning up in Grosvenor Square, and on the flimsiest of pretexts. I was quite certain he was going to ask Robert for permission to pay his addresses to you."

"That was all some time ago." Eugenia sighed, not pleased with her sister for sharing her sentiments. "We have

practically been in seclusion at the Priory while we have been in mourning. You could hardly expect the interest of a gentleman of his stamp to remain keen after so long a time.''

''I would have expected him to renew his suit!''

''Well, perhaps he will. We are still in mourning, you know. It would be most improper of him to speak now.''

''Improper? But surely that would not signify to him if he loved you!''

''Lady Sophia!'' Miss Minton exclaimed in ominous accents. ''I will thank you not to express yourself in so vulgar a manner. Young ladies of your order do not permit violence of feeling to sway their actions. Your sister's sentiments do her credit.''

''Genie!'' Sophia, ignoring this reprimand, rounded on her. ''Do you not *love* Brockton? Would you marry him when your heart is not engaged?''

''Sophia!'' Miss Minton cried again.

''Please, keep your voice down,'' Eugenia urged, neatly covering her confusion beneath an airily unconcerned attitude. ''Certainly I would not, if I did not have a *tendre* for him. But we were not necessarily speaking of marriage, you know. Whether or not I chose to accept, just to receive an offer from a gentleman of Brockton's standing would be quite a triumph, I assure you!''

''You *did* have a *tendre* for him,'' Sophia accused triumphantly.

Gentle color flooded Eugenia's cheeks. Had she? He had sought her out in the most gratifying way, flattering and courting her to the envy of every other marriageable female in town. How could she help but have her head turned? He dressed with unquestioned taste, his manners were such as to make him a welcome guest at any gathering, his abilities in all sports made him popular with the gentlemen, while his finesse on the dance floor assured his popularity with the ladies. He was, in fact, the most eligible gentleman in town. And never before had he lavished his gallantry upon only one lady.

''Perhaps I did, once,'' she murmured, more to herself than in answer to Sophia's question. She forced an artificial

smile to her lips. "You must admit, I had the most amazingly successful Season, thanks to Lord Brockton's attentions. I was quite the envy of all." She ignored Sophia's searching look and her ex-governess's sniff. She was not sounding like herself, she knew, but at the moment she was not at all sure what "herself" was.

It must be the uncertainty of their situation, this waiting to find Edward and worrying where they would live if their cousin George were to inherit the title and estates, that left Genie feeling so insecure. Lord Brockton's casual attitude had rattled her composure more than she cared to admit, for during these last stressful months she had counted on seeing him again, counted on his support—regretted, in fact, that he had not come to offer his assistance to her.

Her long absence must have dulled his interest. Undoubtedly the long winter months had brought their share of amusements, in which she had played no part. He was still inclined to admire her, at least, and if he were willing to indulge in a light flirtation, so much the better. Whether it was pride or honest desire she was not sure, but, despite being in half mourning, she determined then and there to bring Charles, Lord Brockton, up to scratch this Season.

The sisters continued their walk, exchanging greetings with several more people, nodding to others. But Eugenia no longer saw the surrounding shrubbery or expanses of green of Hyde Park. Her thoughts were focused on the coming Season which promised to be an excellent introduction for Sophia—and it appeared to hold a considerable challenge for Eugenia herself.

Their arrival back at Grosvenor Square brought a return of the worries Eugenia had sought to escape in the bustle of the beginning Season. A letter resting on the silver salver in the entry hall bore her name in Mr. Mackelson's prim, precise copperplate. Handing her bonnet and pelisse into a footman's care for conveyance to her room, she shooed Sophia up the stairs to attend Charlotte while she herself retired to the book room with the missive.

It took only a few minutes to peruse. Mr. Mackelson believed, according to his message, that it would be best not to rely wholly upon Mr. Reginald Jessop for news of her

brother, but to insert notices in every major American newspaper, advertising for news of him. This would take time, which could only be beneficial for them. It would also, as much as he hated to mention so sordid a subject, take a fair sum of money that could not, under the circumstances, properly come from the estate. If she wished to pursue this course of action, she should let him know at her earliest convenience, and he remained, as always, her most obedient servant.

She stared at the closely written sheet for several minutes. Time she could spare, and gladly. She would do whatever was necessary to postpone George's taking possession of the Priory, the estates—even Latham House. She looked about the book room, forcing herself to imagine this comfortable room with its walls lined with books as the property of her cousin. The very idea was too depressing to contemplate. But it would take money . . . She went in search of Sophia and Charlotte, hoping inspiration would come.

The only idea that came to mind gave her a pang of regret, but locating Edward was of far greater importance to her than her only pair of diamond earrings. She removed them from her jewel case the next morning, holding them up to the light and watching the sparkling glints of color that danced off the square-cut stones. Robert had purchased them for her at Gray's in Sackville Street only a short year and a half ago. She would buy them back when Edward took possession of his properties, she vowed. Without allowing herself to regret her decision, she placed the jewels into a small velvet pouch and thrust this into her reticule.

She would not tell Sophia of her errand that morning. Her sister, so easily overset, should not know that she was reduced to selling her jewelry. Somehow, until Edward was found, she would shield the delicate little Sophia from the harsher aspects of the life they were now forced to face.

She had no choice but to take Miss Minton into her confidence. An unusual and distasteful errand this might be, but she must protect her name from any shadow of impropriety. Accompanied by the prim governess, Eugenia hurried down the stairs at an hour when she could be quite certain that her sister—and most of the polite world, whom

she would not care to meet upon such an errand—still lay abed, sipping hot chocolate and reflecting on the pleasures of the day ahead.

She awaited the arrival of the carriage in the book room. A slight commotion at the door brought her to her feet, and she started across to the door just as it opened, admitting the butler.

"If you please, my lady, there is a Captain James Harrington come to see you." The elderly man's tone expressed the disapproval his training would never allow him to voice. "A sea captain, I believe. I informed him you were on the point of going out, but he is quite persistent. He says that he has a letter for you."

"Very well, Langley, show him in." Genie sighed, sinking back down onto the deep blue upholstered sofa. If she did not get away quickly, Sophia would come in search of her. It would be hard enough to fob off her questions concerning her absence after her return. If she were once caught, she would never be able to leave without her inquisitive sister.

The door opened again, and Eugenia looked up to behold the embodiment of every romantic fantasy in whch she had ever indulged. Captain James Harrington's height, his energetic, confident bearing, and his indefinable air of command swept over her like a wave from the wake of his ship. He took a step into the room, leveling his gaze upon her.

She blinked, tried to recapture her breath, and forced herself to consider him in a more realistic light. He was tall, strikingly so, and his breadth of shoulder seemed to fill the doorway behind him. Blond hair curled back from a wide forehead in very tight waves, dark near the scalp but bleached on the tips by the elements to the color of pale wheat. A reddish sheen highlighted bushy sideburns. His eyebrows were thick, his nose patrician, his chin square and jutting. The eyes that rested on her in frank admiration were of a deep sea green, alight with dancing golden glints, arresting against the bronzed tan of his skin.

"Lady Eugenia Wolverton?" He spoke with a strange accent, which surprised her and left her rather taken aback. No gentleman, this, from his speech, though his appearance

might have deceived her. He approached her, holding out
his hand, his every step an indication of his strength and
vitality. "I am Captain Harrington. I am the bearer of a
letter to you from Mr. Reginald Jessop."

"My uncle!" Eugenia exclaimed. She jumped to her feet,
taking his proffered hand in a warm clasp. He was American. That explained the peculiar tones that had sounded so
ill-bred to her. She tore her gaze from his rugged countenance and focused instead on the folded white sheets he
held out. She took them with trembling fingers, then raised
her eyes to meet his, so far above her own. "Forgive me, I
am quite anxious to hear his news. Would you . . . would
you perhaps care for some refreshment?"

He gave a slight bow. "No, I require nothing. But please,
by all means read his letter." He strode over to the window
with an easy, swinging gait and stood looking out onto the
square.

Genie returned to the sofa and broke open the seal,
unable to wait a moment longer. Carefully she smoothed the
three sheets of closely written paper, but her hands shook so
that she was barely able to make out the words. Finally she
closed her eyes, lowering the letter to her lap.

"I am sorry I could not have brought you better news."
He moved uncommonly quietly for such a large man, for
she had not heard him until he stood directly before her.

"You . . . you are aware of the contents of my uncle's
letter?" Her eyes narrowed in patent disapproval of her
uncle's apparent indiscretion.

"I have the honor of being in Mr. Jessop's confidence,"
he said, nodding. If he noted her reaction, he gave no hint.
"I fear he has been unwell a great deal during this last year.
He requested that I personally express his sincere regrets
that he was unable to conduct a more thorough search for
your brother."

"He says he believes him dead," Eugenia murmured in a
very small voice.

"I am sorry."

She rose, walking over to the window to stare out with
unseeing eyes. She could not believe it. There was too

much life in the Edward she remembered, too much vitality to be so easily laid to rest. She *would* not believe it.

But what of the lawyers? They would pay no attention to her inner certainty. They wanted only facts, and so far this letter was the only evidence she possessed. Was this enough to allow George to inherit, for that odious Mr. Rotherby to have Edward declared legally dead?

Was this, in fact, the end?

✳ Chapter 3 ✳

E ugenia's fingers clenched with violent force on the pages of the letter she still held, crumpling them. "I won't let them!"

"That's the spirit," Captain Harrington spoke up behind her. "Never give in."

She flushed as she turned to face him, for she had not realized she spoke the thought aloud. "Indeed?" she asked. Her finely arched brows rose slightly at this impertinence.

He refused to be abashed. His generous mouth parted in a broad grin, displaying even white teeth. The effect, devastating against the deeply bronzed skin, caused Eugenia to draw in her breath, then to look quickly away.

"Of course," he assured her, her growing hauteur causing the sparkling lights to dance merrily in his eyes. "Fight with every ounce of energy you possess."

She swallowed the biting retort that rose to her lips, for she found herself in complete agreement with this disturbing man. Instead she concentrated her attention on smoothing the wrinkles from the sheets she held.

"What won't you let them do, by the way?" he asked, still smiling in that disconcerting manner.

Genie pulled herself up to her full height, a process which appeared to afford him still more enjoyment. Her anger

rose. "I do not believe I need bore you with my problems, Captain Harrington. Allow me to thank you for delivering my uncle's letter, and I shall say good morning." She crossed to the door on this note of dismissal, but he made no move to follow her.

"Well, that has put me in my place, hasn't it?" His smiling eyes continued to rest on her in a manner calculated to cause her color to deepen. "No, don't fly out at me." He held up a hand in a gesture to silence her angry response. "I have not yet fully discharged my errand. I am under orders from your uncle to offer any assistance you might require. Indeed, it will be my pleasure!"

"In England we expect a certain measure of respect from our servants. Are all Americans as . . . as impudent and unmannerly as you? Or is it merely my uncle's folly to employ such a . . ." She broke off, at a loss for a word of sufficient force to convey her outraged feelings.

An arrested gleam lit his eye, and a queer twist played at the corners of his mouth. "Oh, it is your uncle's folly, I assure you. But only consider that he told me you would be a meek and timid young lady, so we must hold him excused. His judgment is obviously at fault."

"Of all the impertinent, disagreeable, odious—"

"Certainly, anything you like," he interrupted her, and she broke off with a gasp. "Now that you have vented some of your pent-up spleen, do you not feel better?"

"You are quite insolent!"

"Oh, utterly beyond the pale! My cousin Cassandra tells me so quite often."

"You must congratulate your cousin for me on her perspicacity," Eugenia managed to say with commendable aplomb.

"And now, I repeat: Is there anything I can do to be of assistance? You would not like me to get into trouble, would you?" he asked with an anxiety that was so obviously assumed that she felt an almost irresistible temptation to giggle. "Your uncle will be quite vexed with me if you can think of nothing."

"I imagine a good number of people are frequently vexed with you," she declared frankly, then bit her lip, annoyed with herself for allowing his free and easy manners to lead

her into an indiscretion. He was dangerous company for her, for his carefree energy awoke a responsive chord deep within her, one that it had taken her governess a great deal of time and strenuous training to subjugate.

She sank down onto the sofa. "Oh, do be seated," Genie exclaimed. She watched as he lowered himself into the delicate Queen Anne chair. For a servant, he seemed surprisingly at his ease in the drawing room, but perhaps American society showed a certain measure of permissiveness to sea captains that their English counterparts did not enjoy.

"You say you are familiar with the contents of my uncle's letter?"

"I am a great deal in his confidence," he explained on a note of apology which the amusement in his eyes denied.

"He says that his indifferent health has made it impossible for him to conduct as thorough a search for my brother as he would wish. He also says that he believes him dead. Does he have any reason for this?"

The captain seemed to consider. "Reginald Jessop is not the sort of man to say something lightly, but his health has been very poor, and that might encourage him to take a pessimistic view of the situation."

"Were—are—you acquainted with my brother?"

He shook his head. "Not well. I believe I met him at your uncle's home when he first arrived in Providence. He was rather restless, though. I do not believe he would remain in one place very long."

"What an odd thing for a sea captain to say!" she exclaimed, realizing too late that she had once again spoken her thoughts aloud.

He laughed, a deep, reverberating sound of pure enjoyment that sent a quivering response through her. "Not as odd as you might think," he remarked enigmatically; then his expression altered. "You want to know if your search is hopeless, don't you?" he asked bluntly, serious for the first time.

She nodded wordlessly, her eyes not wavering from the compelling strength of his countenance.

"I can't answer that, I'm afraid. I can only tell you that

your uncle has no real proof, just the fact that his letters of inquiry brought no results. Are you a fighter?''

Eugenia stared at him. No one had ever asked her such a question. ''I am a Wolverton,'' Genie informed him, as that seemed to be the only correct reply.

''Then fight. Don't give up until no doubts remain in your mind, one way or the other. That's what you meant when you said you wouldn't let them, wasn't it?''

Eugenia nodded slowly. ''But my uncle's letter will please my cousin immensely,'' she said with a sigh.

''I'll add my piece to it, if that will help any,'' he offered.

''It . . . it might.'' She stood suddenly, taking an agitated turn about the room. ''Oh, I cannot let George win so easily. Will you?'' she implored as she turned to the captain. ''Will you testify to the solicitors that not nearly enough has been done?''

''If you like.''

''I shall send for them, then. That is—are you free? Can you stay for a little?''

''I am completely at your disposal,'' he assured her, the disconcerting twinkle once more in his eye.

Eugenia sat down at the desk, wrote a quick note, dusted it with sand, and sealed it. She wrote Mr. Mackelson's name with a flourish, then crossed to the bell pull and gave it an energetic tug.

When Langley arrived, she handed him the letter. ''And I won't be needing the barouche this morning, after all. Please convey my apologies to Miss Minton. And bring some refreshment.''

The butler departed on his errands, and Eugenia turned back to her disturbing guest, suddenly uncertain. She was not accustomed to receiving men of inferior social standing, and she found herself rather at a loss for conversation. Resuming her seat upon the sofa, she raised large, wide-set blue eyes to his face. To her surprise, she found herself being subjected to a critical appraisal.

''How . . . did you have a pleasant crossing?'' she asked, rushing into speech to hide her embarrassment.

He controlled a quivering lip with effort. ''It is never dull at this time of the year,'' he said simply.

She flushed, lowering her eyes. "Have you made the trip often?" she tried again.

"A number of times," he admitted. "It can be pretty stormy at this time of year, but I seem to like the spring best anyway."

They continued in this vein, talking the merest commonplaces, until a commotion in the hall alerted Eugenia that her solicitor had arrived.

The door opened to admit not only Mr. Mackelson, but also Mr. George Wolverton and Mr. Rotherby. Eugenia's eyes narrowed at these unwelcome visitors, but her solicitor strode forward, taking her hand.

"They were with me when your note arrived, Lady Eugenia. It seemed expedient for us all to come at once."

She nodded, holding back her vexation with difficulty as she introduced Captain Harrington to the other men. She handed Mr. Mackelson her uncle's letter, and returned to her seat on the sofa. Her eyes remained anxiously on her solicitor's face while he perused the contents.

Without a word, Mr. Mackelson handed the document on to Mr. Rotherby. George, obviously impatient, read over this man's shoulder.

"So Edward is dead!" George exclaimed, unable to hide his jubilation.

"It does not definitely state that," Mr. Mackelson said cautiously. "Merely that Mr. Jessop believes this to be so."

"Well, that is enough, is it not? I don't see how he is to be found if his uncle believes it to be impossible."

Eugenia's fingers clenched together, but before she could speak, the captain's large form shifted in his chair.

"That doesn't mean anything," he commented in a slow, lazy voice oddly at variance with the energy Genie was aware he possessed.

George turned on him. "You have delivered your letter, my good man. I believe your business here is at an end. Cousin"—he directed himself to Eugenia—"is there any need for him to remain?"

"Indeed there is," the captain informed him. He rose, towering over George. He looked the smaller man up and down, then apparently dismissed him from his consider-

ation. He turned instead to Mr. Mackelson. "Mr. Jessop has been very ill for some time now. As he states in his letter, his search has been limited to writing a number of letters, which produced no results. There is much more that can, and should, be done. I believe your search has only just begun."

"This could drag out indefinitely!" George exclaimed. "Mackelson, we agreed at the start that we would await this letter and make a decision based on what it said. And Jessop himself says he believes my cousin is dead. I think this settles the matter."

"It is not settled!" Eugenia exclaimed, alarmed. Instinctively she turned to the captain, her eyes begging him to intervene.

"It would be a bit premature to declare him dead," Captain Harrington pointed out. "Nor would you have much of a case in a court of law, based solely on responses to a dozen or so letters. You will have to do much more than that to have your claim upheld in court, unless English law differs that much from American."

Mr. Mackelson smiled. "I do not believe it does. And you are quite right. I cannot allow this to be sufficient proof. We would have to fight it."

Mr. Wolverton threw his solicitor a look rife with meaning, and that individual cleared his throat.

"We do not deny that every effort must be made to try and locate Mr. Edward Wolverton. But you must also acknowledge that if he is not alive, we may never have definite proof. Therefore, for the sake of the estates, we suggest a time limit. If no proof can be found of his continued existence within, say, six months, then Mr. Wolverton must be declared legally dead, and my client will inherit."

"Six months!" Genie breathed, dismayed.

Mr. Mackelson, to her horror, nodded. "I agree, a time limit ought to be set, under the circumstances." He turned to Eugenia, who glared at him as she would a traitor. "It has been six years, Lady Eugenia. And America is far from being a civilized country, what with all those red Indians."

"Edward would thrive in an environment such as that!" she asserted stoutly.

A slight noise escaped the captain, whose deep green eyes were dancing. Tiny lines at their edges crinkled in suppressed merriment. "Communication between England and America is not as swift as you appear to think," he said with creditable composure. "I would suggest that you set your time limit at one year. Six months is hardly long enough to get word there and back again, without having any time left over for a search."

"There is also the possibility that he might not wish to return—if he is alive," Mr. Rotherby added hastily.

"*Not* wish to be Latham?" Genie and George spoke almost in unison, exchanging a glance that for once registered full accord.

"Edward might be careless," Genie continued coldly, "but he is a Wolverton. Even if he did not love the Priory—which he does—he would recognize his undeniable duty."

"Quite right," Mr. Mackelson said quickly. "That is not in question. Rather, we must decide how best to set about this. I believe advertisements requesting news of him should be placed in every major American newspaper."

"Are you paying for this?" George turned to Eugenia, his tone cordial but his words pointed.

"Certainly," she replied smoothly. "Edward will reimburse me."

Her cousin snorted, but said nothing.

"We are settled, then?" Mr. Mackelson asked, allowing his questioning gaze to rest on each in turn. "Very well, then. We shall write the letters and see to it that an appropriate notice is inserted in the newspapers." He took Genie's hand, bowing low over it. "Lady Eugenia, would you care to see a copy of the advertisement when it is ready?" When she nodded, he said, "Then I shall do myself the honor of calling upon you in the morning."

Eugenia rang for Langley, and the three men were shortly shown out. She turned back into the room to find the captain lounging back in his chair in a negligent manner, one booted leg crossed over the other knee. She stiffened slightly, unaccustomed to a man behaving in so casual a manner in her presence.

"I must thank you for your assistance," she informed him, her tone a perfect blend of the politeness and condescension she would use to one of her own servants who had done her a special favor. "You may be sure that I shall write to my uncle and express my satisfaction with your help."

"Thank you, ma'am, I'm much obliged." The amused sparkle faded from his eyes, leaving them dark and compelling. "You are not pleased by the lawyers' decision, are you?"

The surprisingly gentle note in his voice commanded her confidence, and she found herself responding to it despite the inner voice that warned her against such an impropriety. She leaned back against the sofa, closing her eyes. "No, I am not. They do not know Edward; they have no idea what he is like! I simply cannot imagine him sitting quietly in some large town, making the proper sort of acquaintances who would answer their advertisement."

"What do you think he has done?"

"I don't know," she replied with a sigh. "I don't know America, or what would appeal to him there." She sat up suddenly. "You tell me. What would an adventurous young man do in your country?"

The captain considered. "It would depend on his tastes and on his fortune. Had he much money?"

"I have no idea," Genie answered, surprised. "Some, I should imagine, but not a great deal."

"Then it is very unlikely he would remain in a town. I doubt he was raised to hold down a job, and if he didn't have enough money, he couldn't buy land. Was he a gambler?"

"A gamester? No . . . at least, I don't believe so."

"Then I'd say he probably headed inland, across the Cumberland Gap, to Kentucky or beyond. It's a big, open country, free for the taking, if you have the courage and spirit for it. See to it that they check that area."

Eugenia nodded, confused by the unfamiliar names but unwilling to admit it. "One year," she murmured, gazing off into space, trying to envision the vast, unknown lands of America. "Do you think it will be long enough?"

A soft knock sounded on the door, and it opened to reveal

Langley. After apologizing for disturbing her, he informed her that her aunt, Mrs. Lydia Yately, had arrived to pay a morning visit, and he had ventured to have her wait in the Gold Saloon as Lady Latham and Lady Sophia had gone out for a drive.

"Show her in, please," Eugenia directed.

She rose, moving forward to greet a small, plumpish woman in an elegant gray crepe walking gown. The little lady glided across the room, taking Genie's hands and kissing her cheek.

"So sorry to burst in on you when you have a visitor," she apologized to her niece, peeping over Genie's shoulder to get a glimpse of the blond giant who had stood upon her entry. She looked questioningly at Eugenia.

"My aunt, Mrs. Lydia Yately, Captain James Harrington. Captain Harrington is a . . . a friend of Uncle Reginald's and has brought me a letter from him."

"A friend of Reginald's?" Mrs. Yately exclaimed, obviously pleased with this news. Immediately she crossed over to him, extending her hand as she gazed up into his rugged countenance. "You must know that dear Reginald is my brother." She bestowed her most brilliant smile on the captain.

He responded in a way that set the middle-aged matron's heart fluttering, bowing deeply over the fingers that he raised briefly to his lips. He met Genie's outraged glare over the lady's shoulder with a look of such bland innocence that Eugenia was forced to fight back a smile.

Mrs. Yately seated herself on the sofa, patting the spot beside her encouragingly. Either the captain did not see this action, or he apparently suffered a lapse in manners, for he reseated himself in the Queen Anne chair.

"You must tell me how my brother goes on," Mrs. Yately demanded, leaning forward with an eagerness that had more to do with the captain's compelling charm than with any interest in her long-absent sibling. "Is he well?"

"He has been a trifle unwell of late, but nothing to give rise to any alarm," he told her smoothly. "You are quite like him, you know," he added, after subjecting her to a brief scrutiny.

This apparently pleased her, for she continued to ask him questions, laughing and calling him naughty when he assured her with every appearance of sincerity that Mr. Reginald Jessop was still a handsome figure of a man.

"As if he ever was," she declared, looking as if she longed for a fan with which to playfully rap his knuckles.

Genie leaned back on the sofa next to her aunt, observing this exchange. The captain seemed to be accustomed to flattery and drawing room dalliance, though how he could be was a mystery. His company manners were excellent and his good looks and latent charm undeniable. In fact, he seemed quite the gentleman at the moment, not at all what she would expect of an American.

Only a hint of his restrained power and energy could she detect, but it was enough to make her vitally aware of him, to her discomfort. He possessed a virile attraction that she found fascinating. It was apparent here in the refined atmosphere of a gentleman's book room. What it would be like on board his ship, she did not dare to contemplate.

She tore her eyes from him. He was a mere seaman, after all, and in *trade*! It was quite shocking of her to be so taken with a man so far beneath her.

"Charlotte and Sophia will be sorry to have missed you," Eugenia commented to her aunt, just to be saying something.

"Yes, I was so sorry they had driven out. Is Charlotte feeling more the thing now? A gentle airing is always so beneficial. Oh, and that reminds me why I have come." She bestowed on her niece a smile that still produced a dimple in her rotund cheek. "I shall be holding a small musical *soirée* the day after tomorrow. Nothing elaborate, you know, not while we are still in mourning. But quite unexceptionable, I assure you. We shall have a delightful time, I am sure. Do say you will come, Eugenia, and little Sophia also. I daresay she will enjoy herself immensely. There will be one guest who, I am sure, you will be glad to see." She gave Eugenia an arch smile that filled the girl with foreboding. "And, Captain"—she turned to him, gazing up into his arresting face—"I do hope you will come also. You are a friend of my brother, after all! We must do our utmost to ensure that you enjoy your stay in London."

Genie bit her lip. Having once introduced him as a friend of her uncle, she could hardly now speak up, calling him a servant. If he had any sense of proper behavior, he would cry off from this party, plead some previous engagement, make some excuse not to thrust himself into a society in which he did not belong.

"I will be honored, madam." Captain Harrington smiled down on Mrs. Yately in a way that made this grandmother of three blush like a girl in her first Season. Eugenia glared at him, but he did not seem to notice.

"Well, that is settled, then." Mrs. Yately stood, her mission accomplished. "I must be leaving you now, my dear. So many little details to see to. I shall look forward to seeing you again in two days' time." With a last beaming glance at the captain, she took her leave.

"A most charming lady," he commented as the door closed behind her.

Genie cast him a speaking glance, but refrained from commenting. Instead, she asked, "Are you quite certain you will enjoy her party? It will be a most select gathering. I am sure you will find little in common with the other guests."

"On the contrary. I shall know my hostess, and I shall know you."

She fumed inwardly at his audacity, but kept her tongue. From her very brief acquaintance with him, she felt quite sure that he would get the better of her in this verbal battle. If she were forced to see much more of him, she would have to sharpen her skills.

"Is my uncle really like her?" she asked suddenly, curiosity getting the better of her irritation with him. "My mamma was not, you see, not in the least."

"Oh, yes. There are many similarities, and not just in appearance. Mr. Jessop will be most pleased to hear news of her—and of her kindness to me."

Laughter rippled through his sea-green eyes, creating eddying pools of light that beckoned to her. Filled with a sudden need to escape, Genie stood.

"I must not detain you any longer. I am sure you must have many . . . many business deals to transact. We shall meet again in a couple of days."

He took her hand, bending over it. For a moment she thought he would kiss her fingers, too, but he merely released her, straightening again with that glinting merriment in his disturbing eyes.

"Until then," he said softly. Three powerful strides took him to the door, and Eugenia was left not quite alone, for the force of his presence seemed to linger after him.

For the remainder of the day, either Charlotte or Sophia seemed to be with her every moment, so it was not until early the following morning that Genie set off, accompanied by Miss Minton, to the jeweler's in Sackville Street. Although the proprietor of this establishment seemed somewhat surprised by the necessity for Lady Eugenia Wolverton to sell a pair of diamond earrings, her unusual situation was not unknown to him. The price she received was not as much as she had counted on, but it would be enough, she hoped, to finance the search for Edward.

She need not have worried about Sophia noticing her absence. The seamstress arrived shortly after Eugenia and Miss Minton departed, and Sophia was lost to everything but her enjoyment at being fitted with her first truly "grown-up" gowns.

Mr. Mackelson had arrived in Grosvenor Square shortly before Eugenia returned, so she was unable to join her sister. Instead, she went directly to the book room, where her solicitor awaited her. He had brought with him a copy of the advertisement he had drafted and a list of the papers into which he planned to insert the notice.

"Have you heard of Kentucky?" Eugenia asked him, not seeing this name anywhere among the others.

He stared at her blankly. "I believe there are a number of sparsely inhabited territories in America," he said at last. "But is it likely that Mr. Edward Wolverton would settle in such a place? He is, after all, a gentleman."

"It was Captain Harrington's suggestion. He believes that my brother may have sought a life of adventure, and I agree with him."

Mr. Mackelson looked skeptical, but did not give voice to his reflections. Instead, he merely said, "I do not believe I have sufficient information on the more outlandish reaches

of America to help us. What I would suggest, with your permission, is that I engage the services of a solicitor in America to conduct the inquiries and follow up on any leads. I will hardly be able to do so from here. I fear this may run into additional expense.''

He paused discreetly, and Eugenia reached into her reticule, withdrawing from it most of the bank notes she had obtained that morning. ''Will this be sufficient?'' she inquired in the cool, disinterested tones her governess had insisted she use when referring to such a vulgar subject.

He accepted them, leafing quickly through the folded pieces of paper to determine how much she had given him. ''This should get us started.'' He placed the thick roll into his pocket.

Started? That uncomfortable uneasiness gripped Genie again. She had little to sell, only the strand of pearls which she intended to give to Sophia and the large square-shaped sapphire pendant set in gold and held by a choker necklace of pearls that she never took off. Her fingers rose to touch it in an involuntary gesture, as if to reassure herself it was still there. They would have only one necklace each, and their acquaintances would quickly become aware of it if one—or both—had to be sold. It would be extremely difficult to maintain appearances if that happened.

She was in no mood for joining Sophia in the fitting of the new gowns. Her own three dresses now seemed an unnecessary expense, while Sophia's seemed inadequate to allay any suspicions the *ton* might have concerning the exact circumstances of the Wolvertons. The uncertain succession to the Latham title and fortunes was too well known, and Eugenia feared the consequences of gossip on Sophia's chances for marriage. The announcement of her own engagement to Brockton—if he could be brought up to scratch—would be one very welcome solution.

❅ Chapter 4 ❅

Genie's fear that Sophia's appearance would betray the humble origin of her gown was for naught. The following evening, when she went to see how Sophia did with her dressing for their aunt's *soirée*, no fault could be found in the delicate vision that greeted her critical eye. A fluttering concoction of white muslin, flounced and with a demi-train, made Sophia appear to be floating instead of walking as she moved about to display the creation. If the bodice was cut a trifle lower than Eugenia would have liked for a very young lady, the careful placement of a lace fichu, over her sister's protests, rectified this. Sophia's eyes, a translucent, sparkling blue in her excitement, seemed too large for the fragile face, and the white riband threaded through her dusky curls added the crowning touch.

How proud Robert would be, Eugenia thought. Her sister's fragile loveliness would draw instant admiration and, providing her excitement did not carry her away into unbecoming behavior, her success was assured.

"How *elegant* you look!" Sophia exclaimed, eyeing her sister. "But, Genie, you *should* crop your hair. Did you not study the fashion plates? Curls are quite the thing now."

"For you, definitely. I would merely look a figure of fun."

Had Sophia been given to rational consideration, she would have seen the truth of this. Her sister's small, classically straight nose and large, wide-set eyes would hardly have benefited from the frame of fluffy curls that so admirably suited Sophia. Eugenia's dark brown hair, burnished with mahogany highlights, was worn very long, swept smoothly back to cover her ears, then pinned up to the crown of her head. From there it was allowed to fall in thickly rolled ringlets to below her shoulders.

Over an underskirt of white sarcenet, she wore a simple open robe of lilac crepe, cut very low and square over the bust and with full puffed sleeves. No flounces or ruffles marred its beautiful simplicity. The sapphire pendant lay against the depression of her throat, sparkling in the candlelight.

She stepped forward, a half-smile crinkling the tiny laugh lines about her deep blue eyes. "This is for you, my dear, for your first party. It was Mamma's, you know." She fastened the pearl strand about Sophia's neck, then stood back, casting an approving eye over the effect.

Sophia's fingers rose to touch the necklace. "Oh, Genie!" she breathed. "But they are yours!"

"Not any more," she said, keeping her voice light. "Why, you could hardly go about in Society without a jewel to your name! And pearls, I assure you, are the only eligible ornaments for a girl in her first Season."

Mrs. Yately had assured her niece that this was to be only a very small party, so Eugenia was rather surprised, upon entering the house in Berkeley Square, to find upwards of a hundred people in the drawing rooms. Mrs. Yately herself swept forward to greet them.

"Delightful, is it not?" she whispered to Eugenia. "I believe almost everyone in town has come! Such a success, and so early."

"But . . . are so many people proper? We are still in mourning," Genie protested.

"Quite unexceptionable. It is not a party, really, merely a musical evening. And it shall not last late, I promise."

A string quartet played softly in the saloon, and Eugenia and Sophia moved toward the sound. On the far side of the room, engaged in conversation with Miss Amabel Clayton,

stood Captain Harrington, leaning against the mantelpiece with one booted toe crossed over his other foot. Genie swallowed. It had been only two days since she had seen him—since she had met him, actually—and yet she had forgotten how powerfully arresting his mere presence could be. He towered over every other person in the room, his energy emanating from him in almost tangible waves.

Miss Clayton gazed up into his bronzed face with rapt attention. Eugenia could not hear what he said, but she could almost see those dancing lights in his sea-green eyes. Miss Clayton giggled, waving a hand at him in a flirtatious manner that Genie considered shockingly forward and unbecoming. She turned abruptly from them, scanning the room for other acquaintances.

"Genie, who is that man?" Sophia touched her arm, then gestured towards the captain.

She looked around in assumed surprise. "Why, it is Captain Harrington. You did not meet him the other day. He is the one who brought my uncle's letter to us. An American," she added in a casual tone, "so you must excuse his unusual manners."

Sophia floated her way up to him, her hand firmly holding Genie's as she pulled her sister along with her. Miss Clayton did not appear to welcome their arrival, but she did not depart either, remaining as a listener as Sophia bombarded the captain with questions about her uncle and America in general.

Eugenia, having discovered Lady Clayton, moved to join them. Shortly Amabel Clayton took up her position at the piano, singing a popular ballad in a soft, clear voice. Several times she cast languishing glances at the captain, but must have been disappointed, for Sophia still held his attention. Eugenia vowed to take her sister to task as soon as possible, for it was not at all the thing to talk during a performance. The girl's sole interest appeared to be a flirtation with the captain.

Genie rose as the ballad came to an end, but before she could take many steps she felt a hand on her elbow.

"Eugenia, my love," her aunt purred, "look who has come to join us."

Genie turned and found herself face to face with Charles, Lord Brockton. His elegant attire—a blue coat with very long tails, satin knee breeches, and striped stockings—was a model of the correct dress for a gentleman at an evening party. His neckcloth was beautiful to behold, being tied in the intricate folds of the Mathematical. His brown locks were carefully combed into the Brutus style. For once, his dashing appearance raised only a feeling of mild approval in Eugenia.

"My dear Lady Eugenia, how pleasant to meet you again, and so soon. I am relieved to see you have finally put off your black gloves." His brown eyes moved over her in appreciation, and Eugenia felt her color rise at the manner in which they rested on the full curves of her slender figure. There was a light in the eyes that met hers, but she was not sure that it was one she wanted to see.

"Why so silent?" he asked softly, raising her fingers to his lips in a gallant gesture. Still holding her hand, he placed it on his arm. "Let us go in search of the refreshment I saw in one of the rooms. What this house needs, of course, is a garden. Would you not care to take a moonlit stroll?"

The bantering note in his voice made her hesitate, but to drop his arm and leave him would cause a scene, which she had no desire to do. Better to permit him his flirtation. She could quite easily hint to him that this was not the sort of behavior she had come to expect from him.

A familiar laugh, a shade too loud, caught her attention, and she turned to see Sophia, with two gentlemen at her side. Her high color and quick, wildfire movements warned Eugenia, and she detached herself from Lord Brockton without a second thought.

"You must excuse me. My sister is becoming over-wrought," she murmured. She crossed over to Sophia, separating her from her admirers with difficulty. "Do not, I pray, tire yourself, my dear," she told her mildly, but there was a hint of firmness underlying her tone.

Sophia laughed again, a high, excited giggle. "Oh, Genie, you worry too much! I vow I am having the most delightful time. And I am not in the least fatigued. And in a

moment the music will begin again,'' she added, casting a covert, coy glance back over her shoulder.

Eugenia's concerned eyes scanned her sister's countenance. In spite of her frail constitution, she seemed to be standing up to the strain of her first party quite well. Aside from the obvious signs of excitement, there appeared to be no harm done.

Eugenia watched as her sister resumed her flirtations. She turned back to Lord Brockton, only to find that he was now engaged in what appeared to be a very enjoyable conversation with Amabel Clayton. His interest in her had waned indeed, for before she had been able to command his undivided attention. His easy dismissal hurt her pride, but she found herself disconcertingly unsure whether her feelings went any deeper.

Just then a harp was wheeled into the center of the room, and a young lady stepped forward to take her place before it. Eugenia started to join the others in search of a seat, when a hand touched her elbow, and she almost jumped. She looked up into the gleaming eyes of Lord Brockton. A great weight lifted from her heart, so relieved was she to have him seek her out.

"If we hurry, we should be able to escape in this commotion,'' he murmured. "Come." He drew her hand through his arm, leading her towards the door. "Would you care for some punch?'' he asked her loudly to cover their departure.

Outside the door they paused, and she looked up at him, her heart skipping a beat in her nervousness. Would he offer for her? He had come so close barely six months before. And marriage to him would relieve so many worries, for he would help them find Edward. And even if her brother did not turn up, her social standing—and that of Sophia—would be secure and unassailable.

"Where can we be alone?'' he murmured, one eyebrow raised in a knowing glance.

"The conservatory. I don't believe my aunt has opened it this evening," Genie replied, though her voice held a note of caution. He bore more of the manner of an ardent flirt

than an ardent suitor, but she was no faint-heart and would see this through.

She led him down the hall and opened the door into a room filled with plants. A ring of benches bordered a large round flower bed in the center, and Eugenia sat on one of these. She turned her large blue eyes on Lord Brockton. "And what did you wish to say, my lord?"

He placed one foot in its neat black kid leather shoe on the bench beside her, leaning over her in a most attentive way. His eyes wandered from her face to the low-cut neckline of her gown, and Eugenia found herself leaning back, not pleased.

"It has been some time since I have had the pleasure of your company. Need I have any other reason to whisk you away than this?"

"It is hardly proper, my lord." Her tone held little encouragement.

A broad, sensuous smile settled over his features, and he leaned closer to her. "My dear little Eugenia," he murmured. One arm slipped around her nearly bare shoulders as he drew her closer. He apparently had no doubts as to his reception as he bent his head to find her lips.

Whether or not this was a preamble to a proposal, Eugenia no longer cared. Not only her rigorous training, but also every instinct revolted against such an approach. Drawing back as far as she could, she delivered a stinging slap to his face.

He jumped back, startled, and Genie was able to slip off the bench. "Your manners, sir, are more fitted to the taproom than to a lady's conservatory!"

"Then why did you come here with me?"

She flushed, for she knew her conduct to be reprehensible. Had she not been so certain that a proposal was imminent—but then, why had she been? And why had she wanted him to offer for her? Because he provided an easy solution to her difficulties? Because, in her intolerable, strict upbringing, she had been taught that only such a leader of the *ton* as Brockton would be a suitable match for a Wolverton of Wolverton Priory?

For once she hated that loathsome phrase, hated the pride

that had been drilled into her, hated herself for living up to her governess's—and Robert's—expectations for her. She longed to forget appearances, to enjoy herself without worrying about maintaining standards, to give in to such an ungenteel emotion as love, even if it was for a commoner.

"Call it an error of judgment. It will certainly not be repeated." And it wouldn't. That Brockton no longer considered her as a suitable bride he had made abundantly clear. She stalked off with what dignity she could muster, slamming the door to the conservatory behind her as she left.

Her hopes of reentering the saloon without being noticed died instantly as she stepped through the doorway. The harp piece concluded, and the noise of the door shutting behind her sounded loud and ominous in that momentary pause between the cessation of music and the onset of applause. All eyes turned towards her flaming cheeks. She thrust behind her the hand that still tingled from its sharp contact with Brockton's face. With her head held regally high, she swept into the room, taking the nearest seat as the applause began. She clenched her hands together in her lap as another young lady seated herself at the piano.

"Would you care for a glass of punch?"

Startled, she turned to see Captain Harrington holding out a cup to her. She took it with a murmured "Thank you" and sat sipping it until she felt her anger and embarrassment receding. She was now grateful for the training which a few minutes before had seemed so odious to her. She would now behave as if nothing untoward had happened, her carefully cultivated social manners standing her in good stead.

At that moment the door opened, and Eugenia knew that Brockton had entered the room. She stiffened, her color rising again, angrier with herself than with him for having allowed such an intolerable situation to arise. The music ended; Genie joined in the polite applause and then rose quickly to find her sister.

Sophia met her halfway across the room, apparently bent on the same purpose. "Genie, quickly!" her sister hissed. Her eyes still sparkled and her color was high, but her manner was no longer that of a lighthearted flirt.

"What is wrong?" Genie matched her hushed tones, allowing herself to be led aside into a small alcove.

"I saw you leave with Brockton. What happened?"

"Is that all? Really, Sophia, nothing happened," she lied. "What should?"

Sophia looked disappointed. "I wasn't the only one who noticed. Genie, I overheard two men talking! Do you realize that your chances of capturing Brockton are being bet on at White's?"

The color drained from Eugenia's cheeks. She had heard that gentlemen bet on the most unseemly events, but to be the subject of one herself! Every feeling must be outraged!

"And Genie," Sophia went on, agitated. "They said the odds were heavily against you, that he merely dallies with you!"

Eugenia swallowed. So few thought she could bring him up to scratch. And with good reason, it appeared. But the nerve of those so-called gentlemen to bet on the possibility! There was a great deal of impropriety in the "polite world," and it did not please her.

"Men are quite odious!" Sophia exclaimed. She glared at two of the ones she had been flirting with earlier. "I wonder if Americans are as bad?" she asked suddenly as her gaze, scanning the room, came to rest on Captain Harrington, who was talking with their aunt. Sophia gave a long, rapturous, affected sigh. "I must say, if all Americans are as . . . as handsome as he is, I think we ought to go there and search for Edward ourselves."

Eugenia's smile at her sister's half-humorous sally froze. Go to America? The idea seemed preposterous—at first. But who knew Edward better than she? She recognized, buried deep within her, that same adventurous spirit that she knew dominated Edward. But hers had long been kept under restraint, as befitted a lady of her station, subjugated to the rules of society—until Captain Harrington had arrived on the scene, and she had felt the stirrings awaken.

Genie glanced across the room at Lord Brockton, who had singled out the harp player for an elegant flirtation. She had no more illusions in that quarter. He obviously had been hanging out for a rich wife to support his notoriously

expensive habits. Lady Eugenia Wolverton, with her brother alive and his pockets wide open, was a very eligible choice—and far more desirable than she was now. If her cousin George should inherit, the chances of his bestowing a generous marriage sum on her were very slim. And Brockton was not likely to throw the handkerchief to a poorly dowered female.

She gritted her teeth in vexation. Brockton should not see her languishing or repining at his defection. Let him pursue a wealthier lady. As prestigious as such a match might be for her, she had no desire to be leg-shackled to a man whose concerns were so obviously monetary.

Weighing all of these considerations—Brockton's shocking behavior, Edward's unpredictable movements, and her own spirit longing to be free—the answer was simple.

America it would be.

❋ Chapter 5 ❋

Sophia, Eugenia quickly found, did not share her enthusiasm. The plan, confided to the girl as she climbed into her bed that night, brought instant protest.

"Genie, you are out of your mind! I was not serious, I assure you!"

"But I am. I have no desire to remain here, the object of every vulgar bet in town. And we stand a much better chance than a perfect stranger of guessing Edward's probable actions. For his sake, we must go!"

"We?" Sophia almost squealed. "Oh, no! Genie, I don't want to go! You've had two Seasons already; I haven't even had one! Let me stay with Charlotte," she cajoled. "Aunt Lydia will take me about, you know. I've only just escaped the schoolroom. Let me have some fun!"

"A party given by a relative is one thing. Sophia, we are still in mourning! You cannot go to the parties you are envisioning, not for another six months. You might just as well go to America with me," she added as inspiration struck. "I believe it would be quite proper for us to put aside our mourning there, and by the time we return, it will be all right here as well. And you will have had the experience of American society to carry you through."

Sophia considered, apparently taken with this idea. Eugenia

47

watched her sister closely. It would be better to take her along willingly, though come she would. Having observed the budding little flirt in action, she had no intention of letting Sophia out of her sight.

"It is such a very long way," Sophia finally said. "Eugenia, is not the sea quite rough? It is only just turned to March."

"The sea air will do you good," Genie informed her. "You know how the doctors always directed Mamma to take you to the seaside after you had been ill. You will need a great deal of strength to withstand the rigors of a Season."

With Sophia's reluctant acquiescence, only one problem remained. Money. The fare to America could not be small. Eugenia retired to her bed, considering the matter, until a novel element crept into her thoughts. After living so many years under the domination of her brother Robert, it was rather frightening—and fascinatingly fun—to tackle her problems herself. And she would solve this one, she decided, with newly discovered courage and determination.

The only solution at which Genie was able to arrive during the long watches of the night did not exactly please her, but she was not going to allow anything to interfere with her plans to find Edward. She rose early, donned her most conservative gown, and ordered the barouche to be brought around.

In a very short while, she was put down in Albemarle Street, at Grillon's Hotel. Gathering her courage, she went up the stairs and crossed the lobby to the main desk.

"I should like a message carried to Captain Harrington, if you please, that I am here to see him," Genie informed the man who appeared before her. She fixed him with her most compelling gaze.

One look at her obvious quality did much to assuage that man's uneasiness at the unusual circumstance of a lady visiting a gentleman at a hotel. Bowing, he informed her that it would be done at once.

"Is there a parlor where I might await an answer?" she inquired, raising haughty eyebrows.

Within minutes she found herself established in an elegant chamber on the first floor, boasting a large table, several

comfortable chairs, and a long sofa facing a huge, gaping fireplace. A fire burned merrily in this against the chill of the March morning.

She had not long to wait. Captain James Harrington strode into the room with that swinging, easy gait that spoke of the freedom of the deck of his ship.

"Lady Eugenia?" The deep timbre of his voice resonated through her as he spoke her name. He moved to join her before the fireplace, holding out his hand. If he felt any surprise at her unconventional behavior in coming to see him, he gave no indication. His raised eyebrows implied nothing but polite inquiry.

Coming to Grillon's to visit a single man was bad enough. If word of this got out, she would be the object of just the sort of gossip her governess had most decried. But it was not this thought that held her speechless. Her pride, she discovered, was a very difficult thing to swallow.

"Shall we be seated?" the captain suggested.

"Thank you," she replied coldly. She selected one of the straighter chairs, sitting primly upon the very edge. Her reticule she kept clasped in her lap. "I have come, Captain Harrington, to arrange for my passage to America."

He was in the act of seating himself. As Genie stated her purpose, he checked momentarily in midair, then sat down smoothly. He leaned back, crossing one booted leg over his knee.

"My sister goes with me, of course," she hurried on, determined not to lose her courage. He appeared to be a straightforward sort of man. She would deal with him in that way and lay her cards on the table. If he turned her down . . .

"I have come to you, rather than booking passage in the normal way, for a very simple reason. I have very little money. And what I do have, I am quite certain I shall need in my search for my brother." She kept her tone formal and haughty, trying to hide from him—and herself—how distasteful it was to her to beg. "I would ask you to carry us on your ship." She met his gaze squarely, but could read nothing there. "Since my uncle owns this ship, I hope that our lack of fare will not matter."

Captain Harrington regarded her through half-lidded eyes. The corners of his lips quirked slightly, and she tensed at his amusement. The thought that he laughed at her made her angry, and her chin rose slightly in indignation.

"Well, now, Lady." He emphasized the bare title, his teasing tone making the single word a disrespectful nickname. Genie's temper flared, but his next words drove the thought from her mind. "It seems you're under a bit of a misconception here. Mr. Jessop does not own my ship."

Eugenia's heart sank to the bottom of her stomach. All of her plans . . . She could never afford to buy passage for both Sophia and herself. She clutched her reticule, which held the pitifully few bank notes that remained from the sale of her diamond earrings. Would they be enough for one passage, for her alone? She raised her eyes defiantly and encountered the captain's intent scrutiny.

He rose, taking a quick, restless turn about the room that she sensed was more from a need to be active than to give him time to think. He spun around to face her with suppressed energy. His shoulders quivered slightly, and the golden lights of amusement danced in his eyes. "Are you quite sure you want to go to America? A fine lady like you in that wilderness? What is your plan?"

Again, she sensed that he mocked her, but she was determined to make the voyage, no matter the cost to her pride. "I have none, at the moment," she said steadily. "But I am certain that I have a better chance to find Edward than some complete stranger. And when I do, I intend to make him face up to his responsibilities, to his estates and to his family."

His cool green eyes seemed to bore through her for a moment; then he nodded. "All right. I'll take you both. I believe I can manage to square it with the ship's owner." Again, she sensed his laughter, but at the moment she did not care. He had agreed, and that was what she wanted. After all, she reminded herself, a Wolverton of Wolverton Priory should not care for a mere seaman's amusement.

"If there is any problem, I am quite certain my uncle will reimburse you."

He gave her a mocking bow. "There should be no problems."

"Well, then." She stood, drawing a deep breath of relief at having this business settled. "When do we sail?"

"We must leave for Bristol in two days' time."

"Two days . . ." She stared at him for a moment, aghast. Only two days, and so many things she must take care of . . . Then, with the fighting spirit she was only just discovering in herself, she squared her shoulders and faced him. "We will be ready. Tell me, is there anything special we should pack for a long sea voyage?"

His deep laugh of pure enjoyment boomed forth. "Lady Eugenia," he declared, "it will be a pleasure—nay, an honor—to carry you on your quest."

Only the thought of speed buoyed her as she set about her frantic preparations. She had only one year in which to find Edward somewhere on the vast continent of North America, only twelve short months, and some of that time would be taken up with the voyages back and forth. That made every day precious, and she regretted those that had already been wasted.

The task of getting underway became considerably more difficult with Sophia's sudden, though not unexpected, change of heart. Nothing, that weeping damsel declared, would induce her to undertake so arduous a voyage at this, one of the roughest times of year. In this resolve she was aided and abetted by Charlotte, whose own delicate health made her feel strongly for the considerable sufferings that were undoubtedly in store for her frail sister-in-law.

It was Miss Minton's desertion, though, that served Eugenia the most severe blow. In all of her hasty plans, it had never once occurred to her that her strict preceptress, so rigid in all concerns of propriety, would not travel with them as chaperone. Indeed, Eugenia's training had been so thorough that for a moment she believed she would be forced to abandon her resolve. The prospect of so long a journey totally unsupported by an older female she found not only daunting, but also quite shockingly reprehensible.

"We cannot go!" the distressed Sophia wailed. "Without

so much as a vestige of a chaperone what . . . what would people *say*?''

"We shall have my maid. Sophia, you must not allow such a . . . an unimportant consideration to stop us from finding Edward! How much more improper of us to allow George to inherit without even trying to locate our own brother!'' Her long-suppressed spirit and determination had emerged, and she refused to allow any obstacle to stand in her way.

Although she kept the reflection from her sister, Genie had a shrewd notion that if the exact circumstances of this journey were known, the young ladies would be ruined. A month earlier such a possibility might have wholly borne her down, causing her to abandon such an obviously unsuitable plan. But her courage—stubbornness, Miss Minton called it—carried her through, and she waved such paltry considerations as propriety aside with an assumed airiness she was actually far from feeling. Her training went very deep—but so also did her resolve to find her missing brother.

At least they would not be the lone females on a ship whose only other inhabitants were the male crew. They would have her maid. The young woman recently hired to care for Sophia had refused roundly, but Eugenia's own lady's maid had been with her for several years, and she relied on that woman's loyalty. This thought carried Eugenia through the final hectic hours as she made all the arrangements with Sophia's tearful, halfhearted assistance.

Somehow, though, it was with only a mild sense of dismay that Genie greeted her maid's arrival in her bed-chamber the night before their departure.

"I *couldn't*! Not even for you, miss,'' the woman cried, dabbing at the corner of her eye with her handkerchief. "I meant to go with you, honestly I did. I didn't want to desert you, unlike some I could name, but when it comes right down to it . . .''

"It is all right.'' Eugenia sighed. "I am not helpless, you know. My sister and I shall manage very well on our own.''

These words haunted her throughout the night and the next several days of their journey to Bristol. Miss Minton

accompanied them in the Latham chaise to lend a note of respectability, at least on this leg of their journey. Her attitude appeared to be that what they did after they left English soil was their own problem, but while they remained within this sacrosanct country, they must maintain their appearances as Wolvertons of Wolverton Priory.

Eugenia's first glimpse of the *Cormorant* did much to bolster her sagging confidence. It was a large gray three-masted East Indiaman merchant ship, built deep and broad for carrying cargo rather than passengers and designed for safety and stability rather than speed. Its size and clean lines, along with the sparkling brass and gleaming paint, bespoke its newness, its immense value, and the loving care lavished on it by its crew.

"Captain Harrington must consider himself lucky to be permitted to command such a ship," Eugenia murmured to Sophia.

"Perhaps that is why he swaggers so," Sophia suggested with a touch of asperity, both unkindly and untruthfully.

Eugenia threw a reproving glance at her sister but, seeing her drawn eyes and set mouth, decided not to speak. Although she herself was quite willing to find faults in the overpowering captain, swaggering was something she could not accuse him of. Over-confidence and brazen bearing, certainly, but not swaggering.

They would stay the night at an inn near the quay, the captain informed them, while the ship was readied for its unanticipated passengers. This reminder that she was, in fact, imposing upon the captain and his crew served only to raise Eugenia's defenses. Her guilt was partially assuaged by the fact that she still retained enough money to cover their expenses—as long as they sailed within two or three days' time.

The following morning dawned cold and gray. Eugenia, roused early from her sleep by one of the maids at the inn, was greeted by the news that the tides and the winds were with them, and they would sail within the hour. She crossed to the window of her room, gazing out over the whitecaps that tossed even in the confines of the harbor. She must see

to it that Sophia was bundled on board before the girl realized how rough this first day at sea would be.

Life began at an early hour along the docks. Sophia, fascinated by the commotion, proved far more docile than Eugenia had anticipated, and the only strain of Genie's ingenuity proved to be in the dissuading of her younger sister from buying a monkey, dressed in a cap and jacket, which took her fancy.

When she at last stood on the deck, Eugenia found herself gripping the rails, her knuckles white, in her tension and excitement. What had seemed like such an obvious and simple plan in her aunt's drawing room a scant few nights before now loomed like the momentous occasion this really was. To leave England, with only her younger sister, headed for a strange land on a quest that might well prove hopeless...

She laid cold fingers over Sophia's, and her sister's sparkling eyes met hers.

"I don't believe it," Sophia whispered in awe. "Oh, Genie, do you realize what we have done? I...I never thought you had it in you, you have always been such a...a pattern card of propriety!"

"I didn't know I did either, Sophie. But I'm not going to let solicitors or George push us around or decide our futures for us. We're going to give our dear cousin a fight he won't easily forget."

The last of their trunks was carried on board to be carefully stowed belowdecks. Near the ramp leading to the ship Eugenia could see Miss Minton standing primly, her pelisse buttoned to her throat, her bonnet tied down with a long scarf. She raised one hand in salute, then turned, leaving them, and wended her way through the milling crowd, back to the Latham chaise that would be waiting to return her to London.

The ramp was pulled away. Genie could hear Captain Harrington's deep voice shouting orders as the ropes that fastened the great ship to the dock were thrown off, the sails positioned, and crew members ran to ease their passing from the berth. The deck lifted and heaved as the bow was turned to point out to open sea.

Captain James Harrington's laugh boomed across the

cold, crisp morning air, and Genie felt an answering surge of exultation rise within her. She was heading towards freedom, towards the unknown . . . towards adventure.

The ship rocked with some force, buffeted by the heavy wind and rising waves as they maneuvered free of the harbor. Genie pulled the soft woolen folds of her hooded cloak more closely about her and found it was all she could do to hang onto the smooth wooden rail to keep her balance. Sophia huddled at her side, silent, watching the roiling waters as they slapped up against the sturdy gray hull.

"Let her go!" The captain's ringing cry reached Eugenia, and she turned to see that the ship was clearing the last line of wharves. Dark, churning water lay ahead as far as she could see, the low-hovering clouds matching its dreary color. She felt the ship jerk and pick up speed as the whipping wind filled the now fully raised sails. As she watched, a bank of fog drifted closer and closer until the *Cormorant* pierced its heavy folds and was enveloped within its shrouded closeness.

Captain Harrington ran lightly down the steps from the bridge, jumping the last few and landing quietly on the deck. There was a spring in his swinging stride that had been absent at their last meeting, and energy vibrated from him in waves as tangible as those that were pierced by the speeding prow. Beads of salt spray clung to his brow, and his curling hair lifted slightly in the wind.

"Oh, Genie." Sophia caught Eugenia's hand. "I . . . I don't feel very well."

In the moment's silence that followed this pronouncement, the creaking of the ship and the eerie moaning of the wind could be clearly heard. Gulls squawked above, swooping low to inspect the waters churned by the passage of the *Cormorant*. Eugenia stared in horror at her sister's pallid countenance, enhanced now by tinges of green about her mouth.

"Are you warm enough?" The captain stood at her elbow.

Eugenia spun around. "Can we get my sister below? She is quite unwell, I fear."

"Better keep her up here, then." There was no trace of

sympathy in his bracing tone. "The cold and fresh air will be much better for her than a stuffy cabin."

"Oh, no!" the sufferer wailed. "Please, Genie!"

"Keep her here." The captain snapped the order at her, turning back to his crew and obviously dismissing them from his thoughts.

"You will show us to our cabin, if you please." Genie straightened up with her most regal bearing, fixing Captain Harrington with a haughty gaze. She might be leaving England, she reminded herself, but she was now and would always be a Wolverton of Wolverton Priory. It was best to let Captain James Harrington know at once that she was not to be ordered about as if she were of little importance.

He stopped, turning back to her, amusement glinting in the depths of eyes as dark as the heaving sea all about them. In two steps he was before her, towering over her like one of the masts over the deck. With one finger he tilted her chin up so that he could look squarely down into her face. "Now listen to me, Lady. As long as you are on this ship, you will do as I tell you. And quickly. You will learn why soon enough."

Eugenia shivered beneath his piercing gaze. She had no doubt that he would be capable of forcing her compliance, no doubt that those strong hands could compel her into obedience. The thought was frightening . . . and just a bit exciting, though she was loath to admit it. The power and sheer magnetism that emanated from him were exhilarating, and the temptation to defy him, to experience that energy unleashed, to stir the smoldering embers of what she was sure would be a blazing temper, was almost irresistible.

Sophia sagged limply against her, reminding her of her more pressing responsibility. *The Captain is a servant; do not let him disturb your thoughts,* she ordered herself. Now she had Sophia to worry about.

"If you please"—she kept the haughtiness in her tone, unwilling to let him see that the strength of his masculine vitality had its effect on her—"I believe my sister will feel more comfortable in privacy. Unlike you, she is not accustomed to such . . . such openness."

He released her chin and swept her a mocking bow. "But of course, Lady. On the instant. You'll learn."

Before Eugenia could protest, he had swept the swaying Sophia up into his arms and carried her effortlessly to the door leading down the narrow stairs to the cabins. Eugenia opened this for him, then hurried along in his wake.

Belowdecks, the reek of bilge and tar struck her like a physical blow, and she felt her own stomach turn. She would not admit that the insufferably arrogant captain might have been right, so she continued after him.

The cabin he stopped at was a small apartment, but comfortably appointed with two narrow bunks, a small table, two chairs, and a colorful braided rug. A small porthole gave a view of an endless stretch of gray sea. Two of their trunks and their dressing cases were stacked against the outer wall.

The captain laid Sophia down on one of the bunks, then straightened. "You'll find a basin in there." He gestured towards a small door on one side of the room. "If she gets too bad we have a doctor with us, but the best thing would be to take her up on deck. And now if you will excuse me?" He repeated his mocking bow, backed out the door, and shut it firmly behind him. Eugenia could hear him singing an unfamiliar, lively air as he went back on deck.

The next hour and more were wretched ones for Sophia and Eugenia. The smelling salts had been quickly found in Sophia's reticule, but even they were insufficient to keep the girl from being violently ill. Once her paroxysms were over she sank limply back onto the bunk, and Eugenia wrapped her in blankets, trying to warm her against the shivering that set in.

It was with relief that a little while later she responded to a knock on the door. On her call to enter, a slight man of middle years stuck in his head.

"The captain suggested I give you a look-in. How is the young lady doing?"

"Not well," Genie snapped, irritated by the unnecessary nature of the question and feeling a bit ill herself. Sophia lay limp and pale, moaning softly with each pitching toss of the ship.

The man came into the room, carrying a small case. "I am Dr. Crofton," he informed her, holding out his hand, ignoring the rude nature of Genie's reply. "Now if you will move aside just a little bit? Yes, there, next to her head. I will now see what can be done to make her more comfortable."

He began by pulling the blankets off with what Eugenia felt to be ruthless unconcern for her sister's chills. He felt the tumultuous pulse, looked at her eyes, then stood up.

"Nothing more than seasickness, I should think." He looked down on the delicate girl who moved restlessly in the bunk. "She would probably feel better in the cold wind up on deck. Or is she susceptible to illness?"

Eugenia nodded. "Terribly. We have always taken the greatest care to prevent her from catching a chill."

The man nodded. "Then wait until she is stronger. You might loosen her garments after I have left, and I shall have a potion brewed that will ease the feeling of queasiness and help her sleep."

"How long will this last?" Genie asked softly as she accompanied him to the door.

"Hard to say. She looks to be very frail. I take it she has been invalidish for some time in the past?"

Eugenia stepped out into the narrow passage with him. "Her whole life. Oh, I should never have forced her to come with me!"

"She may surprise you. This might be just the thing to bring her around. Never knew much harm, aside from seasickness, to come from a good, long voyage. Now, get her out on deck as soon as she is strong enough; make her walk about a bit. It will be much easier for her once she gets her sea legs. May take a few days, but she'll come around and enjoy the trip, don't you worry. I'll send that potion around as soon as I can." With a quick nod he moved off down the passage, swaying with the rocking of the ship so that he bumped against the walls.

Eugenia returned to Sophia and unfastened her gown and the stays beneath. This accomplished, she sat back in her chair, patting her sister's thin hand in a comforting gesture.

In a very short time, another knock sounded on the door, and it opened to reveal a slender lad of no more than

thirteen years. A shock of reddish-brown hair hung over a freckled forehead, and his eyes, large and brown, stared at the occupants of the cabin.

"Excuse me, miss. I mean, my lady. Doctor sent this." He edged into the room, bearing a large steaming mug on a round wooden tray. He stared at Eugenia wide-eyed as she rose and went over to him, taking the tray.

"Please thank the doctor for me," she said, smiling at the boy.

His wide mouth broadened into a grin as his color deepened. He sketched an uncertain bow to her and bolted from the room.

"Genie!" Sophia's wailing cry brought her instantly back to the bedside.

"Yes, my dear, I'm here."

"Oh, Genie! I'm going to die, I know it!"

"No, you may wish you would right now, but I assure you, you will not." She lifted her sister's shoulders slightly, slipping another pillow behind her. She lowered her gently, smoothing the lank strands of dark hair back from her forehead. "Come now, drink this. Dr. Crofton made this up especially for you."

Sophia opened one eye, regarded the steaming mug, and a shudder wracked through her feeble frame. "Take it away," she said in a hoarse whisper.

"That I will not. Now, he understands far more of what you are feeling than you do. I expect he has had to deal with this hundreds of times, and with men needed at their jobs. You may be sure it will do you only good. Now drink."

The commanding note in Eugenia's voice did the trick, and Sophia took a tentative sip. As this did not prove fatal, she was emboldened to try another, and through this slow process she consumed most of the contents of the mug.

When Dr. Crofton next checked in on them, Sophia had dropped into an uneasy doze. He checked her pulse, which, although it was still rapid and light, was no longer as alarmingly tumultuous. He nodded his approval of her progress, then turned his attention on Eugenia.

"You had better get up for some fresh air, or you'll be sick as well," he told her encouragingly.

"I don't dare leave her. And I no longer feel the least bit ill. I'm ashamed to admit it, but I'm actually hungry."

He nodded approvingly. "That's the girl. Well, keep an eye on her, but when you want to get out, you just send for me or Sandy. You won't be able to stand being cooped up in here without a break."

His words soon proved true. When Sandy, the cabin boy, next knocked on her door with a tray bearing her luncheon, she was sorely tempted to take it up and eat it on deck. Only Sophia's soft moaning, which had just resumed, kept her from leaving her post.

It took another mug of the doctor's brew to settle the girl. This time she took it gratefully, swallowing the contents in a gulp that must have scorched her throat. She did not complain, merely sipped it more carefully, then settled back down. Eugenia, peering at her with concern, thought that a touch of color had returned to her pale, clammy cheeks.

Sophia's periods of restlessness seemed to come about every two hours. Another one was just beginning when Sandy once again stuck his head in the door.

"If you please, miss—my lady," he corrected himself again, embarrassed by his continued mistake. "Captain's compliments," he went on with his rehearsed speech, "and will you join him in his cabin for dinner?"

Eugenia's eyes widened. This was an aspect she had not thought about. Where would she and Sophia take their meals? Certainly not among the crew. But the idea of dining in the captain's cabin shocked her.

"His . . . his cabin?"

"Yes, miss. That's where the officers eat."

"I . . . oh, dear. Please give the captain my regrets, but my sister is too uneasy. I do not feel I should leave her just now. Could I have a tray in here, as I did for lunch?"

"Yes, miss—my lady." The door shut, and she could hear his footsteps as he ran lightly up the passage.

The response to this message arrived a few minutes later. With only a token knock, the captain swung the door open and entered, his broad shoulders filling the small entryway.

"How is she?" He crossed to the bed, looking down at the tossing figure of the girl.

"Quite unwell, Captain Harrington. As you can see." Her fingers searched for her sister's pulse, and she was alarmed to find it once again beating lightly and erratically. "Please, could you send Doctor Crofton to us?"

"Why won't you join us for dinner?" he demanded.

"Captain," she began, exasperated. "You can see very well for yourself why I can't come."

He continued to watch her, his piercing gaze demanding the truth. "It isn't that you find some problem with dining in my cabin?" he asked, and the teasing light that came to his eyes had its usual disconcerting effect on her.

For a female to dine alone with a number of unknown men was a shockingly forward thing to do. Her courage quavered beneath the weight of her careful tutoring, but she tried to hide this fact, saying merely, with a mild attempt at humor and what she hoped sounded like her customary well-bred ease, "Dining alone with your . . . your officers is not the sort of thing to which I am accustomed."

His eyebrows flew up as he misinterpreted her formal tones. "My apologies, Lady, but I am afraid the duke and duchess have made other plans for this evening. But I assure you my officers, though merely rough louts by your standards, will endeavor to do or say nothing to put you to the blush."

The mockery in his tone caused her to bite off the apology that had risen to her lips as she realized how her words must have sounded. "Indeed?" she said instead, her voice chill. "I shall not put them to so much trouble this evening. I do not wish to leave my sister's side."

"Have you been locked away in here all day?" he demanded.

"I assure you, it does not signify. My only concern is for my sister's welfare."

"Very noble, I'm sure. And what will she do when you are too ill to tend her?"

"I shall do very well," she retorted.

"Just see to it that you get out before you turn in tonight. You'll sleep better for it." With a curt nod, he left her.

❊ Chapter 6 ❊

Visiting the ladies after dinner, Dr. Crofton endorsed the captain's order, telling Eugenia that she would be the better for some fresh air. The sea was calmer, he coaxed her, as she would have noticed for herself had she not spent the day immersed in so much worry. The sky was almost clear, he added, and the stars well worth a look.

In the end she took this advice. When Sophia's uneasy tossings finally stilled and her breathing came deeply and slowly, Eugenia at last felt safe in leaving her—as long as it was for no more than a few minutes.

She wrapped her hooded cloak warmly about her and slipped out the door. It was only a short distance up the rocking companionway, and in moments she emerged onto the deck. Cold, salty wind whipped her hood up and back, leaving her once neatly arranged hair open to the buffeting of the elements.

She was not daunted. The opposite, in fact, held true. Her spirits, depressed by Sophia's suffering, soared, leaving her with a sense of elation. She strolled first towards the stern of the great ship, staring back the way they had come. Somewhere in that vast darkness stretching out behind them lay England, her family, her life . . . everything she knew. And ahead of her . . . ?

She walked along the side, holding on against the pitching of the *Cormorant* as the ship mounted each assaulting wave. Ahead of her, across the far reaches of ocean, lay America. And what, she wondered, would it be like? She leaned her arms on the railing, staring ahead, lost in thought. Somewhere in that vast wilderness she must find Edward . . .

She didn't hear Captain Harrington approaching, and she almost jumped when his deep voice sounded so very near her ear.

"It's a beautiful night," he commented. There was a deep contentment in his voice, and Eugenia felt she could understand his mood. If it were not for her worries, she might even share it.

"I don't believe I have ever noticed so many stars before." She sighed, tilting her head back to gaze upwards. The captain shifted by her side, and the rough material of his heavy coat sleeve just brushed her cheek. She tensed, vividly aware of the vitality that lay beneath his current serenity. There was such strength and energy in the man that it seemed impossible it could be contained even in a frame as large as his.

"Is your sister asleep?"

The question startled her, and she realized she had surrendered to the magnetism that emanated from him and allowed it to sweep over her. She moved slightly away from him. "Yes, finally. It has been a terrible day for her."

"For you, as well. If you mean to sit in that cabin all the way to Providence, you will be mighty bored."

"Hardly that, Captain Harrington. I would remind you that we have been in mourning, and our clothing reflects this. I would hope to beguile the time by making new dresses, in colors, more suitable to America."

"You can sew?" He turned eyes that held a lurking smile down upon her, and she flushed, glad for the paleness of the moonlight that hid the soft tinge on her cheeks.

"We can embroider, certainly. Every young lady of quality can do that. And as for sewing, how difficult can that be? I admit I had thought I would have my maid's

assistance, but there is little a Wolverton cannot do, if she sets her mind to it."

He laughed at that, and her color darkened. "You doubt my word, sir?" she asked, her haughty tone informing him of his great piece of impertinence.

"No, I don't think I should dare," he remarked, his shoulders still shaking gently with his amusement. "Rather, I was admiring your courage. That is something you Wolvertons seem to have in great quantity."

"Thank you." She acknowledged the compliment coolly. *He is a servant. Do not think of him as a man,* she reminded herself with difficulty. She must not allow her standards to slip away as silently and irrevocably as did that great land of England. She was—and always would be—a Wolverton of Wolverton Priory, a fit consort for a duke. A mere sea captain—be he ever so potently alluring—was far beneath her touch. And penniless and alone as she was, she must never, under any circumstances, forget that fact, forget what was due her name and consequence, or she would become a nobody!

"It grows late. I had best turn in," she remarked. Giving him a nod of dismissal, she turned her back and hurried away, afraid to remain—and afraid to admit this fear even to herself.

Sophia's illness continued unabated throughout the next two days, and Eugenia found plenty of time to regret her decision to bring the girl along. Guilt was her predominant emotion, and it led her to be far more uncivil to the captain as he made punctilious inquiries than she otherwise might have been.

By the afternoon of the fourth day, Sophia was finally convinced, much against her will, to come up and take a turn about the deck. Supported by young Sandy on one side and Eugenia on the other, they made their slow promenade. Their progress was watched with considerable interest by the various sailors who stopped their work to observe them, and Eugenia made a firm resolve to speak to the captain about such impertinence.

The walk was repeated the following morning and, to Eugenia's relief, Sophia consented to Sandy's placing a

chair for her in the prow of the ship, where she could sit in the sun, gazing out over the waves, the mere sight of which apparently no longer caused her any queasiness.

The following afternoon, Eugenia welcomed with pleasure her sister's plaintive complaint that she was bored. This meant the girl truly felt better, and she could at long last relax the nerve-wracking vigil she had kept.

"And what would you like to do?" she asked, willing to humor almost any request, so glad as she was to see this improvement.

"I don't know. Anything. I'm hungry!" she suddenly exclaimed, her large eyes widening even more at the absurdity of such a situation. "Genie, I am! Is that not ridiculous? I don't think I have had a proper meal since we came on board."

"I am quite certain you have not. If you will remember, you almost threw your plate at me the other night. You can hardly expect us to keep trying when all you do is wail that we are trying to kill you."

Sophia giggled. "Well, I shall say that now if you do *not* feed me."

"Would you care to eat with the *Cormorant*'s officers tonight?" Eugenia asked with forced casualness. Not for anything would she admit her own desire to do so. But they would be on this ship for what appeared to be an endless number of weeks, and it would be silly to forego the only offered amusement for a scruple. And if it would amuse Sophia, then so much the better.

They dressed with care, taking their time so that Sophia would not be overtired. It was a novel experience, dressing without the assistance of a maid, but they helped each other and found, to their surprise, that a creditable appearance could in fact be achieved on their own.

"Oh, I wish we had a pot of rouge!" Sophia exclaimed, peering into the looking glass at the hollows in her cheeks left by her illness. "I look an absolute hag!"

Eugenia had no need to tell her that that was not true. Her sister had chosen to wear the fluttering lavender muslin that gave her fragility an ethereal loveliness. Her complexion, though pale from her long incarceration, needed little im-

provement, and her blue eyes seemed to dominate her face.
Her curls might be lank and lackluster for once, but Eugenia
helped her disguise this fact with the careful arrangement of
ribbons threaded through the natural curls.

Eugenia herself wore her favorite white crepe gown, cut
low over the bodice and almost off the shoulder. Her only
adornment—indeed, the only one she possessed—was the
large square sapphire held in place with its choker of pearls.
Her hair, which so far on the voyage had been braided and
wound about her head in a crown, she swept back in her
more usual style, smoothed over her ears and pinned up on
the top of her head. With Sophia's inexpert help, several
thick ringlets were arranged to fall becomingly to below her
shoulders. A single blue ribbon was tied into a bow, covering the knot at the top.

When the call came for dinner, they were ready. Sandy,
speechless at the transformation in the two ladies, escorted
them to the cabin next door, where he threw open the door
dramatically.

They needed no introduction. Three men were seated in
high-backed chairs about the carved wood table in the
low-pitched room. Two lamps hung on chains suspended
from the beamed ceiling. Captain Harrington, magnificent
in a deep blue coat with large gold buttons over white
pantaloons, stood as he saw them, and the other two men
did the same. Dr. Crofton stepped forward, taking Sophia's
hand and bowing gallantly over it.

"My dear ladies. I am so glad to see you willing to eat!"

Captain Harrington moved around the table, offering his
arm to Eugenia. "We are most pleased to welcome you. We
have had places set for you nightly, in the hope that you
might honor us with your presence."

Eugenia shot a quick look at him from under her long
lashes, but could detect no trace of the mockery that had
been present on the first night when she had refused to join
him. She moved forward with him.

"The honor is quite ours, I assure you. Now, please tell
me, which of you two gentlemen have we thrown out of
your cabin? This is not a passenger ship, I know. Someone
must have been forced out of his quarters."

"A pleasure, I assure you, to be of so trifling an assistance to two such lovely ladies," declared the other man, whom she had previously seen only at a distance on deck.

"My first officer, Mr. Giles Beverley," the captain introduced him. The young man executed a sweeping bow, quite creditable considering the way in which the ship continued to sway. "I believe he is what you would call an amusing rattle," the captain continued. "I hope you may find him entertaining."

Sophia gave every indication of doing so. As the meal wore on, she ate sparingly from her plate but cast frequent, mischievous glances at the gallant Mr. Beverley on her left. Eugenia, unable to catch her eye, hoped that the aftereffects of her long sickness would keep the girl's spirits in check. They did, but her growing tiredness, coupled with her unwillingness to give in to it, lent a glitter to her eyes and spots of bright color to her cheeks.

These signs were not lost on Dr. Crofton. As the meal drew to a close, he rose, turning to Eugenia. "My lady, it has been a pleasure. But we shall not keep you from your rest. You, my dear," he added, turning to Sophia, whose disappointment at having her evening cut short showed clearly, "we must not tire unduly. Until tomorrow?"

"Indeed." Eugenia smiled at him in gratitude. "It would be most proper for us to retire now, anyway, to leave you gentlemen to your brandy and snuff—or whatever it is American seamen prefer. We shall bid you good night." Fastening a compelling eye on her sister, she started for the door.

An arm reached over her head, opening the door for her. Startled, she looked up into Captain Harrington's smiling eyes. Flushing slightly, she lowered her face, more aware than she liked of his commanding presence.

"We shall look forward to your company every night," he told her. His strong fingers grasped her hand, raising it to his lips. "And when Sophia feels stronger, you must not retire immediately after dinner. I believe we might make up a card table for your entertainment, should you wish it."

She pulled her hand away, unpleasantly aware of the

tingling up her entire arm caused by his touch. "That would be quite nice," she murmured, and hurried out the door.

The following morning they set about the time-consuming chore of making paper patterns from Eugenia's gowns. Whereas the sleeves and bodices might be interchangeable, the skirts would for the most part be identical, a plan which greatly simplified their task. When they tired of this, they went up on deck, but to Sophia's disappointment she did not see Mr. Beverley.

Captain Harrington, though, jumped down from the stack of crates that stood near the center of the deck. He tossed the handful of papers he held to the sailor who stood nearby and strode across to them with that free, springing gait that Eugenia found so disturbing.

"Ladies." He nodded to them. "No ill effects from last night?"

"Oh, no," Sophia assured him. "We quite enjoyed ourselves. We look forward to an evening of cards."

"If Mr. Beverley can keep his mind on them," the captain murmured, causing Sophia to blush adorably.

His amused eyes turned to Eugenia to share the joke, but they met only her disapproving gaze. Immediately his expression turned to one of mute apology, to which she found she was not immune.

His entire countenance continued to bespeak such extreme contrition that she strongly suspected him of insincerity. Under her cool eye, he took on the mien of a hopeful puppy, and she felt an answering quiver of mirth rising within her. Firmly she tried to repress it, but a twitch of her lip seemed sufficient to alert Captain Harrington. His expression remained solemn, but the golden glints danced in the depths of his sea-green eyes.

They did not try their hand at cards that night. Instead, Sophia retired early to bed, as she found, to her dismay, that she still tired far too easily. Eugenia was therefore once again left to her own devices.

She wandered up on deck. The night was not as chill as before, but she wrapped the soft woolen folds of an ivory cashmere shawl closely about her. Standing in the prow, she gazed off across the moon-drenched sea, where the silvery

light sent sparkling shimmers along the crests of the swells. She was not surprised when, only minutes later, booted footsteps sounded behind her and a large, dark shape moved to join her.

She turned ever so slightly, enough to see his profile silhouetted against the light from the moon. The line of forehead, nose, and jaw were rugged, compelling—what a real man should be. No drawing room dandy, this. The very contours of his face bespoke strength of character and will.

She was far too attracted to him. His mere presence could send thrills through her, cloud her judgment, make her desire to remain at his side when she knew very well she should not. She must, for her own protection, keep him safely at a distance.

He turned, leaning his back against the railing, looking down at her with that disturbing half-smile. "Beautiful night," he observed.

"It is," she replied curtly. It was too tempting to remain, to listen to his deep voice, to experience the power that fairly vibrated through him. "If you will excuse me, I wish to be alone." She strode off quickly, before she could give in to her desire to stay.

During the day it was easy to avoid the captain. His duties and concern for his ship and crew kept him occupied on deck, while Eugenia's sewing took up far more of her time than she had anticipated. Decorative embroidery, she quickly discovered, was one thing. Stitching a seam so that it did not instantly unravel was quite another.

With Sophia's assistance, the job quickly took on the semblance of a game rather than a chore. Together they giggled over every mistake and praised themselves loudly whenever something went right. It took them well over a week to complete the first gown, a soft mint-green cambric round dress with a flouce at the hem and a simple braided trim about the bodice. Sophia, spinning about the small cabin while she held out the narrow skirt, could find no fault with her new gown and instantly set about searching for ribands of a matching shade to thread through her curls when she wore it at dinner that night.

The evening meal, and the card games that generally

followed, was the most difficult time for Eugenia. Night after night, week after week, Genie sat at Captain Harrington's right, with Dr. Crofton at her other side. Thus trapped beside the captain, she found herself desperately trying to make cool, polite small talk when every part of her being seemed to respond to him.

The attraction was mutual, she was sure, a fact that alarmed her considerably. Whenever she succumbed to temptation and stole a glance upwards into his laughing eyes, she encountered a gleam of interest there, a spark that lit a similar flame deep within her. His deep, rich laughter seemed to caress her when they shared a joke, an occurrence which was becoming all too frequent for her comfort.

Realizing this, she snubbed his next sally in self-defense and turned her shoulder on him. Searching desperately for a subject—any subject—with which she could monopolize Dr. Crofton, she asked about the ingredients for the brew he had concocted for Sophia's seasickness.

"No secret." He beamed at her. "No secret at all." He went on to list a number of various herbs and spices, whose exotic names assured her they had not come from any English garden, or if they had, it was under another name. He went on, pleased to have her interest and attention.

Sophia, across the table, took full advantage of the doctor's being engaged. Fluttering her eyelashes in a gesture she was trying very hard to perfect, she turned her large blue eyes on Mr. Beverley. From the look on that young gentleman's face, Eugenia doubted he had any idea what she said to him—or even that he cared.

She excused herself from the card game early, going up on deck to stand looking out over the dark sea. She should be safe from the captain, at least for a little while, for he would hardly break up the foursome to follow her.

The voyage seemed to stretch out endlessly, though she knew, at least intellectually, that they were already well over halfway across the Atlantic. In her heart she saw no end in sight, for a very large problem dominated her thoughts. He was large, she reflected, almost a foot taller than she. And so very broad and muscled, with energy to fill two such men. And hopelessly beneath her.

Had the weeks that separated her from England so undermined her upbringing that she dreamed, day and night, of an underbred foreigner? A Wolverton of Wolverton Priory, longing for the touch of a rough seaman? And one in the service of a tradesman, at that? Her only recourse was to snub him, and at every turn. Not for a moment could she allow him to suspect that she found his company very much to her liking.

The opportunity to demonstrate her cultivated indifference to him came sooner than she would have wished. The brush of nailed boots on the wooden deck alerted her, and he leaned against the rail at her side before she could move.

"You seem preoccupied tonight," he said, his eyes gazing out into the blackness.

"Do I?" To her dismay, her cool resolve crumbled and fell about her in a disordered heap. "I suppose I was thinking." With difficulty, she kept her voice steady and repelling.

"About?"

His gentle question caused her to waver, and in retaliation she snapped, more curtly than she intended, "Surely that is none of your concern."

He turned to look at her, his brow furrowing. The darkness veiled the expression in his eyes. "I suppose not," he replied. He pushed himself away from the rail, moving off with his swinging stride partially leashed. She found it easy to tell when he was vexed, but this knowledge did not please her as it should.

Sophia, observing Eugenia's continued callous rejection of Captain Harrington's overtures, finally asked the question that burned in her mind. "Why?" she demanded one afternoon as they sat together embroidering the bodice of an evening dress.

"Why?" Eugenia repeated, smiling the question at her sister.

"Oh, don't pretend to misunderstand, Genie. Why are you behaving so . . . so disagreeably to Captain Harrington? You were abominably rude to him last night. I was never so shocked. *You,* of all people, to so forget yourself. Really, Genie, it is most unlike you."

"The Standards of the Wolvertons?" Eugenia asked, the smile fading from her eyes.

"Certainly. It does not seem at all proper, under the circumstances, to treat him so uncivilly. I am sure Robert would not approve."

"You, speaking of propriety?" Genie tried to force a smile. "But, Sophia, you would find nothing wrong with depressing pretension?"

"Certainly not, but . . . is *that* what you are doing with Captain Harrington?"

"He is most particular in his attentions," Eugenia told her, trying to assume a nonchalance she was far from feeling. "You would not have the daughter of an earl encourage the advances of a mere seaman, would you?"

"Genie! He would not be so impertinent, would he?"

"I fear he would. Certainly you see how . . . how ineligible the idea must be. Every sense of . . . of breeding must be offended. I discourage him as I must, that is all."

"Such a pity he is not better born," Sophia agreed with a sigh. "He is quite the most exciting man, is he not? Of course, he lacks the polish of Lord Brockton, or any of our other acquaintance in London, but still . . ."

But still. Eugenia sighed and concentrated on her sewing. They should reach Providence in another two weeks, with luck. The wind had been with them, the captain said, and the crossing swifter and easier than was to be expected at this time of year. And once she reached Providence, and her uncle's household, she never need see Captain James Harrington again.

For some reason, this cheering thought threw her into a vast depression.

❊ Chapter 7 ❊

E ugenia's concerted snubbing of Captain Harrington
had its effect. She had the questionable satisfaction
of seeing the warmth fade from his sparkling green
eyes, to be replaced by the mockery she had seen when she
first knew him. She felt a pang of regret, but it was
something that must be done, and she tried very hard not to
allow herself to dwell on it.

The excellent sailing weather they had experienced finally
gave way. Every day now seemed darker and more ominous
than the previous one, the freezing cold from the salt air
boring through her very bones. The rising wind whipped her
cloak about her ankles, and she found herself going up on
deck only when the four walls of their cabin pressed in on
her until she thought she would scream if she did not escape
them.

She stood gripping the rail as the ship tossed in the rising
waves, drenched by the spray and mist that made the heavy
air as wet as if it rained. Captain Harrington, as he had done
so often of late, stood in conference with his helmsman and
several others. As they talked, they cast uneasy glances at
the charcoal-gray clouds that seemed to sink as she watched,
hovering lower and lower.

Captain Harrington turned and saw Eugenia where she

stood eyeing them with concern. Giving a dismissive word to his crew, he walked towards her with determined strides that took the rising and falling of the ship with accustomed ease.

"Better get below, Lady," he directed. "Storm's coming up."

Eugenia swallowed, nervous in spite of her outward calm. "I think Sophia would feel less ill here on deck, then."

"Look here, Lady," he snapped, his brow heavy with concerns that were of greater importance than her feelings at this moment. "I've put up with a lot of nonsense from you, but I won't have an order ignored. Now get below with your sister and stay there. Do you want to get swept overboard?"

Her eyes flashed at his tone, but her resolve wavered under the fierce determination she read in his eyes. She started to pull herself up, to meet him with defiance, but he forestalled her.

"You get below," he ordered, his fingers closing about her wrist in a painful grasp, "or I'll carry you down and lock you in!" He jerked her away from the rail, and she stumbled against him as the ship, buffeted by the waves that slammed with growing violence against the hull, seemed to lift up out of the water.

More than half-supported by him, she staggered towards the companionway. She clutched at the frame of the door-way, almost reeling down the stairs as the ship pitched violently.

"Get to your cabin," he snapped. "And don't come out. It's going to get a great deal worse."

His words proved prophetic. By afternoon the plunging and lurching of the ship became intolerable, as torrents of rain pelted down on them. Sophia, who had been growing paler and paler, suddenly stood, gripping at a bracket that stood out from the cabin wall for support. Her eyes seemed unnaturally large in her distress and fear.

"I—I've got to get on deck," she gasped.

"Sophie, no! It's not safe."

"I can't stand it! I feel so—so sick and so closed in! I've got to get some fresh air!" Ignoring Eugenia's cry of alarm,

Sophia released the bracket, almost fell as she lurched to the door, and threw it open. She staggered up the companion-way, falling once, finally dragging herself up by the railing.

Eugenia started after her, but the unpredictable heaving of the ship tossed her to the cabin floor. She clambered to her feet, seriously alarmed over Sophia's wild start, but was thrown down again before she could gain her balance. Frantic, she crawled until she reached the open door, using the frame to pull herself up.

Here she clung for a long minute while the *Cormorant* seemed to lift up out of the water and then dive, nose first, into the angry waves. For the first time she, too, experienced the unsteady lightheadedness of motion sickness, and she gripped the door until her world steadied a trifle. Then, half running, half staggering, she pursued Sophia.

Eugenia was halfway up the stairs when the ship threw violently to the starboard and she almost fell again, saved only by the rail. Her right wrist ached from taking her weight as she caught herself, but nothing mattered now but finding Sophia and bringing her back to safety.

She clambered on, balancing herself with the railing on either side of the stairs. Reaching the doorway, she held on tightly as the force of the winds caught her, almost lifting her off her feet. Freezing rain stung her face and arms, battering her backwards. She leaned forward into the driving torrent and plunged ahead.

She had taken only a few steps before the force of the wind threw her backwards against the cabin wall. Here she rested for a moment, trying to catch her breath, her eyes anxiously peering around the deck through the blinding rain for a glimpse of Sophia. The sky was almost as dark as if it were night, and she could see only a few yards away with any certainty. As far as she could tell, her sister was nowhere to be seen. She shouted, only to have her words whipped from her throat and tossed back at her, useless and unheard.

Real fear gripped her. If she could so easily be tossed about by the storm, what might have happened to Sophia, so light and frail, with so little strength? Eugenia slid along the

cabin wall, passing the open door that led down the companionway, and toiling around to the other side.

There she saw her sister, huddled amid the pile of crates that stood near the center of the deck. She crouched low, her head buried in her arms, leaning against the giant boxes for some measure of protection against the lashing rains.

"Sophia!" Eugenia screamed. She still clutched the edge of the cabin, barely maintaining her balance. "Sophia!"

Her words were again whipped away. Several sailors stumbled past, clinging to each other and anything else they encountered to keep their footing. They were oblivious to her, bent on urgent errands of their own.

Somehow she had to reach Sophia. Her fingers, numb from the cold and wet, slipped from the wall and she nearly fell. Deprived of her meager security, she decided to risk it and started on her staggering way across the pitching deck towards the crates and Sophia—and possible safety.

Genie barely managed three unsteady steps, fighting the wind, the rain, and the wild rocking of the ship. A violent plunge threw her back to her knees, and it was a minute before the ship settled enough for her to struggle back to her feet. She started forward again, half-blinded by the rain that beat in her face and poured from her hair into her eyes.

The port side of the ship seemed to fall away beneath her feet, and a wall of water rose in its place, towering above her for an instant before it came crashing down across the deck. She screamed as it swept over her, slamming her back against the cabin wall. She clutched at the wooden frame, hanging on for her very life, gasping for a breath that eluded her.

The water dragged back, pulling at her sodden skirts; then another wave washed over her. As this one receded, she felt its sucking power, as strong as a hand trying to haul her along with it.

Then real hands were upon her, clutching her slender waist, pulling her to her feet, sweeping her against a rough, drenched sea coat. She clung to the strong arms that held her, sobbing in her terror, unwilling to let go—or be released.

"Sophia!" she gasped. "Where is Sophia?"

"You idiot!" Captain Harrington's deep voice vibrated through his body, and she felt the warmth of him, even through that cold, sopping wool. She held tightly to him until he forcibly set her away. "What the devil are you doing up here? I told you to stay below!" His strong hands gripped her shoulders, shaking her with uncontrolled fury.

"Damn you!" he hissed. "Do you want to get killed?" He pulled her back against him, gripping her slight frame with a strength that bruised her ribs and drove her breath from her body. His mouth sought hers in a savage kiss, and salt and rain and sweat mixed with the blood drawn to her lips.

She clung to him, her response absurdly natural in the midst of this raging tempest. She met his kiss with a force she barely recognized as her own, and they were both shaking when he finally released her.

"Get—get below!" he shouted, trying to make himself heard over the howling of the wind.

"Sophia!" she yelled back. "She came up on deck! I have to find her!"

The captain swore with a force that should have startled the gently bred Eugenia, but she found herself sharing his sentiments.

"Where?" he shouted again. Somehow she was back against him, his body shielding hers from the stinging rain.

"There, by the crates! I—I couldn't reach her!"

Strong hands gripped her upper arms, and he propelled her around the corner of the cabin, through the door of the companionway. "Stay here!" he mouthed, the wind robbing his words of sound. He turned, fighting his way back around that corner into the full blast of the gale.

It seemed an eternity as she waited, shivering with cold and wet and anxiety, until finally he reappeared, carrying the quivering form of Sophia. The ship reared as he reached the doorway, throwing him sharply against the corner. A sharp exclamation escaped his lips, but the rage of the storm carried it away.

On the stairs he tried to set the girl down but she clung to him, wracked with terrified sobs. He shifted her weight, getting one arm up to protect her head as he was thrown

from side to side. With Eugenia hovering barely one step ahead of him, he managed to traverse the companionway and reach their cabin.

Another violent lurch of the ship sent him reeling across the cabin, clutching his delicate burden. He caught his balance, steadied himself, and lowered Sophia safely to the floor. She collapsed there in a drenched heap, her shoulders heaving.

Eugenia dropped down beside her, gathering her into her arms, murmuring soft, comforting words into her ear, and Sophia turned in her embrace, throwing her arms about Eugenia.

"You two look like a couple of drowned rats!"

Eugenia's head spun around, focusing with difficulty through the dripping hair that clung to her face. She glared at Captain Harrington's broad grin.

"If that is all you have to say, Captain..." Eugenia snapped at him.

He held up his hand, forestalling her. "I have a great deal more to say to you, Lady. Be glad I haven't the time. I would suggest you two get into dry clothing and stay where you belong." He turned on his heel, slamming the door behind him as he left.

Eugenia, despite her fiery temper, was not one to scorn good advice. As soon as she determined that Sophia was unhurt, she released the shivering girl and began the difficult process of unfastening their drenched gowns. It took some time in the rolling cabin, but finally their clothing lay in a sodden heap on the floor.

The towels set out by their basin looked pitifully inadequate, but they proved large and soft and very welcome.

"Rub yourself briskly," Eugenia directed, and Sophia, rallying a bit, responded.

"There is some feeling returning to my feet," she declared presently, her voice still quivering.

Wrapped in a voluminous nightgown, Sophia was easily persuaded to climb between her sheets. Eugenia carefully spread the fluffy eiderdown quilt over her, then added a rough woolen blanket as well. What the girl really needed was a steaming mug of coffee or tea and a hot brick in her

bed, but Eugenia strongly doubted there would be a fire burning in the kitchens at the moment.

A knock sounded on their door as Eugenia, now wearing a woolen traveling gown, tried to comb the tangles out of her towel-dried hair. Too exhausted to fight her way across the pitching cabin, she simply called, "Come in."

Captain Harrington opened the door, holding onto it for support. "How is she?" he demanded. Water dripped off him, collecting in a puddle by his booted feet.

"Cold, though I have her dry," Eugenia told him. His blond hair turned a deep, burnished gold when wet, she noted. His eyes sparkled and energy still emanated from him. With a shock she realized that he was enjoying himself!

He came into the small cabin, lurching slightly with the tossing of the ship. "Brought you something." He crossed to the bed where Sophia lay shivering beneath her covers. "Help me lift her up," he directed.

Eugenia joined him, kneeling on the floor by Sophia's head. Gently she eased one arm behind her sister's shoulders, supporting her as the girl tried to sit up.

The captain produced a small chased silver flask from the depths of his capacious pocket. He opened this, pouring a little of the amber liquid into the tiny cup that served as a lid.

"Drink this. Careful," he added as Sophia's trembling hand reached out eagerly. "This is brandy. Don't gulp it; just sip slowly."

She followed his advice, but the first swallow sent a choking cough through her. Gamely she tried again, and this time it went down more smoothly. At last she drained the cup and lay back against the pillows. Gentle color rose in her cheeks, and she appeared a trifle less drawn.

"Now you, Lady." The captain turned to Eugenia.

She wrinkled her nose in distaste, but accepted the tiny silver cup from him. A burning sensation ran down her throat, biting at the pit of her stomach. She took another, less tentative, sip and experienced the same uncomfortable result. Then a welcome warmth spread through her. She

swallowed the last bit and felt the chill seeping out of her aching bones.

"Both of you, stay here," he ordered, and there was a note in his voice that allowed no defiance.

He rose from the floor beside the bed, and Eugenia stood also. She fell against him as they tried to walk to the cabin door, and instinctively his arm went out to support her.

"Better sit down," he recommended.

"Is there any sign of this letting up?" she whispered, not wanting Sophia to hear her concern.

He hesitated, then shook his head. "No telling, really. We may sail right through it at any time."

"Or we may not?"

"You just stay here. I'll send Dr. Crofton along to have a look at your sister as soon as he can get free."

"Get free? Are many of your men ill? Or injured?"

"A few," he admitted.

The dark sky lit up with a blinding flash, illuminating the dark cabin through the round porthole. A thundering crash accompanied it a second or two later. The ship pitched angrily towards the starboard, and the room faded into dimness again.

Eugenia, regaining her balance by grabbing the edge of the doorframe, raised frightened eyes to Captain Harrington's.

He strode out of the room. Moments later she heard the booted steps running up the companionway, and his muffled shout drifted down to her.

"Genie?" Sophia sat up in bed. "Genie, it's getting worse!"

Eugenia crossed to her sister and sat on the bunk, curling her cold feet up underneath her. "It always does, before it gets better," she said soothingly, then could have bitten her tongue for mouthing anything so palpably silly.

Sophia began to cry, and Eugenia wrapped comforting arms about her again. The *Cormorant* continued to rear and toss with increasing force, battered by the raging waves. With growing frequency, heavy walls of water slammed against the side of the ship, covering the porthole until Eugenia feared it would break. The great merchant ship

might have been a toy, so little power did it now seem to possess.

Above them, the shouts of the crew could be made out over the howling of the wind and the constant drumming of the rain on the deck of the *Cormorant*. Her wooden planks creaked alarmingly, sending shivers through them and causing Sophia to cling more tightly. They heard a weird clanking, grating sound which Eugenia finally identified as chains being dragged along overhead. And in the foreground, ever louder, the thunder boomed with resounding power as the flashes of lightning sent momentary glimpses of illumination across the raging waters.

It was the strangely incongruous sensation of hunger that finally roused Eugenia to a sense of how much time had passed. The storm continued with unabated vigor and, between the luminous streaks of lightning, the darkness outside was now completely impenetrable. It was night.

If Genie were hungry, how much more so must be the poor men who had slaved all that long, terrible day? And from the sound of howling wind and beating rain, no relief was as yet in sight. She might be of some assistance, if she could find her way to the galley.

Sophia, resting in her arms, had drifted off into an uneasy sleep. Eugenia lowered her back onto the pillows, covered her, and stumbled away, leaving her sister in the darkness of the cabin.

She found the galley by gripping the walls and following her nose. Someone was attempting to cook, and that fact seemed promising for her empty stomach. She descended another flight of stairs and saw a light burning through an open doorway just ahead.

Here she found Dr. Crofton working side by side with a man he called, simply, Cook. Genie's arrival was welcomed with relief by the doctor, who begged her to take his place and free him to go back on deck. He would send the men down, he promised, one by one, to get something to warm them. The tension in his tone warned Eugenia that they could ill be spared from their posts.

The ship continued to lurch and toss, causing the contents of the massive stew pot to slosh out and scald her hand as

she tried to ladle a serving of the steaming stew into the tin cup that the first of the sailors held out to her. He grabbed it back, shivering and grateful, and stood by the carefully contained fire as he gulped the burning mouthfuls.

This was the beginning of what seemed like a never-ending line of men. By the time she had served the fifth, she almost had the knack of not spilling the stew on her fingers. She had plenty of chances to practice as the night wore on.

When Sandy appeared, she sent him to check on Sophia. Her sister, he assured her not many minutes later, still slept, though he offered to look in on her whenever he could. Grateful, Eugenia thanked him and returned to her ladling.

It didn't seem possible, but the tossing of the ship grew worse. Cook reluctantly put out his fire, saying it was no longer safe. As there were no crew members present for a moment, Eugenia helped herself to the hearty stew, at last easing her own hunger.

Last of all, when she had begun to despair of his arrival, Captain Harrington came into the galley. One look at his haggard face was enough to tell her that things were not going well.

She handed him a cup, and he took it in silence, swallowing the contents in an eager, gulping manner that spoke more of the ordeal they were suffering than mere words could ever have done. Finishing, he tossed the empty cup on a table and, trying to match the fevered rolling of the planks beneath his feet, headed back out of the room.

"Captain!" Genie tried to run after him, but she slammed hard into the table and knocked over one of the chairs as she was thrown between them.

He turned in the doorway, bracing himself against it as he caught her shoulders to steady her. She looked up into his face, so very close above her own as he bent over her. His eyes shone brightly and for a moment, in spite of her fear, time seemed to stand still.

"Captain," she finally gasped. "I—how is it up there?"

"Everything will be fine," he told her soothingly. "Don't—"

The ship heaved hard to starboard, almost throwing them

off their feet. Captain Harrington swore softly, and he set Eugenia aside.

"Excuse me, Lady, it would seem—"

They could not see the lightning, but the thunder exploded in a resounding clap right on top of them. And there was another crack, as of the snapping of wood, that brought the captain's head jerking up. That same creaking, splintering sound came again, and he turned and ran up the passage, bouncing off the walls in his haste.

Eugenia didn't think. She simply ran after him as best she could. She heard that creaking sound again, loud even above the raging storm. She started up the second flight, now well behind Captain Harrington.

The rain and wind slammed into her as she emerged onto the deck. A group of men stood with ropes about the main mast. As she watched, unbelieving, the top half of the great wooden pole, which leaned at an odd angle, shifted its position. The splintering sounded once more, and the mast, yardarms, and furled sails came crashing down upon the men.

A scream tore from Eugenia's throat. Rumbling thunder roared in her ears as a ragged branch of lightning lit up the sky, illuminating the tangled heap of canvas, wood, and bodies. Conscious thought suspended, Eugenia ran forward.

She was pushed aside as the deck crew raced to help. The sail-covered pile heaved—or was it the whole deck that rose, then sank away?—and a man dragged himself out from underneath to collapse barely a yard away. Eugenia fell beside him, reaching out to turn him over.

"Don't touch him!" Dr. Crofton's voice bellowed somewhere near her ear, and she turned to him, filled with horror.

"Is—is he dead?" She had to scream to be heard over the pandemonium of the storm and yelling men.

The doctor placed his hand about the man's wrist, then released it. "Just unconscious. No, don't try to turn him." He stopped her impulsive gesture. "First have to see if he's broken anything."

Something dark seeped from the right side of the man's

forehead, and Eugenia realized it was blood escaping from a long, ugly cut.

The doctor ran an experienced hand over the man's arms and legs, then under the great sea coat, feeling his ribs and shoulders. "Lucky, this one." He stood as another man was dragged free of the wreckage.

This one had not fared so well. Eugenia, peering with frightened eyes over the doctor's shoulder, saw in a flash of lightning the crooked angle at which his knee bent.

She swallowed sickness and caught Dr. Crofton's arm. "What can I do to help?" she cried over the howling wind.

He looked her over, then nodded. "Think you can bandage?" he shouted back. Sandy appeared near her elbow and was sent running for the doctor's emergency supply of linen.

Eugenia, not overly familiar with the sight of blood, had a strong notion she was not going to stand up well. In this she wronged herself. She stumbled after Dr. Crofton, her sodden skirts tangling between her legs, tripping her. Four men now lay on the deck. She watched as he assessed the injuries, then bandaged what she could.

A ripping noise sounded behind her and she started, eyes wide with fear, as the rain-soaked canvas near her bulged and jerked, then separated eerily. An arm holding a knife emerged, briefly illuminated by a glittering streak of lightning, and her heart settled back from her throat. A moment later, Captain Harrington's head emerged.

Instinctively, Eugenia sprang to help him, but his first words, emitted loudly though in a purely conversational tone, shocked her by the breadth of his vocabulary. The knife dropped from his fingers, and his hand came down shakily to grip his upper arm. Two crewmen pushed her aside and helped him from the mess.

He sank to the deck beside Dr. Crofton. Eugenia hugged herself against the fear and cold that swept over her as freezing rain poured unheeded down her straggling hair and the wind whipped it across her face and neck. His breathing was too ragged . . .

"Better cut the sleeve," the captain directed the doctor, who tried in vain to ease him out of his greatcoat. His eyes

narrowed and teeth gritted as the man complied. Carefully the shreds of the sleeve were pulled back. The remnants of a fine lawn shirt followed, exposing an arm covered in blood. Automatically, Eugenia reached to wipe it away, then became aware of the fragments of wood embedded in the skin. A gasp escaped her and, horrified, she turned to Dr. Crofton.

"Well, Lady?" Captain Harrington asked. In spite of his pain, there was a dancing, teasing spark in his eyes, reflected in the intermittent flashes. Rain washed down his face and shoulders, and the blood thinned, flowing away.

"Wrap it in a towel and put it in a sling," the doctor told Eugenia, breaking the spell that had frozen her. "We'll have to get him below before we can see to clean that."

"The devil you will." The captain grinned at them, and Eugenia again felt that suppressed energy about him. He swung himself to his feet, staggering before he caught the motion of the deck.

"Stand still!" Eugenia surprised herself by snapping at him. "And hold your arm out!"

He raised his eyebrows, but submitted to her wrapping the towel loosely about the injury. Next she knotted a sling from a strip of the doctor's linen. She had to stand on tiptoe, but she managed to throw it around the captain's neck. Although she braced herself for trouble from him, he made only a token objection as she eased his arm into position.

"Thank you, Lady." He bowed to her, keeping his balance on the rain-drenched, plunging deck with difficulty. The mocking tone was back in his voice, and Eugenia's temper flared.

"Go below and get that cleaned!" she ordered him, yelling to be heard.

"Lady, it pains me to disappoint you," he shouted back. "Were you hoping to dig a dagger into me yourself? I have a ship to see to." He left her seething, dashing the wet hair from her face, and wishing very much that she might have a chance with that dagger.

A loud moan from one of the sailors recalled her attention, and she made her way, half-crawling on the slippery,

heaving planks, to Dr. Crofton. As they worked, she could hear the captain's energetic, cheering voice booming forth over the storm, rallying his tired crew as they attempted to tie down the wreckage before more men were hurt.

In spite of herself, Eugenia could not help admiring his spirit and courage. He staggered back and forth, wherever an extra hand was needed most, to all intents oblivious to his left arm, which hung in a blood-soaked sling. Nothing seemed to tire him, nor drain his seemingly endless supply of vigor and strength.

"That is all we can do for now." Dr. Crofton sat back, rubbing a weary forearm across his streaming face. "Go below, ma'am. Best get out of the way." A stretcher had been brought up on deck, and the doctor turned his attention to the man with the broken leg, directing his removal to shelter below.

Eugenia, too exhausted to think clearly, took his advice. She followed the men down as they carried the stretcher, turning in at her own door. She sagged against the cabin wall, rolling with the erratic pitching of the ship, and watched as the rain dripping from her skirts formed a puddle on the floor. She shuddered uncontrollably from reaction and cold.

As the door clicked closed behind her, Sophia stirred, murmured softly, then opened her eyes.

"Genie?" she cried as awareness of the storm flooded back to her.

"Yes, dearest." She crossed to the bed, catching her sister's extended hands. "I am dripping wet, Sophia, but I am here." Still talking, she unfastened her gown, letting it slump to the floor in a wet heap. That made two dresses she had ruined that day, she thought.

"Genie, what is happening?" Sophia demanded in rising panic. "Are . . . are we going to be all right? Will the ship go down?"

It was a question she herself had asked, and the smile she forced to her lips slipped awry as she realized she was giving Sophia the same meaningless answer she had received.

"Everything will be fine," she declared, forcing conviction into her tired voice.

"Light the lamp, Genie. I can't see!"

"Not while the ship rolls so. It's not safe," she said with a sigh, though she herself would have felt better with a warm, friendly glow in the cabin. Pulling on a warm wrapper, she sank down on her sister's bunk. "We shall have to wait until it is calmer. Captain Harrington has everything under control." With an effort, she refused to yield to the temptation to fall over and just go to sleep.

Sophia sank back onto the pillows, the darkness hiding her expression from her watchful sister. "I suppose he does," the girl finally breathed, though her voice still quavered. "It's—it's a pity he is not more well-bred," she added with a touch of humor that bordered on the hysterical. "He—he is quite the most capable and—and *manly* man I have ever met."

Her sister returned no answer, for she found this echoed her own sentiments too closely.

With the felling of the main mast, the storm seemed to have exhausted its fury. Eugenia, huddled on the bed beside her trembling sister, suddenly sat up, her eyes widening.

"Genie?" Sophia sat up also, gripping her sister's arm.

"It's all right, Sophie. Can't you feel it? The ship is not heaving as much. And the wind . . . Listen, is it not quieter?"

Sophia did listen, but the only result was that she hugged her sister's arm more tightly. "It—it *howls* so, Genie!"

"But less! And we have not heard thunder—or even seen lightning—for some time now, have we? We are through the worst of it!"

Unconvinced, Sophia still hung onto Eugenia's arm, but even she finally felt the change. The ship did indeed rock less violently, the sounds of the wind and rain became less and less, and there seemed to be a general lightening of the sky outside. The hideous storm was passing.

As Sophia relaxed, Eugenia carefully untangled her arm from the girl's grip and moved across to her own bunk. She fell onto this, pulling up the warm eiderdown and wrapping it tightly about her. Rolling over, she gazed out the tiny porthole, up into the dark sky. High above her, one tiny star peeped out, blinked, then continued to shine.

❋ Chapter 8 ❋

What images haunted her dreams she did not remember, but Eugenia's first conscious thought on awakening was of Captain Harrington's courage. Visions of him striding about the rain-swept deck, shouting encouragement, his arm hanging useless in that blood-soaked sling, flooded back to her.

Proof that it had not been just a horrible nightmare lay on her cabin floor. Propped up on her elbow, Eugenia eyed her ruined dresses with dismay. It would perhaps be easiest simply to drop these garments overboard. Even as she recognized the urge, she knew she would not. The gowns would be washed and ironed, and most likely saved.

"It is calm!" Sophia exclaimed, thus announcing that she, too, was awake. "And, Genie, just look at the sky! There are only just a very few clouds, and it is such a lovely blue."

They had barely finished dressing when Sandy knocked on their door, bearing a tray laden with a hearty breakfast. Sophia, who had not eaten the night before, went immediately to work on hers, but Eugenia could not rid herself of the memory of the mast and yardarms toppling, and the men caught beneath the wreckage as it crashed to the deck . . .

"Sandy!" She stopped the youth.

"Yes, miss?"

"The mast—how much damage was there?"

"Well, miss, you'll have to ask the captain. There's been some, sure enough, but he's looking things over now to see what needs doing."

She thanked him, allowing him to return to his duties, which must be numerous on such a morning as this. Applying herself to her own breakfast, she soon caught up with Sophia, and the two finished very rapidly.

"Can we go on deck?" Sophia returned to the porthole and peered out.

"We should see where we can be of help," Eugenia decided. "I suppose we must find Captain Harrington."

Their first glimpse of the deck provoked a gasp of alarm from Eugenia. She had been out there during the storm, she had seen the top half of that massive mast topple, but somehow, in the darkness with her eyes blinded by the rain, it had not seemed so bad.

"Oh, Genie," Sophia's small hands gripped her arm with a painful, convulsive hold. "Do—do you think we shall sink?"

"No," Eugenia replied. Her gaze moved slowly about the wreckage before her, and a sick feeling of shock engulfed her. One of the yardarms, from which the canvas had already been cut free, lay across the broken cargo crates and out over the edge of the deck, where a large expanse of railing was missing. Splintered wood seemed to be everywhere. Even in the captain's arm . . . She swallowed hard.

His deep, resounding laugh boomed across the fresh, crisp morning air, and Eugenia's heart lifted with the infectious energy that emanated from Captain Harrington. In a moment, his swinging stride brought him into their sight. His head was turned as he looked back over his shoulder, shouting encouragement to the crew members who carried on the clean-up work. There was no blood on the sling in which his left arm rested, a silent testimony to the fact that he had at last allowed the wood fragments to be removed and his wounds to be treated. He sidestepped the splintered chunks of wreckage as if by instinct.

"Captain!" Genie stepped forward, hailing him as he walked past without a glance at them.

He stopped, raising questioning eyebrows. "Well, Lady?"

"Is it? Well, I mean?"

That dancing light sparkled in the green depths of his eyes. "It is, Lady. You need have no fear."

"We are hardly afraid, Captain," she retorted, irritated by his teasing demeanor. "We wish to know if we may be of service."

"Stay out of the way." He started to walk off.

"You did not seem to think I was in the way last night!" She almost stamped her foot in her growing anger. Was he the egotistical sort who believed women belonged in the drawing room—and bedroom—but had little value otherwise?

He looked her up and down, his amusement growing. "I believe I gave you the same advice then."

"And you saw how much good I did by ignoring it!" she flashed back.

He raised skeptical eyebrows, then shrugged. "Go consult Dr. Crofton, if you're having an attack of *noblesse oblige*. I am sure he will allow you to sort bandages, or something else equally safe. Now if you will excuse me, I have a few urgent matters to see to."

Genie spun on her heel and stormed back down the companionway, a perplexed Sophia scuttling along in her wake. They stopped at the small cabin that Dr. Crofton had converted to a makeshift infirmary the night before and knocked lightly on the door. His voice bade them enter, and they were soon engrossed in assisting him with tearing linen and rolling new bandages.

Women's work, Eugenia fumed to herself. It might be true she was not as strong as a man, but she had been raised in the tenet that a lady assisted those less fortunate than herself. Ladling soup and tearing sheets into bandages was indeed the sort of occupation that was not only proper but expected. Still, it galled her that the captain felt she could do no more.

By the time morning wore into afternoon and the sounds of sawing and hammering ceased on the deck above them, a new thought had intruded to temper Eugenia's anger. She had, she knew, quite intentionally played the Great Lady before the captain. In every way possible she had let him know that she was infintely above him, every inch a lady. And she had tried

to hide from him the almost forgotten embers of adventurous spirit that no longer lay dormant within her.

He had every reason for behaving in an insulting manner towards her, for she had done the same to him. And even if he were the employee of some tradesman, even if he were socially beneath her, he was in so many ways a vastly superior creature, a man worthy of the respect she had denied him, a man in every sense of the word. She had sensed his power, recognized his boundless energy, experienced his gentle consideration. And last night she had witnessed the indomitable courage that kept him pacing the deck, working side by side with his crew, rallying them with his unwavering vigor, even though badly injured himself. He was a man to whom she owed her humblest apology for her haughty behavior.

Apologizing for her conduct was not something Eugenia had ever had to do before. Nor did it come easily for her. Leaving her sister quietly sewing in their cabin, she swallowed her pride and went back up on deck in search of him.

She found him overseeing the repair of the main sail. Biting her lip to rally her failing courage, she approached him, her bearing stiff to hide her inward quavering at this unusual task.

"Captain Harrington?" She stood near him, embarrassment holding her rigid. "If you please, I would like to have a word with you."

He raised questioning eyebrows but made no movement to leave his work.

"In private, if you please, Captain." Her voice, even to herself, sounded brittle and edgy. She swallowed, trying to quell her nervousness, but succeeded only in appearing haughtier than ever.

He executed a mocking bow, then gestured for her to precede him to the prow of the ship. She swept along before him, her bearing regal to hide her uncertainty. Reaching the comparative privacy of the prow, she turned to face him.

"There is something I wish to say to you, Captain Harrington," she began.

"I'm not much interested in anything you have to say to me, Lady." He cut her off abruptly, misinterpreting the

reason behind the cold formality of her words. "But you're going to listen to a few home truths from me."

Genie's head snapped up. Startled by the sneer in his tone, she started to speak.

"Be quiet. You're not going to believe this, but it's for your own good, and you're going to hear it whether you want to or not. There aren't many Americans who'll be impressed by your fancy airs and graces. Your snobbery may have been overlooked in England for the sake of your title, but it won't do you any good where you're going now. It'll only win you enemies in Providence."

Eugenia gasped and took a step backwards, away from the fiery lashing of his words, but he gripped her wrist, pulling her back. He gave her a grim smile.

"Told you you wouldn't like this," he continued, "but you're going to stay and hear me out. While you're in America, you will simply be *Miss* Wolverton, a lady no more, without rank or breeding to make your atrocious manners acceptable. In America you'll be no better than anybody else, and pretending you are won't make anyone like you."

Now it was shock and rising fury rather than embarrassment that held Eugenia rigid. One hand swung out and up, but he caught her wrist before she could strike him, forcing her arm back down with infuriating ease.

"Temper, Lady. I'm not done yet. There may be some people in Providence who will receive you for your uncle's sake, but if you continue to play off your airs, they won't put up with you for long." He dropped her wrist as if contact with her burned him. The captain gave her one long, comprehensive gaze, his lips quirking up into a sardonic smile.

"And I, for one, Lady, will be damn glad to see the last of you."

He turned on his heel, leaving her where she stood, in the frustrating position of being unable to think of a single insulting setdown to hurl at his retreating back.

❋ Chapter 9 ❋

Eugenia's fury at Captain Harrington's unjustified rakedown left her trembling. Had he remained before her, she could have strangled him with her bare hands and known only pleasure in doing so.

She spun about, grasping the railing of the prow in lieu of his neck, her fingers crushing against the wood until they hurt as she stared unseeingly across the endless sea before her. How could he have said such untruthful, hateful things about her? That she had succeeded in her aim to set him at a distance and make him realize that she was a lady did not now weigh with her. Only his abominable, odious misinterpretation of her attempted apology mattered, and she would make him regret it!

So he thought her proud and detestable, did he? And he would be only too glad to see the last of her? Well, she would see about that. No man spoke to her in that manner, no matter how highly born he might be. And as for a mere sea captain, a mere servant . . . !

He must be brought to rue those words, to realize how utterly and contemptibly wrong he was about her. He must be brought to . . . to love her! A slow, angry smile lit her brilliant blue eyes. She would make him fall in love with

her and then laugh in his face at his heartrending entreaties. *That* would teach him to insult her!

She released her stranglehold on the rail, leaning forward slightly to rest her elbows on it instead. Her hands clasped together, she bent her mind to evolving the details of her retribution. He had been disposed to admire her, which was why she had been obliged to snub him in the first place. That should make it easier. It was highly unlikely that he had ever before been acquainted with a lady familiar with the ways of London's polite society. And as such, he would be the more easily captivated by the calculated charms, enticements, and flirtations that were a necessary part of every young debutante's repertoire.

She would begin by presenting herself to him in a chastened mode. Let him believe she had taken his words to heart and was repentant. And then, when he felt complacent and forgiving, bent on showing her he held no ill feelings, she would spring her trap.

She remained in the prow of the *Cormorant* for some time, then went below to her cabin to begin preparations. There she found Sophia, just finishing the hem on a flounce.

"What do you think?" the girl asked, her eyes shining with pride at her accomplishment. She held up an evening dress of the palest mint green crepe, of a simple but elegant cut, with a low, curved bodice, puffed sleeves, and a double flounce.

"Quite the thing," Eugenia told her, nodding in approval. Her eyes narrowed, watching Sophia's smug gaze as the girl admired her handiwork. *Only a few short months ago we were shocked by the idea of visiting a linen draper. And here we are creating our own gowns!* And doing a very good job of it, too, she was forced to admit. Well, if they failed to find Edward, she and Sophia could always shock the family and disgrace Cousin George by setting up as mantua-makers.

In another hour, she calculated, it would be time to dress for dinner. She strolled to the cupboard and threw open the door, considering her meager collection of dresses. She wanted something simple and demure for tonight. Her eyes lit on a white muslin trimmed with lilac ribands from their

half mourning. She would retrim it with the sapphire blue ones she had brought.

She finished in time to dress her hair in its usual fashion, swept back, then up to the top of her head. With Sophia's assistance she arranged large ringlets to fall over her shoulders. Giving her appearance one last, searching glance in the mirror, she was satisfied.

When Sandy knocked on their door to announce the evening meal, she picked up the ivory cashmere shawl and draped the soft folds of wool across her elbows. Together she and Sophia went to the captain's cabin next door.

The men stood as the young women entered. Sophia cast her brilliant smile on all of them, then moved to join Mr. Beverley as was her wont. Eugenia hesitated momentarily in the doorway, her eyes just brushing the captain's dominant figure before she lowered them, noting his clean, pressed sling and the complete indifference with which he wore it. She moved gracefully across the small room to take her accustomed seat. She turned to greet Dr. Crofton, then kept her eyes on her plate, as if afraid to raise them to meet Captain Harrington's gaze.

"Has the damage been repaired now?" Sophia asked.

Mr. Beverley smiled at the naiveté of her question. "As much as we can do while at sea, at least," he told her. "There is no way we can raise a new mast." He lifted the lid from a serving dish and offered her some of the sauce-covered fish that lay within.

"Does that mean we are still in danger?" Sophia's large, frightened eyes turned instinctively towards the captain.

"Not in the least. We merely are not sailing under full power, and it will take us a little extra time to reach port. But we are perfectly safe." The captain reached across, taking the platter of fish and offering it to Eugenia.

She raised her face to his, then lowered it immediately, allowing her eyelashes to flutter as if in confusion. "Please," she murmured. "I . . . I am indeed grateful that we find ourselves in such capable hands. The ship might have been lost had it not been for such bravery as I witnessed last night."

"They are a good crew," the captain agreed, deliberately

misinterpreting her meaning. "But as I said, we were in no real danger. The *Cormorant* is designed to weather worse storms than that one, I assure you. She is of a new design, incorporating many of the better features of earlier ships. That stroke of lightning was a piece of ill luck."

"You must be proud indeed to sail her," Eugenia said.

"That I am. A man likes a ship that responds to his hand, that yields to his will. Like a woman."

She bit her tongue, choking back her retort. She could sense his eyes resting on her, could feel the amusement that remained just in check. She kept her eyes determinedly on her fork, though she felt the color rise in her cheeks from the effort of restraining her speech.

"Exactly like a woman," Mr. Beverley responded, nodding his head in agreement.

"We are embarrassing Lady Eugenia, my dear Beverley." A rich chuckle rumbled through the captain's massive form, and Eugenia clenched her fingers together to keep from slapping that comical smirk from his lips.

"How many more days will we be at sea?" Sophia asked the question that had been dominating her thoughts ever since they had set out from Bristol.

"Hard to guess," the captain replied. "It should have been only three or four days more. Now perhaps a week."

Mercifully, the remainder of the conversation dwelt on such innocuous topics as the probable weather and the damage sustained to the cargo in the crates on deck. As soon as they finished eating, Eugenia rose, signaling with a slight motion of her head for Sophia to join her.

"If you gentlemen will excuse us, we are quite tired. We—we had rather a disturbed night." She smiled at Dr. Crofton and Mr. Beverley, then raised wide eyes to the captain's face. Giving him a shy, trembling smile, she looked away and hurried out of the cabin. Before she turned, though, she had the satisfaction of seeing a puzzled expression narrowing his brooding, sea-green eyes.

Sophia was bored, but the storm had taken its toll on her, and she put on only a token protest at not remaining with the gentlemen for an evening at cards. Instead, she occupied herself with rereading her copy of Byron's *The Corsair,*

already quite tattered in spite of the fact that it had been published less than a year before.

Eugenia retired to her bunk and, despite every intention to plan her enthrallment of Captain Harrington, she fell quickly asleep.

She encountered Captain Harrington again sooner than she was ready. She stood on deck the following morning, the soft ivory woolen shawl wrapped warmly about her shoulders as she stared ahead as if seeking her first glimpse of the new land. He came up behind her, the sounds of his energetic, springing step muffled by the gentle splashing of the sea as the prow cut through the swells.

"Well, Lady?" His deep voice startled her.

She faced him, then turned quickly away again, remembering her intentions. She must seem tentative with him, almost afraid, so that her flirtation, when she began it, would prove all the more enticing to him.

"Captain Harrington?" She kept her eyes on her hands.

He leaned against the rail at her side and was silent for several minutes. Then he said, "They are quite pretty."

She looked up at him, perplexed. "What are?" she asked tentatively, not sure whether or not this was another calculated insult on his part.

"Your hands. You have spent a great deal of time looking at them of late. Do you not find it boring?"

"If I did, surely I would look elsewhere!" she retorted before she could stop herself.

His broad smile spread across his deeply bronzed face. "Now that's more like it, Lady. You didn't say a single cross word to me last night. I was afraid you were ill."

"It pleases you to insult me." With difficulty she controlled her voice, though the slight quaver that remained could have been taken for hurt instead of anger.

"It pleases me to talk to you, though I'm damned if I know why," he told her candidly. "It does not please me when you sag there like the wilted flower I know very well you are not."

"I have displeased you a great deal lately." She was not at all sure how to take his comments and hid behind this

gambit. It seemed to be he who flirted with her, and it made her uneasy.

"You have certainly tried."

She bit her lip, then raised her face to his, allowing her chin to quiver slightly. "Then I must certainly apologize, Captain."

His brow lowered, a strange expression on his rugged countenance. His eyes searched hers, then roamed slowly over her features, as if memorizing every detail.

She felt soft color rise, heating her cheeks, but she did not move. Apparently she had responded correctly to him, for she once again had his interest. A flicker of nerves danced within her, causing a quickening of her pulse. She could not deny his virile presence—but she would not forget that her sole intention was to punish him.

Something sparkled in the depths of his eyes, and a quickly repressed twitch of his lip betrayed his emotion as amusement. Eugenia stiffened, her indignation rising once more.

"Lady, as always your company is most entertaining. But you must hold me excused." He gave her a deep bow that she strongly felt mocked her and strode off.

She turned back to the rail, seething. Had he been taken in by her contrition? She was not at all sure. And if he hadn't, then it would seem that his own intention was to amuse himself at her expense. He would not get away with it! He would learn to respect her—and love her!—before she was through.

She did not have a chance to see him again until dinner that evening. Once more she dressed carefully, though this time a bit daringly. She selected her cerulean blue gauze, with the lace-trimmed bodice cut low and square with tiny sleeves that almost came off the shoulders. Her sapphire necklace she fastened about her neck and again draped the cashmere shawl across her arms. The effect was quite sophisticated and more than a little alluring.

She was not disappointed in Captain Harrington's response. She had worn the dress many times before during the lengthy course of the voyage, and each time she had seen that provocative gleam in his eyes as they rested on her. Tonight she allowed a similar spark to flicker in her

own as they met his, then turned away in haste. For she saw something else there, something she could not quite identify, but that might almost have been suppressed humor.

The topic of conversation at dinner remained purely literary, with Sophia proclaiming her admiration for Byron's works. Mr. Beverley, it seemed, was not overly familiar with these, but was only too ready to second any opinion put forth by the lovely Sophia. The discussion quickly devolved into the girl's raptures, Mr. Beverley's agreements on her every pronouncement, and Dr. Crofton's occasional criticism on the whole subject of cynicism and remorse.

"And pride," the captain interjected. "That is a quality I could never admire."

Stung, Eugenia turned her large, seemingly innocent eyes on him. "But surely you have pride in the *Cormorant*, Captain?"

"Ah, but that is not *false* pride. You have seen for yourself what a seaworthy vessel she is. There is substance there, worthy of admiration. But it would be sheer folly in me to be puffed up in my own conceit because of her."

She digested this, for she had little doubt that it was a pointed comment directed at her. It was certainly a different viewpoint from that with which she had been raised. In the eyes of her family, to be a Wolverton of Wolverton Priory meant the Priory, the earldom, and all of its vast trappings and consequence. To envision herself as separate from all of this was almost impossible . . . and also very frightening.

She peeked up at him, only to find golden glints of amusement again dancing in his eyes as they rested on her. Anger rose within her, both at his subtle jibe and at the entertainment he seemed to find at her expense.

They played several hands of cards that night and, though she tried, Eugenia found she had little taste for her flirtation with Captain Harrington. She wanted to punish him, now more than ever, but he had the unnerving habit of maintaining the upper hand. As soon as she reasonably could, she extracted Sophia from Mr. Beverley's side, and they retired to their cabin. Leaving the girl to her preparations for bed, she donned her heavy pelisse and slipped out on deck.

Standing in her favorite spot in the prow, she gazed up at

the stars that peeped out from behind the drifting clouds. Thin, pale light from the crescent moon filtered down, streaking the dark sea with fingers of silvery blue. *If only my thoughts could be so peaceful . . .*

There was no mistaking the captain's step. He moved quickly, with surprising lightness for one so large, and energy always seemed to emanate from him so that she could almost feel his presence before she either heard or saw him. She did not turn, but waited instead to see what his mood would be.

"Looking at the sky tonight, it's hard to believe we had such a raging storm only two days ago."

This opening sounded innocuous, but she did not trust him. And he must pay for his humiliating rakedown of her the day before. Oh, how he would pay . . . And flattery should be a good way to begin.

"You never let me apologize to you, Captain." She lowered her eyes, not wanting him to see how distasteful the words were to her. "Never have I been privileged to see such bravery as you displayed that night."

"But then you have led a very sheltered life, have you not?"

That surprised a choke of laughter from her, which she tried very hard to turn into a cough. Even to her it did not sound very convincing.

"Do you know, you are quite the most odious man of my acquaintance? Can you not have the decency to permit me to apologize and try to make amends?"

"Was that your intention, Lady? Then it is I who am at fault." He had been standing slightly behind her, but now he stepped forward and leaned on the rail by her side.

He did not sound the least bit contrite. If anything, she thought, he was still amused. If he had not insulted her so grievously, she might have found it difficult to remain angry with him for long. But he had struck at the very basis of her upbringing, of her being, and if she were a man she would have called him out. But she was merely a woman, and forced to resort to purely feminine wiles.

She turned slightly to face him, allowing her shoulder to just brush against his arm as she did. "I meant what I said.

It is not many men who could have kept their injured crew working as efficiently as you did. I am quite sure we owe you our lives.'' And the really irritating part of it was that she spoke the truth.

The eyes she raised to his must have reflected this, for his own narrowed slightly as his brow lowered, and for a moment she had the satisfaction of seeing that demon of mockery fade slightly. It was back in a moment, and dancing more lively than ever.

"Lady, you will make me conceited. If this is to be a night of compliments, I should undoubtedly be the one making them. Should I say that the stars compare unfavorably with your eyes, or has that been tried too often?''

She turned away, wondering if anyone ever got the upper hand with this maddening man. "More likely you would compare my temper to the rising waves.''

His deep, hearty laugh broke from him, sending unwanted shivers through her. Oh, he was a man, all right, in every sense of the word. Virile, powerful, masculine to the very core . . . and utterly infuriating. And when he had kissed her in that raging storm . . . But that was part of another existence, something that had been absurdly natural and right at that moment and had no substance in the present reality. Nevertheless, her fingers clenched on the railing, and she was glad of the chill breeze and salt spray to cool her flaming cheeks.

This flirtation was not turning out quite the way she had hoped. But he was a man who would play only by his own rules, and to make her conquest complete she must adopt them and beat him at his own game. For a game, a simple diversion, was all she seemed to be to him. He should be made to regret ever having taken her so lightly.

Humor appeared to be the way to his heart, and it had already occurred to her that she shared his sense of the ridiculous, no matter how much she had been taught to suppress it. If entertainment was what he wanted, then it was what he would have. And let him ponder which of them was the true butt of the jokes. Why should he be the only one to laugh—openly—over their encounters?

The following morning, Sophia joined Eugenia on her

promenade about the deck. Stopping near the stern of the ship, the younger girl pulled her shawl closer about her and stared back the way they had come.

"I never dreamed I would ever go so far from England." There was a catch in her voice, almost of fear, and Eugenia slipped an arm about her. "Do you know," Sophia continued, "at times I almost think I can see the green cliffs, there in the distance."

"We'll go back," Genie promised, "as soon as we find Edward."

"And how long will that take? Mr. Beverley has been telling me how very *vast* America is."

"We have only a year, and almost seven weeks of that are gone already. That leaves us only ten months. But don't worry so. We may find we can trace him quite easily. I don't intend to bother with the city newspapers that Mr. Mackelson thought would do. I think we should find out what equipment is necessary to go into the—the backwoods, I think it is called, and go direct to the suppliers of such things. That will be the best way to find Edward."

Sophia nodded her agreement, turning away from her wistful contemplation of her faraway homeland. "He was always so—so restless, was he not? Do you suppose he could have gone to sea?" she asked suddenly. "I can think of no one more restless than Captain Harrington."

"Not restless, energetic," Eugenia corrected. She considered this. "I cannot see Edward as a mere sailor, can you? He may be careless, but he is a Wolverton, and I do not see him taking orders from anyone. Nor do I see him taking on the responsibilities of command."

Here her eyes strayed to the powerful figure of the captain, who bounded up the stairs to the bridge two at a time. He had abandoned the sling, but the bandage about his upper arm must have been bulky, for his coat merely hung over that shoulder. The wind rippled through the flaxen ends of his sun- and salt-bleached hair and stirred the thick reddish-tinted curls of his sideburns.

Infuriating, insufferable man, she reminded herself and turned back to Sophia. "Let us go inside. The wind is coming up."

"Good, if that means it will get us to America faster."

They went back to their cabin, where they occupied themselves with their sewing. This pastime left Eugenia's mind uncomfortably free, and it began to turn towards journey's end.

One problem she had stoutly refused to think about before, but with every passing mile they came closer to their destination—and their uncertain reception. Her Uncle Reginald had no notion at all that they were coming. From his letter and Captain Harrington's comments, she knew that he had been in poor health of late. What if he was not pleased to see them? What, in fact, if he was not able to welcome them into his home at all?

She had very little money left and only her sapphire and pearl necklace to sell. And what if the captain were unable to convince his employer to waive the cost of their passage? Could she count on an uncle she had never met to defray this expense? And that, inevitably, brought her to her underlying fear.

What if they did not find Edward? She had not seriously considered this possibility before. While in England they could rely on George to support them, no matter how grudgingly. But what if they were stranded here in America, with no means to pay their return passage? Would her mother's brother take on the same responsibility of caring for them? The thought of imposing on anyone was repugnant to her pride.

She still pondered these questions as she stood alone in the prow that night after dinner. It was a fruitless occupation, for answers eluded her and the only thing she found was increased worry. It was actually with relief that she heard the captain approaching to take up his accustomed position at her side. Yet again he had seemed to know where she could be found.

"You have been very quiet tonight," were his opening words. For once she could detect no teasing note in his voice, no hidden barb to draw her into heedless argument.

"Tell me about my uncle," she directed him cautiously. "You said you know him well."

"Regretting the impulsiveness of your journey, Lady?"

That sarcastic tone was back, and she turned on him, arming herself for a battle royal. He had no right to make fun of her fears, and so he should learn! The only thing that modulated her tongue was the infuriating fact that he was right.

"I can hardly regret searching for my brother, Captain. I have little faith in the lawyers' abilities to track down one so unpredictable as he."

"What makes you think you will have more success?"

"I know him. But more importantly, I believe I know how he thinks. My ability should lie in following up leads."

"I wouldn't be surprised if you do it, Lady. You've already shown a great deal more courage and determination than I would have expected from someone with your up-bringing. But why is it so important to you?" He leaned on the rail with his good arm, looking at her through half-lowered lids.

She flushed, unnerved by his sudden and unexpected praise. Without thinking, she threw up her shield of haughtiness to protect herself. "Edward must be found. I would hardly expect you to understand a family pride that goes back hundreds of years. The title of Latham is one that is revered in England, and it must go to the rightful bearer."

"And not to that fubsy-faced cousin of yours?" He did not bother to hide the humor in his tone.

She stamped her foot in anger. "Will you stop mocking me? Only a fool makes fun of something he cannot understand. I had done you the credit—wrongly, I see now—of assuming you were not a fool."

"What a wonderful opinion you must have of Americans," he marveled. "So you think I have no comprehension of family pride? Maybe you're right. What I, and most Americans, for that matter, esteem is individual worth. Just because a man's father was a good landlord or employer doesn't mean his son will be, too. In America we feel a man should earn his own way. Then he really is a man to be respected, because he has won that right."

He paused, his eyes narrowing as he regarded her. "But as enjoyable a pastime as it may be, let's not argue for a minute. You asked me about Reginald Jessop."

"Yes." Eugenia was considerably shaken by his words, for the subject they had been discussing was one she had never before considered. The law of primogeniture was so deeply ingrained in her that to question it seemed anathema. With relief she tried to banish this from her mind and return to the safer topic of her unknown uncle.

"What's worrying you?" he asked and, to her surprise, she could detect nothing but solicitous concern.

"Will he—will he mind unexpected and unknown relatives dropping in on him like this?" she asked, trying to force herself to use a casual tone.

His hand moved towards hers, but then returned to the rail. "You have no need to fear your welcome. He'll be only too glad to have you stay, and for as long as you like. His wife, too. Mary Jessop is a kind-hearted soul."

"You said my uncle was ill."

"Recovering, I hope. He has had a very serious time with an inflammation of the lungs, but we believe he is now improving. He was most sorry that he couldn't do more to search for your brother."

She lapsed into silence, the worst of her fears allayed. For some reason she did not doubt Captain Harrington's word.

"What is America like?" she finally asked.

At that he laughed, but not unkindly. "Lord, how can I explain it? It is bigger than you can possibly imagine, and every area is different. I believe you will like Providence. Do you, like that lawyer of yours, expect us to live in log cabins and fight Indians daily? I'm afraid you will be in for a disappointment if you do. Providence is a very respectable city, a major shipping port, in fact, with newspapers, libraries, theatres, all that sort of thing. And you will find ample social entertainments."

"We have not come to be entertained, but to find my brother," she pointed out, hiding her embarrassment at having her opinions of his country so clearly read. "You must excuse me, my sister awaits." She left him quickly, afraid of how many more of her fears he might guess.

❧ *Chapter 10* ❧

T hree days later, the lookout shouted that land was in sight. Both Eugenia and Sophia rushed to the prow, peering eagerly ahead into the westering afternoon sun. It was almost an hour more before they could make out the dim, grayish outline that indicated America.

The *Cormorant* continued its slow but steady progress, and America seemed to grow out of the horizon before their eyes. The following morning they actually entered Narragansett Bay. Eugenia, once more in the prow with Sophia at her side, stared at the strange country that greeted her nervous eyes.

The bay, she soon discovered, was dotted with islands of varying sizes, looking mostly to be mixtures of rock, forests, and fields. There seemed to be some debate whether or not to put in for repair at the docks of Newport on nearby Rhode Island, the largest of the islands in the bay and named for the state. Captain Harrington, though, with one long, searching examination of his makeshift mast, decided to press on the twenty-odd miles to his own home port.

The ship wended its way between the islands of Rhode and Conanicut, then slowly, always hugging the coast, on past the smaller islands Mr. Beverley told them were named Prudence and Patience. What land Eugenia could see

appeared to be devoted to farming and grazing, and she longed for the captain to come and act as guide.

Sandy, at last freed from his own chores, came to serve this function instead. Eagerly he pointed out Greenwich Bay, no more than an alcove, really, off the larger Narragansett, and finally they approached the Providence River.

Eugenia was not sure what she expected, but it was with considerable relief that she saw that the harbor they entered was not that dissimilar from Bristol's. To her chagrin, she realized she had allowed herself to adopt the view shared by so many of her fellow countrymen that America was a mere colonial outpost, backward in every way.

The port of Providence teemed with life, however, even in the growing dusk of the early evening. Ships beyond number were anchored about the harbor, and more were tied snugly into their berths along the quay. Men lined the docks, heavy carts and carriages seemed to fill the streets, and beyond, through the dim light, Eugenia glimpsed buildings of both brick and wood. And everywhere children and dogs darted about, engaged in games that were probably the same in every port in the world.

Sophia moved closer against her sister's side. "It—it all seems so *civilized*!" she whispered.

"Were you expecting shacks and red Indians roaming the streets?" Eugenia quizzed her, though she realized that this possibility had lain in the back of her own mind.

"It is all so very big! And so many people! How shall we ever find my uncle?"

"I am sure we can rely on Captain Harrington to assist us, as soon as he is free. Unless he must check in with his employer first." Eugenia hesitated, suddenly unsure. Already the sun was setting. Would they spend the night on board the ship, one last night in its relative familiarity, before setting forth on what she dubbed their Great Adventure? Or were they to be pitchforked into it immediately?

"Are you ladies packed yet?" So absorbed had she been in these reflections that Eugenia had not heard the captain's approach. She turned quickly, her eyes betraying her uncertainty as she looked up into his easy, smiling face.

"We are to go ashore, then? Immediately? Can—can you contact my uncle for us?"

"Go pack," he told her, that irritating amusement back in his eyes. "We still have to dock; then we can worry about such things. But have no fear, I won't desert you in the streets." With a mocking bow, he strode off.

Packing was not difficult, for most of their belongings they had already stowed away the night before. Eugenia, glancing out the porthole, could see the dock coming closer and closer as the great ship was maneuvered into a position along the wharf for unloading. Soon the ropes would tie them securely to the dock, the sails which already hung limp would be furled, and the gangplank pushed into position. Then they would leave the refuge of the *Cormorant*.

At the door of the cabin, Eugenia stopped and looked back at the little room that had been their home for fifty-one days. The only traces of their presence were the trunks and their dressing cases, now resting in a neat pile against the outer wall, the same place, Eugenia realized, where they had been the first time they entered this room. It didn't seem possible that they had really dared make such a momentous journey. But the voices she heard shouting in the semidarkness outside echoed the accents of the crew members, not the more familiar ones of England. They were indeed in America.

They emerged onto the deck to find Captain Harrington waiting for them. The *Cormorant*, resting quietly by the wharf, apparently needed little supervision, for the majority of the crew were nowhere to be seen. The captain gestured to two men who stood waiting, and they headed down the companionway. From the thuds that sounded from below, they appeared to be bringing the trunks.

"If you will come with me?" Captain Harrington motioned towards the gangplank that led to the dock. "I have sent Sandy to find us a carriage. Your uncle's house is a little ways outside of town, but it will not take us long to get there."

Eugenia inclined her head and started forward, trying to stifle her nervousness. A slight commotion occurred, and the crowd of spectators who had gathered to watch the

docking separated to make way for a carriage. It appeared to be a large and comfortable one, if the dim image she could make out in the increasing darkness was to be trusted, and she suddenly felt considerably cheered. Somehow, she had imagined traveling in one of the great cargo wagons that lined the dock, but she now saw her error. America was definitely not as backward as she had supposed.

The door of the vehicle opened slightly, and a grizzled, portly man leaned out. "Harrington!" he cried, waving one arm.

Eugenia stiffened. Would this be the captain's employer? Would they be forced to stand there listening as the captain explained why he had carried two passengers, and ones that had not paid at that? Or would he be forced to leave them, to attend to business? Fear replaced the relief she had just begun to feel, and she turned in anxiety to the captain's reassuring figure.

He waved one arm in a return gesture. "Brought you a little surprise, Jessop!" he called, and Eugenia looked quickly back to the dock. No employer, this, but her uncle! A different set of worries assailed her, and suddenly she hung back.

Sophia apparently shared her trepidation, for Eugenia felt a small, cold hand slipping under the folds of her shawl and gripping her arm. Eugenia covered her fingers with her own trembling ones, tried to quell the quivering of nerves that rushed through her, and failed.

"A Wolverton, afraid?" The amused voice sounded softly behind her. "He doesn't bite, you know."

Eugenia stiffened at this calculated comment, taking it as an insult. With her head held high, she led the way down to the dock, pulling the reluctant Sophia along with her.

Mr. Reginald Jessop had by this time left his carriage and awaited them at the foot of the gangplank. His keen pale eyes peered through the dimming light at the girls, then turned on the captain.

"New come-out for you, ain't it, James?" he asked, a low, rumbling chuckle sounding in his voice.

"Just so. May I introduce Lady Eugenia Wolverton and

Lady Sophia Wolverton?'' The amusement in the captain's voice was barely repressed.

Mr. Jessop's jaw dropped. He stared at the two girls for a moment in disbelief, eyes narrowed as he studied their features with care. "Bless my soul!" he exclaimed. "Julia's girls!"

Eugenia started to offer her hand in tentative acknowledgment, but found herself engulfed in a massive bear hug. The sincere warmth and delight of the gesture left her breathless, with tears starting to her eyes. After all of her fears of not being welcome, the reality left her weak with gratitude.

Sophia returned the embrace with alacrity, inspecting their uncle with every bit as much interest as he had shown. What she saw apparently pleased her, for Eugenia felt her relax and saw her brilliant smile flash.

"Lord, such a delicate little thing you are!" Mr. Jessop exclaimed, beaming on Sophia with avuncular pride. "Best get you in out of the evening air. James, you send that cabin boy of yours on up to my house to tell my Mary to see that we get rooms prepared for these two. Bet you'll be glad to sleep on dry land, eh, puss?" He positively beamed on Sophia, then on Eugenia.

At this point Sandy returned, hopping out of another carriage. He was quickly dispatched on his errand, and Captain Harrington once again turned to Mr. Jessop.

"And what brings you down to the wharf?"

"You, my boy. Soon as I heard the *Cormorant* was heading into dock I came to see if you had any news of my girls here. No notion at all you'd bring them, but it was a dashed good idea." Here he subjected Eugenia to a further inspection. "And who'd have thought you'd be such pretty little things? Don't believe Julia was above average, and as for Latham, well!"

Eugenia's features relaxed into a smile, liking this man, sensing the similarity in warmth and expansiveness to his other sister, their beloved Aunt Lydia. "I—I hope you don't mind our coming, Uncle Reginald. Captain Harrington assured us you would not, but . . ."

"Mind? Certainly not! Delighted! And so Mary will be,

too. Don't you give it another thought.'' He patted her shoulder, and Eugenia found she could not doubt his words.

The first of their trunks now safely strapped to the back of the carriage, Mr. Jessop guided them over to this vehicle. Eugenia, suddenly aware that the captain had not accompanied them, looked about in sudden anxiety, irrationally not wanting to lose his comforting presence. The sight of him starting back up his gangplank without giving them so much as a farewell irritated her, reminding her of her unfinished punishment of him. As she was uncertain whether or not she would have another chance to give him his much-needed setdown, she decided she had best administer as much of one as she could manage now.

''Captain!'' she called.

He paused, turning back to look down on her as she walked towards him, staggering slightly with the unaccustomed stillness of the ground beneath her feet. After it had taken her so long to become accustomed to the constant movement of the deck, it seemed absurdly ridiculous that she would have to go through another adjustment on land.

The captain hesitated just for a moment, then moved to join her. ''Lady?'' He smiled at her in a manner that set her errant senses jumping, but she stifled this feeling firmly.

''I wish to thank you for bringing us safely to my uncle. It was a most . . . enjoyable voyage. Good-bye, Captain.'' She inclined her head slightly, her manner every inch that of the grand lady graciously thanking an inferior.

''Oh, this is hardly good-bye, Lady.'' His eyes danced with his amusement. ''I am frequently a guest in your uncle's house. I very much fear that you will be seeing a great deal of me.'' His great shoulders shook slightly with his suppressed laughter at her obvious discomposure at his unwelcome words.

He extended his hand, and she responded by placing her own in it, still taken aback by this piece of information. He raised her fingers to his lips for a lingering kiss she sensed was mocking, and her indignation swelled.

''*Au revoir,* Lady,'' he murmured.

She left him abruptly, her head still high, her bearing stiff, the sounds of his rich chuckle sounding in her ears. He

would pay for his insults, and pay dearly. If this were indeed not good-bye, if she were to see more of him, then her original plans must be brought back into play. He would learn not to make sport of her!

She joined Sophia in the carriage, and her Uncle Reginald climbed in after her. The darkness of the vehicle prevented the flaming color in her cheeks from giving away her anger and, as they were quiet for several minutes, she had time to bring this emotion under control.

"Uncle Reginald," she ventured, not sure how to begin. "I want to thank you for trying to find my brother Edward."

"Does this mean you've come to have a go at it yourself?" he asked. "Good for you. It came up at a dashed bad time. I'd been laid up for a good six months with an inflammation of the lungs and could hardly do a thing. I have to tell you, though, I've not been able to find any trace of him at all."

"Captain Harrington thought he might have gone to a place called Kentucky."

Reginald Jessop considered this for a minute, then nodded slowly. "It's possible, I suppose. Wouldn't care to do that myself, but there's no telling what a restless young man may decide to do. You've got your work cut out for you, my dear. But I'll give you any help I can, you can count on that."

"Thank you. I—I'm afraid we're already taking you up on that, just by coming."

"Told you not to let that bother you. Glad to have the chance to get to know you. You'll stay as long as you like, remember. Consider this your home. I don't want you rushing back to England a minute before it's necessary."

A lump welled in her throat at his heartwarming welcome of them. "Uncle Reginald . . ." she began.

He held a finger up to his lips, then nodded towards Sophia's slumped figure. Eugenia glanced across at the girl, hearing her deep, even breathing.

"She has had a difficult time with the crossing," Eugenia told her uncle softly. "She—both of us—will be grateful for a real bed again."

"We'll see to that soon enough, don't you fear. Get you a

good dinner, then let you sleep. We'll leave all our talking for tomorrow."

They lapsed into silence, and Eugenia found herself hard put not to follow her sister's example. The strain and fear had taken their toll, and the gentle rocking of the carriage was a welcome change from the rolling of the ship. When the vehicle slowed for a turn, then started up a gravel path, she noted with relief that their journey was ending at last.

"And here we are," Mr. Jessop declared unnecessarily, with a jovial heartiness.

Eugenia shook Sophia's shoulder, and the girl yawned and rubbed her eyes. They clambered out of the vehicle, slightly unsteady as they tried to accustom themselves to solid ground.

They stood in a wide drive surrounded by dark shapes that might have been shrubs. The house before them was large, fashioned from brick, with numerous mullioned windows, most of which seemed to be lit. The double front doors were thrown wide and two young men, obviously servants, hurried down the shallow steps. They were followed by a stout little woman who wrapped a shawl tightly about her shoulders and peered out into the darkness.

"Mary!" Mr. Jessop called. "Come and meet our guests!"

The woman, lifting the fronts of her long skirts, seemed to float down the stairs. Eugenia gained an impression of fluffy gray hair surrounding a sweetly pink face before she was gathered into a smothering, motherly embrace. Her cheek was kissed; then she was held slightly away.

Mary Jessop appeared to be the perfect companion for Uncle Reginald. She beamed at Eugenia in much the same manner as her husband had, then turned her attention to the sleepy Sophia.

"Inside, my dears," she declared, putting her arm about the tired girl and drawing her towards the welcoming lights of the house. "You will be shown to your rooms immediately; then we shall see to your dinner. Come, Mr. Jessop. We must not keep them standing out here in the cold."

The two servants were just disappearing through the front door with the first of the trunks. Instead of going straight to the rooms that were still being prepared, Eugenia and

Sophia were escorted into a drawing room, where Mr. Jessop poured each of them a glass of lemonade. While they sat quietly sipping, Mr. and Mrs. Jessop held a quick, low-voiced conversation.

The only details of the room that Eugenia took in that night were the comfort of her chair and the cheerfulness of the great fireplace so very near her. She sat there, allowing the warmth to envelop her, with no idea how much time passed.

She was roused from this pleasant state by Mrs. Jessop, who, taking an arm of each girl, announced that their rooms were now ready. They went back out into a wide hall, then up the carpeted staircase with its heavy black walnut banister that curved its graceful way to the upper hall.

They stopped on the first floor, which Mrs. Jessop called the second, and headed down a hall that intersected the main one. A door stood open to reveal a bedchamber decorated in white and pink rosebuds.

"Sophia?" Mrs. Jessop suggested.

The girl took one look about the room, turned towards her aunt, started to thank her, then broke down into tears.

"Oh, my dear," Mary Jessop declared, embracing her exhausted niece. "Now you just lie down, and I'll send my maid to you. No need to come back downstairs tonight. I'll send you your dinner on a tray. Now, your sister will be right next door, so you have nothing to worry about. To bed with you."

Eugenia was relieved to see her sister comply. The journey had tired Sophia more than the girl realized. Genie herself was forced to fight back the lump that rose to her throat, for there was nothing more conducive to tears than to find comfort and welcome after a long, wearisome—and worrisome—journey.

The room to which Eugenia was conducted was decorated in white and blue. She looked about it, noting her combs and brushes laid out on the dressing table. Her gowns, she was sure, would already be hanging in the clothes cupboard.

"Aunt Mary . . . ," she began, but that troublesome lump in her throat caused her to break off.

"Dinner will be served in about twenty minutes," Aunt

Mary told her warmly. "If you're too tired to join us, just tell the maid. Don't stand on ceremony with us, dear. Just make yourself at home. Now, I've forbidden your cousins to bother you, so if they dare peep in here, you just send them about their business. I'll leave you now to make yourself more comfortable. Oh, I am so glad you have come," she added with her beaming smile. Kissing Eugenia's cheek again, she bustled out of the room.

Left alone at last, Eugenia sank down onto the chair before the dressing table. The image that stared back at her out of the mirror looked unfamiliar. Exhaustion, she supposed. Never had she been so glad to arrive somewhere before. It was best not to think tonight, not while she was so tired. She would just be grateful that her relatives had proved so wonderful, eat her dinner, and sleep.

She removed her bonnet and pelisse, cast a rapid glance over her wrinkled gown, then cast this aside as well. From the cupboard she drew out her white muslin with the blue ribbons and was in the process of trying to hook this when a knock sounded on her door and a young maid entered.

The girl bobbed her a curtsy, then deftly set about the task of fastening the gown. Eugenia, suppressing a sigh of gratitude, allowed the girl to finish. When she was propelled to the chair before the mirror and her hair unfastened and allowed to tumble down about her shoulders, her only feeling was that of relief to be once more in the hands of a competent maid.

In a surprisingly short time, Genie was ready to go downstairs. She opened the door to Sophia's room, but the girl lay motionless on the bed and did not stir. Closing the door softly, Eugenia continued on her way.

At the head of the stairs, her courage nearly failed her. The enormity of what she had done, of arriving uninvited for an indefinite stay, struck her once again. Her aunt and uncle seemed to be wonderful people, but that did nothing to lessen her shocking behavior. Feeling very much alone, she started down the steps.

Voices sounded in the drawing room, where the family apparently gathered before dinner. She started towards this room, only to be brought up short in the doorway.

Captain Harrington's deep, rich laughter boomed forth, announcing his presence. Eugenia stepped forward quickly, eager in spite of herself to see his powerful, commanding figure, the one familiar person among the sea of new faces.

No trace of her own exhaustion marred his bearing or lined his features. To look at him, one would never guess that he had just completed an arduous, round-trip voyage. He looked up and saw her, his eyes bright and dancing, his energy unabated. A broad, devilish smile lit his countenance.

"Well, Lady?" He smiled, satirical amusement rife in his eyes. "We meet again, so soon." He swept her a mocking bow, and Eugenia recognized the opening of Round Two in the ongoing battle between them.

❋ Chapter 11 ❋

Eugenia gathered together the remnants of her strength, formed her mouth into the semblance of a condescending smile, and swept forward, one hand extended.

"Captain? I admit I had not expected the . . . the pleasure of seeing you again so soon." She raised her eyebrows a fraction in a gesture she hoped indicated sublime indifference.

He raised her fingers to his lips, the twinkle in his eye belying the courtliness of his manner. "And your sister? Are we not to enjoy her company this evening?"

"She is asleep, Captain. I fear the journey proved rather tedious and tiring for her. I am sure it was not your fault," she added kindly. Favoring him with a dismissive nod, she crossed over to where her aunt stood near the sofa.

"Is everything in your room to your satisfaction?" Mary Jessop asked. There was a note of anxiety in this lady's voice, and her eyes appeared unnaturally wide as they rested on the slight but regal figure of her niece.

She had impressed the wrong person! An almost hysterical desire to giggle welled within Eugenia, making her realize how tired she was in truth. Not for the world would she have this sweet, homey little woman think her high in the instep.

"Dear ma'am." She held out both hands, and Mary

Jessop instinctively took them. "Everything is wonderful! You are being so kind to us, and I cannot but feel we are imposing on you in the most dreadful way." Sudden tears rose to her eyes and a lump swelled in her throat as her exhaustion caused an erratic swing in her emotions.

"Nonsense, my dear!" The ready tears of the soft-hearted filled Mrs. Jessop's eyes, and for a moment Eugenia feared they would both indulge in a crying spate. "You should not have troubled yourself to come down this evening, as tired as you must be," her aunt continued. "Is little Sophia indeed asleep?"

Eugenia nodded. "She probably will not wake until morning, and then shock you with all she will desire to do. Her plans always exceed her strength, I fear."

"Well, you need have no worry." Mr. Jessop, who had been pouring Eugenia a glass of wine, handed it to her, then gestured for her to take a seat. "We shall not tire her, not for a while yet, at least. We must let you recover a bit. James has been telling us that you had a bit of a rough voyage."

"Oh?" Eugenia asked, turning a deceptively sweet smile on the captain. "I had not thought it that bad."

"Eugenia!" Mary Jessop exclaimed, shocked. "He says the main mast came down, and on top of several of his men! I vow I would have been terrified and quaking in my cabin!"

"I fear he exaggerates," Eugenia murmured. She cast a covert glance at the captain's amused countenance, and her irritation with him swelled.

"Oh, our lady wasn't the least bit afraid. She was right out there on deck, helping the doctor."

Eugenia felt soft color burn her cheeks for, although his expression seemed to taunt, she could detect no trace of a teasing note in his voice. She raised her eyes to his and encountered a look that merely increased her confusion, for she was not sure what it contained.

"You kept assuring me there was nothing to cause concern." She shifted her position on the sofa, trying to hide her uncertainty. "I merely do you the honor of believing you."

His deep laughter rumbled forth, and golden lights danced merrily in his eyes. "Now, why should you have chosen to believe that, Lady, when I swear you never believed anything else I told you?"

Her eyes flashed, for the mockery was back. She could not relax her guard with him for a moment, for his wit and humor were always at the ready. She struggled for a retort, but found her tired brain unequal to the task.

She was saved by the opening of the door and the entry of the darkest-skinned man she had ever beheld. He was almost black! She stared at him, taking in every detail, from his tightly curling hair to the austere propriety of his dress and bearing.

He bowed slightly to Mrs. Jessop. "Dinner is served," he intoned, then stood to one side, stiffly erect, awaiting their passage from the room.

"You seem surprised," Captain Harrington murmured in Eugenia's ear.

She jumped, for she had not heard him come near her. He offered her his arm and she rose, grateful in spite of herself for his support. "A . . . an African?" she whispered, her eyes still wide.

"Were you expecting a red Indian?" he asked, the slight tremble in his voice betraying his inner laughter. "Rhode Island is well known in the slave trade. Did you not know? Newport, in particular, is a major port."

The revulsion in Eugenia's expression set his shoulders shaking again, and his fingers came to rest over hers. "You disapprove? Now, one might have been pardoned for expecting you to consider slavery natural."

She tried to pull away from him, but he retained his hold on her hand, his eyes gleaming with infuriating amusement, and too late she realized he again teased her.

"Have no fear," he continued quietly as he drew her forward. "Our good Thomas there is not a slave. Your uncle holds your views, and all who work on this estate are free."

"Are you a slave trader?" she demanded in a hushed but savage undertone.

"Nay, Lady. That's a commodity I take no part in. I fear I

also share your views. And we are not alone. There will come a day when the trade will be illegal.''

They passed into the hall behind Mr. and Mrs. Jessop, who turned in at the dining room door. In spite of herself, Eugenia stole another look at Thomas's frozen face, and a shiver went through her.

If her uncle's servants were all free, in an area that not only accepted but relied on slaves, then he must have very strong convictions—and be comfortably well off. And that reminded her . . . Eugenia's fingers squeezed the captain's arm, holding him back.

''Captain.'' She found it difficult to raise her eyes to meet his. When she did, it was to find a gentle smile lurking there. ''Have you spoken to your employer yet? About our passage?''

The golden flecks brightened in his eyes as the creases at their corners deepened. ''Lady, you shame me. In truth, I did not mention you.'' He hung his head in mock contrition.

''But, Captain! Surely you must! He . . . will he not be quite angry, if he learns of our voyage from someone other than you?''

''But who is there to tell him?''

''Any of your crew! Oh, not on purpose, but surely it will get about that Sophia and I arrived on the *Cormorant*!''

''Do you worry so about me, then?''

''I am shocked by your perfidy!'' she exclaimed, stung by a question that held more truth than she would care to admit. ''And I am sorry to have been a part of it. I insist that you tell him, or . . . or I shall! I never meant him to be deceived in this matter.''

His deep, wholehearted laugh shook his frame, causing her aunt and uncle to turn back to look at them. He grinned at the couple, then drew Eugenia's clenched fist back through his arm and led her on. ''Is this a matter of honor for you, Lady? Does a Wolverton not steal passage?'' he murmured.

''They do not, indeed!'' she hissed back. ''I am shocked by your behavior!''

''Are you, Lady? I thought you had already credited me with every dishonorable trait.''

They entered the dining room at that note, and she was relieved to be spared the necessity of answering him. She had not expected him to run shy on this business of their not paying their fares—or on any other, for that matter. It had never occurred to her that he would behave in any but a purely honorable fashion—and to admit that he might not disturbed her deeply, almost as deeply as discovering that his character had flaws. In spite of her determination to dislike him, he had won her reluctant respect. And the shattering of this respect unnerved her.

Her silence during the meal was ignored by the others, who had every reason to believe her too tired to take part in the conversation. Only Captain Harrington knew the real reason for her pointedly ignoring him and, she believed, he would hardly tell the others.

Eugenia was relieved to discover that her uncle maintained the custom of the ladies retiring to the drawing room after dinner and leaving the gentlemen to their port and brandy. She followed her aunt to the same room where they had gathered before the meal. Mary Jessop seated herself on the sofa, patting the spot next to her invitingly.

"Now, my dear," she began as Eugenia sank down into the cushioned softness at her side, "do not let us keep you up longer than you would wish tonight. You must make yourself at home and do exactly as you wish. And do not feel you must stay up because James is here. I assure you, we do not stand upon ceremony with him."

"I . . . I was rather surprised to see him here. I would have thought his employer would have wished to hear all the details of his voyage and cargo."

"His employer? James does not work for anyone."

Eugenia stared at her Aunt Mary, her eyes widening as the import of this disclosure registered in her tired mind. "But . . . the *Cormorant* . . . is it . . . surely it is not *his* ship?"

"Of course it is. Why, whatever gave you the idea it was not?" Mary Jessop laughed. "Has he been roasting you? You must pay him no mind. He is such a complete hand! He can say the most outrageous things."

"He can, indeed!" Eugenia said hotly, trying to control her fuming anger. To have led her on in such a way was

unpardonable! She ignored the fact that it was she who had simply assumed he worked for someone else. A gentleman would have told her the truth immediately instead of baiting her for his own amusement. But Captain Harrington was no gentleman. He might not be a servant, as she had first—and quite naturally—thought. But he was in trade, which was no better—and undoubtedly deceitfulness was a trait carefully cultivated by that class of persons, she added to herself with savage force.

"Does . . . does he dine here often?" she asked, controlling with care the angry trembling of her voice.

"Why, yes. He and your Uncle Reginald are very good friends, despite the difference in their ages. And we could hardly let him spend the evening alone, when he has just returned from such a long trip, and his family not here to greet him."

"His . . . his family?" It had to be her exhaustion leaving her feeling chill and faint, causing the blood to drain from her cheeks. A family. Why had it never occurred to her that a man as virile and overpoweringly attractive as the captain would have a wife and children . . .

"Yes, his aunt, uncle, and cousin have been spending several weeks in Boston. If only they had had some warning he would come back today, I am sure they would have tried to return." Aunt Mary shook her head sadly over this inability to foretell the future.

Eugenia took a deep breath and realized it was the first she had taken in almost a minute. "He . . . he lives with them, does he?" she managed to ask, and was pleased that her voice sounded calm, with only polite interest.

"Oh, no. He lives on the estate he inherited from his father's family. Ah, and here come dear James and Mr. Jessop now."

Eugenia also heard the deep voices in the hall and had time to compose her features before the door opened to frame the captain's tall, muscular figure. His brilliant smile flashed, the whiteness of his teeth standing out in sharp contrast to his deeply bronzed skin. The suppressed, restless energy radiated from him, and Eugenia, in spite of her

determination not to let him affect her, experienced the tug of his undeniable attraction.

She marshaled her defenses, denying her answering smile by setting her lips with firm resolve. He may not have actually lied to her, but he certainly hadn't been truthful— and he had been laughing at her! She longed to rake him down in rare style, but realized she was far too tired to do justice to his perfidy. Nor did she relish an audience for this pleasurable venting of her wrath.

"Well, Lady, not asleep yet?" The challenging note in his voice invited her to join battle.

She teetered on the verge of informing him that she was made of sterner stuff than that, but thought better of rising to any fly of his casting that night. She would undoubtedly come off the worse from any encounter with him until she was rested. Instead she rose, brought one delicate hand up to cover her mouth, pretending to yawn, then gave him her sweetest smile.

"I knew I was forgetting something. I must thank you for reminding me. Dear Aunt, Uncle Reginald, please excuse me. I am rather tired." She started to the door, then paused as she reached Captain Harrington. "Good night, Captain. I am told I must not stand on any formality with you, so I do not. I am assured that I shall have the . . . the pleasure of seeing you again soon."

He took her hand, once more raising it to his lips. His sparkling eyes met and held hers. "Retiring from the lists, Lady?" he murmured for her ears alone.

"I fear I should bore you this night," she replied, and was irritated with herself to discover that this was the truth.

"That you could never do, but I won't press you. Good night, Lady." An odd gleam shone in his eyes as they held hers for a moment before her courage wavered and she broke the gaze, hurrying from the room.

The gentle creak of her bedroom door awakened her the following morning, and she raised her tired head slightly, trying to focus on the source of this sound. A quick movement and the soft click of the latch told her the door had now been closed.

"She's still asleep!" she heard a child's voice hiss in a not very quiet whisper.

"Quiet, Sammy!" came another, even louder whisper. "You'll wake her, and you know what Gramma said!"

"*Me* wake her! *You're* the one shouting!" came the ready retort. "It's your fault!"

The rapid beat of running footsteps reached Eugenia as the querulous voices faded. Her cousins? She wracked her still-befuddled memory. Aunt Mary had spoken of cousins last night, but surely her children were grown and married. But one of them had said "Gramma." She forced her mind to start working. Sammy. Were these the children of their second daughter? No, their son, the one who had died along with his wife in a carriage accident. The children lived with them now. This question settled, Eugenia closed her eyes and rolled over again. She would make their acquaintance soon enough, she was sure.

She had no idea how much time had passed when her door opened once again. Her intention to ignore the intrusion was thwarted, as slippered footsteps brushed softly across the wooden floor.

"Genie?" Sophia perched on the edge of the spacious bed. "You cannot *still* be sleeping, surely!"

"I can try." Eugenia stretched and sat up, yawning. "It can't really be morning yet, can it?"

"Genie!" Sophia giggled. "It is going on ten o'clock!"

Eugenia stared at her, honestly shocked. "Ten? No, you're teasing me. It cannot be!"

"Oh, do get up!" her sister begged, ruthlessly pulling at the blue and white quilt that Eugenia hugged near her chin. "I am quite hungry." She reached up to the head of the bed and tugged the cross-stitched bell pull that hung there. "Oh, it is so wonderful to have a maid again!"

Sally, the same young woman who had helped Eugenia dress the night before answered the summons, bearing a tray containing a teapot, a cup and saucer, and a covered basket. These she set on the bedside table and excused herself as Eugenia thanked her.

Sophia lifted a corner of the cloth and extracted a roll

from the woven basket. "She's gone for your dress," she explained.

Eugenia, in the act of pouring a cup of tea, raised her eyebrows, and her sister indicated her own fresh, neatly pressed gown. Their eyes met, and Eugenia let out a long, heartfelt sigh of thanksgiving as Sophia giggled again.

"Do you know, I never really appreciated Silton," Eugenia declared, reflecting on the many little services her maid had performed of which she had never really been aware. "I don't think I ever knew just how much she did until I had to do it all myself."

"Or I did it for you," her sister added. "I hope I never have to be without a maid again!"

Eugenia picked up the other roll before Sophia could and bit into it with appreciation. "Oh, real food again! Sophia, you should have come down for dinner last night. It was sheer heaven! I do not believe we have had a single *fresh* thing to eat—except fish—for ages!"

Sophia shuddered. "Well, I hope my aunt offers a selection of dishes at each course, because I assure you I shall never touch fish again!"

Eugenia smiled her understanding, but her reply was cut off by Sally's return. She carried Genie's favorite sprigged muslin morning gown, newly washed and pressed, the tiny puffed sleeves starched so that they stood out from the shoulders with a becoming pertness.

In a surprisingly short time, Eugenia was fastened into the dress and her long dark hair arranged in its usual style. With sincere thanks to the maid, she and Sophia set forth in search of breakfast.

As they descended the broad black walnut staircase to the main hall, their aunt bustled in from the back reaches of the house. A warm smile lit her face as she saw them, and she hurried forward.

"Ah, my dears! Have you slept well? Are you rested?"

"I don't believe I stirred the entire night," Eugenia assured her as Sophia, her bright eyes wide with interest, looked about.

"You'll be wanting your breakfast now, I'll wager. This way." She took an arm of each and led them back the way

she had come. "Sally—my maid—alerted Cook when she fetched your gown from the laundry girl, so you'll find fresh dishes all laid out for you."

"We must be making a great deal of extra work for your staff." Eugenia followed her aunt into a sunny breakfast parlor with a long row of windows looking out onto a garden just coming into bloom.

"Don't let it worry you, my dear. If those two rascally grandchildren of mine haven't upset everything around here, then you certainly won't be able to."

Mary Jessop settled the girls at the places that had been set for them, then lifted the lids from a selection of serving dishes. Plates of eggs, sausage, and ham met their eager eyes.

Sophia drew in a deep breath, sniffing with undisguised pleasure at the magic aroma that came from the last of the plates. Thin round cakes fried to a yellowish brown lay within.

"You've never had johnnycakes?" her aunt demanded in response to her question. "These should pluck you up a bit, my girl." She heaped several of the steaming cakes onto Sophia's plate, then liberally covered them in butter and maple syrup for her. Eugenia watched in amusement as her sister went to work on this treat with enthusiasm. Despite her fragile appearance, the girl had a ravenous appetite.

Mrs. Jessop, after making sure that Eugenia really did not want as large a portion as her sister, seated herself across the table from them and poured a cup of chocolate.

"Such fun we shall have!" She stirred the swirling dark liquid, then added a dollop of sweetened cream to it. "We have held only the smallest of parties since my girls were married. And little Sukey won't be ready for balls or routs for many years yet to come."

Eugenia raised large eyes to regard her aunt. "We have not come to be entertained, Aunt Mary. You are aware that we are searching for our brother? You cannot know, though, that the solicitors have placed a time limit of only a twelvemonth for finding him. And already over two months of this are gone, and we have made no progress."

"Of course you have. You are here, are you not?" Mrs.

Jessop dismissed her worries with an airy wave of her hand. "But you won't be spending every minute looking for him, and I quite long to introduce you to our friends. Real titled ladies! Why, everyone will so look forward to making your acquaintance!"

Sophia choked, but maintained her countenance. Eugenia lowered her own eyes, her indignation giving way to amusement. As if they were one of the sights of Bath—or whatever curiosities there were in this country to point at and marvel over! Would people come to ogle them and make rude, impertinent comments well within their hearing, if they did not live up to their expectations for the British nobility?

"Just a small party at first, I believe," their aunt went on, oblivious to their reaction to her naive comment. "Just to let you meet some of the young people. Should you like a dance? Or would you prefer a musical evening?"

"Oh, a dance, please!" Sophia exclaimed. "That would be the most delightful of things, would it not, Genie?"

"It would, indeed," Eugenia agreed, though with caution.

Their aunt positively beamed on them. "I must make plans immediately. Oh, and we must have picnics and take you to all the local sights, and to the theatre... I wonder how many couples we should invite?" Still murmuring to herself, Mrs. Jessop bustled off, her half-full cup of chocolate forgotten.

"You were right, Genie." Sophia sighed happily. "I shall have ever so much fun here. Only think how tiresome I should have found it, having to remain in mourning all Season at home!"

Eugenia nodded absently. Their aunt seemed to be a born hostess and must have sorely missed the excuse to entertain lavishly once her own children were grown and gone. But she must not allow that lady's plans to interfere with her finding Edward.

Leaving Sophia to a second helping of the delectable johnnycakes, Eugenia went in search of her uncle. Questioning the first maid she encountered, she was directed to a library on the other side of the house. Tapping on what she

hoped was the correct door, she was reassured to hear her uncle's voice bidding her enter.

He looked up from a stack of papers and smiled as he saw her. "Ah, Eugenia. Rested, my dear?"

"Yes, thank you, Uncle Reginald. Are you free?" She closed the door, then glanced about the spacious apartment. Leather-bound volumes filled the shelves that lined the room, giving it a comfortable, homey appearance. Candles in branched candelabra were set about on the desk and tables, though at the moment light flooded through the long French windows that opened onto a small garden.

Mr. Jessop stood, then drew up a comfortable chair opposite his large mahogany desk. She took this and waited while he reseated himself.

"And what may I do for you, my dear?" Absently he picked up a pair of wire-rimmed glasses and polished their lenses.

Eugenia bit her lip, once again marshaling her courage. In England she had not given herself time to think. On the voyage her search had still seemed so safely far away. Now, at last, it truly would begin, and she had to admit she felt rather afraid and overwhelmed by the task that lay ahead.

"I . . . I have not a minute to lose in trying to find Edward, Uncle Reginald." She told him of the time limit and watched with growing unease as his brow furrowed in perturbation.

"You've got quite a job, my girl, but I'll do everything I can to help."

"Captain Harrington believes he might have gone to Kentucky, or some such place. I thought we should perhaps check the suppliers of the equipment he would need for such a journey."

He nodded slowly. "There are several jumping-off places where he might buy things—if he indeed went that way. I'll get someone to find the names for us, and we can write." He lifted the glasses, breathed on the lenses, and rubbed them more thoroughly. "I think we shall have to get James to help us. Don't know why I didn't think of it before. Must have been too ill." He shook his head, then balanced the spectacles on the bridge of his nose. He peered at Eugenia,

then took them off and briskly rubbed the lenses with his handkerchief again. "We'll get him to talk to the other captains, see if anyone remembers carrying the boy anywhere."

Eugenia frowned. She had to admit this was a very sound idea, but she had no desire to feel grateful or obligated to the perfidious captain. The knowledge that he would enjoy the situation immensely did nothing to reconcile her to it.

"That's settled, then," her uncle declared, smiling. "I'll send a message to James this morning and get someone to work on the names of those suppliers. Now, don't you worry. We'll find that young rascal."

Eugenia stood. Apparently she would have to put off any plans for revenge on Captain James Harrington. It seemed she needed him yet again. With reluctance, she banked her anger, but left it smoldering.

"When he left here, did Edward give you *no* indication of where he might be headed?" she asked, her uncle's confident air only partially reassuring her.

He shook his head. "I've searched my memory, m'dear. Can't think of anything that would give us a clue. Seemed keen on making his fortune at first, until he figured out how much work it would be to set himself up in trade. Adventuring was much more to his taste. More like we'll find him in Kentucky—or beyond."

She was still pondering her uncle's words when she found her sister in the formal gardens, being given a tour by a boy and girl. All three saw her immediately and hurried over.

For a moment, Eugenia stared at the children, startled by their almost identical size and features. Sukey was perhaps a shade shorter than her brother and her eyes more gray than blue, but her long white-blond hair, which she wore in thick ringlets, matched Sammy's exactly. Twins, she remembered.

"Cousin Eugenia?" Sammy extended his hand, taking hers and bowing over it in a courtly manner that would have delighted his doting grandmother, had she seen it. He could not be more than nine years old, Eugenia thought, quite taken with the boy.

"Now, would you be the Sammy who peeked into my room this morning?" She smiled at him as one sharing a joke.

"I told you you'd wake her," Sukey put in with sisterly spirit.

"Did you tell Gramma?" Sammy asked, raising wide, worried eyes to hers.

"Of course not," Eugenia told him with solemn assurance. "*I'm* not a . . . a squealer."

She had the satisfaction of seeing the critical gleam fade from both pairs of eyes, to be replaced by a confident light.

"I told you she'd be a right one, lady or not," Sammy flung at his sister.

"You just said that! How could you know?" Sukey demanded, ready to do battle over anything.

"Shall we show Genie the garden?" Sophia, who had been standing quietly, enjoying this exchange, broke in on what promised to be a lively argument.

"Yes, please," Eugenia agreed. "It's quite lovely."

"I'm glad you've come." Sukey tucked her little hand into Eugenia's, pulling her along down the gravel path between carefully pruned hawthorn shrubs. Tiny pink flowers were liberally scattered across them, with numerous buds promising a profusion of blooms in the near future.

"Are you really glad?" Genie asked encouragingly.

"Of course. Now Gramma will hold a lot of parties, and Cook always makes the stickiest tarts, and she'll save a *whole* plate of them for us!"

Eugenia resolutely bit her lip, met Sophia's sparkling eyes by accident, and burst out laughing. What a delightful setdown for her—and how Captain Harrington would have loved to hear it! She sobered, remembering that she was furious with him.

She did not see or speak with him again until four days later, when he came to the informal cotillion her aunt had arranged in remarkably short order. Although he had twice called at the house in the intervening time to speak to her uncle, both times she was out with her aunt, assisting with the rapid but thorough arrangements for the party. If she felt any regret at missing him, she was able to convince herself that it was only because she was unable to give him his instructions for his part in the search for her brother personally.

The problem of what to wear on this, her first appearance

in American society, plagued her for the better part of the two days before the event. She was, after all, Lady Eugenia Wolverton, daughter of an earl, representing not only her lineage but her country as well. As such, it befitted her to be as regal as possible.

But the captain's words haunted her. America had broken with England and English traditions—including the nobility— and another war had ended only a few short months before. Unless she wished to be a constant reminder to her tempo-rary neighbors of the conflict that lay between their two countries, she had best simply be Miss Wolverton, not Lady Eugenia.

The idea frightened her. Stripped of title and position, she found herself uncertain of how to behave, how to interact— in short, she had very little confidence in herself. London society provided such safe guidelines for etiquette. She herself had been assured of her reception and role by virtue of her birth. But here? Was Captain Harrington right? Would she, because of who she was, be toadied to or shunned?

In the end, she selected a simple half-robe of celestial blue crepe over an underskirt of white silk. Betty, the maid assigned to her by her aunt, brushed her glossy dark hair until mahogany glints shone through it, then dressed it in its usual style, arranging the thick curls so that they fell forward over her shoulders. With the large sapphire held at the hollow of her throat by its pearl necklet, Eugenia felt a certain measure of confidence creeping back. The result, which she examined with care in the cheval glass, she felt to be sophisticated without being overstated.

Peeping in on Sophia, she was relieved to find that the girl had donned the fluttery white crepe that she herself had selected for her. They shared Betty's ministrations, and the maid now went to work with the curling iron on Sophia's short, thick curls. A pink riband threaded through these produced a result that made Eugenia's heart swell with justifiable pride.

They descended the broad stairway just before the first of the guests arrived. Eugenia stood stiffly beside her aunt, forcing a calm smile to her lips as she acknowledged the

introductions to people whose names and faces she quickly confused.

One face, though, she sought in vain. Though loath to admit it, she longed to see the one person she knew who would be familiar. Typical of Captain Harrington, she fumed, that he should absent himself on the one occasion she might actually welcome his presence.

One fact did help—a little. With considerable relief, she noted the gowns of the ladies and the quiet propriety of dress among the gentlemen. Her expectations of the backwardness of America faded further. It might not be so very different from England after all.

❁ *Chapter 12* ❁

Aunt Mary had invited enough young people to make up eight couples to form the sets for the country dances, along with their parents and chaperones. These latter Reginald Jessop took in charge, guiding them to the drawing room, where several card tables had been set up. Here he presided in perfect contentment, seeing to it that everyone had the necessary partners for the various games and that the wine flowed freely.

Mary Jessop's abilities as a hostess for a young people's party quickly became apparent. As soon as they were released from their position in the receiving line, Eugenia and Sophia were drawn into a game of Speculation. Several young gentlemen tried to outjockey one another for a position near Sophia's side, and the girl colored adorably under the lively and sincere attention. At home she undoubtedly would have scorned the game as too juvenile. Here she quickly abandoned her dignity and entered into the spirit of the game with enthusiasm.

By the time the musicians were ready to strike up the opening chords of a country dance, Sophia was on sufficiently easy terms with the other young people to seek out her partner and drag him, laughing, into the set that formed. Her fragile appearance, belied by her lively manner, capti-

vated that young gentleman, who followed her with an expression that reminded Eugenia strongly of a lovesick puppy granted a wish beyond his wildest dreams.

Eugenia was led into the same set by a rather sober-faced young man whose gentle expression held just a hint of humor. His manners were excellent, and though his eyes strayed occasionally to Sophia's ethereally lovely figure, Eugenia could not fault him on his attentions to herself.

"Do . . . do you live in Providence, Mr. Sands?" Eugenia asked. In spite of herself, her gaze strayed enviously to her sister's glowing face, Sophia seemed so relaxed among all these strangers. Eugenia, with two London Seasons behind her, realized she was far more nervous and ill at ease than her little sister, who had yet to be formally presented!

Her question drew a smile from her partner, and when the motion of the dance brought them back together again, he said, "My parents own the estate that borders your uncle's."

Eugenia flushed, for she remembered—belatedly—that she had she been told this when they were introduced. "My shocking memory," she apologized to him as soon as she could. "Please forgive me."

"There is nothing to forgive. I am in fact honored you were able to remember my name. There is nothing more unpleasant or unnerving than to meet so many strangers all at once."

The dance came to an end, and he led her from the floor. "Lemonade?" he asked. As if against his will, his eyes drifted to where Sophia stood in the middle of a laughing group.

"Allow me." Captain Harrington's deep voice interrupted them, sending a quivering sensation through Eugenia. Insensible relief flooded over her that he had come, that she was not alone, and she found it difficult to hide the surge of exultation his presence caused. For that one moment, it almost did not matter how very angry she was with him.

"Captain?" The thick blond waves of his hair, sun-bleached almost to white on the tips, curled back from his forehead in a manner that played havoc with her peace of mind. With difficulty she schooled her features into a cool

smile. "How pleasant. I feared you were unable to make it."

"Only a little late, Lady. I had some . . . some business to take care of."

"I am sure I do not have to present you to Mr. Sands?" she asked, hoping he would believe he was interrupting her from a pleasant dalliance.

"No need at all. How have you been, Gregory? Aren't you just about finished with school now?"

"Graduated last term, James." He grinned up at the elder man, not in the least discomposed by the captain's impressive height and bearing.

Eugenia glanced from one to the other, wondering suddenly about the easy terms on which all of these people stood with each other. Gregory Sands was the son of a wealthy landowner. His family's friendship with her uncle's she could understand. But the captain's people were in trade, she had gathered. Did the social constraints that bound British society not hold here? Were people, as the captain had declared, really accepted for themselves?

"Lady, may I have a word with you?" The captain looked down at her, amused, and she realized that he had addressed her more than once while her thoughts had been wandering.

"Of course. Excuse me, Mr. Sands."

The young man bowed, then walked quickly away. Glancing over her shoulder, Eugenia saw him join the circle about Sophia.

"What may I do for you?" she asked, allowing a haughty, condescending note to creep into her voice, at odd variance with the gratefulness she felt at his comforting presence.

The captain seemed to be aware of her conflicting moods. "Why, nothing, Lady. But poor Gregory was practically chomping at the bit to escape from you and pay court to your sister."

Odious man! She suppressed her mixed sensations and glanced over at the group to discover that Mr. Sands had neatly ousted Sophia's last partner and was leading the girl

towards the refreshment table. "I seem to be getting constant setdowns of late."

"Impossible, Lady. Sophia might be a fairy princess to beguile a callow youth, but you are a lady to captivate a grown man."

She flushed under the obvious sincerity of his words, hiding her confusion in a rallying tone. "You . . . you flatter me, I fear. I have it on good authority that my greatest value in this household is in forcing my aunt to entertain, thus making it necessary for Cook to prepare sticky tarts."

The captain's deep laugh boomed forth, rich and infectious, causing several people to glance at them. "Setdown indeed, Lady. Who could have had the impertinence to say such a thing? Sammy?"

"Sukey. I also have the dubious honor of being the only person she can beat at jackstraws."

"My poor Lady." He had led her to the refreshment table and now regarded its contents with disapprobation. "I know Mary Jessop. Where has she hidden the champagne?"

"In the card room. She thought it best not to leave it about for the younger guests." She bit her lip, her eyes dancing suddenly. "Perhaps you would be more comfortable there, with the . . . the older members of the party?"

"Cat," he murmured, his eyes resting on her in appreciation. "Shall I go and fetch you some punch, or do you fear they will hold me there among the doddering relics where I belong?"

"I don't want any at the moment, but by all means get yourself a glass. If you do not return in a few minutes, I shall know you are lost," she told him, then turned away as an unnerving thought occurred to her. She had turned to Captain Harrington as if to an old and dear friend! It was only because she felt shy and insecure without her rank and position, behind which she had always hidden in the glitter of the London *ton*. It was only because he, amongst this sea of strangers, was familiar to her. Once she became better acquainted with her new neighbors, the captain's presence would become a matter of indifference to her.

He did not reappear, and Eugenia at last allowed herself to be led into a new set by a young man whose name she

did not catch, but whose manners were easy and relaxed. Under his rambling, bantering conversation, she felt some of her stiffness begin to fade, and by the time the dance ended she was much more comfortable. A tentative, joking sally she directed to the other young lady in the set produced an unaffected laugh and a warm response and, with a sense of surprise, Eugenia realized she was beginning to enjoy herself.

In a moment her hand was claimed for the next set and, over her protests, she was whirled back onto the floor. Although the music was familiar to her, the steps were not always the same as those she had learned in England. After her second blunder, Eugenia was ready to sink with mortification, but her pride kept her going. Her attempts to correct herself were greeted by a mixture of hilarity and praise that soon made her realize that the laughter was not *at* her but *with* her.

"Well done!" her partner exclaimed as the last notes of the music faded away.

"How dreadful to find steps that one knows *changed*! However did you manage?" put in a young lady.

In London, even armed with an excuse for not being familiar with the dance, she would have been ridiculed behind her back or worse—been the object of insincere pity—for her faltering efforts. A smile trembling on her lips, Eugenia acknowledged the praise, warming to her aunt's guests.

The musicians rose to take a break, and Mary Jessop hurried forward, bent on arranging parlor games for everyone's entertainment during the interval. Eugenia caught a glimpse of Sophia in the center of one group and, reassured that her sister was enjoying herself, remained with the dancers from her last set.

When she looked about again, she saw that Captain Harrington was engaged in conversation with her aunt, whose watchful eye never strayed far from her guests. With so many of the young people having known each other most of their lives, she had little to do as hostess except make sure that their high spirits did not get out of hand.

Eugenia wished to speak with him herself about the

search for Edward, but he did not give her the opportunity. She was once again engaged in a dance when he took his leave and, though she knew he saw the speaking look she threw him, he left before the music ended.

Typical! she fumed to herself. Captain James Harrington really was the most infuriating and insufferable man she had ever met. She turned back to her partner with vigorous enthusiasm, determined not to let the captain's desertion— absence, she meant—disturb her.

The party did not begin to break up until well after midnight, and by then Eugenia found herself yawning. Sophia, she noted, appeared as lively as ever, apparently carrying on two flirtations at the same time. The girl's eyes glittered with an unnatural brightness, though, and it was with relief that Eugenia finally was able to lead her up the stairs to bed.

Sleep did not come readily. For a long while, Eugenia lay staring at the canopied top of her four-poster bed, deep in thought. Never before could she remember enjoying a party quite as much—except for the captain's irritating presence, of course. She had felt welcome and at home, and *comfortable* among these people.

Suddenly the reason struck her with blinding force. She had not been courted and flattered because she was *Lady* Eugenia, sister of the earl of Latham; she had been offered honest friendship by very nice people who came to the party because they liked her uncle, not because they wished to ingratiate themselves with him. No one there cared that she was Lady Eugenia Wolverton of Wolverton Priory. There had been no standards to maintain, no rigorous code of behavior to follow. She had simply had fun. The whole experience was novel to her, and she found she liked it very much. On this thought, she finally drifted off to sleep.

In spite of the late hour at which she had sought her bed, Eugenia was up the next morning at almost her usual time. When she peeked in on Sophia, the girl was still asleep. It seemed best to leave her, for late nights frequently brought on her headaches and nervous palpitations.

"Should we call a doctor for her?" Mary Jessop asked, concerned when Eugenia informed her of this.

"No," Eugenia reassured her. "It is best to let her have her sleep, then keep her quiet for the day. Perhaps we could take her for a drive when she wakes?"

Her aunt agreed, though she was clearly not convinced. "We must take care not to keep her up late, though I know how that will vex her. She seemed to have such fun last night! Do you think she will be better in three days' time?"

"I am sure she will be better tomorrow," Eugenia soothed her aunt. "But why? Is something going to happen?"

"Oh, to be sure, you did not hear! Mrs. Sands has invited us all to a dinner party. You will enjoy it immensely, I assure you, for she has the most wonderful cook, and she always invites the most amusing guests!"

"I am quite sure Sophia will not wish to miss that," Eugenia murmured, more to herself than to her aunt. Her sister's coy glances at young Mr. Gregory Sands had not been lost on her.

They were just rising from the breakfast table when Captain Harrington was announced, causing Eugenia to catch her breath and force her unruly emotions back under firm control. It was ridiculous to respond like that when she was trying to convince herself that she did not like him.

Mary Jessop stood irresolute for a moment, then turned her hopeful gaze on Eugenia.

"Will you see him, my dear? My housekeeper has been waiting this age for me! Tell him I shall be there as quickly as I may." Thanking her niece, she hurried down the back hall towards the kitchens.

As much as she might like, Eugenia could not—yet—give vent to her anger with him, not while she needed his help in finding Edward. Steeling herself in anticipation of the outrageous comments she was certain he would make, she made her way to the drawing room. There she found Captain Harrington leaning negligently against the mantel-piece as he stared down into the fire. He looked up as she entered and came forward to take her hand.

"Rested after your late night?" he asked.

She raised her eyebrows slightly. "I am hardly such a poor creature as to be laid up after a single party. Were you

hoping to see my uncle? I am afraid you are too late. He has driven into town already.''

"No, I came to see you. Now why should that surprise you? I had thought that look you gave me as I left last night to be an order to present myself without the least delay.''

She colored slightly. "Pray, don't be absurd.'' It was disturbing to have him continually reading her feelings so accurately. "I did wish to speak to you,'' she admitted. "About Edward,'' she hurried on as those glinting devils of merriment danced in the depths of his eyes. "My uncle tells me that you have been making inquiries.''

"To no avail yet, Lady. But I have no intention of giving up. New ships arrive almost daily, and I have considered taking the *Sea Horse*—my schooner—down to Newport, or perhaps even to Boston.''

Why should the thought of the captain sailing off trouble her? She tried to ignore it, instead concentrating on her search. Every day brought her that much closer to Cousin George's usurping the earldom. She had no time for delays.

"That would be an excellent idea! Will you be able to go soon?'' she asked with forced eagerness.

He looked at her through narrowed eyes. "I hope so, Lady. I am quite at your disposal.''

She flushed at the warm amusement that sounded in his voice, turning so that he could not see how he affected her.

"Would—would you be gone long?'' she could not stop herself from asking.

"A week or two, I should think. But if you do not mind, I won't leave for a few days. I am waiting to see someone here. The captains I have spoken to have all promised to spread the search in every port they stop at. Someone, somewhere, must have heard of your brother,'' he added with firm conviction.

Eugenia sighed. This was a start, but she felt lost, not knowing what to do next, unable to do anything by herself.

There was little she could do but wait for some word, some clue, to point out the next direction. Waiting seemed intolerable, but she had little choice. She drove out sedately with her aunt and Sophia, walked in the gardens, and longed for some diversion to take her mind off her worries.

The evening of the Sands' dinner party arrived not a moment too soon for Eugenia's restless nerves. Even if it did nothing to assist her search, it at least would provide her with a much needed distraction.

Although their estate bordered that of the Jessops', both were very large and the houses were actually situated over a mile apart. The Jessop party was among the last to arrive.

It was not to be the small, quiet affair Eugenia had anticipated. Twenty couples, most of whom had not been present at her aunt's dance, took their places at the long table in a dining room that rivaled that of Wolverton Priory in its magnificence. Eugenia found herself seated between a Providence merchant and a visiting Boston lawyer, and fell back on her company manners to carry her through a dismally boring meal.

Formal dinner parties, she realized, appeared to be a universal fact of life. In England, she had accepted them as one of the obligations that went with her position in Society. Here she found herself wondering how much longer she had to wait before she would be able to escape. Had she changed that much in such a short time? She, who had been brought up practically from birth to take her place at State occasions? What could have so undermined her training?

Involuntarily, her eyes drifted up the table to where Captain Harrington sat, engaged in what appeared to be a highly entertaining conversation with a lively and quite pretty young lady. He glanced up at that moment, his gaze roving down the table, and his eyes met hers. Eugenia felt the power and energy that emanated from him, felt again the tug of that undeniable, disturbing attraction, and hurriedly looked away.

She was able to escape his presence shortly when the ladies retired to the suite of connected drawing rooms that had been thrown open for the evening. Here she sat with Sophia and two of the young ladies whom she had met at her aunt's party, deep in a discussion of the latest fashions in London and Paris.

She felt the captain's approach before she either heard or saw him and looked up while he was still several paces away, meeting the cold determination in his eyes. Something

seemed to crush down on her heart, a great weight that pressed in her chest. Not knowing why, she stood to meet him.

"Lady, may I have a word with you?" He led her slightly aside. "I would like you to meet Lieutenant Patrick Connerly."

She stiffened, but inclined her head in polite greeting, not quite sure of the etiquette involved in meeting a member of the military in a country recently at war with her own.

The blue-coated, slim young man appeared to feel no such constraint. He bowed briefly over her hand, and his unruly orange-red hair bobbed and his watery blue eyes shone brightly—from the after-dinner brandy, Eugenia guessed shrewdly.

"So, you'd be Ned Wolverton's sister, then?" he asked, a wide, lopsided smile on his freckled face.

"Ned..." Eugenia broke off, her eyes widening as the import of these words sunk in. Her knees felt unaccountably weak, and she barely noticed when the captain pressed her gently into a chair.

"Easy, Lady," his voice murmured softly near her ear. His hand remained gripping her shoulder tightly—in warning? A sudden fear gripped her, holding her rigid.

"Yes," she managed. "You know him, then, Lieutenant?"

"That I do. Or did, I should say. Haven't seen him for several years now," he added in the contemplative manner of one a trifle above par. "Great gun, though. Always prime for any lark."

At least he was not telling her that Edward was dead! But why did the captain's hand remain with such a firm, reassuring grip?

"Has—has Captain Harrington told you that I am trying to find him? Then perhaps you would tell me where you saw him last and what he was planning to do?"

"With a man like good ol' Ned, that's hard to say. Las' time I saw him was the night before he left our... our unit." His words began to slur a bit. "Dead drunk, we were. Don't really remember what he got so excited about. Somethin' 'bout how we weren't doin' anythin', an' he wanted t' be in the thick o' things. He was sort of an informal volunteer, so I guess he jus' up an' left."

Eugenia stared at him, trying to make sense out of this rather confusing speech. "Do . . . do you mean your unit in the army?" she finally asked, wholly bewildered.

"O' course. Can't think o' any other unit I'd be in," he told her, beginning to succumb to the amount of brandy he had drunk.

"Edward joined the *American* army? But . . . but when?"

"When the war broke out," the very bosky Lieutenant Connerly explained patiently, as if to a child. "Tol' you, he wanted t' fight those stinkin' Brits!"

✾ Chapter 13 ✾

Eugenia felt the blood drain from her face, leaving her cold and trembling. Lieutenant Connerly could not have said what she thought he just had; it could not be true. Edward? To have joined the American army? To have fought against England—his homeland?

The pain in her shoulder caused by Captain Harrington's steely fingers recalled her to a sense of her surroundings. Her first response, to accuse this man of lying, to scream her revulsion at the very idea of what he said, she managed to stifle. She drew a deep, quavering breath and felt the captain's grip relax.

"Perhaps you had better tell me a bit more," she said as steadily as she could.

"Not much t' tell," the lieutenant said, completely unaware of the devastating impact his words had already had on her. "Met him back in the summer o' 1811. Had some good times together, too. Leastways, I think we did. Weren't sober very much," he added with a halfhearted apology. "When we declared war on the Brits in 1812, he started talkin' wild about lathes . . ."

"Latham," Genie corrected automatically.

"That's right. Latham." He nodded vigorous agreement. "An' priorities. Talked a lot o' nonsense, then suddenly he

up an' signed on as a volunteer. Nothing much happened, an' I guess he got . . . got fed up.'' The lieutenant swayed slightly, then with an effort pulled himself together. ''Heard him yellin' at the officers one mornin' an' never saw him again.'' He looked from Eugenia to the captain, then back again, obviously pleased with himself for completing his recital.

''Thank . . . thank you. He gave you no hint as to where he might be going?''

''None. Had no idea he planned t' leave. Jus' never saw him again.''

While the captain guided the faltering lieutenant back to a group of his friends, Eugenia rose unsteadily and made her way out through the long, open French windows into the garden. There she stood, staring unseeingly up at the stars, trying to make sense out of what she had just heard. Could Edward's hatred for Robert have gone so deep that he would have struck back against England? Or could his rebellion against tradition, against being a Wolverton of Wolverton Priory, have taken this form?

She pressed her hands over her face. What did she really know of her brother? Could his careless gaiety have hidden a rebellious, lawless spirit? He had committed a treasonable act! Even if she found Edward now, could he step forward and claim the title, or would he be arrested and shot?

She heard steady, purposeful strides approaching from the house. She swallowed, trying to force her frantic emotions back under control. Even if her brother could have been so lost to all sense of decency as to fight against his homeland, she, at least, would maintain the standards of the Wolvertons!

''I'm sorry, Lady.'' The captain's deep voice came from directly behind her, gentle and serious. His leashed energy emanated from him in tangible waves, enveloping her with his boundless strength.

''It seems my brother may be a deserter as well as a traitor,'' she declared, her voice brittle, almost breaking. She bit her lip. *Those words should not have been said!* she told herself firmly. *He is not to be judged by lesser men.* But she, a Wolverton herself, judged him and found his behavior disgusting.

"You now have one clue as to what he has been doing," the captain mused. He gave no indication of having heard her outburst, and for this she was silently grateful. "You now know his whereabouts in the fall of 1812. That's three years ago instead of six."

She turned to face him. "Do you not scorn my brother's behavior?" she demanded.

"Nay, Lady. It's not for me to judge his actions. And until you know the truth behind them, you should not torment yourself either. Would you rely on the word of a drunken soldier who dislikes your country?"

Her eyes dropped to study the large silver buttons of his blue coat. "No," she said at last. "That Edward joined the army as a volunteer we do know—or at least we can confirm. Why is another matter and does not concern us at this moment. But why he left might. What do I do now?" She raised her large, troubled eyes to his and encountered a look of smiling approval.

"That's the spirit, Lady. I believe we should next check the military records to discover everything we can about him. How long he was enlisted, where he was sent, and hopefully why he left and where he went."

"Will it be difficult? For me, I mean? Is the American army likely to let a British subject inspect their military records?"

The captain's massive shoulders shook with sudden mirth, and when he spoke there was a slight tremor in his voice. "Lady, you would undoubtedly be shot as a spy. I think this may take some discretion."

"Which you think I do not have?"

"Lady, you could never disguise your accent. And I do not believe any government would allow a subject of a nation with which it was recently at war access to military records."

"Then . . ."

"You will do best to leave it to me."

She straightened up regally. "Captain, I already find myself deeply in your debt, and—"

"And it galls you to let me help further?"

"Yes!" she declared baldly.

He laughed, his rich chuckle sending shivers through her as she responded instinctively to his magnetism. "I'm sorry, Lady, but I believe I know how we may get the information you need. And I'm afraid I can get it more easily than you."

She clenched her teeth together, biting back the retort that sprang to her lips. The most infuriating thing about Captain James Harrington was his insufferable, irritating habit of being right! She took a deep breath, trying to regain her composure.

"Thank you, Captain," she managed at last, forcing a condescending smile to play about her lips. Her manner was every inch that of one conferring a favor on a servant, of permitting him the honor of doing her a trifling service.

It was not lost on him. His eyes glinted with amusement, reflecting the light that washed over them from the stars and half-moon. "That's my Lady."

Her cheeks warmed, and she turned away in confusion. "We had best to go back inside," she told him, striving to keep her voice cool and indifferent. He had an unnerving effect on her, though why calling her "his" lady should affect her so was ridiculous! The sooner Edward was found and she returned to England the better.

It took Captain Harrington four days, a number of visits, and two letters of introduction before he gained permission to examine the military records, and even then Eugenia suspected it would not have been approved of in Washington. In comparison, the actual searching of the documents took very little time.

Eugenia awaited the captain's report with considerable anxiety. The suggestion that she go with her aunt and sister to pay morning visits she turned down immediately, preferring to pace about the garden or sit in the drawing room, a book open in her lap, staring with unseeing eyes into the fireplace.

When the sound of hoofbeats crunching up the gravel path finally reached her, she sprang to her feet, allowing the forgotten book to drop to the floor.

The captain's tall figure strode into the room only minutes later. He came to her immediately, taking the hands that she

held out to him. Her wide eyes asked the question she found difficult to put into words.

"I found the records, Lady. He was with the army for less than a month."

Her knees trembled and gave way, and she sank back down into her chair. "Oh, thank God!" she breathed reverently. The idea of Edward's fighting against England had sickened her. Relief that he had apparently regained his senses before it came to that flooded over her, leaving her weak.

Captain Harrington seated himself on the sofa across from her, his eyes resting on her averted countenance. "Would you care for some sherry, Lady?" he finally asked.

At that she looked up and smiled, for the first time since she had spoken with Lieutenant Connerly. "No, I do not stand in need of a . . . a cordial. What a miserable, missish creature you must think me!"

"Indeed I do not."

One of the things she most disliked about Captain Harrington was his continual ability to put her to the blush. Every time she began to relax and feel at her ease he would say something to throw her into confusion, to make her long to forget his despicable behavior on the *Cormorant*—not to mention the tenets of her upbringing—and engage in most reprehensible repartee with him.

She schooled her features into a semblance of dignified reproof. "Please tell me what you learned, Captain."

"Yes, ma'am." His eyes twinkled at her, mocking the serious note he forced into his voice. "Your brother signed on as a volunteer in Newport, took part in training, and resigned again before the month was out. There was no record of why, or where he went."

"So we are back where we started—except now we have proof that he was alive three years ago."

"We have a little more than that. I took down the names of several others who joined at the same time, who were in training with him. If we talk to some of these men, we may learn a bit more."

"Oh, Captain!" Real hope shone in her eyes. "How can we find them? When do we begin?"

He met her gaze, his compelling eyes holding her mes-

merized within the magnetic force that emanated from him.
"My name is James," he said softly.

James. But that could be only for a lady whom he could
approach on equal terms, whom he could court, to whom he
could pay his addresses, whose hand he could solicit in
marriage . . . And she was a Wolverton, though for the first
time she felt a measure of regret for her august lineage. Her
position in Society, in the ranks of the nobility, precluded
the degree of intimacy that he offered her.

"Captain." Her voice, even to herself, sounded hollow,
and it hurt her more than she had anticipated to see the
glinting light fade from his eyes.

"I know the family of one of the men," he continued.
"I'll call at their house when I leave here. As for the
others . . ." He paused, his brow wrinkling as he considered.
"I believe our best move will be to write to their people, try
to get word of their current whereabouts."

"I . . . I'll draft a letter immediately." He had accepted
her snub quite smoothly, even acted as if that brief exchange
had not taken place. It would be much easier to look down
on him if he were not so considerate of her at the most
unexpected moments!

They wrote the letter together finally, a short and simple
statement that they were searching for any clue that would
lead to the whereabouts of one Edward Wolverton, known
to have joined the army as a volunteer at the same time and
location as the person addressed. Eugenia copied this message in her elegant copperplate seven times, once for each
of the men on the captain's list, and he took the letters with
him when he left.

The first response came sooner than Eugenia expected.
The following afternoon, as she and Sophia were being
initiated into the mysteries of skittles on the south lawn by
Sukey and Sammy, Eugenia saw the captain cantering easily
up the long drive towards the house.

"Aim at the *pins,* Cousin Genie, not Gramma's rose
bushes!" Sukey exclaimed as Eugenia rolled the ball with
incredible inaccuracy.

Sammy, who had run after the wayward balls that now lay

scattered about among the roses, looked up as Captain Harrington reined in barely fifty yards away. "It's Uncle James!" he cried, abandoning his mission in favor of one of his favorite adults.

Uncle James? Eugenia watched as Sammy hurtled over the grass and locked chubby arms about the captain's elbow. A groom hurried forward to take his horse, and Sammy triumphantly dragged his captive back over to where the others stood waiting.

"Uncle James will show you!" Sammy declared.

"How can he, stupid? You didn't get the balls!" Sukey informed him. They went off together to retrieve them.

Eugenia, granted a moment by the twins' argument to recover the composure that seemed to slip whenever she found herself face to face with the disturbing captain, extended her hand to him in greeting.

"Captain, I had not expected to see you again so soon."

"And I had not expected to have word for you so soon."

"You've learned something? That man whose family you know?" she asked quickly.

"Word?" Sophia asked, looking from one to the other. "Oh, Captain, have you news of our brother?"

"A little, not much, I fear. I now know why he enlisted and where he was heading when he resigned."

"Uncle . . . Uncle James, *show* Cousin Genie how . . . how to throw the ball!" Sukey, breathless from running, came panting up to them.

He ruffled her fair curls carelessly. "In a bit, Sukey. I need to talk to your cousins for a minute."

"*Now*, Uncle James! Oh, please, she wouldn't listen to me!"

"Well, can you blame her? If that last toss I saw you make was a sample . . ."

"It landed in the bushes by . . . by the merest chance!" Sukey declared hotly.

"Hah!" Sammy stuck in with true brotherly spirit.

"Well, I didn't see *you* do any better!" Sukey turned on him.

"Practice!" Captain Harrington commanded. "You may spend the next half-hour polishing your skills, and when I

return with your cousins, you may show us what you can do.''

His tone brooked no argument, and though the twins showed him rebellious faces, they made no objections. As Eugenia started towards the house, she saw Sukey taking careful aim and rolling her ball to within only a few feet of the untouched pins.

Eugenia barely waited until they had entered the drawing room before turning on the captain. "Please, tell us. What possessed Edward to join the army?''

"He was foxed." His face was solemn, but there was a twinkling imp of mischief in the depths of his eyes.

"Inebriated! Of all the irresponsible, *stupid*"—she borrowed the word from Sukey's vocabulary—"idiotish thing to have done!''

"As you say. He was apparently out with a few *choice spirits,* several of whom were soldiers, and woke up in their camp. The army was eager for men, and somehow both he and another fellow found themselves enlisted without being sure how. He apparently found the experience novel and entertaining, because he stuck around for a few weeks before he decided to leave. And since he was a British citizen, and we were at war with the British . . .'' The captain let the sentence dangle. His eyes danced, inviting her to share the joke.

"He was lucky they did not shoot him as a spy!'' she exclaimed.

"As you say. But I must suppose by then they had become somewhat familiar with his . . . eccentricities,'' the captain suggested.

Eugenia stared at him. Sophia, at her side, began to giggle, and Eugenia joined her, releasing her tension and worry. How like Edward! How could she ever have believed he would have joined on purpose! Not when there was a chance his enlistment could have been the result of a prank gone wrong, or even sheer accident!

"Captain, I am so glad! Indeed, I am very grateful to learn the truth of this. But did you not say that you also learned where he was going?''

"I did, Lady.'' A serious note crept into his voice, and it

was not lost on her. She tensed again, waiting. "He fell in with a regiment from Kentucky, going to Canada."

Her knees buckled, dropping her onto the sofa which was luckily at hand. She stared at him, unable to speak, letting this information sink in to her bemused brain. "Canada..." she whispered.

"Why?" Sophia demanded, bewildered. "With a regiment? But he resigned from one. Why should he join another?"

"That I'm afraid I cannot tell you—yet."

"Canada..." Eugenia repeated. She raised her eyes to meet the captain's. "Must... should I go to Canada?" she asked, feeling overwhelmed, lost in the seeming hopelessness of the task before her.

"Do nothing yet," he directed her, his voice firm and reassuring.

She took a deep breath. "Do... do you think..." she began.

"What I think is that you have had too many nasty shocks of late. You may be sure his reasons for joining another regiment are going to be very interesting and probably highly diverting, once we learn what they are."

"Canada," she repeated, but this time thoughtfully, without the earlier panic she had felt. "He might have picked a regiment as the easiest means of getting to British territory during a war. We won't know, though, until we learn how and where he left them."

"Good girl," he said, smiling in a way that caused uncomfortable sensations in the pit of her stomach.

"So we should go to Canada and try to find word of him there," she said slowly.

Sophia drew in her breath audibly and dropped one hand onto Genie's shoulder. Eugenia raised her own to cover her sister's, hoping she had enough courage to carry them both. She had known their search for Edward would not be easy, but the reality was proving far more frightening than she had ever guessed. And would she have enough time...

"I don't think you need bother quite yet, my lady," the captain said gently. "If you agree, I believe it would be best to write letters to the military headquarters in Kentucky and

see if there is any proof that he actually did join one of their regiments. He might have only thought about it. And I have a business acquaintance in Quebec. With your permission, I will write to him also.''

She felt Sophia's relief in the relaxing of her fingers. With their limited funds, this would be the most practical solution. For if it were found that Edward had *not* gone to Canada, she would have wasted precious money . . . and time.

''How long do you think it will take to hear back?'' Eugenia asked.

''I'm afraid it will probably take close to a month. But you can't go to both Kentucky and Canada yourself, and there's a chance we may learn more from the other men who enlisted with your brother.''

Eugenia considered this, nodding slowly. He was right—as always. She must wait and not squander her dwindling funds until they had definite proof, not just conjecture or rumor. But a whole month! When every day mattered . . .

''I know, Lady. But what good would it do you if you hurried off to Canada, only to hear someone else thought he went to Virginia?''

She looked up to meet an unusual seriousness in his eyes. Why did his continually being right irritate her so? Just once she would like to see him uncertain of himself, vulnerable, for once not so insufferably capable.

The door opened slightly, and a straw-blond head peeped in. ''Aren't you coming *yet*, Uncle James? You promised!''

The captain raised questioning eyebrows towards Eugenia. ''Would you like to think about it, Lady?''

''No.'' She sighed. ''Write your letters. Please. The sooner we get them off, the better.''

''I will see to it that they go with the morning's post.'' He bowed to her slightly, then turned his attention to the small figure of Sukey, who almost danced in the doorway in her impatience. ''Do you want me to help you bowl down your grandmother's rose bushes?''

With Sukey pulling the captain along, they returned to the south lawn. Eugenia followed, relieved that some action was being taken, but disturbed that it was the captain of all

people who quietly took command and helped her. She wished heartily and uncharitably that he might not prove as adept at this game of skittles as she very much feared he would.

❊ Chapter 14 ❊

Weeks of waiting stretched ahead of Eugenia. With not one single thing she could actually do to look for Edward until the letters were answered, she turned with a restless enthusiasm to the various entertainments offered to pass the time. Her aunt, who had begun to worry about her preoccupation with her brother, was relieved by this change in her and immediately set forward plans for a dinner party and a visit to the theatre.

Eugenia welcomed anything that diverted her mind from her worries. She paid morning calls with her aunt and sister, went on lengthy shopping expeditions, and found herself looking forward to even the smallest and dullest event. More than once she accompanied Sukey and Sammy into Providence to watch the docking and unloading of one of the great merchant ships that arrived frequently at the port.

It was on one of these expeditions, in the company of her uncle and Sophia as well as the twins, that they saw Captain Harrington striding about the deck of a newly arrived ship, shouting orders and inspecting the cargo crates as they were hauled into position for transfer to the wharf.

He looked up as a great block and tackle lifted one of these crates and spotted them where they stood along the quay. Tossing the sheaf of papers he carried to the man who

followed him, he crossed to the gangplank and down to the wharf. The twins squealed with delight and took off running to meet him.

The others waited, and within minutes Eugenia could see his tall, impressive figure wending its way through the crowded street, one twin pulling on each of his arms.

"Grampa," Sammy shouted as they approached. "Uncle James says we can go on board when the ship is unloaded!"

"You're sure you want them?" Mr. Jessop asked, smiling indulgently on the happy trio.

"Oh, they know better than to get underfoot. I'll just throw them overboard if they do," the captain said cheerfully. The twins giggled at this dire threat, hugging his arms more closely.

Eugenia studied him through lowered lashes. With his boundless energy and air of strict command, it surprised her how he indulged the children. His deep, hearty laugh and joking nature assured him his place as the twin's favorite, but he never seemed to tire of their dogging his footsteps, hanging on him, or asking a never-ending string of questions.

"If you would like, I can return these two to you later," he suggested. "I'll just lock them in a cabin until the men are done."

Reginald Jessop smiled as Sukey and Sammy giggled again. Then his gaze moved thoughtfully to Eugenia and Sophia. "There is someone I wish to speak to this morning," he said slowly.

"Do not worry about us," Eugenia immediately spoke up. "Sophia and I can walk about here or meet you somewhere later."

"The dock is no place for unescorted ladies," the captain said sharply. "Would you care to stay and help me look after these two rascals?"

His method of doing this was quite simple. He led his charges along the wharf until he reached a shop with a confectioner's sign hanging over the door. Here he purchased a bag of peppermint candies and chewy sticks. They then returned to the ship, where he ordered chairs placed for them on the bridge, where they would be sure to have a good view without being underfoot.

Eugenia positioned Sophia's and her own chair so that their backs were to the sun that peeped out through a low covering of gray-tinged clouds. Pulling her woolen shawl tighter about her shoulders, she sat back, feeling the gentle rocking of the ship at rest. Surprisingly, Sophia made no protest at this motion, merely leaning forward, watching the unloading process as eagerly as did the twins.

There was such a comfortable, familiar feel to being on a ship again, even if it was not the *Cormorant*. Their voyage had been restful—and adventurous—all at the same time. And there was the captain, crossing and recrossing the deck with his purposeful, forceful gait, shouting orders no one would dare disobey—except her.

A reminiscent smile played about her lips. They had argued and laughed and teased each other; he had infuriated her and . . . The light faded from her eyes. He had lied to her and laughed at her, insulting her beyond endurance. In the past couple of weeks, she had almost allowed herself to forget this. She was relying on his help in her search for Edward, and somehow her equally important punishment of the captain had slipped from her mind.

She rose, crossing over to lean on the railing that ran about the bridge. Sukey and Sammy, who knelt on the deck peering through the wooden posts, huddled closer to her skirts for warmth against the chilling breeze that came up. The captain, glancing up, waved to them, and the twins flapped their hands wildly in response.

Why did Captain James Harrington choose to help her? Because it amused him, of course. She could think of no other reason for him to do anything. She had declared a covert war on him, he had enjoyed their battles, and he was not a man who would casually abandon such an entertaining pastime. His helping her must be just another tactic in their ongoing game.

A cold, empty sensation swept through her. He merely played a game, while she had been engaged in the urgent matter of finding Edward. She had allowed herself to be distracted, thus giving him the advantage. Well, if he still fought her, she would not retire from the lists. A Wolverton

did not surrender, but it might be prudent to take a few minutes to regroup her forces.

On consideration, she decided that she had been playing neatly into his hand. He now held the dominant position, commanding her gratitude and reliance. Briefly she considered refusing any further assistance from him, but dismissed this as impractical. Such a blatantly childish act would only afford him more amusement—and reinforce the low opinion of her he must already hold. No, it would be far better to make as much use of him as she could, thus advancing her search and displaying superior sense.

That decided, she turned her attention to her original plot to make him fall in love with her. The idea still appealed to her—disturbingly so, in fact. She forced her thoughts to gloss over this and move on. The admiring glint in his eyes had returned when he thought her pride humbled. But it was no fun playing a shrinking flower, and she strongly doubted that sort of woman would appeal to him. He seemed to be a creature wholly devoted to his own amusement. So amuse him she would—and herself, at the same time.

This time Genie would declare her war openly, playfully, making it clear to him that it was she who found him amusing. That should shake up his complaisance. He must be humbled, as he had tried to humble her. He would pay for despising her, for saying those hurtful things to her on the *Cormorant,* and he'd pay with his heart. And when he knelt before her, offering her his love, she would reject it, scorning his entreaties.

She turned away from the rail abruptly, suddenly aware of the squawking of the gulls and the shouting of the men. Of course she would reject the captain's love. She had her own life in England, her own position in Society. A Wolverton was ineffably above a sea captain. Such an alliance was unthinkable.

It was with considerable relief that she welcomed her uncle's return to the ship shortly before noon. Sophia, who had begun to shiver, was only too ready to return home, but the twins were made of sterner stuff. Loudly protesting their fate, they refused to listen to Mr. Jessop's remonstrances. Captain Harrington took charge. Over their complaints,

he forcibly removed Sammy and Sukey to the waiting carriage and ruthlessly thrust them inside. One soft word from him was enough to silence their wails that they wanted to stay, and he then turned back to hand in Sophia.

"Thank you, Captain, I had a lovely morning," the girl declared.

He bowed slightly. "You shall have to come down whenever I have a ship come in. Though you should perhaps dress more warmly."

Whenever he has a ship come in? The thought barely had time to register in Eugenia's mind before he turned to her. Was this his ship? But he had not been gone . . . did he *own* another merchantman besides the *Cormorant*? If so, he must be better circumstanced than she had supposed.

"Have you received the invitation to my aunt's ball?" he asked as he took Eugenia's hand to help her step in.

"Your aunt's ball?" she repeated blankly, trying to recollect her scattered wits. "Why, no. Your family has returned from Boston, then? We shall look forward to it."

And she did. To her dismay, she found she was curious about the captain's family. She had automatically assumed he was merely a sea captain in someone else's employ when she first met him, and she had learned of her error. Now it seemed that he owned more than one ship. What would his people be like? Would they be of low origin, climbing the social ladder through success in trade? Or would they be genteel, well-bred, unexceptionable, as was her Aunt Mary's family?

She had to admit, now that she was more familiar with the ways of Americans, that Captain Harrington was far more the gentleman than she had first believed. He was, in fact, becoming a considerable problem for her. The force of his presence haunted her even when she did not see him for days on end. His deep laugh reverberated through her, making her vitally aware of him, making everything fade into insignificance except the sensations he created in her. The sooner she found Edward, gave the captain his much-deserved setdown, and returned to England, the better.

Their next meeting came on the night of his aunt's ball the following week. The intervening six days were full of

boredom, which she beguiled by polishing the fine points of her plan for revenge and wishing that the captain would appear so she could try them out.

She also spent this time in adding to her sparse wardrobe. As her Aunt Mary planned a number of social events, and the rest of Providence society seemed only too anxious to do the same, it quickly became clear to Eugenia that she and Sophia stood in crying need of ball gowns. They had not brought any with them, for they had not expected to be spending their time in America in this manner. Sophia was delighted with the way things were turning out and entered with enthusiasm into the hiring of a seamstress.

The price of fabric in America was considerably more than it had been in London, leaving Eugenia relieved that they had purchased several ells of different cloths before their departure. While on the ship, they had mostly been concerned with appropriate day and dinner gowns for Sophia, whose emergence from the schoolroom had been rather abrupt. Their satins and lace had been untouched, and Aunt Mary, eagerly entering into the unpacking of their working trunk, exclaimed in delight as these were brought forth.

A week's work resulted in Eugenia's being dressed for the ball in a new slip of sapphire blue satin worn under a half-robe of white lace. Sophia, demurely attired in a simple gown of the pale peach satin that so became her, met with approval from her sister's critical eye, and together they went down the stairs to where their uncle and aunt already awaited them.

The home of Captain Harrington's aunt and uncle was located a little more than two miles beyond that of the Jessops', along the Boston Post Road. Despite telling herself that there was no reason why it should matter, Eugenia was obscurely pleased when the carriage pulled off the main road onto a neatly raked gravel drive. By the brilliant light of the colored lanterns that had been hung to illuminate the way for the guests, she could see that it was lined by tall hedges winding their way up to the imposing front of the house.

Lanterns were scattered about here also, lending a friendly and welcoming glow to the red brick facade. She was handed down by a footman, who stood back to allow her to

proceed up the path before turning to assist Sophia. The massive front door opened as they started up the wide white-painted steps, and a butler, as dark-skinned as her uncle's Thomas, bowed them in.

A tall, regal lady swept towards them, almost floating across the marble-tiled entry hall. Eugenia, casting a quick eye over her hostess, was pleasantly surprised. There was nothing backward or provincial about the elaborate French gown or the modishly cropped and curled graying hair. Mrs. Quincy, her sweet smile genuine, welcomed each of them in a warm, friendly voice. When she laughed at a compliment from Mr. Jessop, it was as wholeheartedly and infectiously as her nephew.

Her husband joined them a moment later, the quiet propriety of his dress winning Eugenia's instant approval. No dandy or mushroom, this, she realized. Mr. George Quincy was undeniably a gentleman, by anyone's standards.

"Mrs. Jessop!" A tall, laughing girl hurried towards them, hands extended. Her thickly curling blond hair bobbed about her lively face as she moved with that same restless, suppressed energy Eugenia knew so well from her acquaintance with the captain. This must be his cousin, Miss Quincy.

"Cassandra, my dear." Mary Jessop offered her cheek for the kiss that was clearly coming. "Now, do be still for a moment. I want you to meet Mr. Jessop's nieces. Lady Eugenia Wolverton and Lady Sophia."

Cassandra took Eugenia's hand. "I feel I know you already, Genie. Oh, may I call you that? And Sophie. James has told me all about you, and I've been longing to ride over to meet you. Oh, I must not keep you out here. Do come into the ballroom. I hear the musicians warming up. Do you know many people yet? Shall I introduce you around?"

On her tumbling words, they entered a lofty, elegant room decorated with potted plants and vases of flowers. Chairs were arranged in clusters about the edges, half hidden by the gold velvet hangings. A surprising number of people were already gathered, sipping from glasses and talking. Cassandra paused just over the threshold, looking about.

"Oh, there is James. Do you mind if I turn you over to

him? I should get back to the hall to greet latecomers. James!'' she called.

It would be difficult not to notice the captain, no matter how full the room might be. Eugenia's eyes had been drawn to him the moment she entered, his powerful figure dominating those about him. His simple but elegant evening attire fit him as naturally as did his rough woolen sea coat. It was not every man, she thought, who could look as at home in a ballroom as on the deck of a ship. He turned as his cousin hailed him, and Eugenia swallowed, trying to control the surge of emotion that swept through her as their eyes met.

He crossed the tiled floor with his free, swinging stride, then bowed before them. ''Well, Cassy, you have met my Lady and her sister.''

''I have indeed. But I must go back to my post, and I don't want to desert them among so many strangers. Honestly, I believe we have half of New York and Boston, as well as Providence and Newport, here this evening. Don't let them get lost in this crowd, James.''

''My pleasure, I assure you. Run along now, before you get in trouble.''

She wrinkled her nose at him, but hurried off.

''She is quite like you,'' Eugenia informed him, watching the lively girl's departure.

The captain chuckled softly. ''Don't let Cassy hear you say that. Lord, she wouldn't thank you in the least!''

''Oh, I didn't mean she shared your more disagreeable traits,'' Eugenia assured him promptly.

His shoulders shook from the effort of containing his merriment, and golden lights danced in the depths of his mesmerizing eyes. ''Lady, you wrong her. She—'' He broke off, for the determined figure of Gregory Sands made its way up to them.

''Lady Sophia,'' he breathed, his attention riveted on the delicately frail young lady. His expression could be described only as besotted. Belatedly, he turned to greet Eugenia and the captain.

Eugenia glanced at her sister, prepared to share the joke of her first conquest, only to see that the girl stood with

hands folded before her and eyes cast down in adorable confusion. The look she gave Gregory from beneath her long, lovely dark lashes would have caused envy in an accomplished flirt. Its effect on the young gentleman was staggering.

Eugenia frowned, not at all pleased. It seemed her little sister was learning the arts of fascination all too quickly. Captain Harrington apparently found it amusing, and the corners of his mouth twitched as he tried to restrain his smile.

"Would you care for a glass of punch?" young Mr. Sands asked Sophia.

"Oh, yes, please," she murmured, smiling tremulously up at him, her sparkling eyes belying her demure stance. She accepted his arm, and they strolled off together.

"Don't scowl so," the captain murmured softly. "The little bird is merely trying her wings. She will come to no harm with Gregory Sands."

"True. At least *she* has the escort of a gentleman." Eugenia, to her annoyance, was unable to think of a better, more stinging retort. He would hardly understand her worry for such a frail and unsophisticated creature as Sophia. She felt deeply her responsibility for the girl. Sophia had been kept so sheltered, and now here she was, in the wilds of America, with only a sister for protection. That they had a very capable and respectable uncle and aunt did not at the moment weigh with Eugenia's sense of guilt.

"Does that mean I should have offered you some punch?" he asked, his bearing that of one anxious to please.

"Oh, don't be absurd. Tell me instead if you have received any answers to your letters yet. I have not seen you for almost a week."

"Alas, no, Lady. Are you promised for this dance? It is one with which you should be familiar."

The music had started, and sets were forming rapidly. Curious to see how he would perform as a partner, Eugenia accepted his hand and permitted him to lead her into a line near them.

Despite his size, he moved with a surprising grace. She quickly discovered she had no need to fear lest he tread on

her toes or lead her wrong. He proved to be as accomplished on the dance floor as he was on the deck of his ship.

He was not permitted to remain by her side after the music ended. Mrs. Quincy bore down on them, bringing another partner for Eugenia and whisking James off to do his duty by the other females present. Eugenia next spotted him sitting out the dance with a matronly woman who seemed to giggle excessively and unbecomingly at everything he said.

Eugenia, keeping a surreptitious eye on Sophia, was pleased to discover that Mr. Sands was truly a gentleman. After leading Sophia into the first set, he had taken her to her aunt, then quite correctly solicited another young lady's hand for the next dance. If his glance strayed rather often in Sophia's direction as she danced with others, it was not so noticeable that anyone could complain that he had sat in her pocket all evening.

Sophia appeared to enjoy being a sensation far too much to allow her thoughts to dwell on any one gentleman. She was never without a partner, Eugenia noted with pride, and, if she did display a tendency to flirt, it was not done in an outrageous fashion. Only the highest sticklers might have found fault in her behavior.

After several dances, Eugenia escaped to sit quietly with her aunt, sipping a glass of ratafia procured for her by her last partner.

"Oh, what a relief to be off my feet for a moment!" Cassandra, appearing by her side, laughed as she sat down. "Just look at James! How does he keep going, dance after dance?"

"He doesn't. He has been sitting out with the chaperones. I don't believe he has danced more than three times," Eugenia informed her.

"I'll roast him for that! He told me he had not rested for a moment!" She paused, looking about the room. "Did you like your last partner?" she asked abruptly.

Eugenia considered. "A Mr. Selkirk. Yes, he seemed quite amiable."

"He is!" Cassandra asserted. "I am going to marry him.

Though don't mention it to my papa," she added confidingly. "I have not quite convinced him of it yet."

Eugenia stared at her. "Did . . . did he not speak to your papa first?" she asked, quite shocked. That was hardly the behavior of a gentleman, unless the proprieties differed in America.

"Oh, yes. Papa did not forbid it, you understand, though he is not quite *pleased*. Jasper used to be only one of James's clerks. Now he's in charge of the warehouses, and he'll go much further, I assure you." Her eyes twinkled in merriment.

"Does . . . does your cousin have many people working for him?" Eugenia tried to make the question sound merely polite.

"Oh, yes. I don't see how he can keep track of them all. What with the sailors and clerks and agents and dock workers . . . Heavens, I hardly know what all he needs. There are dozens of them, though."

"Then why does he captain his own ship?" Eugenia looked down at the delicate fan of pierced ivory she clasped in her hands.

"He only does that when he is restless or bored. He owns a fleet of ships, you know. Whenever he gets tired of life on land, he just selects one that is headed somewhere interesting and takes over. We never know where he will be off to next." Her eyes narrowed suddenly. "Has he been teasing you?"

"He . . . he let me believe he was merely a captain, working for someone else, when I first met him."

Cassandra's merry peal of laughter rang out. "Oh, if that is not just like him! He is the most absurdly shocking creature! I hope when you learned the truth you gave him a sharp setdown."

"He does not make that an easy thing to do," Eugenia declared candidly. "But I'm working on it."

"Oh, good!" The lovely green eyes, so like her cousin's, glinted with mischief. "It's just what he needs. So many people just give in to him, you wouldn't believe it!"

"That is something I will not do, I promise you."

"Excellent! Oh, before I forget. Do you ride?"

"Yes, though I haven't since we arrived. My uncle does not keep any ladies' mounts, except for Sukey's pony."

"Then we shall provide the horses. We are arranging an expedition tomorrow, into the countryside. Do say you and your sister will come."

Cassandra's eyes sparkled with an unshared joke, and Eugenia, glancing sharply at the captain, who was leading his partner from the dance floor, found that his gaze rested on them. So it was Captain James Harrington who wished her to go riding, was it? Well, she would not disappoint him—not in that respect, at least.

"We shall look forward to it." Eugenia turned back to Cassandra, meeting her eager look with one of simple politeness.

Eugenia did not have an opportunity to speak to the captain again before they left, which was just as well, she reflected. She needed some time to digest what she had learned about him—and his family—that evening. Not that it made any difference to her plans, she assured herself. It might, however, assist her in her tactics.

They left the ball early, over Sophia's protests, but Eugenia was anxious that the girl not overtire herself. When she disclosed the promised treat for the morrow to her sister, the girl brightened considerably, and she even agreed that a good night's rest would be necessary before venturing out on an all-day riding expedition.

They were dressed and waiting in the drawing room the following morning when Sophia, who stood near the window to keep a lookout, shouted, "Here they come!"

Eugenia crossed over to join her, peeping out over her shoulder. Captain Harrington, astride his powerful, raw-boned bay, led the way, holding the reins of a riderless, quiet-looking chestnut. He was followed by Cassandra, Mr. Jasper Selkirk, and Mr. Gregory Sands. A slightly built man with the unmistakable aspect of a groom rode behind, leading a neat little gray mare.

Sophia almost ran to the door in her eagerness, and Eugenia hurried after her. As they emerged, the captain was just swinging down from his horse, having handed the reins of both mounts to Mr. Selkirk.

Gregory Sands, seeing Sophia, almost leapt from his saddle. He signaled the groom forward and, taking Sophia's hand, led her up to the gray.

"Ravishing." Captain Harrington bowed slightly to Eugenia, his eyes glinting his eternal merriment.

"Thank you." She smiled at him, allowing her own amusement to show clearly. She cast a considering eye over the riding habit of her favorite sapphire blue, allowing herself a reprehensibly smug smile. It had been the highest kick of fashion the year before, as was the hussar hat that crowned her head.

He tossed her lightly up in the sidesaddle, and she hooked her knee over the pommel. While she settled her skirts neatly about her, he examined the stirrup leather, shortening it by two holes. She tested it, then thanked him politely.

"Genie! Is she not lovely?" Sophia already walked the gray mare up the drive, testing her mount. "I vow, she is above anything great!"

Eugenia, smiling at her sister's pleasure, pressured her heel gently against the chestnut's side, touching the rein slightly to turn him so that she could join Sophie.

There was no response. She tried again, this time with more force, and managed to get a shambling walk out of the creature. Indignation swelled in Eugenia's breast. That this was the captain's latest insult to her, she had no doubt. But it would work only if she allowed herself to be upset. If she could laugh it off, it would be *he* who would be discomposed.

She turned the reluctant animal back to the captain, who once again sat in his own saddle. His jaw seemed to jut out more firmly than usual, and Eugenia guessed shrewdly he was having difficulty in controlling his laughter.

"How delightful of you!" Eugenia called to him. "Did you guess I should be so worn out by last night's ball that I did not really wish to ride? Why, I have only to sit here, or go to sleep if I desire, and I shall be carried right along at this steady pace!"

That brought a laugh from the others.

"I *told* you, James," cried Cassandra. "But you would insist."

His shoulders shook with his effort to control his merri-

ment, but his voice was almost steady as he replied, "You must forgive me. But how was I to know," he went on glibly, "whether or not such a fine lady as you would be accustomed to spirited animals?"

As she was considered a notable horsewoman, she was prompted to deliver a stinging retort. "To be sure, you are a sea captain, are you not? It would be unjust to expect you to also be a judge of horseflesh or horsemanship." Her smile was sweetly condescending as she prodded the reluctant chestnut into position. Sophia rode up on the gray, and the whole party started down the drive.

"*Touché*, Lady," the captain murmured as he brought his bay up beside her.

"Oh, do you fence, as well?" she asked innocently.

"A little. Do you?"

"I think my brother would have been shocked if I had expressed a wish to learn any such thing." This was said not without a certain regret, for she had always secretly thought it might be a great deal of fun.

"What, there is something a Wolverton cannot do?"

The teasing note in his voice stung her, and her chin came up. "Say rather that there are certain things that it would not be proper for a Wolverton to do."

"How dull for you," he said, his voice holding so much understanding and sympathy that she suspected him of insincerity and longed to strike that quirking smile from his lips.

"But then I cannot expect you to understand living within Society's rules," she said, her tone indicating vast pity for such an unfortunate as he.

"True." He was quite agreeable. "I never allow anything so ridiculous to interfere with me. After all, I am only a sea captain," he added on a note of apology.

She struggled against her sense of the ridiculous and lost. It really was too much, to have her own taunt thus thrown back at her. She choked back a laugh. "Are you by any chance the bane of your family?" she demanded.

"Oh, undoubtedly the black sheep. Just ask Cassy. The two of you may abuse me soundly for hours on end, I make no doubt. And probably enjoy yourselves immensely."

"We undoubtedly should," Genie agreed promptly. "It would be delightful to talk to someone with so much proper feeling."

It was his turn to laugh, a deep, hearty sound that set his massive form quaking. His horse sidled skittishly as his weight shifted, but Eugenia's chestnut, to her disgust, plodded along undisturbed, not even flicking an ear at the disturbance.

She stole a glance at the captain through her lowered lashes, only to find his eyes resting on her, the glinting lights in their depths bespeaking his amusement. Was he never serious? She looked away, studying the long, coarse hairs of her mount's mane. Was she fascinating him or merely entertaining him? He was not an easy person to punish, she reflected.

They stopped for lunch at a lovely old inn deep in the country. It proved a lively and protracted meal, for all were bent on enjoying themselves. As they started back, Cassandra, who was in the lead, reined in and turned to the others.

"Oh, let us race! I am longing for a good gallop." Her horse seemed to share her enthusiasm, for it danced beneath her, eager to be off.

"Go ahead," her cousin called. "I will keep Eugenia company. I doubt her horse can go faster than a trot!"

"It was really quite despicable of you, you know," Eugenia informed him conversationally as she watched the others tear off. The groom accompanied them, following closely behind Sophia, which relieved Genie of that worry.

"Of course it was," he replied with great affability. "What, by the way?"

"This . . . this slug! I don't share your optimism by calling it a horse."

He laughed again, sending a shivering response through her. "It was indeed. And I do apologize."

Her startled gaze flew to him, for he seemed sincere. "What? You? Apologize? I must be hearing things," she said unsteadily, forcing a teasing note into her voice.

"What an opinion of me you must have!"

"And quite justified, too, as you know very well!" she snapped. "Come, let us try the paces of this animal. Do you

think we can manage a semblance of a trot?'' She dug her heel into her mount's side and was rewarded by having him amble along slightly faster. She repeated the action and, to her surprise, he broke into a trot for several steps before shuffling back into a walk.

''Oh!'' she declared in disgust. ''This animal is as stubborn as . . . as *you* are!''

''Or you, Lady,'' he said softly. ''We neither of us give an inch once we have begun something, do we?''

She refused to meet his gaze, for there had been no trace of his customary lighthearted teasing in his words. And what did they mean? Did he know what she was up to, that she intended his enthrallment solely to bring about his downfall? Did he laugh *at* her, not with her, whenever they joked, knowing full well why she played along with him?

She went cold inside, as if a cloud had settled firmly before the sun. Her hands clenched at the unresponsive bridle. Of course. He had been playing her for a fool, and she had been helping him every step of the way.

❈ Chapter 15 ❈

Eugenia lay awake long into the night, tossing fitfully as she sought a sleep that steadfastly eluded her. She had handled things badly that afternoon, and she knew it, which only made an intolerable situation even worse.

Captain Harrington had noticed the manner in which she had withdrawn from him. Well, how could he help but notice? She had been so blatantly obvious about it. Rather than treating him with the contempt she felt he deserved, she strongly suspected that she had merely given in to a fit of the sullens.

He had seemed puzzled at first, but made no attempt to draw her out. As the minutes stretched out, silent and stilted, she had become aware of his growing amusement, of the quirk of his lip that indicated that once again he laughed at her.

Her suspicion that he was aware of her intention to make him fall in love with her haunted her. Now what was she to do? Was he indeed aware of her game, or was his amusement nothing more than a mannerism, a habit, as natural to him as his air of command?

More important, did she have the nerve to continue it? If he knew what she was up to, then there was no point in it;

she might as well treat him with cool civility and avoid his company whenever possible.

The prospect did not please her. Such behavior, she told herself, bore more than a hint of childish sulks. The unfortunate truth, that she enjoyed her arguments with the insufferable captain and was loath to give them up, she tried to ignore. He enjoyed them, too, she reminded herself. Too much. The conviction grew within her that he might very well be laughing *at* her, and that was something her pride could not tolerate.

Eugenia remained in this uncomfortable state of mind, unable to decide on her best course, for the next several days. She was relieved that she did not immediately see him again, for this respite, she hoped, would give her time to consider her future actions and demeanor.

As she sat in the garden one morning watching Sophia playing at skittles with the twins, her spirits still cast down, the sound of hoofbeats on the gravel drive reached her. Hope, that treacherous, traitorous emotion, welled up, and she jumped to her feet, hurrying eagerly along the path to see who had come. But it was not the captain's tall, vigorous figure that swung lightly down from a well-ribbed chestnut, but that of his cousin.

Cassandra looked across the expanse of lawn to where the twins laughed and shouted, and saw Eugenia. She waved and, with a quick word to the groom, who took her horse, she crossed over to Genie.

"How are you?" Cassandra called gaily, then hurried on without waiting for a response. "I have been meaning to ride over these past several days, but something always seems to crop up. Have you received any word yet of your brother?"

"None." Eugenia took the hand that was held out to her, then led the way back to the bench where she had been sitting. The twins and Sophie shouted greetings but did not leave their game. "I was rather expecting to hear something from your cousin."

"James? Did you not know? He has gone to New York, on business."

"No. He . . . he did not mention it." Irritation with him

for not telling her vied with a vast feeling of emptiness at knowing he was nowhere near. While she knew he owed her no explanations, Eugenia had hoped to be included in his plans. With difficulty, she forced her irritation to overpower her softer, more confusing feelings for James Harrington. "He might have at least sent me a message, so I would not sit here waiting for word! He knows how anxious I am, how very little time we have."

"Oh, he is quite famous for being aggravating. We are all accustomed to his high-handed ways," Cassandra told her merrily. "You will get used to him, too, never fear."

This idea appealed to Eugenia far too strongly. "I doubt I shall be in America long enough," she countered.

"Will you be coming to the musical *soirée* tomorrow night?" Cassandra abruptly changed the subject.

"Why, yes, we are looking forward to it." Eugenia blinked, trying to tear her thoughts away from the infuriatingly absent captain. "It . . . I am sure it will be quite enjoyable."

"Oh, it will. Mrs. Sands' parties always are. Do you sing or play an instrument?"

"Both. That is, I can accompany myself on the pianoforte. Sophia prefers the harp."

The twins, finally tiring of the game, ran over and threw themselves down on the grass at the base of the bench. Sophia followed in only a slightly more dignified manner, caution for her new gown preventing her from following Sukey's example.

Sophia looked forward to the following evening with enthusiasm and bombarded Cassandra with questions as to what sort of music was preferred here and the instruments and variety of songs they might expect to hear. To listen to her, Eugenia mused, one might almost believe music to be her entire life. Her sister was quite proficient on the harp, but Genie had never before noted that her enthusiasm carried her away.

Eugenia remained in her dissatisfied, almost petulant, mood for the remainder of that day and most of the next. She attributed her listlessness to the frustration of waiting for news that did not come and directed her anger at the

captain for not being present so that she could vent some of her tension in a rousing argument with him.

The prospect of diversion at the *soirée,* coupled with Sophia's bubbling enthusiasm, finally coaxed her into a better mood, and she spent some time helping her sister select just the right dress for the occasion. Her own appearance she did not worry so much over, selecting at random the white crepe with the blue ribands. She did not admit, even to herself, that her lack of care in selecting her gown might be due to her not expecting to see the captain.

In this, though, she was wrong. From the moment she entered the drawing room of the Sandses' impressive mansion, she was aware of Captain Harrington's presence. As always, he dominated his company, not only by his size, but by the sheer force of his personality. Her eyes were drawn to him as if by magnetic force, and an elation she could not quell surged in her heart.

He looked up, almost as if he sensed her arrival, and his eyes scanned the doorway. They rested on her momentarily, and her heart seemed to drop as his gaze moved on after he gave her only the briefest of nods. He returned to his conversation, and Eugenia noted that it was with a young and quite pretty blond.

Sophia drifted off, seemingly without direction, but in only a few minutes Eugenia noted that she had joined a group of which young Mr. Gregory Sands was a part. Eugenia's brow lowered thoughtfully as she studied her sister. Her manners were those of a practiced flirt rapidly making progress, but Eugenia finally decided she could detect nothing more, nothing that might indicate her sister stood in danger of losing her heart. She was so young, so inexperienced. It would be terrible if she threw herself away on an American before she could be brought out in London.

For once, Eugenia found that she was not enjoying the evening. Even Cassandra's cheerful, confiding prattle failed to divert her, and the performances, though of an unusually high caliber, did not lift her sagging spirits. Even when a harp was wheeled out and Sophia shyly took her place at it, Eugenia's depression did not wholly dissipate. The response to the lovely performance was all that a fond sister could

have desired, but she left the smug looks to her aunt and uncle. This night she felt far from complacent.

She stole a look at Captain Harrington, only to discover that he was once again in conversation, this time with a lively brunette. If she had ever wondered whether or not he was much sought after, her observations tonight would have settled the matter. "Assiduously courted" by the ladies might be a better term. And why not? He was wealthy enough, according to Cassandra, to cause even the most fastidious damsel to overlook his irritatingly humorous manner. She could only be grateful that she was a Wolverton and thus above such mercenary considerations.

Her unpleasant reverie was interrupted by her hostess, who hovered near her elbow. "Lady Eugenia," Mrs. Sands said, and Genie realized that it was not for the first time.

She turned to the woman, silently cursing the captain for causing her to be inadvertently rude. "Yes, Mrs. Sands? I am sorry, I fear I was thinking."

Her hostess's eyes flickered in the direction of the captain, but if she guessed Eugenia's preoccupation, she had the tact not to mention it. "Will you sing for us, my dear?" she asked. "Sophia assures us that you are quite renowned in London."

"A sister's exaggeration, I assure you," Eugenia demurred, but this was in fact the truth. She had not taken part in her Aunt Lydia's musical evening in London because she had still been in mourning, and she had felt a pang of regret, for playing and singing were normally a source of joy or solace to her. Tonight, though, she had her doubts.

Seated at the exquisite pianoforte, she ran loving fingers over the keyboard, then struck a rich and carrying chord. She began the verse for "The Elfin Knight," then, on impulse, switched and sang instead "The Golden Vanity," a lovely old ballad that dealt with the perfidy of a sea captain.

She held the final note long, her soft, musical voice carrying across the stillness of her audience. She released it at last and sat back, flushing softly at the warmth of the applause from her audience. Unable to restrain herself, her eyes searched for the captain, eager to see his response. To her fury, he appeared not to have paid any attention,

indulging himself instead in an obvious flirtation with the
lovely blond again.

The end of her performance signaled an interval, and the
guests rose, mingling, heading for refreshments. Eugenia,
quite thirsty after the effort of maintaining the purity of
some of the more difficult notes, went in search of something to drink.

She almost collided with the captain in the doorway to the
drawing room in which the refreshments were laid out. He
appeared to be alone—for once—and carried only one glass.
He was frowning, his eyes dark and cool.

Eugenia stepped back in feigned surprise. "Excuse me. I
did not see you."

At that his brow lightened, an appreciative gleam setting
golden glints in his sea-green eyes. "Lady, your wits must
have been wandering. I am not easy to miss."

Suddenly the evening did not seem so drear. It must be
the aftermath of singing, she told herself, and allowed a
slight smile to play about her lips. "If I may pass?"

"Forgive me." He bowed in an exaggerated manner.
"Do you wish something to drink? Allow me to escort
you."

"Thank you. It is so far, I would be afraid to go alone
and unprotected."

His deep chuckle rumbled within him. "Lady, are you
trying to put me out of countenance? I was merely trying to
be civil."

"Pray, do not strain yourself. And I doubt if anyone has
ever put you out of countenance."

"Not often," he agreed. He worked his way forward
through the crowd, reappearing moments later with a glass
of ratafia, which he handed to her. Then offering his arm, he
led her to the next room, where they found an unoccupied
sofa.

"You do not take part this evening?" Eugenia asked
between sips.

"Nay, I have no turn for music," he replied with studied
casualness.

In spite of her determination not to care for his opinion,
she was annoyed. Knowing herself to be a very fine player

and singer, she had expected at the least a word of appreciation for her performance. His deliberate unconcern irritated her. "How can you say that?" she demanded with mock astonishment. "I frequently heard you singing sea chanteys on board the *Cormorant*."

He smiled to indicate his inner amusement, but he did not release it in the deep, wholehearted laughter that never failed to send a shiver through her. Instead, his attention seemed to wander, then settled on someone on the other side of the room. In a moment he excused himself and made his purposeful way towards the ravishing blond to whom he had been speaking earlier.

Eugenia sagged into the cushioned softness of the sofa, considerably taken aback. Never before had the captain hurried away from her, preferring the company of another lady. She had come to expect his undivided attention and support, and to be suddenly deprived of it was no pleasant thing. She considered his behavior to be an act of callous desertion, though she was not quite sure why. Why should she care that the captain wished to speak to someone else? He might do as he pleased. But to leave her like that was little more than an insult, adding to the score that already lay between them.

Three days later, she was still trying to come up with a suitable revenge when she saw him ride up to the house. As he dismounted, he glanced over to where she sat on a bench amidst the roses. He could see her clearly, but he did not wave or nod. Instead, he made his purposeful way towards her.

"Good morning, Captain." She tried to stifle the uneasy feeling that settled over her with disconcerting force. "And to what do we owe the honor of this visit?" Her finely arched eyebrows raised a fraction. Only the slightest hint of indifference colored her tone, but surprisingly it did not please her to see an irritated muscle twitch at the corner of his mouth.

"This, Lady." He drew a letter from his coat pocket and handed it to her.

She reached out to take it, only to find that her hand

trembled too much. Her eyes, large and frightened, flew to Captain Harrington's face.

"No, Lady," he said quickly. "My acquaintance in Quebec says merely that he has been unable to locate any trace of your brother."

Eugenia let out a long breath in a ragged sigh. "No, well, we never really expected much from him, did we?"

The captain sat down next to her, again offering her the paper. She took it, scanned the few lines, then handed it back.

"He promises to make further inquiries," she said, her voice flat even to her own ears.

"You may be sure he will. He is a very thorough man. He will do everything possible."

Eugenia nodded absently. "Do you know, I cannot see Edward remaining in one spot for very long. It is possible that he is somewhere near Quebec, but not very likely, even if he did go there when he left the army."

"You're sounding defeated. That's not like you." The gentle note in his voice caused her to raise her eyes to his face, then lower them again quickly in confusion. She felt annoyingly breathless.

"Not defeated," she corrected. "Just frustrated. I sit here, week after week, doing nothing except attend parties!"

"I am sorry you find Providence society dull."

"Oh, don't be absurd!" she snapped. "You know perfectly well that is not the problem. Everyone and everything has been quite delightful. I just feel that I have come so far to contribute absolutely nothing to finding my brother!"

Too late she saw the dancing lights in his eyes and realized once again he teased and laughed at her. She rose, angry, and he followed suit, taking her agitated hands. She tried to pull them away, but his grip was firm.

"Must you always mock?" she demanded.

"Only to make you laugh, Lady. Do you truly believe I meant offense?"

His tone was curious, and this time when she tried to remove her hands from his, he released her without protest.

She turned away from him. "I am sorry, Captain. It is just that the time runs out, and I do so little."

"We have not yet heard from Kentucky, Lady," he said, his tone as casual as ever.

She sat down again abruptly. "No, we . . . we haven't." With a concerted effort, she willed her agitated mind to be calm. "That is undoubtedly the more promising of the inquiries you made. From what I have heard of frontier life, it might suit Edward."

"It might, indeed. There's a challenge there for an adventurous young man."

She looked at him, wondering. "Might you have gone there, if you hadn't gone to sea?"

At that he laughed, but she did not sense that he teased her. "I don't know. The sea is my kindred spirit. It's my love, in my blood. I can't imagine life without the wind and the spray . . . the feel of being on a ship." His mysterious green eyes reflected his emotion, becoming luminous pools that beckoned her into the whirling vortex of their depths. With difficulty, she struggled back to reality.

"But . . . oh, would a *normal* man, one who wasn't obsessed, seek such adventure?" she demanded, trying to disguise her soaring response to his words. Such an obsession, in her mind, made a man complete. A man without a vision, without a driving force, seemed empty and shallow. And she longed for such a man, to share his dream, to be part of his motivation, his life. Any lesser man would be dull in comparison.

The captain's deep, rich chuckle sent a shiver through her, and those disconcerting eyes bore into hers as if finding the truth behind her mocking words.

"There would be adventure in both lives, Lady. Had I been born inland so that I never saw the sea, I might easily have been drawn to the mountains, the forests, the challenge of making my own life." He considered for a moment, then: "It would take a strong man to go on, to survive. One without enough determination would turn back, find an easier way to live."

Eugenia nodded slowly. Edward would undoubtedly have the spirit and desire for adventure to try . . . but would he bear up under the hardships? To consider her own brother as less of a man than the captain was hurtful, but it would do

her no good in her search to lie to herself. Edward, as she remembered him, was wild and lively, but she strongly suspected that he lacked dedication to any cause but his own welfare.

"I am sorry I could not bring you positive news, Lady."

She stood again. "Thank you for trying, Captain. We never held out much hope for Canada, though."

He took her hand. "That's the spirit. Don't let it discourage you. Do you go to my aunt's party? Then I shall see you in three days' time."

She watched him stride off towards the stable, where his horse had been taken, and in only a couple of minutes she saw him ride down the drive. She sank back down onto the bench, her eyes following the tall, muscular figure astride the great bay until he disappeared around a bend.

What did she really know of Edward? She had come to America because she had been so convinced she could predict his movements. But he had been young, and in many ways immature, when he left England. His spirit she could not doubt. But his courage? She had heard stories of red Indians, horrible tales. Would Edward really have placed himself in any serious danger?

❧ *Chapter* 16 ❧

E ugenia's uncertainty about her brother's probable
activities gave way to another, even greater, concern.
As she reviewed everything she could remember
about Edward's character, a new doubt rose in her mind.
Was finding her brother actually the best course—not only
for him, but also for the estate?

With the earldom, Edward would have the money, influ-
ence, and importance she knew he would enjoy. But he was
proven footloose and irresponsible, a gay adventurer at
heart. Would he be willing to settle down and be a responsible landlord? The captain's words returned to haunt her. Just
because Edward's father and brother had been deeply concerned with their land and tenants did not necessarily mean
that he would be the same. What if it bored him? Or, even
worse, what if he wasted the Latham estates?

The alternative, though, was dear Cousin George, and
she had no doubt whatsoever that he would be a terrible
landlord. Fancying himself a Go amongst the Goers, he
would soon waste the estate on ill-judged flights on the turf
and fall prey to every ivory-turner or Captain Sharp in town.
She knew him well enough to guess shrewdly that he would
find himself run off his legs in no time, without having

invested so much as a single groat back into the land, where it was sorely needed.

Even more important than the estate was Sophia's future. The sister of an open-handed and wealthy earl stood in a far more secure social position than the impecunious cousin of a close-fisted and wastrel earl. Lord Brockton's abrupt change of attitude had made that fact abundantly clear to her.

And the title of Latham must go to its rightful heir. She was a Wolverton, and so was Edward. When faced with his responsibilities he might be reluctant, but she was sure he would recognize his duty. Edward must be found—and soon.

Restless, Eugenia wandered off in search of her sister. She finally located the girl in the children's parlor, seated at a card table where she was engaged in a card-house-building contest with Sammy and Sukey. Three small, wobbly creations stood before them.

"Eugenia, don't close the . . ." Sophia began, but it was too late. The air current caused by the opening of the door proved too much for the unstable constructions. All three teetered and collapsed.

"Oh, Genie, look what you've done!" Sammy exclaimed. "And mine was the biggest!"

"It was not, mine was!" Sukey instantly asserted.

"Enough!" Eugenia prudently stopped the argument before the two combatants could get properly warmed up. "They were both beautiful, and I am sorry. I will leave the door open so there won't be any trouble when I leave."

"What is the matter, Genie?" Sophia asked with uncustomary astuteness.

"Captain Harrington was just here." She silenced the twins' exclamations at having missed him. "His friend in Quebec has found no word of Edward."

Sophia nodded wisely. "Gregory said it was unlikely."

"Gregory?" Eugenia asked, momentarily bewildered. "Oh, Mr. Sands."

"He thinks Edward probably went to Kentucky, or even beyond."

"Beyond! Oh, Sophie." She sank into a chair. Could

Cousin George have been right, and they would never find their brother? "Do you really think Edward would be willing to face red Indians?"

"Oh!" Sophia looked at the twins as if to find inspiration, but none came. "I . . . I don't know. I'm sure he would want adventure. But *danger* . . . ?"

Eugenia watched her sister through narrowed eyes. It was not like the girl to confide in someone—as unusual, in fact, as her own reliance on the captain. She tried to shake off this errant thought, but found it difficult. "Did Gregory consider the danger?" she asked.

"As if he would care for that!" Sophie exclaimed. "If he had elder brothers to inherit, I am sure that is what he would have done. He is really quite dashing and brave."

The twins hooted their opinion of such a soppy statement, but Eugenia prudently kept her lips closed firmly on her own retort. She had been so preoccupied with the search, and with her ongoing battle with Captain Harrington, that she had not been aware of the changes taking place in her once frail and wilting little sister.

Perhaps Dr. Crofton on the *Cormorant* had been right. After her initial seasickness the long sea voyage seemed to have done wonders for the girl's health. She would always be fragile in appearance, but there was now a bloom in her cheeks and an unfamiliar energy about her. The delicate prettiness that had always characterized her had blossomed into an ethereal beauty, with a promise of better things still to come.

Eugenia was already aware of Sophia's tendency to flirt, but she had allowed herself to hope that it was merely the pastime of a fledgling trying out her wings. She knew there was depth of character hidden beneath her sister's fluttery surface, but it had not occurred to her that it was ready to emerge, marking her transition from a lighthearted child to a young woman. Sophia, she realized suddenly, would be seventeen in another month, the age when many young ladies of birth and breeding were married. And she had taken her from England, where she might meet a young gentleman whose birth and circumstances matched her own.

This new problem, which Eugenia had been too preoccu-

pied to notice before, now hovered over her like a dark, ominous cloud. She began to watch Sophia covertly with renewed concern, listened to her casual, lighthearted chatter, and saw a very disturbing picture developing.

Sophia's enthusiasm for searching for Edward, never particularly keen, had now faded into insignificance. For the next two days, her talk was of little but the Quincys' party and their own *al fresco* luncheon scheduled for a few days after. And, interspersed with increasing frequency, came the name of Gregory Sands.

Eugenia did not have the opportunity of observing these two together again until the night of the Quincys' informal ball. Unlike the previous occasion, when the rooms had been disconcertingly full of strangers, Eugenia found she knew most of the other guests, had danced with a number of the young men, and felt on fairly easy terms with several of the other young ladies. On the whole, it should be a very pleasant evening for her.

Sophia, within moments of their arrival, was drawn into a small circle of which Gregory Sands was a member. Eugenia noted this, her eyebrows lowering thoughtfully.

"If you aren't careful, you will give my aunt a reputation as a poor hostess." Captain Harrington stood at her elbow.

Eugenia almost jumped. She had been so deeply troubled that she had not heard his approach. "I . . . I am sorry. What did you say?"

"Merely that if you scowl so, my poor aunt will be blamed and her popularity as a hostess dimmed."

"You are being absurd, as always," Eugenia declared roundly, trying to maintain a straight face and failing.

"That is better," he told her encouragingly. "You have such a pretty smile."

She blushed, trying to determine his purpose behind this compliment. It must only be to tease her into a better humor, though why he should bother escaped her. "Is that why you laugh at me so often?" she countered.

"You make me sound a monster, Lady." He chuckled softly. "Why should I laugh at you?"

"For your own amusement, of course. You seem to enjoy laughing a great deal."

"I do. But I prefer someone to laugh *with* me."

"I doubt that few dare to laugh *at* you." She attempted a light response.

His heavy brow lowered in a puzzled frown. "You are worried this evening. And it is more than your brother, is it not?"

"What concern is it of yours?" she demanded, distraught, wanting to confide in him but knowing it would not be wise. A long-time friend of the Sandses, he would not understand her anxiety for her sister's heart. Involuntarily her eyes sought out Sophia, only to find her leaving the room on the arm of young Mr. Sands.

"Is that it?" the captain asked. "Then I can relieve you of this worry, at least. Young Gregory is a gentleman to be trusted in every way. He will not take advantage of your sister's inexperience."

"But will be respect her youth? He is quite young himself."

The captain's chuckle rumbled once more, irritatingly. "Do you fear that his intentions are honorable, then?"

"Of course I do. I would not want his affections to become too deeply engaged, for she shall not be remaining in America for very long. She will return to London and be brought out properly among people of her own rank and position."

"Don't you feel the Sandses are good enough for her?" There was a curious, pointed edge to his words.

"Do you enjoy being ridiculous?" she asked with a sweetness she did not feel. "The Sandses are quite excellent people. It is you who do not understand. We do not belong here. We have our own lives, our family, everything waiting for us in England. This is only an interlude."

The captain bowed slightly. "My apologies, Lady. But what if your sister forms a lasting attachment?"

"At sixteen? It is hardly likely."

"And so your worries are pointless?"

"Oh, you are abominable!" A half-laugh of exasperation and vexation escaped her. "Of course I worry too much about her," she conceded. "It has become a habit over the years."

She glanced to the doorway where Sophia stood with Gregory and saw the unmistakably flirtatious tilt to the girl's head. As she watched, Sophia gave a trilling laugh, and Eugenia saw trouble. Sophia's heart might not be engaged, but her manners were becoming those of an ardent flirt, which was not something that Eugenia cared to see.

"She will outgrow it, you know," the captain murmured. Eugenia spun back to face him, but he held a finger up gently to her lips. "I do not speak without experience, I assure you. My dear cousin started out in much the same way."

"Yes, and look at her now, engaged to a mere clerk."

His eyes narrowed. "You have met Mr. Jasper Selkirk. He has been in my employ for less than six months, but I can safely tell you that he will end up my second in command, unless I am very much mistaken. He may have come from humble origins, but he is a man to be reckoned with."

Eugenia flushed under this rebuke, for she knew, from her very brief acquaintance with Mr. Selkirk, that the captain spoke the truth. "I spoke in anger and did not mean it. I am sorry, Captain Harrington."

His eyebrows flew up in exaggerated surprise. "What? My Lady apologizing? Does it not hurt?"

"I have been betrayed into the necessity of it. As a general rule, my acquaintances are far too well bred to lead a conversation into such channels."

"Was that meant to excuse your lack of practice, or to give me a setdown?" he wondered. "At any rate, how very dull it must be for you. Does no one let you exercise your wit?"

She sighed, realizing his was a hopeless case. "If you find me so unworthy an opponent, I wonder that you bother with me."

"Oh, not unworthy, Lady. Merely inhibited. The wit is there, but I fear your strict upbringing has restrained it."

She looked up into his warm, smiling face. "Is that such a bad thing?" she challenged him.

"For a person of lesser humor or intelligence, no. But for

you, Lady . . . I should imagine your governess almost despaired of ever achieving a prim and boring result.''

"Which she did in the end?'' she demanded.

"Nay, Lady. But your strict upbringing appears to be engaged in a constant struggle against your lively spirit, and I hope the latter wins out. You must excuse me. I see my aunt trying to attract my attention.'' He bowed and walked away, leaving Eugenia seething in speechless indignation, unable to find words of suitable force with which to express her complete indifference to any opinion he could possibly hold.

That his views on the subject coincided with her own, she tried to ignore. How often of late had she felt that wild, adventurous spirit within her longing to be free? She had felt the first stirrings shortly before she met the captain, and she blamed his restless, barely leashed energy for bringing out this reprehensible side in herself. It was responsible for her breaking away, flouting convention, coming to America—and perhaps discovering her true self buried somewhere in that ridiculous, drilled-in knowledge that she was a Wolverton of Wolverton Priory. She was also, as she was beginning to discover, simply Eugenia. Exactly what that meant she had still to learn.

Several days later, Eugenia's thoughts remained in a whirl. She was troubled enough with worries about her brother, and now she had her sister's budding flirtatious nature to deal with as well. Her uncertainties about herself were best put aside for the moment.

Sophia, when taken to task about her behavior, merely laughed. "But, Genie, this is only America! Don't take on so!''

"It may not be London, but—''

"But that is exactly the point! Oh, Genie, did you never flirt, not in the least? It is such fun! Oh, I know it wouldn't do for . . . for Almack's! But what can it hurt here, in rustic Providence? And I am learning how to go on at parties, just as you wished. When we return to England, I shall have had my fun and shall engage to be just such a pattern card as you.''

As they were promised to ride out shortly with a party of

friends that included Gregory Sands as well as Cassandra, Eugenia was forced to abandon the argument. She continued it with herself, though, as she changed into her riding habit. So far her sister had not gone beyond the bounds of propriety, such as by slipping out alone into the garden with a man, and, against her will, Eugenia trusted the captain's summation of young Gregory's character. If either urged a clandestine meeting it would be Sophia, and she thankfully suspected that Gregory would be shocked at the suggestion, nipping it neatly in the bud.

Sophia, possibly aware of her sister's critical eye on her, behaved with unexceptionable propriety on the expedition, causing Cassandra to ask Eugenia whether her sister was suffering from fatigue.

"Guilt," Eugenia replied in the same half-whisper so that the others would not hear. "I fear I reproved her for flirting."

Cassandra let out a laugh that was disturbingly reminiscent of the captain's. "The poor girl! But I assure you, her manners do not go beyond what is pleasing. She is considered a lively, spirited little thing and has won general approval among the adults. Had you not realized?"

"I . . . I *hoped* it was so," Eugenia stammered, more relieved to hear this than she would have believed possible. "I could not be sure."

"You are merely critical because she is your sister, and you are so anxious for her. James was the same about me. You should have heard the thundering scolds he gave me! He has been more of a brother to me than a cousin, you must know."

"How . . . how interesting for you."

Cassandra's ready laugh rang out again. "You are quite absurd! I would rather depend on him than anyone! And he is the most delightful creature, for he is always ready for fun. You seem to laugh often enough in his company."

Eugenia flushed slightly, urging her horse forward. "Oh, he can be amusing," she said lightly. "Come, since I am not mounted on a slug today, I am dying for a canter."

Cassandra's words continued to bother her. Captain Harrington was entertaining, always laughing—though too

often his laughter was directed at her. By the tenets of her upbringing, he behaved in a reprehensible, shocking way that made her long to be as free as he.

And he was the sort of person that one naturally turned to when in need. It was because of his size, Eugenia told herself firmly. There was no good reason for her to trust him, yet she did, and she relied on his help in her search for Edward.

The extent of her reliance on him still bothered her when, several mornings later, she and Sophia descended the stairs to find Thomas sorting the newly arrived mail in the entry hall. He looked up as they neared the foot of the stairs and bowed slightly to them.

"Good morning, Thomas," Sophia called lightly.

"Good morning, miss. And Miss Eugenia, there is a letter for you."

Surprised, Eugenia accepted the folded and sealed sheet he held out on a silver salver. "Thank you." She turned the letter over, reading the mark of the military authority in Kentucky. She swallowed hard as a wave of nervous apprehension swept over her. "Go ahead, Sophia. I will join you in a few minutes. This . . . this is probably another dead-end trail for Edward."

"Don't be long," her sister threatened, "or I shall eat all the johnnycakes."

Gathering her courage, Eugenia crossed to the drawing room. Its sunny warmth was inviting, but she felt chilled. Still afraid, she sat down on the sofa and tore open the letter, spreading out and carefully smoothing the two sheets.

The opening words brought some measure of relief to her. There was no record that Edward had ever joined a contingent from Kentucky, even informally. There was no mention of him, or anyone answering his description, among the papers of the officers who had led the Kentucky units to Canada. She had not really expected that he would have joined, even to escape over the border from America, but there had always been the possibility. Feeling more relaxed, she continued to read.

The officer who had received the captain's letter had gone far beyond any required duty. Recognizing the urgency of

their search, the letter said, he had requested his men to make inquiries wherever they went. And one of them had turned up something. It might not be her brother, of course, but the similarity of the name made him feel that he should mention it. A Ned Wolfton was reported killed in an Indian raid.

Eugenia choked on a rising sob, unable to read the polite closing of the letter. Edward . . . Was he dead? Her shoulders shook with the force of her emotion as she tried to deny the words before her. *This cannot be Edward!* her mind screamed, over and over. But was it? Was he indeed dead and her search pointless, over? Cousin George would be so delighted . . .

It was not the thought of her detestable cousin inheriting the title and estates that solidified her resolve not to give up without more definite proof. It was her new-found courage, her determination to learn the truth. If this was Edward, she would give in with good grace and accept the inevitable. But if it were not . . . She would never rest until Edward was found.

But what was she to do now? Go to Kentucky, find people who had known Ned Wolfton, try to get positive proof that he was—or was not—Edward? The thought terrified her. The journey to Kentucky would make the ocean voyage, complete with storm, seem a trifling matter. There were red Indians, determined not to allow the invasion of their lands, who did not hesitate to kill anyone they could . . .

She lowered her head into her hands, her slender body trembling. Could she do it? Did she have the courage to face the many dangers, to face the possible truth at the end of so terrible a quest?

✻ Chapter 17 ✻

Shock numbed Eugenia and she sat there shivering, clenching the pages with icy fingers. *It cannot be true! It cannot!* kept running through her mind, over and over. But the names . . . Edward Wolverton, Ned Wolfton . . . And she had thought the adventure of Kentucky would appeal to him, that he might readily go there . . . but might not the dangers have turned him back . . . ? Would they turn *her* back? Could she brave them, to find the truth? She must not give up, not without being certain one way or the other . . . She was a Wolverton; she must not give in to her fear, not when her duty was clear. Not even for a moment could she admit to the terror that took root within her at the thought of barbarous red Indians.

The door opened silently, and Thomas coughed gently to announce his presence. She raised her head from her hands, turning her wide, troubled eyes to the man.

"Captain Harrington, Miss Eugenia." He stood back, allowing the great form of the captain to pass into the room.

The captain hesitated a moment in the doorway, his expression one of concern as his gaze rested on her. In four long, quick strides he reached her, dropping down on one knee as he took the chilled hands between his own large, warm ones.

"Lady, what has happened to distress you?" he demanded. "Not Sophia?" he added suddenly.

"No, it . . ." She broke off on a quavering sob, and his grip tightened in encouragement. "This!" she managed, removing one hand from his and picking up the pages that had fluttered to her lap.

He reached out one finger and wiped away a tear that threatened to slide down her cheek. Then he took the letter and walked to the window, where he read it.

Eugenia remained on the sofa, but her eyes followed him, hopeful in spite of herself. Somehow the captain's presence made everything easier. He would know what to do; he would help her. This she did not doubt.

He looked up, gazing in abstraction out the window, then swung about to face her. "You think this Ned Wolfton is your brother?"

"I don't know what to think!" she exclaimed. "His nickname is Ned! I . . . I must go to Kentucky and find out!"

"No, Lady, that you must not." He crossed over to the sofa and sat down beside her, once again taking her cold hands. "Think of all the danger, not to mention wasted time, if it proves not to be Edward. The name is not identical. There is a very good chance this is just a false trail."

She squeezed his hand, partly with gratitude, partly with relief. "What . . . what should I do?" she asked.

Gently he stroked a stray strand of her dark hair back into place. "Stop shivering, for one. This has been a nasty shock for you, and probably it will have been for nothing. Have you breakfasted?"

"I don't want to join the others yet!"

"No, not yet," he agreed. He rose, and Eugenia had to restrain herself from reaching out to stop him. It was only to ring the bell, though, and he returned to sit beside her. When Thomas entered, the captain requested that he bring suitable food and beverage, with a pot of rum for adding to the tea. Thomas, that excellent man, did not betray the least surprise and in only a few minutes reappeared with the tea tray, heavily laden.

"Take a deep breath," the captain directed her. "You are still shaking and will spill the tea." There was a gentle, teasing note in his voice that seemed to envelop her in warmth and comfort.

She did as he directed, then poured them each a cup of tea. He selected a silver pitcher from the tray, adding a dollop of a dark, golden liquid to each cup. She looked at it, eyebrows raised in questioning uncertainty.

"Rum," he explained. "Just a little. It will help ease your shock. Now drink." He watched while she did so, then spread butter lavishly on a roll, added a generous amount of marmalade, and passed this to her as well. By the time she finished it, he had a second ready for her, this time spread with a berry conserve.

"If I eat breakfast with you very often, I shall become shockingly fat!" she declared, then colored slightly at the possible connotations that could be placed on her words.

He merely smiled. "It won't hurt you. You have lost too much weight lately."

Her flush deepened. "That is not a proper sort of remark for a gentleman to make," she informed him, trying to hide her confusion.

"Ah, but then we were agreed long ago, were we not, that I am a most improper gentleman."

Her chin trembled, and she pressed her lips firmly together to keep them from doing the same. She longed to cast herself into the safe haven of his capable arms, to rest her head against his massive shoulders, to feel his strength comforting her.

Here was a man, in every sense of the word. Strong, brave, powerful, commanding yet gentle, tender, humorous. His concern and sympathy for her radiated from him as strongly as did his energy. She warmed towards him in a way that she never would have believed possible. He was deserving of her deepest admiration, and she now gave it to him without reservation.

If in America a man was really judged by his character rather than his lineage, then the captain was undoubtedly a very superior person. But she came from another world, she remembered with sudden regret, where birth dominated all.

In her world, any and all character flaws were overlooked so long as a man's family was of sufficient importance.

In her world, she was the daughter of an earl, and the captain, no matter how wealthy or influential he had become, was still a commoner—and an American, his breeding impossibly convoluted.

"Lady?" he asked softly. "There is no need for tears. I will discover more of this Ned Wolfton for you. And if all else fails and we can learn the truth only by going to Kentucky ourselves, I will go with you."

She tried to swallow a sob, but failed. In a moment she was just where she longed to be, her quivering form held firmly against the captain's massive chest as her tears fell unheeded, soaking his coat. One large, powerful hand gently stroked her hair, while his other arm encircled her firmly.

And she despised herself. Here was everything she had ever dreamed of in a man, yet still she sensed the social gulf that separated them. Her years of training were too much for her, and she disentangled herself from the one place she longed to remain. She was a Wolverton, whether she wanted to be or not, and she must behave accordingly. The captain was forbidden fruit, a temptation she must forever deny herself.

He released her the moment she started to withdraw. "I will write more letters this morning, if you wish, Lady," he told her, his tone still one of calm reassurance. "Ned Wolfton must have had friends, possibly family. Someone must have known something about him. And we have another lead."

She looked up at that, surprised. "Another . . . You have heard something?" Hope surged in her.

"It may be nothing. A captain I know remembers carrying a young Englishman to Virginia a couple of years ago. It was just as the war began, which is why it stuck in his mind. No, there is no need for you to go to Virginia." He smiled at her, causing her trembling to begin again, though for a different reason. "I have a ship going there, leaving tomorrow. I will take it myself and find out what I can."

"You . . . you are doing too much for me." She lowered her head, unable to meet his eyes.

"Would you be angry if I told you I enjoyed it, Lady? Finding your brother is a challenge, and life can become unbearably flat without a good problem to solve once in a while."

"How could I be angry? My search is what brought me to America in the first place, " she replied candidly.

The smile lines about his mouth deepened. "My kindred spirit," he murmured. "I shall take my leave of you, Lady. The letters to Kentucky will go off in the next post. I doubt I shall see you before my ship sails, but I shall report back as soon as I return."

She watched him depart, disturbed and discontented, knowing it would be some weeks before she could hope to get further word of Edward—and possibly before she saw the captain again, as well. The days loomed ahead, long and drear, filled only with anxiety.

Sophia peeked into the room, and Eugenia looked up from her contemplation of her hands.

"Well?" the girl queried. She came in, settling down beside her sister. "I saw Captain Harrington leave. Did he have any news for us?"

"Possibly. Virginia, this time." Eugenia sighed. "And there was no word of him in Kentucky. The best they could manage was a Ned Wolfton."

Sophia perked up. "But isn't that close enough to follow up?" she demanded, interested once again now that something semipositive might be in the offing.

"It's not likely. And it was a report of the man's death. But Captain Harrington is following up on it, just to be sure."

"Oh." Sophia sank back against the cushions. "I must say, Genie, this is much harder than I expected. You could never lose a person like this in England."

"We'll find him," Eugenia asserted with an optimism she was far from feeling at the moment.

Sophia threw her a shrewd glance, then stood up. "Come, Genie. Aunt Mary is just making the final arrangements for tomorrow's *al fresco* luncheon, and we need your opinion.

And she has decided to hold a small cotillion ball, too. Won't that be fun?''

Eugenia's answer was drowned by the exuberant arrival of Sukey and 'Sammy, who stormed in unceremoniously. They regarded their two cousins with disapprobation.

"You said you were coming to get her!" Sammy complained to Sophia. "But you're just sitting here!"

"Genie, come on!" Sukey grabbed her arm and started pulling. "Gramma won't decide how many more dishes to have prepared until you look over the list."

"Oh, well," Eugenia agreed, trying to smile for their benefit, "that is an important matter, is it not? But maybe you had better tell me what you think first. I have never been to an American *al fresco* luncheon before. I would hate to suggest too few sweets."

Sammy beamed his approval on her. "There should be more tarts!" he declared.

"And pastries. And *gallons* of lemonade," Sukey added. "And if Uncle James is coming, there must be a raspberry syllabub."

"Oh?" Eugenia asked, curious.

"It's his favorite," Sukey informed her knowledgeably. "At least the way Cook makes it. He said it was the only reason he came to our tea party last summer."

"I see. Well, I am afraid even a raspberry syllabub won't be enough to bring him to our party tomorrow. He is sailing to Virginia."

"Can't that wait?" Sammy demanded. "Maybe we should tell him that Cook will make a special one, just for him!"

"It won't be nearly as much fun without Uncle James," Sukey added, though she seemed to accept his inevitable absence.

"Well, come along. Let us tell your grandmother what we think is necessary." Eugenia hastily tried to divert them. "It is to be on the south lawn, is it not? Will we be able to play skittles?"

That was enough to set the twins off into another hot argument, for it seemed that Sammy had a tendency not to await his turn, but to bowl as soon as Sukey had reset the pins. Sophia stepped in at this juncture, taking a hand of

each of the two combatants and informing them roundly that if either uttered another word on the subject, it would be she who monopolized the bowling. This dire threat drew giggles from both, for although Sophia was becoming a proficient player, she always gave way to the twins' outrageous demands.

The luncheon the following day was declared by all to have been an outstanding success. Only Eugenia seemed to find it a trifle flat, but as she had a number of worries on her mind, it was easy for her to convince herself that it was these, and not Captain Harrington's absence, that cast down her spirits.

The same held true for the tea party held by the Sandses three days later. No one could fault her for her manners, but Cassandra, drawing her aside, made her realize that she must appear distant and withdrawn.

"You mustn't let it worry you so," Cassandra chided gently as she took a seat next to her. "James will do everything he can, you may be sure."

"I fear we impose dreadfully on your cousin." Her gaze met Cassandra's and dropped. The captain's humorous understanding seemed to be mirrored in the girl's clear green eyes, reminding Eugenia vividly of his absence.

Cassy shook her fair head as she laughed, and Eugenia detected the captain's merry, heartfelt tones lurking within his cousin. "Pray, don't be absurd! He is enjoying himself. I have not seen him so entertained in ages! I was quite surprised to hear he was off with one of his ships, until he told me the reason. He only goes, you must know, when he is bored, which he has not been since you arrived with this task for him."

"I am glad someone takes pleasure in it," Eugenia said with a certain measure of asperity.

"You are vexed, and I cannot blame you." Cassandra patted her hand. "The waiting must be unbearable for you. In a way, you are like James. You always want to be *doing* something."

The idea that she shared a trait with Captain Harrington both pleased and appalled her. The less they had in common, the better, she told herself forcefully. But she, too,

had sensed a kindred spirit with him, and the knowledge disturbed her deeply.

Sophia's laugh, unaffected and gay, drifted across the room to her. She looked up, only to be greeted by the sight of her sister seated among a group of children, demonstrating her skills at jackstraws to the admiring group. Sukey and Sammy sat beside their cousin, pointing out her superior technique with pride to their cronies.

Gregory Sands was the only other adult in the group. His tall, slender figure stood just behind Sophia's chair, leaning attentively over her shoulder. He said something that caused Sophia to giggle and throw a roguish glance up at him. The expression on young Mr. Sands's face, even at that distance, was eloquent.

He, at least, no longer bore the manner of a flirt. But Sophia? She still spoke of her impending debut to London Society, which led Eugenia to believe that her heart was not engaged. But Gregory was another matter. This was his world, this was where he belonged, and he was beginning to show every sign of wanting Sophia to share it with him.

Eugenia's worried eyes scanned the room, finding her hostess. Mrs. Sands, she noted, managed to circulate, keeping several groups talking contentedly, and still maintain a surreptitious watch on her son. A novel thought struck her. Did the Sandses disapprove of Gregory's infatuation? Sophia might be penniless in her own right, but Uncle Reginald had a considerable fortune, as did the Sandses themselves. And if Edward could be found, Sophia's dowry would not be inconsiderable.

In England, a marriage with a Wolverton would be considered advantageous in every way. The family was old and important, and only a fortune hunter—such as Lord Brockton—would scorn such an alliance. But what about in America? Here they were stripped of their rank and background. Here they were merely—themselves.

The captain's heated words on the ship, which had seemed so hateful at the time, now rang true once again. She was a lady no more, he had said. Merely Miss Wolverton. And the same was true for Sophia. Here they would be liked—or courted—for themselves, not their family back-

ground. It was a frightening notion. In England, no mother would look askance on Sophia, who was an eligible and desirable bride for the highest in the land. But in America such considerations held no importance whatsoever.

The sooner she and Sophia returned to their own world, the better. This refrain was beginning to underlie Eugenia's thoughts every waking moment. In many ways it was gratifying to be welcomed and liked for herself, but her confidence, she found, was shaky. In England she must always be accepted because of who she was. In America, her position was more tenuous.

To hide her uncertainty, Eugenia threw herself into the plans for the upcoming cotillion ball with an enthusiasm that caused Sophia to eye her with concern. The activity helped to take her mind off her worries, and somehow the time continued to pass. The captain would return soon—with news of this lead on Edward in Virginia, she added hastily to herself.

Two weeks had passed since his departure, and Eugenia found herself anxiously awaiting the dawn of each new day. He could return at any time now, she knew, and the prospect cheered her. This happy state of affairs lasted until the morning of the cotillion, when, as Thomas handed out the morning mail, Eugenia received a letter from the captain.

She tore it open with trembling fingers while Sophia leaned eagerly over her shoulder. Together they read the brief note. Eugenia set it down with a sigh, then looked up to find her uncle's eyes on her.

"He has been unable to trace the Englishman who went to Virginia. And he has been delayed over his return cargo, so he will spend the time asking questions, he says."

Aunt Mary reached across and patted her hand, her soft brown eyes filled with compassion. "That's only one lead, dear. There are other letters that have yet to be answered, you know."

"There is no proof it was even Edward," Sophia said with a sigh.

"Nor do we have proof he was Ned Wolfton!" Eugenia exclaimed, then bit her lip as she saw her aunt's gentle face, surrounded by the fluff of silvery curls, settle into a con-

cerned frown. "I am sorry, Aunt Mary. It is just so very . . . frustrating! I sit here doing nothing, just waiting, and week after week passes. I can just see my dear Cousin George counting off the days back home, willing us to fail!" She rose abruptly and hurried out of the room.

She was acting badly, she realized. Her raw nerves and impatience were no excuse for poor manners. Her aunt and uncle were being so very kind, so helpful. She must make an effort to be a better guest.

With this resolve, Genie entered into all of her aunt's plans with at least a semblance of enthusiasm. Sophia honestly enjoyed their shopping expeditions, the morning visits, and outings with the children. Eugenia tried to share her sentiments, but found most of their activities rather flat and insipid.

The twins proved to be her best entertainment. Always lively, their adventures led them into such predicaments as getting caught in a tree or trying to ride the milk cows. Listening to their excuses proved to be almost as diverting as reading a novel.

Ever since the captain's letter informing her of his delay, she found her interest in the various entertainments to have faded to almost nonexistence. For her aunt's sake, and Sophia's as well, she tried to smile brightly as they set off for a dinner party in Providence one night, just over a week later.

There was always the prospect of meeting someone new, she told herself, someone who might have known Edward. Keeping this thought in mind, she strolled about the large drawing room, her eyes scanning the mostly familiar faces. It was still early, but she held out little hope. This was mostly a political party, the guests of her uncle's generation, their discussions of trade and tariffs. The thought of Edward mingling with such people brought the first lightening of her spirits that she had felt in days.

Cassandra entered the room with her parents and also scanned the crowd. Immediately she moved to join Eugenia, her expression one of thankfulness.

"I am so glad you are here. Whenever the Browns have a dinner, you may be sure only the most boring or politically

important people will be invited. You have no idea how I dread them!''

"Uncle Reginald should enjoy that, but I fear I do not share his taste." Eugenia looked about again, noting that Sophia sat on a sofa, trying to appear politely interested in the lecture being delivered to her by an intent-looking young man of sallow complexion and receding hairline. "Nor does poor Sophia."

Cassandra, whose eyes had wandered to the doorway, was not listening. "James!" she exclaimed. "Genie, he is back! James!" She hurried over to the blond giant who stood on the threshold. "When did you return?"

"We docked barely over an hour ago," he replied, taking his cousin's outstretched hands and raising them to his lips. "As you see, I have made all haste to see you again, dear cousin."

She threw him a teasing glance. "I am sure you did. Come, relieve our boredom. Genie and I have just been bewailing the absence of any lively company." Cassandra dragged him along with her, to where Eugenia stood gazing at him, feeling that life once again had some meaning.

She started forward, her eager eyes taking in the familiar lines of his strong, sun-bronzed features. How she had missed his reassuring company and the dancing, teasing light that lit his whole face when they shared a joke. He was back, and he would have news . . .

He took her hand, raising her fingers to his lips. "I'm sorry, Lady." Her face must have fallen, for his hold tightened briefly, comfortingly. "I could find no trace of the Englishman. It might have been your brother, it might not. His trail simply disappeared. I have not given up, though. There are several people continuing the search there."

A long, ragged sigh escaped her. "Thank you, Captain. It is back to waiting again, then."

Mr. Quincy, seeing his nephew, hailed him, and the captain was drawn away into a circle to discuss the outcome of his voyage. She hadn't asked him about it, Eugenia realized. All she had cared about was his news . . . and the fact that he was back.

And that, she knew, was wrong of her. Captain Harrington

was not for her, no matter how strongly he tempted her. Nor did he seem to wish her to feel differently, and that knowledge pained her. He did not want a proud, aristocratic wife, if indeed he could be tied down by any lady. He had spoken of the sea as his love, his life. She had heard it was often that way with sailors. They might marry, but their brides were as good as widows, for the sea was a mistress with which no mere woman could compete.

"Lady Eugenia!" A deep, surprisingly familiar voice hailed her, and she turned, shaking off her reverie, to face the one person she never would have expected to see in America.

❊ Chapter 18 ❊

E ugenia stared at the tall, elegant gentleman with the carefully curled dark locks, bewildered, his presence seeming incongruous to her. "Lord Brockton?" she exclaimed in disbelief.

Charles, Lord Brockton, laughed, a light, amusing sound very unlike Captain Harrington's. He strode quickly across to her, taking both her hands, raising them to his lips with lingering finesse. "My dear Lady Eugenia," he murmured. "Only the thought of seeing you again sustained me during a most hideous voyage!"

The expression in his gleaming eyes caused her to draw in her breath. Gone was the devil-may-care flirt of her Aunt Lydia's party, bent on kisses but nothing more. A light mood remained, but the underlying seriousness was back— disconcertingly so.

"You are more beautiful than ever, sweet lady," he murmured.

She drew back, confused by the change in his attitude. Had he greeted her this way in London, when they met in Hyde Park, it would have been all that she could have hoped for. But he had been so casual there, bent on erasing the memory of his earlier, determined pursuit of her. Had her abrupt departure wrought this change, renewed his ardor?

"What . . . what brings you to America?" she managed to ask.

"Why, the need to broaden my horizons, what else? At least that makes an excellent-sounding excuse to seek you out, my dear. I cannot tell you how unbearably flat London Society became when you were no longer there to grace it."

She blinked, still trying to adjust to his presence. She tried to withdraw her hands from his, but he retained his hold, his thumb caressing her palm in an intimate gesture that only made her more uneasy.

"How . . . how long do you remain here?" she asked.

"I have no idea, my dear Eugenia. How long do *you* remain?" he countered.

She found herself at a loss, unsure of what to do or say. His behavior—his very presence—was so unexpected that she felt totally disoriented. She looked about, almost frantic, needing a diversion, anything, to gain time to think and compose her mind.

Sophia, she saw, sat bolt upright on the sofa, staring at them. Her prosing companion rattled on, oblivious of her abstraction. The girl's eyebrows flew up in a comical, quizzical gesture, and Eugenia gave the slightest shake of her head to indicate her own astonishment. Sophia giggled, then turned at least the semblance of her attention back to her boring acquaintance.

"May I introduce you around?" Eugenia suggested impulsively. "You cannot know many people. Did anyone accompany you?"

"David Saunders. You are not acquainted with him, but I can assure you I cultivated his friendship when I learned he knew your Uncle Reginald."

"Then perhaps you would care to meet others?" She looked about. Her gaze settled on Captain Harrington. His powerful back was turned to her, but she could hear his voice, serious for once, as he took part in a political discussion. She could use his company and his support right now, but this was denied her.

"I have met the only person who matters," Brockton told her softly. "I have no interest in a pack of provincials."

She stiffened. Those "provincials" he scorned so disdainfully

were her friends! "They are quite excellent people!" she informed him, her tone holding reproof.

"I am sure they are," he replied smoothly. "But having once found you, anyone else must naturally seem dull to me."

The sincerity of his words left her shaken. That he was bent on fixing his interest with her she could not doubt. The only question that remained in her mind—and heart—was how she should respond.

Such fervent compliments could not help touching her. A year before, to have his heart laid at her feet was the height of her ambition. And it was flattering in the extreme to have been sought out, all the way across the Atlantic, by a leader of the *ton* who could easily have his pick of the many eligible young ladies who remained, quite available, in London.

His appearance was as polished and sophisticated as ever. He might be at Almack's, so much care had he taken over his dress. *All this trouble, just for me!* The thought was overwhelming, and she allowed it to sweep over her, to soothe her worried nerves, to fill her heart. She was wanted by a dashing, desirable man who was at pains to let her know she was important to him.

"Ah, Lord Brockton, you have found a friend." Their hostess, Mrs. Brown, joined them. "Lady Eugenia, how glad I am to be able to bring you together with an old acquaintance. It is quite delightful, is it not, when you are so very far from home?" Clearly, the titles of her guests thrilled this little lady. While her husband's love was politics, hers appeared to be Society.

Eugenia nodded, bereft of speech by the glow of Brockton's gaze.

"It is, indeed, Mrs. Brown." He admirably filled the breach. "I cannot thank you enough for allowing me to come this night."

"We are only too pleased to have you, Lord Brockton. Now, I have set you two next to each other at dinner, so you will not feel so lost among strangers."

"An admirable plan," he informed Mrs. Brown, bestowing a practiced smile upon her. She moved on to the next group

of guests, and Brockton turned back to Eugenia. "Is that lovely young lady on the sofa there really Sophia? She is blossoming, is she not?" he asked, establishing himself more firmly in Genie's good graces.

She found her hands released at last, only to be offered his arm. She took it, resting her fingers on his elbow, feeling a grateful wave of familiarity wash over her. Brockton was of her world; he knew what behavior was expected of him. With him she could fall safely back on her rank and family, where she felt secure. As if in a dream, she allowed him to lead her to her sister. Only vaguely was she aware of Captain Harrington, who watched her through narrowed eyes.

With little effort, Brockton rid them of Sophia's talkative admirer. He bowed deeply before the girl, raising her fingers to his lips, his laughing eyes meeting hers over her hand. "Well, Lady Sophia? It seems that America has been kind to you."

"What a pleasure to see a face from home." She smiled, fortunately restraining herself from throwing a speaking look at her sister.

Dinner was announced, making further conversation impossible. Lord Brockton swept her in to the large dining room, found their places near the middle of the table, and seated her ceremoniously on his right. Throughout the meal he kept up a steady flow of polite dinner chatter, entertaining both Eugenia and Cassandra who sat on his left. For Eugenia, he had a ready supply of the latest gossip that circulated through the *ton*.

During a few moments when he turned his attention to the lady on his left, Eugenia stole a glance across the table to where Captain Harrington sat conversing easily with the ladies on either side of him. He appeared to pay no attention at all to Eugenia and her partner. Once, though, when Brockton made a slighting remark about the meager entertainments he had heard were available in Providence, Eugenia caught the captain's brow furrowing in dislike. To her surprise, she was as insulted as he, almost as if she were a native.

Whether Lord Brockton caught her unconscious stiffening

or not, his next comment was about the beauty of Narragansett Bay, and Eugenia found she was able to forgive him. For one so accustomed to the numerous advantages of London, any other city must seem a trifle flat. Here there was no White's, no Boodle's, no Daffy Club, no Cribb's Parlor, no Gentleman Jackson's rooms to visit. Providence was a very small town in comparison.

As the evening ended, Lord Brockton escorted her to her uncle's carriage, kissing her palm as he said good night. With her permisson, he vowed, he would call on her first thing in the morning. Any lingering vestiges of annoyance melted at his gallantry, and she found herself unable to resist his carefully cultivated spell.

The carriage door closed, the horses sprang forward, and Sophia let out a whoop of delight.

"Oh, Genie, Lord Brockton! What did he say to you? Why is he here?" she demanded.

"He says he has come to broaden his horizons," Eugenia replied with demure restraint, though her heart sang. She was flattered—well, how could she help but be? It was enough to sweep any girl off her feet, to be sought and courted in such a way.

"To Providence? No, Genie, that's doing it much too brown! Did he come to find you?"

"He seems quite the gentleman," Mr. Jessop put in, though there was a hint of reservation in his tone. "Have you known him long, Genie?"

"He almost offered for her last Season, before Robert died," Sophia explained, her excitement carrying her away. "What did he say?" she again demanded of her sister.

Eugenia blushed and was relieved when her aunt spoke up.

"He seemed most attentive to you, Genie. If you would like, we shall invite him to dinner soon."

Eugenia was not allowed a moment's peace, for Sophia demanded every detail of his conversation from her. By the time they arrived home, Eugenia longed to be alone to sort out her jumbled thoughts, and she hurried straight to her room. She was tired, though, and her serious thoughts soon gave way to a rather pleasant, hazy dream of returning to

London in triumph, wed to one of the Season's most notable catches.

This happy frame of mind lasted until she climbed between the sheets. Away from his overwhelming charm and her sister's clamorous questions, her brain began working again. Lord Brockton had made no mention of her own reason for being in America—her search for her missing brother. His only thoughts were of fixing his interest with her. Brockton's character was rather shallow, she realized in surprise. Suddenly he seemed a trifle too polished, his manners too punctilious. He lacked the casual but sincere warmth, unpolished though it might be at times, of a man like . . . Captain Harrington. Worldly considerations aside, could she be happy with a man whose primary interest in life was himself?

The subject of so many jumbled thoughts arrived on the Jessops' doorstep promptly at ten o'clock the next morning. Eugenia received Lord Brockton in the drawing room, where she sat with Sophia and Aunt Mary. All three ladies looked forward to this visit, for different reasons.

Lord Brockton, hesitating on the threshold, found himself the target of three pairs of eyes. Being a leader of the *ton*, he was not unaccustomed to being the center of attention and so sallied calmly into the room, raising his quizzing glass to better observe the ladies. He bowed first to Mrs. Jessop, making so pretty a leg as to win her instant approval. Then, after a bow to Sophia, who regarded him critically, he turned his attention to Eugenia.

His purpose that morning, it seemed, was to make himself agreeable, which he did to good account with Mary Jessop. His address could not but be admired, and when he set himself out to charm an aging lady, he did it with such finesse that she could not doubt his sincerity.

Eugenia, for the moment not the object of his practiced gallantry, did doubt it. Was all of London society so artificial, she wondered, or was it just Brockton? Or was she wronging him? Remembering her own insecurity and brittleness the first few days in this strange land, she must have seemed every bit as insincere. Her reservations melted in sympathy, and she responded with warm enthusiasm to his next sally.

"Lady Eugenia," he said as he turned to her. "I have quite an ambition to observe more of the countryside. And I have heard rumors of a riding expedition for the morrow. Might I dare hope . . . ?"

"Of course," Eugenia assured him on the instant. "But I fear we have no riding horses here."

"That will be no problem. I have already ascertained that the livery stable near the hotel were I am staying can provide me with a mount. But you—surely such a notable horsewoman as yourself is not forced to rely on such indifferent animals?"

"No, Miss Cassandra Quincy is kind enough to mount us."

He considered a moment. "Ah, yes. The tall female. It is most amiable of her, I am sure."

"It is, indeed." Eugenia hesitated, not quite liking his dismissive tone when he spoke of so delightful a friend as Cassy. "You . . . you have not told us your plans for your visit to America," she finally said, changing the subject.

"That is because they are not quite formed yet. I admit there was a purpose to my visit, but until I know the outcome of this, my plans must remain unsettled . . . as must I."

The look that accompanied this explanation caused Eugenia to draw in her breath, though she tried to hide this reaction. There could be no doubt. He had come in pursuit of her, and he meant to make her an offer of marriage. Firmly she squelched the roiling emotions within her. She had jumped to this conclusion once before, and it had caused her considerable embarrassment in her Aunt Lydia's conservatory. She would wait—*must* wait, in fact, for she found she was unsure of her own heart.

The drawing room door opened, and Eugenia looked up to see Captain Harrington's tall, muscular form. A surge of elation rose within her. She had seen him only for a precious few minutes the night before, and she had many questions she wished to ask him . . .

He nodded briefly to them. "Good morning, Mary. I'm sorry, I didn't realize you had a visitor." He acknowledged the other man, though Eugenia noted there was a slight curl

to his lip. "I won't disturb you. Is Reginald in his study? Then I shall go straight there. Lady, Sophie, I shall see you later, I am sure." He bowed to the assembled company with more than a hint of mockery and took himself off. Mary Jessop excused herself and hurried after him.

"What a curious man," Brockton declared, lowering the quizzing glass he had raised to better observe the captain. "I must say, his manners are not what I am accustomed to find in a lady's drawing room. Who is he?"

"You have seen him before, Lord Brockton," Eugenia informed him, irritated by his patent contempt for the captain's behavior. "At my Aunt Lydia's musical *soirée,* just before Sophia and I left England. He owned—and captained—the ship that brought us to America."

"Ah, a tradesman—that would explain it. I am surprised your aunt received him." Brockton dismissed him as of no account.

Eugenia stiffened. That these had been her own initial sentiments did not matter at the moment. The captain was in all ways a far better man than Brockton, but his birth would forever separate them. It disturbed her to realize she had come to prefer the free and easy terms on which she stood with the captain to insincere commonplaces and stiff formality.

Brockton quite properly took his leave at the end of half an hour. His good-byes were accompanied by florid compliments to his hostess, who returned in time to bid him farewell. She beamed on him, swept away by the charm he turned on to its fullest. He bowed deeply over her hand, then turned to Eugenia, raising her fingers to his lips.

"I shall see you on the morrow, my dear," he said, but retained her hand in his for a moment. "I shall count the minutes," he murmured for her alone.

Such words and actions could not but please her. To be the object of so ardent a pursuit by such a courted and sought-after gentleman was a compliment of no mean order, and her spirits soared.

They remained high until Sophia began teasing her. The girl saw no other possible outcome than her sister's shortly becoming Lady Brockton, but Eugenia refused to discuss it. She found she was not sure what her response to a proposal

would be, and that fact disturbed her. It was her predicament, she told herself. Until Edward was found—until she knew he was safe—and she could relax, she was in no fit state to make any momentous decisions about her future.

Lord Brockton, complete to a shade in an olive green riding coat that appeared to be molded to his muscular shoulders, was the first of the riding party to arrive the following morning. He greeted her with a murmured comment that he could not wait to be with her again. Eugenia was not proof against such flattery, and her irritatingly vacillating heart swung like a pendulum once again.

Gregory Sands was the next to arrive, leading his mother's own riding horse that she had generously offered for Sophia's use. He swung down from the saddle as soon as a groom took his reins and hurried over to join them.

The introduction was quickly made, and Brockton, raising his quizzing glass, observed the young man as if he had been an insect. Gregory, though, appeared to be totally unaware of this scrutiny, for he had eyes only for Sophia.

"Surely you do not allow that callow puppy to dangle after your sister?" he demanded of Eugenia in an aside.

"There is no harm in it," she replied with a cool unconcern she did not actually feel. "He is of excellent family, and he is a perfect gentleman. She will come to no harm with him." It irritated her further to realize she was using Captain Harrington's own defense of Gregory.

"Excellent family? By American standards, perhaps, but hardly by ours. Really, Eugenia, you could not possibly countenance an alliance between a Wolverton and some foreign nobody!"

She was grateful that at this point the remainder of the party arrived, for she had no desire to discuss the subject when her own views on the matter remained so confused. She was not pleased, however, when she saw that it was not Jasper Selkirk who accompanied Cassandra, but Captain Harrington, and considerably out of temper to judge from his expression.

She moved away from Brockton, hurrying forward to greet the new arrivals, swallowing her uneasiness. A morn-

ing spent in the company of Brockton and the captain, who clearly disliked each other, was not going to be easy.

"Jasper could not make it, so I brought James instead," Cassandra called to her. "I did not think you would mind."

"Of course not. In fact, there are still some questions I wish to ask you, Captain. You have not met Lord Brockton, I believe?"

The captain nodded to him briefly, but Cassandra leaned down from her horse, extending her hand to Brockton with smiling welcome.

"I am glad you are able to join us," she declared, and Eugenia almost smiled. It was comically obvious that Cassy's cousin did not share her sentiments.

They mounted quickly and set off down the gravel drive. At the road they turned away from Providence, heading into the countryside. This was an enjoyable ride; they passed through a beautiful countryside of rolling landscapes and small farms. The clear blue sky promised a pleasant warmth for the day.

Brockton, in contrast to the captain, appeared to be in his most affable mood. His mount, though not as spirited as he might like, he believed to have quite passable gaits, and the estates and fields he pronounced to be either handsome or delightfully quaint. Everything, in fact, pleased him.

Gregory and Sophia led the way, while Eugenia and Brockton followed them. The captain and Cassandra brought up the rear.

"A lovely day, Eugenia," Brockton declared. "Do you remember that morning of hunting we enjoyed last year in Somerset? It was over country much like this, was it not? Not really good hunting territory, of course, but I remember particularly the day—and the company."

Eugenia slowed her horse, sensing what was to come. Cassandra moved up near them.

"Do you hunt, Miss Quincy?" Brockton asked her. She shook her head, and he bestowed a pitying smile on her. "A most enjoyable pastime, I assure you. A true test of horsemanship in every way. To be able to guide a horse safely over rocky and uneven ground, to clear stone fences at a gallop . . . I remember once when I rode with the Quorn,

it was just after a frost, and the ground was so slick that half the riders had fallen by the third fence. Very few of us were left at the end, I fear.''

Cassandra, intrigued by his haughty manner and condescending air, encouraged him, and soon he was relating long tales of his hunting experiences. Eugenia prudently tried to drop back to ride beside the captain, for she had heard these stories before. Once started on the topic of hunting, Brockton could hold forth on his own abilities for hours.

"Captain," she called, reining in and waiting for him. "Please, tell me more of your voyage. I did not have the opportunity to ask you the other night."

His piercing green eyes softened at the earnestness of her tone. "Of course, Lady. What would you like to know? I have no desire to bore you," he added, his eyes sparkling with sudden amusement.

She bit her lip and averted her face for a moment. In truth, Brockton was boring on, though Cassandra appeared interested. But it was most unkind of the captain to comment on this, thus adding to her uncertainty.

"You are delayed. Did you have trouble?" she asked, just to be saying something.

"Eugenia!" Brockton broke in on his answer. "You must remind me. Did we have sleet or merely rain that day in Yorkshire when the major broke his leg?" He turned his smiling, almost caressing, eyes on her, his manner possessive.

He did not again let her drift far from his side. Somehow he managed to include her in the telling of every story, even of runs of which she had not been a part. His attentions were flattering, but she did not feel entirely at her ease. It must be the captain's glowering looks, she decided, that disturbed her so. How could anyone enjoy themselves with his ill temper so obvious?

The situation did not entirely displease her either. Captain Harrington had monopolized her attention since her arrival in America. He seemed to have come to regard it as his due. If nothing else, Brockton's blatant pursuit of her should discompose him, make him realize that she did not need him.

Within three days of this expedition, Brockton declared

himself. Paying her a morning visit, he led her out into the garden, where he lost little time in laying his heart, his estates, and his title at her feet. It was all couched in the most romantic and flowery phrases that might have been calculated to melt the heart of the iciest damsel.

And Eugenia was far from being cold-hearted. A glow of warmth at the tenderness of his pleas vied with triumph at this achievement and won out. Flattered, she realized what this moment meant for her. Her lack of dowry apparently did not weigh with him after all—it was she that he wanted, not her brother's precious money. She could bring out Sophia in style, the girl's place in society assured from the start. This was everything she had wanted—a year ago.

Then cold reality washed back over her. A year ago she had longed for him to offer for her. But now? Now that he actually had proposed? Fickle, unsteady creature that she was, she was no longer sure. Had she dreamed of Lord Brockton, the man, or merely of his position and the security it would bring her?

"If you wish," he continued, smiling tenderly down at her, "I will seek permission from your uncle. I would not want you to feel I had behaved shabbily, just because we are so far from home."

"No. That is . . ." she stammered, breaking off. What did she want? "I . . . I need time to think," she finished lamely.

"This cannot have been unexpected," he told her, and she felt the gentle pressure of his fingers against the backs of her hands. "My feelings cannot come as a surprise to you."

"They don't. That is, I could not be certain, of course."

"Then let us not waste time. I suppose we can be married in this outlandish place just as well as if we were in England. We cannot have St. George's, Hanover Square, but what will that matter, as long as I can have you as my wife?"

She pulled back slightly, confused. "This . . . this is rushing things. Please, do not press me for an answer just now. I have been so worried, I fear my mind does not function properly."

She thought his brow wrinkled in annoyance, but it

smoothed again so quickly that she might have been mistaken. "It is only my eagerness to be united with you. We should have been married long ago, except for your brother's untimely death. Every day that we wait seems an eternity to me."

She lowered her eyes as soft color suffused her cheeks. Who could remain unmoved by such words? "Please, do not press me," she whispered.

His grip tightened for a moment. "Forgive my impatience to call you my own. I shall leave you now, but I shall call on you again, and soon." He raised her hand to his lips, turning it over so that he pressed his ardent kiss into her palm. With a last lingering, longing look, he walked away from her.

Eugenia stood among the roses, watching his retreating figure until he disappeared from her sight. She remained there for fully fifteen minutes; then slowly she came back down to earth.

She must consider Brockton, and with care. She had longed for this proposal a year before, but had it been only for the prestige and worldly advantages he had to offer his wife? Again she asked herself had she ever wanted Brockton, the man, or had her head been turned by being so assiduously courted by so notable a leader of the *ton*?

And what about the months that followed her brother Robert's death? He could have sought her out then, and she would have been grateful for his support during that trying time. But he had vouchsafed not a single word, not even one of condolence. And when they finally met again in London, she was sure that he had merely trifled with her. She could not have been mistaken, for there had been no hint of sincerity in his attitude at her Aunt Lydia's party.

But then he had pursued her across the Atlantic. Had he realized the place she held in his heart? If this was the truth, she could forgive and understand his previous uncertainty, for she shared it now.

He spoke slightingly of her new friends, calling them provincials. She did not like that. On the other hand, to capture the *ton*'s biggest matrimonial prize would be quite

an accomplishment, especially after the betting had gone against her at White's.

Still she hesitated, unsure of her own heart, but sorely tempted by worldly and practical concerns—and the chance to confound the odious betters at the club.

✢ Chapter 19 ✢

Fortunately for Eugenia's confused state of mind, she did not see Lord Brockton on the following day. Instead, she received a note from him in which he begged her pardon for pressing her so ardently. He would visit Boston, the note informed her, and call upon her immediately on his return. Until then, he remained her faithful, loving servant.

She reread the note several times during the day, finding it no help in the decision she must make. In turn she found him first kind and considerate for absenting himself to allow her time to think, then insufferably cock sure that her ultimate decision would be in his favor so that he need pay her no more court.

By the following morning her head ached with an unbearable throbbing. She vouchsafed not a single word of what had passed between herself and Brockton to Sophia, who hovered sympathetically over her.

"You have been worried too much," Sophia informed her, perching on the edge of the bed while she watched her elder sister dress. "There is every chance this Ned Wolfton won't turn out to be Edward, you know."

"I know. But if Edward *is* dead . . ." She shook her head, disarranging the dark ringlets that hung about her shoulders.

"I am just tired, Sophie," Eugenia admitted. "Do you think Aunt Mary will mind if I do not accompany you to the river this morning?"

"She won't mind," Sophia asserted with confidence. She had found much compassion in that quarter for her own megrims, which had occurred less often of late. "It is Sukey and Sammy who will be upset."

Eugenia tried to smile. The twins would certainly prove diverting, but it was quiet she needed, time alone to consider her future, to weigh her few alternatives.

The two children did indeed put up a protest at her remaining behind, but Uncle Reginald called them to order, and Sophia quickly initiated a memory game that required their undivided attention. They waved to Eugenia as the carriage started forward, but the gesture was half-hearted, and she could tell they were already forced to use their full concentration for their feats of recall.

She stood in the drive, watching as they disappeared around the bend, then slowly turned back to the house. The prospect of returning indoors on such a fine, warm morning did not appeal to her. Instead she strolled around to the rose garden, but did not stop there. Walking soothed her restlessness, so she continued, aimless, crossing the lawn until she emerged from a gap in the bushes onto the road. She started up this to where an intersecting lane would lead her around the back side of the estate. If she followed this too far it would lead her to the Sandses, but a gate several hundred yards along it would take her into a thicket on her uncle's property.

She turned onto the lane just as the sound of beating hooves reached her, and she saw Captain Harrington approaching at a canter. He pulled up as he drew abreast of her, and she tried not to notice how the morning sun highlighted hints of reddish gold in his sun-bleached locks.

"A morning walk, Lady?" he asked as he dismounted. He studied her drawn face, and his eyes narrowed. "Has something happened?"

"No, I . . . it is just worry." She forced a smile, welcoming his concern although she knew she should not.

"Will this help?" he asked, drawing a letter from his pocket.

She took it, her eyes flying to his face, trying to read his inscrutable countenance. Quickly she tore open the single sheet, scanning the closely written lines with anxiety.

It was from Kentucky, written by the same officer who had sent the last letter. One of his men had located someone who knew Ned Wolfton's father. His people come from Maryland, the officer informed them, where they still had family living. He went on to say that he was glad this was not the man for whom they searched and that he was sorry he was unable to find anything more for them.

"It is quite enough," Eugenia sighed, handing the sheet back to Captain Harrington. Relief swept over her, the smile that quivered on her lips genuine. "If you knew how I dreaded the thought of going to Kentucky!"

"I could guess."

In her gratitude, she ignored the latent humor she detected in his voice. "I cannot thank you enough, Captain. Your help has been invaluable."

He seemed on the verge of saying something, his expression clouded as he studied her face. "I have not done much, Lady."

"I could not have found out this much without you."

He tilted her chin up with one finger. "Lady, you worry me. Compliments?"

"I can, on occasion, remember my manners," she replied more tartly.

"That's my Lady," he responded with alacrity, his eyes twinkling.

Her shoulders quivered slightly. "You are quite abominable, you know. Have I been boring you?"

"Never that, Lady. I just don't like to see you depressed."

"Meaning that is the only time we do not argue?"

He chuckled, the deep, rich sound that warmed her, wrapping about her like the soft folds of a shawl. "I am glad to see you are feeling better. May I escort you home? I fear I cannot remain. I must see to a ship that sails when the tide turns."

"Then it was kind of you to ride out with the letter. I

won't detain you. I had thought to walk down the lane, then back through the spinney.''

He took her hand, raising it to his lips in a brief kiss. In another moment he had swung back up into his saddle, turned his horse, and cantered back the way he had come.

Eugenia continued on her way, her heart lighter than it had been since she first heard Ned Wolfton's name. It was not Edward! For several happy minutes, this thought predominated. Her quest had not reached a tragic conclusion.

She stopped, her eyes staring unseeing before her. Her quest might not have reached a sad conclusion, but where did she take it from here? Every lead they had uncovered had proven a false trail. For all intents and purposes, Edward had completely disappeared.

She walked slowly, dispirited once again. Time marched on, but she seemed to get nowhere. Should she surrender, admit defeat to Cousin George? It seemed to be inevitable, whether she accepted it now or in a few months' time.

And what would she do then? George as Latham . . . Her mind's eye saw Sophia's dowry disappearing, not to mention her own. What would their futures be like in England? They would always be accepted socially, and George would be forced to support them, but a penniless female's chances of marriage were slim.

The solution was in her hands. Marriage to Lord Brockton would answer all their problems. Apparently her lack of money did not bother him after all. She would be able to bring Sophia out in style, independent of their hateful cousin. Her own marriage to such a noted Corinthian and leader of the *ton* could only add to Sophia's prestige.

So why did she not jump at so tempting an offer? Brockton was of her world, he could offer her every material advantage, it was what she had wanted . . . once. Anger with herself welled within her for hesitating—and for allowing Captain Harrington's handsome, masculine features to disturb her thoughts.

She was a fool to permit him to haunt her dreams, to intrude into her idle thoughts. A gulf as wide as the Atlantic separated them, yet the dancing golden lights in his sea-

green eyes could send her heart soaring, and his deep laugh vibrated through her until she almost resonated in response.

How could she marry Brockton when her very soul was in tune with another man?

Her private arguments started again. Because she would not—could not—fall in love with Captain Harrington. Because she belonged to a different world than his, one in which Brockton was an acknowledged leader. Because she owed it to her family—to Sophia—to make an eligible alliance that would further their standing with the polite world.

That she did not love Brockton could not be allowed to matter. Miss Minton's thorough lessons began to reemerge. A lady of quality did not marry to please herself. She did not wear her heart on her sleeve. She married to oblige her family. A lady of her station did not demean herself by succumbing to such a vulgar emotion as love.

By the time she returned to the house she was, if anything, in a worse state of mind. *Make no decision in haste*, she told herself. *Do nothing that cannot be undone until you are very sure you will never wish to change it*. All right, then, since she did not know what she really wanted, she would make no decision. She would remain in America and continue her search.

She was able to tell Captain Harrington when he arrived to dine with them that evening that she would not give up her hunt for Edward. To her surprise, an approving glow lit his laughing eyes as they rested on her.

"That's the spirit, Lady," he told her promptly. "We'll give that cousin of yours a run for his money. We've barely scratched the surface of this vast land, you know. We're bound to uncover your brother somewhere."

"But where?" She sighed, though her mouth twitched into a wry acknowledgment of his enthusiasm.

"I am still making inquiries among the captains and sailors I meet, and there are quite a few of them, let me tell you. The word has spread already."

Misty tears filled her eyes. "I . . . I am so very grateful to you, Captain," she said softly. "You give me hope when I need it most."

Disturbingly, that was the truth. She moved away, but continued to watch him surreptitiously as he settled himself in a chair to play with Sukey and Sammy, who promptly climbed up onto his large lap. In spite of his constant levity he was a kind man, one on whom she could depend, one to whom children turned naturally and trustingly.

A flood of warmth surged through her, unsettling in its force, disturbing her. She regarded him now as a friend, although she was not quite sure when she had begun to see him in this light. She wracked her memory, realizing that it had been some time since she had actively plotted any revenge on him for the hateful things he had said to her on board the *Cormorant*. In fact, she had more than once admitted the truth of his words, even, in a way, almost been thankful for his warning of how different she would find life here in America.

This fact did nothing to ease her troubled mind, and her spirits sagged. It was with difficulty that she kept up her share of the conversation during the meal. Several times she accidentally met Captain Harrington's questioning gaze, but quickly she looked away, addressing some inane, unremembered remark to anyone who was free.

"Is it an English custom, or merely your own, to retire to a corner and hide after dinner?" the captain asked her when the gentlemen rejoined the ladies after the meal.

"Oh, it is quite the rage in London, I assure you," Eugenia responded promptly, though without her usual buoyancy. Beyond him, she could hear her aunt exclaiming with the twins as they set up a game of jackstraws. Sophia played idly on the pianoforte, her uncle leaning over her shoulder to watch. A pleasant family evening, all in all, but she did not feel up to joining it.

"Lady, do you feel quite the thing?" he queried.

"Why do you ask?" His exaggerated concern made her instantly suspicious, and she eyed him with distrust.

"Normally you would have told me that such behavior is called 'minding one's own business.' It is not like you to miss such a golden opportunity to put me in my place."

She flushed slightly, trying to smile at this sally. "What a rag-mannered monster you make me sound."

"Oh, no, merely out of sorts. I can forgive you—this once—for not arguing with me."

That drew a reluctant smile from her. "Is that all you think of? Your entertainment?"

"Why, no. I also think of yours. And I fear I am failing miserably at it tonight."

"Then we are a pair, are we not?"

"We are, indeed. Can I say nothing to joke you out of this fit of the sullens?"

"I am not sulking!" she exclaimed, then caught the dancing, teasing lights that sprang to his remarkably speaking eyes. A choke of honest, though rather weak, laughter escaped her, and she glanced at him with rueful apology.

"That is much better, Lady," he encouraged her. "Would you like to abuse me soundly?"

"I should, indeed!" she informed him tartly. "You are quite odious!"

"What, not abominable and infuriating? I must be slipping!"

"That you are not—as well you know. Now, go play with Sukey and Sammy. They have been casting the most beseeching glances at you. You must be hardhearted to ignore them so."

"Ah, but your need of cheering seemed so much greater than theirs. They can always argue with each other." As he left and joined the delighted twins, she felt insensibly more at ease.

Drawing her out, teasing her into a better frame of mind, had been one of his acts of kindness. There certainly had been no malice in his attitude, no intention to hurt, only to please. It had been some time, she realized suddenly, since she had felt any antagonism on his part. Or had there ever been? Had it only been on her side, while she had ascribed a baser, crueler meaning to his purpose than really existed? Now, at any rate, she was sure only a friendly banter underlay his words.

She was able to join in a game of jackstraws with more enthusiasm than she would have believed possible only an hour before. Captain Harrington had that effect on her, to make her problems seem less desperate, to make her enjoy the moment. When he finally rose to depart she was sorry

and found herself eagerly looking forward to their next meeting.

Alone in her room as she prepared for bed, she kept thinking about him, looking back on every teasing word he'd said. A warm glow crept over her as she realized how truly kind he'd always been, how his sense of the ridiculous matched hers, how free and happy she felt whenever he was near . . . and the awful truth dawned on her. Her initial antagonism, her attraction, her reliance on him had all boiled down to one inevitable result. In spite of Miss Minton's careful teaching, she had developed a decided *tendre* for Captain James Harrington.

It came as both a shattering revelation and a severe blow to her. It explained why the earth seemed to stand still when his glowing eyes met hers, why it became difficult to breathe, why life became dreadfully flat when he was away. But it did nothing to help with the decision she must make, and soon. Troubled thoughts accompanied her as she climbed between the sheets and kept her awake long into the night.

The following morning brought the problem to the forefront. Lord Brockton, newly returned from Boston, presented himself upon her doorstep promptly at ten o'clock, begging her to indulge him with a drive about the countryside. Once underway, he lost little time in pressing his suit.

Eugenia hesitated, weighing her words with care. It was very flattering, but she didn't really want to marry him. Nor did she want to close the door on this possibility. In the long run, marriage to him might be the best solution for her, but she was not yet willing to accept this, not when her heart yearned for so much more.

"This is not an easy time for me, Lord Brockton," she finally said. "I realize that my not giving you an answer immediately must make me seem quite missish, but in truth, I do not seem to know my own mind. It must be my anxiety for finding my brother, for every day the time limit draws closer, and I worry more." She placed one hand on his elbow, and he quickly covered it with his.

"For the chance to win you, I would wait forever," he said, though the tightening of the tiny lines about his eyes showed that he was not pleased.

"I am sorry. Never before have I been so . . . so foolish!" she exclaimed. "Pray, have patience with me."

"Indeed, I am wrong to press you at such a trying time," he said smoothly. "But I long for the right to protect and help you."

Captain Harrington does both, and by no right whatsoever. She had to control her errant thoughts! How irritating of the captain to intrude into her mind in the midst of another man's proposal! He had no manners at all—and what was worse, he made every other man seem insignificant by comparison.

Captain Harrington continued to hover about the fringes of her consciousness, seriously distracting her. She caught herself contrasting every movement Brockton made with visualized memories of the captain. And when her escort handed her down from his carriage and gazed down into her eyes, she felt no eager response, no tingling sensation as she would if it had been her captain who stood before her.

They were to dine that evening at the Quincys', so she knew she would see him. This thought carried her through the long afternoon and into the evening, when she dressed with care in the celestial blue crepe gown. She should not look forward to the meeting with so much eagerness, she knew, yet still she found it hard to quell the excitement that surged through her.

She saw him as soon as she entered the Quincys' large, elegant drawing room. He leaned negligently against the mantelpiece, listening with a humorous expression to something Cassandra said to him. He looked up, and her worries seemed to melt away as she met his warm, admiring gaze.

He brought his conversation with his cousin to a close, then crossed the room to join her. His searching eyes scanned her countenance, but then he relaxed, smiling at her in his usual teasing manner.

"Well, Lady?" His voice was soft, and there was more to the simple question than was expressed by the words.

"Not so well, Captain," she admitted. He always seemed to know, somehow, by some mysterious means. At times he understood her as clearly as if her face were a page on which her thoughts and emotions were clearly inscribed.

Before she had found this habit disconcerting. Now . . . it was more so, for her unsteady sensations as far as he was concerned were something she had best keep from him.

"Is there ought I can do?" There was no mistaking the sincerity of his words, his honest desire to be of service to her.

Would that he could! But there was no simple solution to her problem. She searched his eyes, his expression, trying to gain a clue as to his true feelings for her. Friendship, concern, sympathy . . . all were present. But was there anything more? Some sign of deeper affection, some sign that the *tendre* was not on her side alone . . .

She could not tell. And worst of all, she was sure that she should not want there to be.

That was not the only incident to occur that evening to disturb her. Sophia, she noted, was at her liveliest, flirting with a handsome young soldier. Her delicate, fragile appearance, coupled with her fluttery manner, lent her a fairylike quality that was not lost on the bright-eyed lieutenant.

Nor was it lost on Gregory Sands, who stood some distance away, ostensibly part of a serious discussion. His gaze never once turned fully on the laughing couple, but Eugenia, watching his grim expression, was quite certain that they were never out of his sight.

Sophia fluttered her eyelashes, peeking up at her new "conquest" in the most outrageous manner. Eugenia wished she could hear what he said to her, but the covetous expression on his face spoke volumes, as did the sudden rush of color to the girl's cheeks. Eugenia drew a deep breath and started to excuse herself from the discussion in which she took a half-hearted part.

At that moment, however, Sophia seemed to regain some semblance of propriety. She stood in confusion, though a word from her companion drew an uncertain giggle from her. She moved off, throwing a look over her shoulder at her dashing blade that was roguish in the extreme. The girl drifted among the other guests for a few minutes, speaking casually to several, somehow winding up near Gregory's stiff figure.

Eugenia's face revealed her concern. She knew that

mischievous expression in her sister's glittering, excited eyes. Sophia was up to something, and Eugenia could only be glad that she had abandoned that rather dangerous-looking soldier to try her tricks instead on the relatively dependable Gregory. She would come to no harm with him.

For once, possibly the first time, Gregory did not appear pleased with his adored Sophia. She detached him from his group, whispering to him in a cajoling manner. His reply must have been sharp, because Sophia's head flew up, her chin tilting in a stubborn, angry manner. *That, more than any words of mine, should give her a hint!* Eugenia thought with satisfaction. Sophia left him abruptly. Her lieutenant was engaged with another young lady, and in only a few minutes she settled herself down next to her sister.

"I have the headache, Genie," she announced, her angry pout and sparkling eyes belying this excuse.

"Have you, my dear?" Eugenia's tone was sympathetic, for it was essential to soothe the girl before her headache became a fact.

"I want to go home." Tears hovered on her lashes, a dangerous sign.

"We will dine in a moment," Eugenia said. "You will feel better when you have had something to eat. If your head still aches after, I am sure we can leave then. I would hate to spoil my aunt and uncle's evening."

Sophia glanced to where their Uncle Reginald was holding forth before a group of his cronies. He was a sociable gentleman, full of warmth and good humor, always enjoying a convivial evening among friends.

The butler entered at that point, announcing the meal, and Eugenia watched with relief as Sophia allowed her partner to lead her in to the dining room. Genie soon had the satisfaction of seeing her sister relax under the attentive compliments of the gentleman seated on her left, who succeeded quite well in coaxing her into a more cheerful frame of mind.

When the ladies retired to the drawing room, Sophia made no mention of desiring to leave. Eugenia was relieved to have this problem solved. She turned her attention to

Cassandra and, until the gentlemen joined them, they discussed plans for a visit to the theatre.

"I doubt it will compare favorably to plays you have seen in London." Captain Harrington leaned over his cousin's chair, his teasing gaze resting on Eugenia.

"Oh, I am not above being pleased," she told him. "The whole evening sounds quite delightful, in fact. Or are you to join us?" she added sweetly.

His shoulders shook with the effort to restrain his deep laughter. "I believe I shall, Lady. How could I possibly miss your first real taste of Providence culture?"

"Oh, do be quiet, James," Cassandra broke in, her own eyes twinkling. "If anyone heard you two, they would not understand! As if Genie looks down on us! Now don't be so absurd."

"Absurd? Me?"

"I am ignoring you," James's cousin informed him. "It is the only thing to do at times, Genie. If you pretend he is not here and refuse to rise to his shocking comments, he will go away."

"Will he?" Eugenia asked, pretending wistfulness.

"I might not be the only person who is going away," he murmured, a sudden, serious note in his voice.

Eugenia looked up, startled, and her eyes followed the direction of his. Sophia, with a far too casual glance about the room, slipped out through the long French windows into the garden. Eugenia waited, her hands clenched on the arms of her chair. A few minutes later, with equal casualness, the lieutenant followed.

"Where is her watchdog?" the captain asked.

"Angry with her, I am afraid." Eugenia sighed before she remembered that it was most improper to discuss her sister's reprehensible behavior with him.

"Shall we take a stroll outside?" Cassandra asked, her eyes alight with amusement. "I fear that lieutenant has a certain . . . reputation."

Eugenia rose quickly. "By all means."

Sophia suddenly reappeared in the doorway, glanced quickly about, and met Eugenia's anxious, frowning eyes. She returned a look of bland innocence, then stepped into the

room. Eugenia sank back into her chair, relieved, and watched as her sister settled herself on the sofa near Gregory Sands. Within a few minutes she had drawn him into a reluctant conversation, which appeared to warm quickly.

"One less worry, Lady?"

Genie looked up to meet the challenging smile in the captain's eyes.

"There is no need to feel concern for Sophia," she retorted. "Although she may be young and inexperienced, she has had a proper upbringing and will remain within proper bounds...unlike some people."

His eyes gleamed with appreciation. "As you say, Lady. But now I see my aunt bearing down on me, and unless I make haste I shall be forced into a card game with the elderly ladies."

That was indeed to be his fate and Eugenia, who was beginning to understand and appreciate his character a bit better, was not surprised when he made no move to avoid it. Instead, he helped maintain a steady flow of entertaining conversation, bestowing his most charming smile on his fellow players and in general making himself agreeable to them.

"He never seems to be bored," Cassandra observed. "I do not know how he manages to be so patient, or what he finds to talk to them about!"

"He undoubtedly does it for his own amusement." Even as she said it, Eugenia knew this was untrue. He would find enjoyment in this pastime, just as he found it everywhere, but his primary object would be to ensure his companions' pleasure.

Acknowledging the captain's many admirable qualities was not what she wished to do at the moment. She was far too ready to admire him, to allow her gaze to rest on his mobile, striking, bronzed countenance, to see his broad, muscular shoulders, the unruly waves of his fair hair, the sea-green eyes that sparkled with a merriment he was always ready to share...But she must not—could not—think of him, for even if she were able to overcome her own rigid upbringing and ignore what she knew to be her duty to her family, he gave no sign that this was what he wished.

❊ Chapter 20 ❊

When Brockton came to call the following morning, Eugenia greeted him with more warmth than had been her wont, a reaction to her uncertain feelings for the captain. Lord Brockton seemed pleased, but prudently did not press the issue. Instead, he entertained Eugenia, Sophia, and Mrs. Jessop with a steady stream of gossip picked up in Boston, then properly rose after a half-hour to take his leave. As he raised Eugenia's fingers to his lips, though, he permitted a possessive smile to light his eyes as they held hers.

This was not lost on Sophia, and Eugenia, seeing the speculation rife in her sister's expression, prudently retired to her bedchamber.

Sophia was made of sterner stuff than that. A few moments after the door shut behind Eugenia, it was thrown open again to admit her sister, who flopped down on Eugenia's bed in a most unladylike manner.

"Well?" she demanded.

"Well, what?" Eugenia said, though she knew it would not fob Sophia off.

"Genie, what did Brockton mean, looking at you like *that*?"

Eugenia hesitated. His proposal was a triumph, even if

she did not know how to respond to it, and her sister was the only other person who could appreciate it to the fullest, the only other person who shared her world. "He has asked me to marry him," she finally said, curious to see her sister's reaction.

Sophia squealed, "Genie! Oh, Genie! *That* will show everyone in London! You have accepted, of course?"

"No. That is, I have asked him to give me time."

"Time? How can you hesitate? Just think of the position you will have as the wife of *such* a noted Corinthian. Why, you will be the envy of all! And think of the Season I shall enjoy next year! Sister-in-law to one of Society's leaders! I shall probably catch a marquess, at the very least!"

Eugenia watched the girl's raptures through narrowed eyes. Her manner seemed unnaturally stilted, a bit forced. The words were right, but the enthusiasm was not quite real. Did Sophia also have her doubts about this scheme? Had she, perhaps, begun to like America—and Gregory Sands—just a little too much?

She did not feel up to facing that potential problem just at the moment. Between Edward, Sophia, Lord Brockton, and Captain Harrington, everything seemed a bit too much for her. She spent the afternoon pacing about the rose garden, oblivious to the twins as they argued loudly over their game of skittles.

She sat, staring with unseeing eyes down the drive, when the sound of hoofbeats penetrated through the shrouded layers of contradictions and worries that surrounded her mind. She looked up to see the cause of much of her inner torment dismounting before the house. She rose quickly, hurrying forward to greet Captain Harrington.

"Have you heard anything?" she called as soon as she came within hailing distance.

He turned and saw her, catching up her extended hands as she reached him. "Nothing, Lady. I have come to see your uncle." When he saw the expression on her face, the pressure of her fingers increased briefly before he let them go. He raised her chin, his compassionate eyes gazing down at her with concern. "What is troubling you?" he asked softly.

She shook her head, biting her lip to prevent the anguished tears from spilling down her cheeks. "I ... I had just hoped ..." She broke off, unable to continue.

"Come." He took her elbow and led her around the corner of the house, into the drawing room through the side door that gave onto the garden. Here he compelled her to sit on the sofa while he poured her a glass of Madeira from a decanter on the sideboard. "There is more troubling you than your brother," he commented as she sipped the wine.

Startled, she looked into his eyes and then down at her lap. "Finding him would solve so much," was all she said. She took a deep breath and set down her glass. "Captain, my time is running out. Is there nothing, no clue ... I *cannot* just sit here doing nothing!"

"So far every clue to his activities has led to a dead end," he admitted with reluctance. "All we can do is wait for answers to our inquiries, or hope to hear news from incoming ships."

"If you were me, what would you do?" she demanded. The gaze she turned on him clearly revealed her turbulent state of mind.

"There is not much you can do but wait. There are notices in every major American paper, and I have men making inquiries in as many places as possible. In truth, Lady, I fear we are already doing all that can be done."

"Has my coming to America been for nothing?" Even to herself, her voice sounded pitiful, hopeless, which disgusted her.

"No, Lady. That it has not. If you had not come, you would always blame yourself and feel that you should have done more. Now, if Edward cannot be found, you will at least know that you attempted to discover his whereabouts."

"Oh, must you always be so ... so reasonable?" she demanded.

A slight smile lightened his countenance. "Whenever possible, Lady. Would it help you if I weren't?"

"There you go again! And the worst thing," she added with sincere indignation, "is that I can get absolutely furious, and you just sit there smiling and unaffected!"

"Only if you feel better for letting off your anger."

Her lips twisted wryly. "I do—as well you know."

"That's my Lady."

She looked quickly away from the teasing light in his eyes. It would be too easy just to sit there, to be with him, to feel the security and comfort of his presence. "You said you had business with my uncle. I must not detain you," she declared with a brightness she was far from feeling.

He nodded. "Don't let yourself get discouraged, Lady. There are still several months to go. We'll find him."

She tried to believe in his words, but once away from his energetic, positive presence, her doubts and fears again took over, and her hopes of finding Edward dimmed. It was time she faced reality, she told herself, time to stop dreaming and seriously consider a future with her cousin George as the earl of Latham.

The prospect depressed her. She had refused to think about it for so long . . . but it could be avoided no longer. She had to make decisions, both for herself and Sophia, and they could not be based on half-truths and avoided issues. These thoughts occupied her throughout dinner, for which the captain remained, and they kept her unusually silent.

Only Sophia appeared not to notice her sister's abstraction. She was dressed in one of her prettiest gowns of peach crepe, and her eyes sparkled with a suppressed excitement that drew compliments from both the captain and Uncle Reginald. She giggled at these, obviously pleased, but did not respond with flirtatious comments of her own as she normally would. Eugenia, finally noting this restraint, felt some concern, but was able to convince herself that it was due to Sophia's having learned a lesson with that dashing lieutenant the night before.

Immediately following the meal, Uncle Reginald rose, signaling Captain Harrington to join him. With one long, piercing glance at Eugenia, that gentleman accompanied his host back to his study, where the two settled down to resume their discussions. Eugenia retired to her room almost immediately, too preoccupied to worry about Sophia's odd manner, and sat by her open window gazing out into the warm, late summer night.

The odds were very good that she would dwindle into an

old maid if she returned to England without marrying Brockton. Such an eligible offer seldom came the way of a dowerless female. Sophia's prospects might be better than hers, as her fragile air and fairylike grace commanded instant admiration from all who beheld her. Her chances would be considerably improved, though, as the sister-in-law of Brockton.

But Brockton, Eugenia admitted to herself as she gazed out across the moonlit lawn leading to the spinney, was not her ideal choice for a husband. At the moment, his offer could only be considered as an emergency solution to her dilemma.

And if they remained in America?

Captain Harrington's tall, vibrant figure intruded into her thoughts, and she was unable to drive it away. His image might be her constant companion, but the man himself was a very different matter. For all his friendliness, he was disturbingly elusive. He sought her out, enjoyed her company, but never had he given any sign that he wished to make a permanent attachment. At heart, she feared, he had the seaman's free spirit. He could never long be tied to one port . . . or one woman. He would laugh and argue with her, never serious, and when another young lady came along who amused him more . . . She considered for a moment. If that happened, then little would change. He considered her no more than a friend, and he was a man who had many of these.

Below her, a dark shadow slipped away from the wall, floating across the moonlit expanse of grass. Eugenia stiffened, peering down, as she recognized Sophia's slight form. She still wore the peach-colored crepe, though now she had a light shawl thrown about her shoulders.

The reason for her recent giggling excitement became clear in a moment. Another shadow detached itself from the bushes on the far side of the garden, hurrying to meet the first. Eugenia noted with growing fury that her sister was a willing participant in a shocking rendezvous.

She had been so sure she could trust Gregory Sands to behave with propriety! That was what truly shocked her, for her sister's reprehensible behavior she was more readily able

to believe. But how could they? Clandestine moonlit meetings might be packed wih all the trappings of romance, but they were not at all the things, and so she would tell the miscreants in a very short time.

She caught up a shawl and hurried out of her room and down the back stairs. No one was about, she noted with relief. So far, Sophia's escapade could be kept secret. Eugenia let herself out the side door into the garden, then paused, looking about.

The young couple were nowhere to be seen. But they would hardly remain in full view of the house, in full sight of anyone who chose to look out a window as she had. With a purposeful stride, she headed for the rose garden, with its surrounding, concealing shrubbery.

No one was there. Perplexed, Eugenia stood for a moment, thinking. Where would they . . . ? Then it struck her. There was an open conservatory, now in disrepair, attached to the other side of the house. Growing anger welled within Eugenia. How could they be so lost to all sense of propriety?

She came within sight of the conservatory in less than three minutes, but that was time enough for her to think up several furious, cutting remarks to make to the couple. As she came closer, she could dimly make out a shadow silhouetted against the arched opening.

Shock stopped her. The couple appeared to be in an embrace, swaying together . . . No, they struggled! Galvanized into action, she raced up the shallow steps, throwing herself against the pair. Sophia bit off a scream, pulling back and away from the man who had held her captive.

"Of all the shocking, stupid . . ." Eugenia broke off, staring in horror at the evil smile of the man before her. This was not Gregory Sands, who would be properly abashed by a few well-chosen words. It was the nameless lieutenant, and his purpose, judging from his expression, was far from innocent.

"How dare you!" Eugenia exclaimed. "You will leave at once!"

His smile grew, and it was not pleasant. "Now, you don't want to interfere with the young lady's fun, do you?" he asked. "You certainly can't say she was being forced."

"I was! Oh, Genie, it was horrible! He . . . he kissed me! And he wouldn't stop, even when I begged!"

"Then what was your purpose inviting me here?" he demanded. "You knew perfectly well what I wanted. And you," he turned to Eugenia, "are in the way."

"Genie!" Sophia gripped her arm, shivering.

"Trouble, ladies?" Captain Harrington's deep voice sounded from the darkness behind them, and Eugenia spun around, wondering how he knew their location yet quite relieved in spite of herself to have his aid.

"Ah, Lieutenant. Were you just leaving?" he asked, his affability unruffled.

The man hesitated. Clearly he wanted to land this intruder a facer, but did not dare. Eugenia, glancing from one man to the other, doubted that many men would dare face the blond giant with the firm, square jaw and determined stance.

The lieutenant was not one of them. He shrugged, attempted a casual laugh, and moved past them towards the door. Captain Harrington reached out suddenly, catching his arm as he passed.

"It wouldn't be very wise to mention this little incident to anyone," he said, his surface calm not concealing the steel beneath his words. "If it became necessary to defend the lady's honor, I would not come after you with pistols, but a horsewhip."

The lieutenant raised his eyes to the captain's grim face, then looked away quickly. He pulled free and almost ran down the steps.

Eugenia let out her breath in a long sigh of relief. "Thank you, Captain."

"For what?" he asked, smiling. "Rather I should thank you two for coming out to say good night to me. But I believe I shall see you safely back within doors before I leave."

Eugenia raised wondering eyes to his disturbingly attractive countenance. Here was a gentleman in the truest sense of the word. He had just told her in his own way that as far as he was concerned, the incident had never taken place.

Sophia hunched an angry shoulder. "Oh, do let us get

back inside. It is getting chilly here.'' She pushed by them, and Eugenia and the captain followed.

He accompanied them to the side door, waiting for them to enter. Eugenia paused, looking up into his face, trying to find words with which to thank him. The situation might not have gotten any worse... but then she did not trust that lieutenant—his expression was not that of a man willing to give way easily. She shuddered suddenly, wondering what might have happened had the captain not appeared so providentially.

''You are getting cold, Lady. You had best go in.'' He raised her fingers to his lips, kissing them gently. She turned her hand, gripping his, and looked at him with every ounce of gratitude she could muster.

''Go inside,'' he repeated and stood watching until the door closed behind her.

Sophia was no longer in the lower hall, a fact that did not surprise Eugenia in the least. The girl would not get off so easily, though, of that she was determined. What had started as a mere flirtatious prank had taken on a serious, possibly terrible, aspect. Sophia must be brought to realize the truth.

She found the girl in her room, already unfastening her gown. Eugenia stepped forward, helping with the last hooks.

''Are you all right?'' she asked.

Sophia turned, almost falling into her arms. ''Oh, Genie, it was horrible! He... he *mauled* me!''

Biting back a retort that it was only what such behavior asked for, Genie instead soothed the distressed girl. It would seem she had learned her lesson, all right. But one thing bothered her. ''Why did you go out to meet him, Sophie? You only just met him last night!''

Sophia pulled away from her, turning her back. ''I only wanted to have some fun, and this seemed like the most splendid idea. But then Gregory was so stuffy, saying it was not at all the thing, and refused to meet me. And the lieutenant seemed so... so dashing and gallant, I thought he would do as well.''

She only wanted to have some fun, Eugenia repeated to herself. So she chose a shameless libertine who it seemed

would not scruple to take advantage of a romantic little idiot. If it had not been for Captain Harrington's interference...

"Sophie, if the captain had not ordered him to keep quiet about this, the whole story would be circulating about the armed forces in the morning. Do you realize how easily you could have been ruined?" she asked as gently as she was able.

Sophia stared at her. "You make too much of it, Genie. No one would ever know!"

Eugenia raised a skeptical eyebrow, and Sophia's mouth firmed in a stubborn line. Slowly, under her steady gaze, the girl's eyes fell, and her chin began to tremble.

"He... he is not a gentleman!" Sophia cried.

"You mustn't do anything like that again, Sophie. Ever. Especially with a man you hardly know. Gregory Sands *is* a gentleman. If he does not approve of something, you may be sure it is not because he is 'stuffy.' I don't believe he would do anything to hurt you—which I cannot say for that lieutenant."

Sophia sniffed, but did not reply. When Eugenia gave her sister a quick hug, though, it was returned with an intentness that did much to relieve her mind.

"Do... do you think the captain is a gentleman?" Sophia asked as Eugenia started out the door.

"Yes." She turned back, the strength of her own conviction startling her. "He will say nothing, you may be sure. And he will make certain that the lieutenant keeps quiet as well."

Eugenia returned to her own room, but did not get ready for bed. Instead she sat once more in the window, staring out with unseeing eyes. *She only wanted to have some fun.* The thought kept repeating itself in her tired brain. What would she try next? She would not mean any harm; she merely was too innocent of the world to realize what might happen—or just how reprehensible her actions might appear to someone who did not know her that well.

A Season in London would do the trick, Eugenia realized. She needed to be presented to eligible young men so that she could select a husband before she set the town on its ears with her flirtatious airs and hoydenish pranks.

She closed her eyes. Edward, disappearing without a trace. Sophia, on the verge of ruining herself. Captain Harrington, attractive, virile, but elusive, disturbing her sleep, unsetting the equilibrium of her mind. The sooner she and Sophia departed for England, the better it would be for both of them. It was time they abandoned this hopeless quest and got on with their lives.

And there was Lord Brockton, who offered her the protection of his name, the security of being his wife. She would be a fool not to take it. She had better tell him that she would marry him before she could change her mind.

Having reached this decision, she prepared for bed. Sleep was long in coming, and she awoke in the morning feeling unrefreshed. She had come to one more conclusion, though. It would be best for her to accept Brockton, pack her belongings and set sail for England as soon as possible— before she had time to regret her choice. For Sophia's sake, she must go through with this.

All of the family were present at the breakfast table. Eugenia found herself looking at each one of them in turn, thinking how very fond of them she had become, how very much she would miss them. Leaving was no easy thing, for she did not know whether she would ever see any of them again. The thought robbed her of her appetite.

"Uncle Reginald," she began as the meal drew to a close, "may I speak to you in your study?"

He nodded. "Of course, my dear."

Together they walked down the hall, only to pause as a commanding rap sounded on the front door. Thomas, who must have heard the approach, appeared almost immediately, swinging the door wide.

"Good morning, Thomas." Eugenia heard Captain Harrington's voice. Thomas stood aside, revealing not only the captain but also another man, dressed in similar clothing. "Is Miss Eugenia—" he began, then broke off as he saw her standing in the hall.

"Yes, Captain?" she called.

"Lady," he said with a smile as he stepped forward, his companion following is his wake. A mischievous, dancing

light sparkled in those mesmerizing eyes, and the captain's whole face seemed aglow with a barely repressed enthusiasm.

Eugenia's heart leapt within her, her decisions of the night before forgotten. Nothing mattered except this vibrant, energetic, masculine man before her, who took her hands, raising them both to his lips.

He squeezed her fingers with an almost painful force as his joy enveloped them both. "Lady," he repeated, warm laughter underlying his words, "your brother has been found."

❖ Chapter 21 ❖

The blood drained from Eugenia's face, and she gripped Captain Harrington's hand for support. A shivering started deep within her, and she shook her head slowly, not able to believe those words she had longed to hear.

"Edward . . ." she whispered. "You've found Edward?" Her voice rose half in disbelief, half in rising hysteria.

The captain slipped one arm about her, holding her up as he guided her into the study. There he settled her on the sofa. "Yes, Lady." He disentangled his hand from hers and turned to his companion. "This is a friend of mine, Michael Boyd, a sea captain. And this, my friend, is Lady Eugenia Wolverton, the sister of the new earl of Latham."

Captain Boyd bowed to her. "A pleasure, Lady Eugenia. I am the bearer of a letter to you from your brother." He drew a sealed sheet from his pocket, and Eugenia took it with nerveless fingers that refused to cooperate.

"As soon as we arrived in America, I told my friends to keep a lookout for your brother," Captain Harrington said smoothly, taking the letter from her shaking fingers and opening it for her before handing it back. "Boyd here was sailing south and wound up with a cargo for Jamaica. It

seems your brother was making a tidy little fortune for himself there in the rum trade.''

"Edward . . . Jamaica . . . rum . . ." Vaguely Eugenia realized that she was repeating the captain's words in the stupidest fashion, but she could not think clearly at the moment.

Captain Boyd took up the narrative. "Mr. Wolverton—I guess I should say the earl of Latham now—was in high gig when I told him everybody was looking for him and why. And since I was sailing with a cargo for England, he asked me to take him along. Could hardly wait to assume his new position, he said. Seemed to think it was a rare joke you were behind the search for him, that you'd gone all the way to America just to find him. And he asked me to bring you that letter when I got back." He gestured towards the single sheet she held limply in her hands. "I would have delivered it to you sooner," he added apologetically, "but I've been held up in Canada, waiting for a cargo to bring back here."

Eugenia swallowed, her shock giving way in indignation at her brother's casual attitude. If that was not just like Edward! He had been sitting comfortably in Jamaica all this time, amassing his fortune, then went skipping off home without bothering to collect his worried sisters—without even contacting them!

With difficulty she mastered her surging emotions. "Thank you, Captain Boyd," she managed to say. "I . . . I appreciate all you have done. If you knew . . ."

"James told me," he interrupted, embarrassed. "Glad to be of service to you." He looked beseechingly at Captain Harrington as tears of happiness threatened to overcome Eugenia.

"Lady?" the captain asked.

"I . . . I am all right. Pray forgive me. Would . . . would you care for refreshment? I owe you so much, Captain Boyd . . ."

"We must needs return at once," Captain Harrington told her. "Michael still has his cargo to see to. He left his ship immediately to bring you this letter as soon as he could."

"And I am indeed grateful," Eugenia declared with more

composure. She rose. "I shall not keep you if you really must leave. But if there is anything we can do . . . ?"

"It was a pleasure to bring you good news," Captain Boyd said hurriedly, almost backing from the room.

"I will call later, Lady, to see what that brother of yours has to say for himself." He took her hand, squeezing it with a firm reassurance. "You won, Lady," he said softly. Their eyes held for a long moment as she drew strength from his inexhaustible store of compassion and support. Then they were gone.

Alone, Eugenia turned her attention to the miserably scrawled sheet that already showed the marks of her nervous grip. It opened, as she might have expected, with a remark about her having run off to America. No word of thanks or of appreciation for her efforts accompanied this.

The next paragraph riveted her attention. "Met Brockton at White's," her brother wrote. "You were a fool to go running off when he was on the verge of offering for you. Promised him you'd have a generous dowry, if you'd have him. Said he'd hop on over to America and fetch you home for me." He went on with a casual closing, but Eugenia took in no more.

So Brockton knew about Edward, knew about the fortune he had made, knew that to marry her was to marry the money she had once suspected he needed. He had not come to America to find her and declare his love, but to guarantee a portion of her brother's wealth!

She felt physically ill. How could she have been so gullible, so ready to believe his false protestations of love? Her pride at her triumph of capturing such a notable matrimonial prize shattered in fragments that left deep scars. Of course he was anxious to wed her—he was afraid she would learn that Edward had been found! And as for Brockton's perfidy . . . ! Angry tears spilled out from between the fingers she pressed to her face.

How could he have done this to her, not told her about her brother and left her to worry herself to distraction? Had he been the one to bring her the news, then courted her on the long return voyage, she probably would have succumbed to his charm. But now . . . ! The mere thought of him

sickened her. He had taken the grossest advantage of her, knowing full well that if Edward were not found, marriage to him would be her best solution. He had counted on her giving up—and giving in! And he would wed a fortune.

A soft tapping sounded on the door, and it opened to reveal her Uncle Reginald. He hesitated, not coming into the room, watching her slight, slumped form.

"Eugenia?" he finally asked.

She looked up, forcing her raging emotions under some semblance of control. "You heard. Edward has been found."

He nodded. "Yes, I heard. Are you all right?"

"Yes. Just . . . I'm all right. I'm sorry, it has all come as rather a shock to me."

"You poor child, of course it has." He sat down beside her, patting her hand. "Have you told Sophia yet?"

"No, I . . . Edward sent us a letter. It must be the first one he has ever written." Eugenia attempted a bit of humor, trying to appear more composed.

Mr. Jessop stood. "You'll want to tell her yourself, then. Now, I don't want you two to hurry off. You've had a trying time. Best to stay and relax a bit before going back. There's no rush, you know, no more time limit hanging over your head."

"No, there isn't." She stared blankly up at her uncle, who smiled encouragingly down at her. No more time limit, no more anxious days of waiting, no more searching . . . no more reason to remain in America. The purpose behind all of her thoughts and actions for the past months had abruptly been removed. She barely noticed when her uncle left, closing the door softly behind him.

Genie felt lost, floundering in a sea with no anchor. Edward was alive and had already taken up his position as the earl of Latham. All those long months of worry were over. In her present state of confusion, she barely spared a thought of her Cousin George and his discomfiture. Her victory over him seemed strangely hollow.

Where was the joy, the celebration, the pride at having accomplished such a difficult task? Her feelings, she discovered to her dismay, were very mixed, and elation did not appear

to be one of them. *What am I to do next?* she wondered vaguely.

There was no longer any need to hurry into marriage for Sophia's sake. They could live with Edward; their dowries were secure—and apparently those sums would be generous, judging by the disgraceful behavior of Brockton, whom she now freely stigmatized as a gazetted fortune hunter. The sisters could return home to England, their lives progressing exactly as they wished. Genie could live in style, the way she had before the death of her brother Robert. But to her consternation, she realized she was not anxious to leave America.

The discovery of Edward's whereabouts meant one more thing. She no longer had a reason to remain near Captain Harrington.

She had no excuse to seek him out, to receive his help, to feel his strength and encouragement. And he had no further reason to be involved with her.

With dragging steps, she went in search of her sister, finding her at last on the south lawn, watching as Sammy and Sukey argued over whose turn it was to fetch the scattered balls. Sophia looked up as she approached, and Eugenia could see her half-frightened, half-excited expression.

"Genie, who was that man Captain Harrington brought? What did they want?" she demanded as soon as her sister came within hailing distance.

"He was a sea captain. Sophie, he found Edward."

Sophia started to stand up from the bench on which she rested, then sank down, the color draining from her cheeks. "Where?" she cried.

So Sophia's initial reaction was not one of overwhelming thanksgiving either. Quickly Genie told her Edward's brief story, watching as her sister's indignation swelled to match her own.

"So he has been safe in Jamaica all this time!" she exclaimed. "You'd think the least he could have done, once he knew we were here and worried about him, would be to send us word before he left for England!"

"I think we were agreed on our opinion of Edward's unreliability," Eugenia commented dryly.

"Oh, but if that is not the outside of enough!" Sophia exclaimed. "To leave us imagining horrible fates for him, while all along he was perfectly safe . . . ! And I doubt he'll even bother to thank us for all the trouble we've been through on his behalf!"

"He didn't. He thought it a lark that we should have come here to search for him."

"How dare he!" Sophia's eyes flashed in her growing anger. "And after all these months! You'd think he might have let us know, so we could call off the search."

Eugenia hesitated, but then she succumbed to the need to share the rest of her shattering discovery. "We might have known several weeks ago, for Lord Brockton knew."

"What? He couldn't have!" Sophia declared. "He knew what you were going through, how upset you were. If he knew, he would have told you!"

"Edward has made himself a considerable fortune in the rum trade," Eugenia explained, her voice carefully even. "Lord Brockton desired to marry that fortune."

"And with Edward found, you'd have no need to marry Brockton." Sophia nodded.

"He must have realized, after his behavior in London, that I would not marry him if I had a choice." Eugenia looked down at her hands, then up to where the twins were once again bowling their balls with haphazard abandon into the rose bushes.

"Of all the . . . the unspeakable cads!" Sophia exclaimed. "I hope you give him a setdown he'll never forget!"

"You may be sure of that," Eugenia informed her grimly.

The opportunity presented itself the following day when Lord Brockton came to pay a morning visit. Eugenia and her Aunt Mary were in the small parlor. From the moment he arrived, Eugenia detected something different about him, a change in his approach that made him seem at once more passionate and more determined.

After bowing low over each of the ladies' hands, he begged the pleasure of a stroll about the rose garden with Eugenia. She met his admiring gaze with one of cool skepticism and had the satisfaction of seeing his suave demeanor falter for a moment.

"My dear Lady Eugenia," he murmured, offering her his arm, once again his familiar, over-confident self. "America must agree with you, for every day you seem more beautiful to me."

"Then perhaps I should remain and not return to England," she replied before she could stop herself. It was difficult keeping her anger with him under control, but she intended to punish him as thoroughly as possible.

"Never that, my lovely Eugenia. How could you think of depriving the *ton* of your company? I, for one, could not bear to be parted from you."

They were now deep into the shrubbery, and he turned to her, taking both of her hands in his. "You have begged for time, my love, but every day that I wait is sheer torture for me. Marry me, and I shall be your slave forever."

"Oh, don't be ridiculous," she snapped, trying to shake her hands from his firm, compelling hold.

He straightened slightly, his eyes opening wide, startled by the disgust that could be clearly heard in her voice. "Lady Eugenia!" he protested.

She pulled herself free. "Why did you not tell me Edward was safe, and in England?" she demanded, unable to restrain herself any longer.

He blinked, taken aback, but made a fairly smooth recovery. He laughed, a forced, unpleasantly grating sound, and tried to look shamefaced. The result, Eugenia thought, was repellent.

"It slipped my mind in the joy of seeing you again," he apologized. "I was quite overcome." He reached for her hands once again. She thrust them behind her, so instead he cupped her shoulders, caressing the soft flesh near her neck with his fingers. "My beautiful Eugenia, my desire to make you my wife eclipsed any other consideration. I feared if I mentioned your brother, you would think of nothing but him, and I would be forced to wait even longer to call you my own."

"But you knew how I worried! How could you be so . . . so cruel?"

"My love for you is my only excuse," he said ardently, trying to pull her towards him.

"Then it is a very poor excuse for a love!" She drew back, trying to shake off his touch, which made her flesh crawl.

"You will soon learn the extent of that love when I possess you and teach you the joys we have in store for us." He managed to get his arms about her, forcing her against him. His warm breath fanned her cheek, and she jerked away as if it scalded her.

"Let me go! I have no intention of marrying you!" She managed to free one arm that had been caught between them and pushed against his chest.

His eyes narrowed, but his hold remained firm. "There, my love, you have punished me. I deserved it, I know. Forgive a heart that loves too deeply," he coaxed. His lips strove to nuzzle near her ear as she tried to pull away from him.

"I am . . . not joking! Let me . . . go . . . this instant!" She struggled, but her slight, slender form was no match for a man famed in sporting circles.

He pinned her easily against him, gripping her chin with one hand, forcing her face up to his. "Be sure of this, my love, I shall never let you escape. You may be angry now, but that only shows how deep your true feelings are for me. I shall wed you, and soon. I cannot deny my desire for you."

It was difficult to speak while she struggled, but Eugenia made the attempt. "You mean . . . for Edward's . . . fortune!"

That caused him to relax his hold momentarily, and she was able to catch a breath before his grip tightened once again. His eyes regarded her with an expression that was cold and calculating. It made her shiver, though she was still held close within his arms.

"My brother wrote to me of what passed between you," she informed him, her words icy. "Are you so badly scorched that you are forced to go to so much trouble?"

A slow smile settled over his face like a mask. "No wonder you have rejected me! My dearest one, you have been given a completely false impression! As soon as you left England, I realized you were the only one I wished for my wife, and bitterly did I rue my behavior towards you. I

was already on the verge of setting out to find you when I learned that Edward—Latham—was in London. I know how you would wish everything to be done with propriety, so I begged his permisson to pay my addresses to you. He was delighted with the match and insisted on providing your dowry. You must know I would wed you this moment without a penny to your name!"

At the end of this speech, his lips descended on hers, catching her off guard. She fought him, but was unable to break free, to rid herself of his revolting touch.

He released her so abruptly that she almost fell. She stumbled, losing her balance, before realization of what had happened sank into her seething mind.

Lord Brockton was being turned about in the purposeful grip of Captain Harrington's massive hands. In another moment one of these, neatly curled into a punishing fist, landed flush on the Corinthian's chin. He reeled, tottered, and collapsed.

The captain rubbed his knuckles meditatively, regarding the immobile form of his adversary. Then his eyes rose to Eugenia, who stood trembling, staring in horror at her erstwhile suitor.

"Good morning, Lady." Captain Harrington bowed to her. "I hope you are well?"

Her disbelieving gaze transferred to his immense, capable form. "Captain . . ." she whispered. She took a shaky step toward him and felt her knees give way.

"Shall we go inside?" he asked, his tone calm, conversational. He slipped an arm about her, barely noticing her sagging weight against him.

"Brockton . . ." she began, looking back over her shoulder at his inert form.

"Will be best left alone to recover. I doubt he will come up to the house to complain."

"Captain, I . . ." She broke off, trembling.

"Your pride has been hurt, Lady. Nothing more." He led her in to the drawing room through the open French windows, then settled her on the sofa. Her aunt, she noted with relief, was not there.

"He . . . he will not be pleased, I fear," Eugenia told the captain.

"What, do you fear for me?" His eyes were alight with dancing, glowing lights, and irrationally it annoyed her that he had so enjoyed playing the knight errant.

She lowered her eyes demurely. "You did catch him off guard," she informed him. "He is quite famous in London as a boxer, Captain, and I fear size alone is no match for science."

His broad shoulders shook. "Lady, I am relieved you are feeling better. Do you also believe that large men are necessarily slow?"

"You, never," she declared with considerable force.

He grinned, showing even white teeth against his bronzed skin. "You flatter me, Lady."

"Do I?" She looked up at him through fluttering lashes, succumbing to the mischievous imp that strove within her whenever the dangerous captain was near. "I must apologize. I had not meant to do so. My wits are obviously still scattered."

That deep, resounding laugh that never failed to send shivers through her rocked his large frame. "On the contrary, my lo—Lady, they would seem sharper than ever. Have you adjusted yet to such an abrupt end to your quest?" he asked suddenly.

"It would have been easier had it been less abrupt," she admitted, somehow knowing he would understand. "It would all seem less frustrating if he had not already assumed his title and position."

The captain nodded, his expression solemn but his green eyes brimful of laughter. "It's like a job unfinished. You do all the work up to the last minute, but aren't allowed to take part in the finale."

"That's it exactly! I feel as if there is something I still must do, but I don't know what!"

"Then you haven't made any plans yet for yourself and your sister?" he asked, and she could detect nothing but a polite interest in his manner.

"No. That is . . . I suppose we shall be returning home. My uncle has asked us to remain for a while, but I don't

know. I shall have to talk it over with Sophia. We should sail before winter makes it too dangerous."

Did he not care? Eugenia studied his face as he rose, saying he must seek out her uncle. After so many months of joking, of sharing the worry, she expected at least an expression of sorrow at her impending departure. All she could detect in his attitude was a certain self-satisfaction that it had been through his inquiries that the search had been brought to a successful conclusion. He seemed not to care about the inevitable fact that she would leave America.

Plunged into depression, the reason for which was all too clear to her, Eugenia decided the sooner they went back to England the better, but this was a decision in which Sophia must share. When the question was put to her later that afternoon, her sister turned away, staring out the long drawing room windows, across the lawn. She was silent for several minutes.

"It will seem strange to leave all of our new friends, won't it?" she finally asked.

"And Aunt Mary and Uncle Reginald, not to mention Sukey and Sammy," Eugenia agreed.

"Oh, dear! I promised Sukey I would help her with her plans for the Harvest Festival next month!" Sophia exclaimed, turning back into the room. "And . . . and the Sandses are holding a ball next week, which we have promised to attend." She raised large, beseeching eyes to Eugenia.

"And the Quincys' dinner party, and the Browns' cotillion, and Aunt's tea party." Eugenia continued the list.

"It . . . it would be quite rag-mannered of us to cry off from so many engagements, would it not?" Despite an attempt at indifference, Sophia's anxiety could clearly be heard.

Eugenia hesitated. To her dismay, she could find in herself no real desire ever to return to England. The honest warmth of American society was more to her liking than the sometimes insincere formality of the London *ton*. That there was no man in England to compare with the dynamic, enticing, impossible Captain Harrington she steadfastly refused to consider.

"Genie, might we at least stay for the Sandses' party?" Sophia asked in a small voice.

Eugenia noted the sad, lost little girl look that lurked in the depths of her sister's lovely blue eyes. What did leaving mean to Sophia? Did she merely flirt with Gregory Sands as she had with that horrible lieutenant—or had that reprehensible little interlude been the result of far deeper feelings for Gregory?

Should she remove Sophia from America and temptation as quickly as possible? Was life in London any better? As long as her sister was able to marry a good, considerate husband of excellent family, what did it matter whether or not he was titled, or on which side of the Atlantic he lived? But they were Wolvertons, there was tradition behind them, there was the family to be thought of . . .

"I don't see why not," Eugenia decided, closing her mind to the raging tide of conflicting emotions and feelings of duty. "It . . . it would be grossly ill-mannered of us to cry off from our immediate social engagements, I suppose," she ventured, offering this sop to her conscience.

Sophia swooped down, throwing her arms about her in an engulfing hug. "Thank you, Genie!" She backed off, biting her lip. "That's silly, isn't it? I . . . I guess I don't want to face another ocean voyage yet."

"Well, we shall have to face one, and before winter. But be of good cheer: Captain Harrington tells me the return voyage will probably take two weeks less time than our previous trip."

Sophia nodded. "It will be funny, seeing Edward again, will it not? I don't know what I shall say to him."

"Well, I shall have a few words for him, I assure you!" Eugenia declared with considerable feeling. "It was the outside of enough to leave us here! He could quite easily have sailed here first before going to England—and so I shall tell him. I suppose we should speak to Uncle Reginald about obtaining passage . . . in two weeks' time?"

"That . . . that will be after Aunt Mary's tea party," Sophia agreed, though without enthusiasm. "We must not disappoint her, not after all she has done for us."

❋ Chapter 22 ❋

Aunt Mary was more than ready to endorse her nieces' decision not to depart immediately. With great zeal, she began plans for their entertainment for these last days that, if half were brought to fruition, would keep them there past Christmas. Eugenia, trying to smile, pointed this out to her aunt, who waved aside her objections.

"My dear, we shall have you only for a few more weeks!" Mary Jessop exclaimed, her large, pale eyes filling with ready tears. "We want you to have fun."

"And we shall, dear Aunt," Eugenia assured her, deeply touched by the sincerity of the little woman's emotions. "But we want to spend time with just you and Uncle Reginald and the children."

Mrs. Jessop pressed Eugenia's hands, then wiped an errant tear from her cheek. "Then we must have an *al fresco* luncheon, just for us, or maybe we should invite the Sandses and the Quincys. Oh, and do you think the Browns would care to come as well?"

Recognizing an unequal task, Eugenia left her to her plans. Between Mary Jessop's determination to make their last days memorable and Cassandra's riding over for morn-

ing visits or to coax them into joining riding expeditions, the days seemed to fly by.

Eugenia did not see Captain Harrington again until the afternoon of the tea party. He was one of the last of the guests to arrive, and she saw him as soon as he entered her aunt's crowded drawing room. He strode up to her immediately with his long, swinging gait. She felt herself swaying towards him, drawn by the magnetism of his gaze.

"Lady?" he bowed deeply over her hand, then raised her fingers to his lips. His eyes held hers, and she had to fight against the sensation of sinking into their beckoning depths.

"Well, Captain?" She managed a coolly polite smile for him, though every part of her being reacted to his nearness.

He drew her fingers through his arm and led her to a chair. "I fear I have been neglecting you of late. I have had some trouble with a shipment of cargo."

"Cassandra mentioned you were busy."

He moved his chair so that he sat closer to her than he usually did, and she found his nearness disturbing. She raised her eyes to his and encountered a smoldering glow in their mysterious depths. Her breath came more quickly, shallow and uneven, and her gaze dropped.

"I . . . I hope you were able to solve your problem?" She rushed into speech, saying the first thing that came to mind.

"Almost. But it kept me from many enjoyable arguments with you."

That drew a giggle from her, which she found hard to stop. *I'm as nervous as if this were my first party!* she thought, shocked by the devastating effect he had on her composure. With an almost Herculean effort, she controlled herself.

"You should be wary. Now that I no longer need your assistance in the search for my brother, there is nothing to force me to be polite to you."

"Is that what you were?" His sparkling eyes invited her

to laugh with him. "And here I have thought you the veriest shrew."

"Why, and so I am," she agreed with cordiality.

"Have you made your plans yet?" he asked suddenly.

The abruptness of the question caught her off guard. "Not . . . not really. We planned to remain only until the Sandses' ball, but after that . . ." She hesitated, for the ball was in only three days' time. "We must leave before the winter storms make the ocean too rough," she finished.

"You will be here for the ball, though," he murmured, his tone almost a caress. He rose, once again taking her hand, his touch warm and compelling. "Lady, I must take my leave of you. As I am sure you have noticed—Cassandra has told you—Jasper Selkirk is not here. He is working late this evening, and I must return to help him. If I do not see you before then, I shall surely see you at the ball."

After the captain's departure, the party suddenly seemed very flat to Eugenia. She walked restlessly about the rooms, seeking out anyone who could take her mind off his lingering presence. Sophia, she noted, sat almost primly in a corner, one of a small group of young people that also included a rather sober-faced Gregory.

By the night of the Sandses' ball, Eugenia had yet to approach her uncle about making the arrangements for their return passage to England. There was still plenty of time, she told herself, and Sophia should have this one more evening to enjoy before their plans were finalized. That it was she who was reluctant to leave, she tried desperately to forget.

Somewhere in the back of her mind the hope lurked that Captain Harrington's continued absence and preoccupation with his work meant that he was making arrangements to sail for England, to escort them home. This vied with the desperate, but unacknowledged, wish that he would somehow prevent her departure and ask her to remain.

It was in this chaotic frame of mind that she entered the lofty and elegant ballroom at the Sandses'. Looking about, as she tried not to search for the captain's dominating figure, it came to her almost as a shock that she was

acquainted with—or at least recognized—almost every person present. More surprising, perhaps, was the fact that she liked an unprecedented number of them.

There was so much less formality here than in England, she mused, acknowledging various greetings as she followed her aunt and Sophia to one side of the room. It was one of the many aspects of American life she was coming to enjoy. Here she could be herself; she could laugh aloud if she wished, and no one would stare or be shocked by such behavior. And when she was seated at a dinner table, her position did not reflect the fact that she was the unmarried sister of an earl of ancient and prominent family.

By the time the orchestra finished their lengthy tuning up and struck the first chords of a quadrille, Eugenia found she was promised for most of the remaining dances. Should she save one, in case Captain Harrington would appear . . . ?

She almost faltered in the steps that she knew so well. He stood in the doorway, tall, magnificent in his evening attire, those disturbing eyes scanning the room . . . for her. Even at that distance, she could sense the warmth of his smile as their gazes met. The sweet strains of the music sounded far away now, and she executed the movements of the dance without conscious thought. Her eyes remained locked with his, lost in the magnetic spell that emanated from him, enveloping her in a private world in which he was the only other occupant.

She paused, unable to remember any more steps, suddenly realizing the music had stopped and the dance ended. Her partner had not noticed her preoccupation with another man. Thanking her, he led her back to where her aunt sat. The captain moved on a converging course, joining them just as they reached the chaperones. Her escort departed to locate his next partner, and Eugenia turned to Captain Harrington, feeling strangely shy and breathless.

"You are late." A poor opening, she knew, but her mind did not seem to work as it should, and it was the only thing she could think of to say.

"Not too late, I hope, to have the honor of a dance with

you?'' A glowing, luminous sparkle lit the swirling pools of his eyes.

"I . . . I believe I still have three free." It took considerable effort, but she kept from drowning in their depths.

"Not anymore." His smile sent that pleasurable shiver through her.

"All three, Captain?" she asked, doing her best to sound skeptical.

"More, if you were free." His compelling gaze held her.

She swallowed and forced herself to resume breathing. "Captain, you would set people talking unkindly."

"Only those whose dances I stole."

At that moment she was claimed by Jasper Selkirk, who bowed deeply before her. If he noticed her bemused manner, he made no comment. "Cassy says she is saving you a dance, James," he informed him.

"A royal summons?" the captain asked, his latent amusement surfacing.

Mr. Selkirk grinned back at him. "I don't think she is taking no for an answer."

The captain glanced across to where his cousin was taking her position in a set that was just forming. "She seems busy at the moment," he replied casually. His gaze took in several unpartnered ladies, but for once he did not move to do his duty. He turned to Mrs. Jessop. "Mary, may I sit this one out with you?"

No one could be insensitive to his charm, Eugenia thought, allowing herself to be led away. He could probably walk up to any lady in the room, partnered or not, and the dance would be his for the asking. Instead he chose to sit among the chaperones, his eyes following her, so that each time she looked across at him—which was uncomfortably often—her eyes encountered the caressing touch of his.

"What is he up to?" Mr. Selkirk asked as the movement of the dance brought them together.

"I had thought to ask you," Eugenia replied. "Surely you know him better than I do."

"Cassy doesn't know either, and it has cast her into high fidgets. She swears he's in the midst of some game or other,

but she's never seen him act quite like this. She thought you might have a guess.''

Fortunately they were separated by the movements of the other dancers in their set, and the soft flush had faded from Eugenia's cheeks by the time she rejoined her partner. ''I wondered to what I owed the honor of this dance,'' she said archly, hoping to divert him.

It didn't work. ''Oh, I'm not Cassy's messenger, at least to you. She'll corner you herself before the night is over, never fear. This is a terrible way to conduct a conversation,'' he added two minutes later as they again approached each other and she took his hand for a promenade.

''It assures that we confine ourselves to the merest commonplaces.''

''Does that mean you know something but aren't going to tell me?'' he demanded.

''Jasper,'' she declared, relaxing her stiff manner, ''have you ever known *anyone* who knows what goes on in Captain James Harrington's addled mind?''

He laughed as they separated and was still chuckling as he again took her hand. ''Genie, I am sorry. No one ever knows until it is too late.''

''And you have to work for him,'' she said with sincere sympathy.

''That's what is upsetting Cassy,'' Jasper told her as the dance ended. They remained on the floor for a moment, and she looked inquiringly up at him. ''He spent all of yesterday and most of today explaining the principles behind his shipping business to me. Cassy says that sounds like he's planning on being away for a while and is preparing me to take charge for a bit.''

''Has he done this before?'' Eugenia asked. *Was* he preparing to captain the ship that would take them back to England? She looked across to where he sat, still with her Aunt Mary, and encountered a special smile meant only for her. It was difficult, but she forced her eyes away.

It is almost as if he is trying to fix his interest with me! Could he be courting her in earnest? A surge of elation swept upwards through her, burning her cheeks and leaving her flesh tingling. But if his intentions were to ask her to

remain in America and marry him, then why did he prepare for an extended absence?

"When he sailed for England back in January," Jasper answered her forgotten question. "He left old Mr. Penniworth in control, but he was pensioned off last month."

"Then it does sound as if . . ." Eugenia began uncertainly, but broke off as Gregory Sands touched her elbow. She looked up at him, surprised, for she had not heard his approach and had even forgotten that the next dance was promised to him. The sets were forming around them, she realized. Jasper left her to seek out his own partner, and she accepted Gregory's arm.

She glanced up into his somber face, surprised to see no lurking humorous glint in his dark eyes. "Would you rather sit this one out?" she asked suddenly. He shook his head and she hesitated, then asked, "Is something worrying you?"

"Is your sister feeling quite the thing?" he blurted out. "When I speak to her, she just casts her eyes down and murmurs the merest commonplaces. And look at her! She has been unusually subdued all this evening."

Eugenia, instantly concerned, turned to follow Gregory's gaze. Sophia did indeed appear more sedate than was her wont, for once not flirting with the gentleman who stood opposite her in the set. Nothing could detract from the delicate grace of her movements, but she lacked the customary effervescence that drew all eyes to her in admiration.

Eugenia glanced back up at her partner, whose lack of interest in her—and the dance that began at that moment—was far from flattering. "I believe she merely dreads the voyage back to England," she informed him.

Gregory stiffened, missing a step. "Do you go already, then?" he asked as soon as he could.

"If we do not sail soon, the approaching winter will make the crossing almost impossible."

"Why not wait until spring?" he asked, his expression clouded. His eye moved past her, seeking out Sophia. "She is so very young," he murmured, and Eugenia realized he was talking to himself.

He did not speak again and Eugenia, knowing his thoughts

were far away from her and his parents' ball, did not try to interrupt him. She was glad when the music ended and he escorted her back to her aunt.

She had barely seated herself when Captain Harrington appeared before her, taking her hand and drawing her to her feet.

"No rest yet, Lady. It is my turn to claim you." His words were a caress, enveloping her into the glow of his eyes. The soft smile that played about the corners of his mouth hinted at an intimacy between them that went far beyond the bonds of friendship.

It was a waltz, the first she had danced in America. She had barely a thought to spare for her sister, for it would not matter if Sophie danced it here without the permission of the patronesses of Almack's. They could both swirl about the room in time with the music, guided by the arms of the gentleman of their choice . . . The captain led her effortlessly, his slightest touch enough to direct her about the floor.

She raised her eyes to his, and there was no need for words between them. Lost in his mesmerizing gaze, she allowed him to sweep her along, only vaguely conscious of the other dancers, the ballroom, even of the soft strains of the music. Nothing mattered but the glowing tenderness in the eyes that held her prisoner.

The music ceased abruptly and they stopped moving. For several long seconds they remained as they were, his arm still about her, her hand clasped warmly in his. Then, breaking the spell with reluctance, she stepped back.

He released her instantly. "The middle of a ballroom is hardly the place to say what I wish to you."

"That . . . that has never stopped you before," she responded as lightly as she could. She took a deep breath, trying to steady herself, trying to resist the desire to sway back into his strong arms, to rest her head against his broad shoulders, to feel the roughness of his sideburns across her cheek as he lowered his head . . .

"Perhaps I am learning more decorous behavior." He offered her his arm, and she placed trembling fingertips upon it. "May I take you in for some refreshment? I fear

your next partner is bearing down upon us, and I do not wish to lose you just yet.''

They sipped punch from crystal glasses in silence, as if neither wanted to lose the sense of togetherness that enveloped them. She allowed herself to be drawn away by the young gentleman to whom she was promised for the country dance that followed, and somehow she must have behaved normally, for he made no complaint. The captain stood where Eugenia had left him, still holding their glasses. When her gaze was drawn to him, she was held by the passionate gleam that lit his eyes.

Every time she turned she could see him still watching her, even when he danced with another lady. At last he claimed her a second time, unfortunately for a quadrille, and she was forced to keep part of her mind on the intricate steps. The dance separated them frequently, which was not at all to her liking.

She was not able to dance with him again until the end of the evening. This one, a round dance, was no more conducive to conversation than had been the quadrille, but the smoldering look in his eyes as they rested on her obviated the need for words between them. The music ended, but it played on in her heart as she walked with him back to join her aunt.

Sophia came up, under the escort of an unsmiling Gregory Sands, pale and with shadowed circles under her eyes. One look was enough to warn Eugenia that the girl was overtired and would be better for leaving early. Sophia agreed to this plan without protest, a circumstance that did little to reassure her anxious sister. While they waited with their aunt, Captain Harrington went to the card room in search of Reginald Jessop.

The captain escorted them to the front door, where they waited for their carriage to be brought around. Drawing Eugenia aside, he tilted her chin up so that she gazed fully into his gleaming eyes. "I shall be paying your uncle a visit in the morning," he told her softly.

The sound of their vehicle drawing up before the door prevented her from speaking, which was just as well. From his smile, though, she guessed that the expression in her

eyes had been sufficient to signify her approval of his intentions.

He handed her in, kissing her fingers with lingering desire. Then he turned her hand, pressing another kiss into her palm in a way that left her trembling. He stood back, shut the door, and the horses leapt forward.

She could not be mistaken. Happiness filled her, blocking out all thought for her sister's exhaustion. The following morning, Captain James Harrington would ask her uncle's permission to marry her, and she would accept. Gone were all thoughts of spurning a love for which she now ardently yearned. The artificial stiltedness of the London *ton* became completely meaningless. At last she could admit to herself that life in America, at her captain's side, was all she could ever want.

Her euphoria still enveloped her the following morning when, dressed with extreme care, she seated herself in the drawing room with her embroidery. Behind her, through the open windows, she could hear Sukey and Sammy arguing. Sophia, who sat reading in the rose garden just beyond, called to silence them with no noticeable result. Genie smiled, setting her next stitch neatly. Captain Harrington, according to Thomas as he cleared away the breakfast dishes, had been closeted with her uncle for well above half an hour. It could not be much longer now, and they would send for her . . . The door opened, and her heart skipped in her eager anticipation.

"Lady, you are alone?" Captain Harrington stood on the threshold, his gay eyes dancing with that familiar suppressed merriment, as if at a joke unshared.

"I am quite deserted," she managed to reply. "Do you come to bear me company?"

"Alas, Lady, I do not. I come to take my leave of you." The mischievous glints danced in those sea-green depths, and a muscle twitched at the corner of his mouth.

"Your leave . . ." Her flesh tingled as the blood drained from her face. She shook her head slowly, not quite believing his words. He was coming to ask her to marry him! He had to be! But he spoke of leaving . . .

"I am sailing with one of my ships in an hour's time,"

he explained. "I find I am bored and fidgety on land and will be the better for the excitement of a voyage."

"Where . . . where do you go?" she asked, not quite believing, not wanting to accept his words.

"I shall take a consignment of your uncle's to Jamaica, but after that, I have no idea. Anywhere where I won't have to see a port for weeks!" he declared. "I must not delay. The tide waits for no one. Lady, it has been a joy."

He bowed deeply and walked out of the room.

❊ Chapter 23 ❊

Eugenia stared at the drawing room door as it closed behind Captain Harrington. A sensation of burning coals, followed by ice seemed to pass over her flesh, leaving her chilled and shivery. It had been a joy, he said . . . he was bored and fidgety . . . he wanted to be free.

She had been right in that earlier guess about him, that he possessed the wanderlust of a seaman, but this fact did nothing to ease the shock that engulfed her. He would never remain long in any one place. No woman could ever compare to the sea; no mere woman could ever tie him down. He was wed to his ship and could only be happy walking her decks, feeling the wind and the salt spray in his face.

Had he started to love her? Did he depart now, so suddenly, because he ran away from a commitment to her? Her heart prayed that this might be so while her mind acknowledged that it did not matter. Whether she had lost him or had never had him, the result was the same either way. He was gone. If he felt any pangs of regret, they would quickly disappear as the prow of his ship crashed through an onslaught of rising waves and the exhilaration of the chill, damp winds replaced any lingering traces of desire for her.

And she? The pain stabbed deeply into her soul, tearing at her until she longed to cry out against it. What could she do to escape a torment that only he could ease? He was gone, and only his presence at her side could heal these wounds.

Slowly her head sank and her hands came up to cover her face. He must have known how she felt, how she had been prepared to place her heart at his feet. She had made no secret of it last night, when she thought her love returned and wanted. Was that what drove him away? At least he had not laughed at her . . .

The irony struck her as hard and unrelenting as a cudgel. Was that not exactly what she had planned for him? To bring him to the point where she was now, then scorn him? Not as she had been scorned, but with disparaging words to make the rejection more complete.

The thought sickened her. She would never have gone through with it, she knew now. Never could she have caused such pain in anyone on purpose. The whole scheme had been thought up in the heat of anger . . . and before she knew what exquisite agony unrequited love could be.

It was some time before she could drag her mind from the depths of despair and focus it on the more practical matter of what to do next. She could not bear the thought of remaining in America, not where everything and everybody would remind her of the laughter and arguments she had shared with the captain. And especially not here in Providence, where she would see him whenever he returned from a voyage.

England it would be. She had a home, a family, friends, a position in Society. She would be a titled lady once more. She could step back into her old life as if she had never been away, except that now it would be Edward who was Latham and not Robert. And Edward would need to find a wife, and she must find Sophia a husband, and Charlotte, her brother's widow, would emerge from mourning and undoubtedly marry again. Life went on . . . but not for her.

She would not marry. She would go through the sham of

the London Season for Sophia's sake; then once the girl was safely wed she would apply to Edward for enough money to live quietly somewhere in a cottage, perhaps in a small village. But nowhere near Wolverton Priory. Robert would never have countenanced such a scheme, but Edward was enough of a loner himself to understand her unconventional desire.

A lady does not wear her heart on her sleeve. A lady conducts herself with propriety at all times. A lady does not display an excess of emotion. Miss Minton's dictums ran through her mind. She must pull herself back together, behave as if her world had not crumbled, be her normal self. To appear otherwise would give rise to questions she did not believe herself capable of answering.

Leaving America was of the first priority. She would see to that at once . . . before she told Sophia of their impending departure. The girl would be loath to give up the planned entertainments. Better to tell her arrangements had already been made than to give her a chance to postpone their voyage.

When she tapped on the library door, she was relieved to hear her uncle's cheery "Come in," for she had been half afraid he had already left the house. Bracing herself, she entered the comfortable room.

He looked up from the pile of papers on his desk and smiled. "Ah, Genie, my dear. What may I do for you?"

"If you please, Uncle Reginald, I would like to arrange for our passage back to England. As soon as possible." Her voice sounded calm and even, a fact that pleased her.

His eyebrows raised. "Already, my dear? We'll be very sorry to see you leave, both my Mary and I."

Eugenia bit her tongue, trying to hold back the tears that sprang to her eyes. There was a disagreeable lump rising in her throat, but she swallowed, forcing it back down. How she would miss them! But it did not bear thinking about, or she would never be able to carry out her plans with any degree of composure. She could cry later, on the ship . . .

"It is time we returned, before we decide to move in on

you permanently," she tried, with an attempt at a light-heartedness she was far from feeling.

"You'd be welcome, you know."

Carefully she did not meet the warmth and sincerity in his smiling eyes. "We must go back," she declared, more firmly than she had intended. It would be impossible for her to remain, waiting, always hoping for the captain to drop by. Would she start haunting the harbor, as did Sukey and Sammy, praying that perhaps on that day she would see his ship sailing into port? "Do you realize," she hurried on, "that it has been almost seven years since we have seen Edward? We must return and help him adjust to his new station."

Uncle Reginald took his spectacles off his nose and began to polish them. "And when would you like to sail? Next month?"

"Today, if possible," she blurted out. "I mean . . ."

"Well, I suppose it's only natural to be anxious to get on with it, once your mind is made up." His tone was casual, but his eyes narrowed and he regarded her closely. "I'll send a messenger down to the docks. I believe there may be a ship preparing to leave within a day or so. Or is that too soon?"

"No, that would be . . . that would be fine. It won't take us long to pack. We could be ready at any time. Oh, Uncle, I do hate to leave you, but . . ."

He came around from behind his desk and slipped an arm about her. "My poor girl, this has been a trying time for you, has it not? But don't think we shall never see each other. You are young, and you can come back and stay with us again. Or who knows? Maybe my Mary and I will come to visit you, and I can show her England."

She nodded, wordless, then threw her arms about him, returning his hug. As the tears threatened to overcome her, she ran from the room.

Her uncle must have acted immediately, for shortly before luncheon Thomas came to where she sat in the rose garden to tell her that her uncle requested a few words with her. She found him in his library, where he paced about, his heavy brow lowered.

"Ah, Genie." He paused in his circumambulation and tilted his spectacles to peer at her better. "Couldn't find you a ship, at least not for some time. No one is sailing towards England."

"No one? But surely . . . I thought one went almost every month. When did the last one set out?"

"Well, there's one due to leave at dawn," he said. "It's too soon for any others to plan a trip, you see. They have to find cargoes and passengers before they go. Another won't leave for several weeks."

"Is there room for two more passengers on the morrow's boat?" she asked, fighting down the sense of panic that rose within her. Every moment she remained in America was painful. Perhaps later, with time, the jagged edges of her wounds would start to mend and she could remember the captain without her heart and spirit being torn apart anew.

"Genie, are you mad? You'd have to board tonight! You couldn't possibly be ready."

She smiled, but it was pitifully thin and tight. "Oh, yes we can. It will be easier on Sophia, not to have time to think. Can you find out, Uncle Reginald?"

He hesitated. "I don't like it, Genie. You won't have time to say good-bye to . . . anyone."

"You and Aunt Mary can give our regrets. It will be easier this way, you know. It . . . it's not as if we will be returning in a couple of months' time. A farewell of this permanence is not easy to say."

"Are you sure you know what you are doing, my girl?" he demanded. "James . . ."

"Captain Harrington sailed this morning. I know; he told me. We . . . we do not wish to wait until he returns. And he may not have a ship going to England when he does. It is better we leave now."

"I suppose you know your own business best," he said slowly, but he did not sound convinced.

"I do, Uncle," she said softly.

His eyes narrowed once again as he studied her carefully blank face. "James is a fool!" he exploded. "Very well, if there is no hope for it, I'll see what I can do."

"Thank you, Uncle Reginald." She kissed him quickly on the cheek. "We shall start packing immediately, just in case."

After sending for her maid to start this lengthy procedure, Eugenia steeled herself to face her sister's inevitable horror at the scheme. She found Sophia by the simple expedient of following the squeals and shouts of Sukey and Sammy. As these had led her to expect, all three were on the south lawn bowling balls that came almost within feet of the pins.

Sophia, upon learning of the arrangement that had already been made, stared at her sister, her complexion unnaturally pale. "Tonight?" she whispered.

"It is best this way, Sophia. If we think about it, we will keep putting it off. There are people we . . . we do not wish to leave, but we must. The sooner we go, the easier it will be."

"I want to stay!" The girl's eyes glistened with unshed tears, and her slender form trembled.

"You . . . you must have a Season in London, Sophie. You owe it to your name and lineage. If at the end of that time you . . . you still wish to return to America, I shall bring you back."

Sophia sniffed and gulped. "You mean if I don't take?" she asked.

"Oh, there is no chance of that. You will probably be a success, and hated by every less favored young lady in town. What I meant," she said steadily, "is if you find no gentleman you wish to marry. Our training—our breeding—makes you an eligible consort for a duke. You must have a chance to select a husband of your own rank and station, from your own world. But if you find there is none you can like . . ."

Sophia kept her eyes on her hands. "And if my . . . my heart is already given?" Her voice was barely audible.

"You will not even be seventeen until next week," Eugenia said gently. "And Miss Minton was right in one respect, at least. Love alone is no basis for marriage. You must be very sure you have a great deal in common with the gentleman you choose to marry. If you do not suit in

temperament and likes, love will quickly die. Sharing the same background is of very great importance.''

Sophia was silent, not meeting her sister's compassionate eyes.

''Betty is already packing for us,'' Eugenia went on after a moment's silence. ''And we have some letters to write. We cannot go without sending word to Cassy and her mother. Or Mrs. Sands. And Gregory has been so very kind to us. I believe, in this circumstance, it would be proper to write a brief note to him.''

Sophia's eyes met her sister's now. ''If you like, I shall write to him,'' she said. ''And to Mrs. Sands. As you say, they have been most kind.''

So it was easier than Eugenia expected. Sophia joined her in the drawing room, where Thomas brought them writing paper and quills, and together they set about the unhappy task of informing their closest friends of their departure. *We will be gone before these are even received*, Eugenia thought as she sealed a wafer on her note to Cassandra's mother. The next, to Cassy herself, would be more difficult, for she had grown honestly fond of the girl. Should she wish her joy in her upcoming marriage? That sounded too final, as if they would never exchange letters. In the end she kept it brief, adding a request that Cassy say good-bye to her cousin for them.

Reginald Jessop found them just sealing the last of their notes. Their passage, he informed them, was settled. They must board the ship as soon as possible.

Eugenia refused to meet Sophia's anguished eyes. Determined to keep busy, she led the way upstairs to help Betty with the packing. Here they found two more housemaids as well as their aunt's maid. Mary Jessop ran back and forth between the two rooms looking distraught and wringing her hands.

''You cannot leave us like this!'' She pounced on them as they came up the stairs. ''Without any warning! We had so hoped that . . .'' She broke off suddenly and stared hard at Eugenia's drawn face. ''Well, that is neither here nor there. If you have already made all the arrangements, then there is

nothing for it but to pack. If only I could be sure that you would come back someday!"

"We will, Aunt Mary." Eugenia took her hands and squeezed them. "Now that we know you . . . And in the meantime, we can write, and you can tell us all about Sukey and Sammy."

Whether it was the shock she had sustained from Captain Harrington that morning or the abruptness of their departure Eugenia was not sure, but she moved about as if in a dream. No, a nightmare. Every dress carefully folded away in silver paper and stowed in a trunk punctuated the fact that they were indeed leaving, but Eugenia could not accept it as true. Barely aware of what she did, she selected which gowns she wanted with her on the ship and which ones could be packed in the storage trunk.

Dinner was a brief, quiet meal, for no one had much of an appetite. As soon as they were finished, Eugenia and Sophia returned immediately to their rooms, where the packing continued. It took hours, but at last all of their gowns were safely stowed and only their hooded woolen cloaks remained. Finally, the maid removed Eugenia's brushes and bottles from the dressing table. All traces of her occupancy were removed from the room, except for the two heavy trunks that stood in the center of the floor.

A large, rumbling wagon, normally used only for farming purposes, drew up in front of the house, and the two footmen started the strenuous task of carrying down the luggage. In a few very short hours it would be dawn and, with or without the last-minute passengers, the ship would sail. Eugenia was determined to be on it.

It was just like Captain Harrington to force her hand, to cause her to leave in such haste without time for proper good-byes. And, as disgustingly always when he was involved, it was probably for the best. This way there was no time to think, no time to regret, no time to back out . . .

In a distressingly short time, they said a tearful good-bye to a sleepy Sukey and Sammy. Mrs. Jessop accompanied them as far as the drive, where she embraced them, then watched as they climbed into the carriage. Their baggage had already been stowed, and their traveling trunks would

be awaiting them in their cabin. Only one had been available, and once again they would share their quarters.

If only I could believe this is real . . . But she would, and all too soon. When the shock wore off, when Eugenia realized that Captain Harrington was indeed gone from her life—forever—the pain would settle in anew, and she would long for this misty semi-oblivion that wrapped about her now.

Somehow they boarded the ship. Reginald Jessop came with them, inspecting their cabin and directing the captain to have a care for his precious cargo. He took his leave of a tearful Sophia, but Eugenia accompanied him back up on deck. He hesitated before making his reluctant way down the gangplank, turning to his niece.

"You shouldn't do this, Genie," he said with a sigh. "What will James say when he hears you could not even wait to say good-bye?"

"We said good-bye this morning, when he told me he was sailing. I am sure he never expected us to wait the six months, or whatever it will take, before he finally arrives home."

"I think you should wait for the next boat," he repeated as he had several times.

"For what, Uncle?"

"Dammit, I thought James was going to marry you!" he exploded.

"Apparently not," she said, struggling to keep a light, airy note in her voice that completely failed to fool her uncle.

He drew a deep breath, puffing out his cheeks as he dispelled it. "I'm sorry, Genie," was all he said, but his voice held a wealth of sympathy and understanding. "We— Mary and I—hoped . . ."

"You reckoned without your host, then," she said, trying to force a laugh into her words. "Could you really see Captain Harrington tied down by anyone?"

He clapped his hand on her shoulder, giving it a quick squeeze. "I'd better leave, my girl, or you'll see your old uncle in tears. You keep in touch, now. Somehow, I'll see

you again.'' With that, he hurried away before his emotions could overcome him.

Eugenia stood by the rail, watching as his carriage disappeared in the dark. She kept her mind blank, concentrating on the glittering stars, the smell of the salt air, the gentle lapping of the wavelets against the hull of the ship, so like the *Cormorant* . . . No. She could not allow herself to think, to remember. Not yet. She turned, making her way down the companionway to their cabin, where she found Sophia already in her bunk, crying herself to sleep.

❋ Chapter 24 ❋

An unfamiliar rocking motion awakened Eugenia not many hours later. Pale gray light seeped through a tiny round window somewhere above her head and fell across her bed. She lay in a state of half-sleep for several minutes, trying to place where she was. The clank of dragging chains reached her, followed by muffled shouts. And there were birds. Sea birds. She was on a boat . . .

But it was not the *Cormorant,* and if she went up on deck she would not see Captain Harrington's tall, dynamic figure striding energetically back and forth. Nor would she hear his deep, booming voice, shouting orders, encouraging his men, calling her Lady and laughing in the way that vibrated through her . . .

Sophia murmured in her sleep and rolled over, pulling the blankets up almost to the top of her dusky curls. It might be morning, but it was still very early, and they had not gotten to bed until an unreasonably late hour. All things considered, it would be best if she copied her sister's example.

Blessed sleep eluded her, and in desperation she rose, donning the same gray traveling gown she had worn the night before. Tossing her cloak about her shoulders, she slipped quietly out of the spacious cabin, leaving her sister peacefully at rest.

As she emerged on deck, the chill dampness of the morning air struck her, the breeze ruffling her hair until she pulled the woolen hood up for protection. She made her way to the stern, where she stood staring back the way they had come, back to the harbor of Providence that could barely be discerned as it slipped away into the misty gray distance.

But Captain James Harrington wasn't there. By now he was well on his way to some foreign port.

The sound of booted footsteps sounded behind her and she spun, her heart stopping for a moment. "Captain..." The name tore from her throat, dying as she beheld the small though powerfully built middle-aged man who had come up behind her.

"Good morning, miss. Did you sleep well?"

"Captain ... Blaine, is it?" she asked, her voice hollow as the shock receded from her. Her fingers gripped the rail tightly as her knees threatened not to support her. "Yes, quite well, thank you," she added, trying to regain control of herself.

"A bit cold this morning, miss," he went on. "Though it looks like you're prepared. Well, breakfast will be served in an hour's time. Dining salon is the last door. If you'd like coffee, I'll send a cabin boy for it.'

"Thank you, no." She shook her head. "I ... I'd like to just stand here, looking at the scenery. It will be my last view of America, you know," she added, and hoped he did not notice the hopeless note that echoed in the emptiness of her voice.

She remained there throughout the rest of the day, staring out across the land that slowly slipped past, feeling shaken and wondering if she would ever recover. Sophia joined her, seating herself in a chair placed for her by one of the crew. Her pale face and unnatural silence spoke volumes for the havoc wreaked on her stomach by the unrelenting rocking of the ship. Eugenia, wrapped in her own private world of misery, for once barely noticed.

Clear at last of the islands dotting Narragansett Bay, the great East Indiaman picked up speed as she faced the open waters of the Atlantic. No answering surge lifted Eugenia's heart as the last sails were unfurled and the wind struck

them fully and drove the ship on. She remained in the stern, huddling into the warmth of her cloak, her eyes fixed unseeingly on the land behind them that grew smaller and less distinct with each passing minute.

Sophia felt no desire to eat but Eugenia, at the captain's coaxing, finally allowed herself to be led belowdecks for an evening meal. She did not stay long, but quickly resumed her vigil beside her sister's chair until the cold and darkness forced them down to the cabin. They returned topside with the first light, seeking relief in the cold dampness, Sophia from her queasiness and Eugenia from the heaviness of her heart.

As the morning fog began to lift under the determined rays of the ascending sun, Eugenia glimpsed the hazy gray coastline. The light and distance played tricks with her eyes, for the rippling water far behind them appeared to swing in a wide, tacking movement.

The odd ripples provided her something to concentrate on. She continued to watch throughout the moving, realizing as she did that each angle the moving water turned brought something closer to them. Not a ripple, then, but a smaller ship, and making admirable speed.

By early afternoon she could make out the clean lines of a trim schooner, a brilliant white against the deep, glittering blue of the sea. Neatly the small boat sliced through the bouncing whitecaps as the wind that roughened the sea sent it flying, skimming lightly across the surface of the ocean.

The ship drew ever nearer, until she could make out the figures of several men on the deck. One waved, as if saying hello, then returned to work shifting a sail as the sleek schooner turned hard about for its reverse tack.

The figures grew larger and clearer. One, a full head taller than the others, raised an arm once again, and Eugenia's clenched hand rose to her throat. A fair-haired giant who waved merrily, who strode across his ship with a free swinging stride . . .

After the ship's next tack, there could be no doubt. The chill breeze lifted the tightly curled blond hair, stirred the reddish sideburns. Captain Harrington waved again, this time shouting something that she could not catch.

"Genie, is that not . . . ?" Sophia's soft voice penetrated through her confusion.

"Yes." Eugenia nodded. "It is. But why?"

Why? The question ran through her mind as conflicting emotions surged within her. Why did he chase her, for surely that was what he did? This was no merchant ship that followed them. But what . . . and why . . . ? Had he, *could* he, have changed his mind?

"What the devil . . . ?" Captain Blaine strode up behind her, leaning on the rail. "They're trying to hail us!" he declared. He turned slightly, shouting over his shoulder to heave to and allow the boat within range. Sailors went running, and in a remarkably short time several of the great sails hung limp. The merchantman slackened speed, and the schooner pulled near.

"Harrington, is that you?" Captain Blaine shouted. "What the hell are you doing?"

"Need to see one of your passengers!" The answer drifted across the sea between them, his deep tones carrying easily.

Captain Blaine waved an acknowledgment to him, and Captain Harrington disappeared from view. In another moment two of his men lowered a tiny rowboat over the side, and the captain climbed easily down into it. He pushed away with one oar, then locked it into position. With smooth, powerful strokes, he pulled across the expanse of tossing water that lay between them.

A rope ladder was dropped over the side of the East Indiaman. Captain Harrington tied the dingy to this, then clambered up, finally swinging over the side.

Blaine strode forward to meet him, looking up into the laughing face so far above his own. They held a low-voiced conversation that Eugenia strained to catch, but without success. Blaine nodded, grinning, and gestured to the stern, where Eugenia stood rigidly, her hand holding Sophia's for support.

"I think you will do better without me," Sophia murmured.

"No, please . . ." Eugenia's eyes, wide with panic, sought her younger sister's.

"Remember Who You Are!" Sophia ordered, mimicking

their ex-governess. "Or Who You May No Longer Have To Be." She pulled her hand free from Eugenia's nerveless grip and slipped away.

Eugenia made the mistake of casting a quick glance at the captain and found to her dismay that she could not look away. It seemed so natural to see him striding energetically towards her across an expanse of deck. So familiar, so . . . frightening.

"Well, Lady, it would seem that the game goes to you, after all," he declared. The laughing devils set golden sparkles dancing in his eyes as he bowed deeply before her. "Lady, I am all admiration."

She swallowed, trying to make sense out of this. "Are you?" she managed to ask. The quivering within her made it almost impossible for her to speak.

"You certainly played the last card. And I made sure I held the trump." There was far more in his eyes than amusement, but at the moment she was too confused to identify it.

"You find you were wrong?" She remained tentative, on uncertain ground.

"Lady, I never dreamed you would call my bluff like this. I admit I suffered some worry when I was held up at the warehouse and couldn't get back to see you that afternoon, but when I finally arrived at your uncle's yesterday morning, to find you had sailed at dawn . . ." He broke off, and for once the strong, undauntable mask of his features seemed to shift, leaving him momentarily vulnerable. "Lady, if it was your desire to punish me, you have succeeded admirably."

A game? Had it all been a joke? Was that why his eyes had danced with suppressed merriment when he told her he was bored? Fury rose within her, with him for so perfectly turning the tables on her and with herself for being so completely taken in. Or was it all a plot? Had there been truth behind it as well? Uncertainty ran rampant within her, and her anger faded into fear. Enough remained, though, so that she faced him squarely.

"I see." She raised one eyebrow in polite disbelief. "So you came immediately to tell me the truth, but it took you

two whole days to catch us in that shockingly slow little tub of yours?''

"No. But it took one to finish the repairs I was having made on her." His eyes narrowed as he studied the stiffness of her expression, and their gleam became arrested. "Lady, you knew what I was about, did you not?"

"Of course!" She forced a casual laugh. The remnants of her pride could not tolerate that he realize the truth, that he should guess how miserable she had been.

"When you set about to captivate me, with your purpose so obvious, I admit I plotted to turn the tables." His hands rose to her shoulders, as if to reassure himself by touching her that she was still there. "But I loved you already—my purpose was solely to add more interest to our game. Only at first did I desire to teach you a lesson. After that . . . after that, I found I enjoyed myself so much that I was loath to end the game. And you enjoyed it, though I had not counted on you reserving this last trick. When I found you had gone . . .''

He pulled her gently into his arms, but she remained stiff, pulling back from him. He did not force her, but neither did he release her. The puzzled look came back into his eyes.

"Oh, God! You did not believe I would sail without my Lady! That I could ever be bored with your company?" This time his enveloping embrace did not allow for protest. "Why did you set sail from America so quickly?"

"Because the next ship would not leave for another month," she informed him coldly from somewhere in the vicinity of his right shoulder. "I was anxious to return home. Why else?"

She had the satisfaction of feeling him stiffen, and he permitted her to pull back slightly. His expression for once was solemn, all trace of his infuriating amusement wiped clean. "Were you, Lady?" he demanded. "Is that the truth?"

She could not meet the intensity of his searching gaze. Her eyes fell, but he dropped one arm from about her waist so that he could use that hand to force her chin up until he held her eyes captive.

"Tell me you do not love me!" he ordered.

This had gone beyond a game. If she responded as her temper prompted her, by complying with his directive, he would not press her. He would return to his schooner, and she would never see him again.

"Why?" she countered, trying to gain time. "So that you may continue to roast me with a free conscience?"

His expression could be described only as exasperated. He jerked her roughly back against him, and his mouth descended upon hers with demanding force. The pressure on her lips relaxed, only to be resumed almost at once, this time gentle, caressing, coaxing a trembling response from her.

When he finally, reluctantly, raised his head, she clung to him for support, breathless and shaken. She opened her eyes slowly, encountering an expression on his face every bit as ardent and passionate as she could desire. No trace of humor or teasing remained. His heart, at long last, lay at her feet. And this time she had best pick it up before it was too late.

"Oh, my love," he murmured, one hand caressing the nape of her neck, then around the smooth skin of her throat. "If I have caused you a moment's pain, I will never forgive myself."

"It . . . it was worth it," she whispered. "For the first time, I can be sure you do not mock me."

He shook his head slowly, the love in his eyes so real that she felt it wash over and through her, warming her in its enveloping glow. "And I was at such pains at the ball to let you know how much I loved you." He drew her back against him so that her head once again rested on his broad shoulder. "I was so sure you guessed that my saying I was leaving was my final play in the game. I thought you would laugh at my clumsy tactics, for I was sure my love must be obvious to all. I expected some reprisal, but not this, and I never thought it could go so wrong." His arms tightened about her, almost crushing the breath from her body.

"You . . . you underestimated my love for you," she replied when she was able.

His response to that left her with three aching ribs and a bruised mouth, a condition that pleased her immensely.

In the silence that followed, as she rested contentedly

against him, the shouts of the crew members reached her clearly. She pulled back, suddenly aware of her surroundings, and flushed deeply.

"We ... we have an audience!" She peeked around the massive form of the captain, only to see her trunks already sitting on deck. The uproar concerned the lowering of one into the captain's rowboat. "What ... ?" she began.

"Transferring your baggage, my love," he told her, the amusement back in his voice. His deep chuckle rumbled through him. "Lady, we have been such fools, I to have carried our game too far, you to have doubted me."

"It seems you ought to do a little doubting," she replied. "I have not said I was willing to return with you."

As soon as the words were out she questioned their wisdom. That devilish gleam lit his eyes, and he loomed above her as she felt his energy partially unleashed.

"In that case, my beautiful love, I fear I am about to abduct you."

The idea appealed to her, but she tried to school her face into a disapproving expression. Out of the corner of her eyes she noted the tiny boat, riding deep in the water, being pulled back to the schooner by a line she had not previously noticed. Another rope was now attached to it, fastened to the merchantman.

"Would you really carry off a defenseless female by force?" she demanded, fluttering her lashes at him.

"Let us say instead *not* against her will."

At that she giggled. "You are quite abominable."

"If you do not mind your tongue, my sweet Lady, I shall have Captain Blaine marry us before we have any more misunderstandings."

"What a dire threat!" she responded promptly. "And what of Sophia?"

"Oh, she has already gone across to the *Sea Horse*. We shall return her to Providence, to the care of Mary Jessop. And then, my love, you shall be at my mercy. I should perhaps mention that the repairs I have been making to the *Sea Horse* have adapted it for a wedding trip that you will not soon forget."

"Do . . . do you prefer to be married on this ship?" she asked.

"Only if you argue with me. Actually, your aunt and uncle are making all of the arrangements at this moment so that we may be married with all propriety as soon as we land."

"You *do* assume a great deal, you know," she informed him with feigned reproof.

He laughed, that deep, dashing sound that sent ripples of merriment through her as well. "Shall we be off, Lady? I find I am impatient to get you back to Providence."

"As you wish, sir," she replied meekly.

He laughed again, his power unleashing fully as he swept her up into his arms and kissed her, filling her with his joy of life. He carried her easily across the deck towards the dingy that waited to transport them home. Eugenia, her arms tightly about the captain's neck, buried her face against his shoulder, as eager as he to reach America once again. Here was her happiness, held safe in his arms. For the inexpressible joy of being plain Mrs. James Harrington, she would gladly be a lady no more.